# The WINDS of CHANGE

*Also by Martha Grimes*
*in Large Print:*

The Grave Maurice
Cold Flat Junction
The Deer Leap
The Dirty Duck
The Five Bells and Bladebone
Help the Poor Struggler
I Am the Only Running Footman
Jerusalem Inn
The Lamorna Wink
The Man with a Load of Mischief
The Old Fox Deceiv'd
The Old Silent
The Stargazey
The Train Now Departing

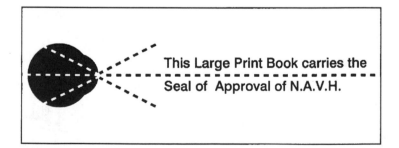

This Large Print Book carries the
Seal of Approval of N.A.V.H.

# Martha Grimes

## *The*
## WINDS
## *of* CHANGE

### A RICHARD JURY MYSTERY

**Thorndike Press • Waterville, Maine**

Grateful acknowledgment is made for permission to reprint an excerpt from "Year's End" from *Ceremony and Other Poems* by Richard Wilbur. Copyright 1949 and renewed 1977 by Richard Wilbur. Reprinted by permission of Harcourt, Inc.

**3 1559 00170 3469**

Published in 2005 by arrangement with Viking Penguin, a member of Penguin Group (USA) Inc.

Thorndike Press® Large Print Core.

The tree indicium is a trademark of Thorndike Press.

The text of this Large Print edition is unabridged. Other aspects of the book may vary from the original edition.

Set in 16 pt. Plantin by Ramona Watson.

Printed in the United States on permanent paper.

**Library of Congress Cataloging-in-Publication Data**

Grimes, Martha.
    The winds of change : a Richard Jury mystery / Martha Grimes.
        p. cm.
    ISBN 0-7862-7186-8 (lg. print : hc : alk. paper)
    1. Jury, Richard (Fictitious character) — Fiction.   2. Girls — Crimes against — Fiction.   3. Police — England — Fiction.   4. England — Fiction.   5. Large type books.   I. Title.
PS3557.R48998W56 2005
813'.54—dc22                                2004062033

To my brother, Bill
1929–2003


We fray into the future, rarely wrought
Save in the tapestries of afterthought.

— "Year's End," Richard Wilbur

As the Founder/CEO of NAVH, the only national health agency solely devoted to those who, although not totally blind, have an eye disease which could lead to serious visual impairment, I am pleased to recognize Thorndike Press* as one of the leading publishers in the large print field.

Founded in 1954 in San Francisco to prepare large print textbooks for partially seeing children, NAVH became the pioneer and standard setting agency in the preparation of large type.

Today, those publishers who meet our standards carry the prestigious "Seal of Approval" indicating high quality large print. We are delighted that Thorndike Press is one of the publishers whose titles meet these standards. We are also pleased to recognize the significant contribution Thorndike Press is making in this important and growing field.

Lorraine H. Marchi, L.H.D.
Founder/CEO
NAVH

* Thorndike Press encompasses the following imprints: Thorndike, Wheeler, Walker and Large Print Press.

# *The* Lost Gardens

# 1

The blood spatter on the little girl's dress mixed with the pattern of bluebells as if someone had thrown a handful of petals across her back.

Richard Jury was down on one knee in a gutter of a North London street, at the end of a dingy street called Hester Street, looking at the body, the face to one side, not quite believing it. He studied her — the pale hair, the eyes his hand had closed, the caked rivulet of blood that had run from the right side of her mouth, running down and across her neck and soaking the small white collar of the dress with the bluebells. His torch had made out the color. Even the blood could have looked blue in this difficult light. He thought it again — that the blood spots could have been petals.

It all seemed miniaturized as if everything — dress, body, blood — were part of some magical tale that reduced proportions, an *Alice in Wonderland* sort of story, so that at any moment the little girl would wake, the blood draw back into the mouth like a vapor trail and the dark stains on the dress dissipate, leaving only the flowers.

No coat. It was the first day of March and she wore no coat.

"A runaway, possibly?" suggested Phyllis Nancy, the police pathologist, who was kneeling beside him.

Jury knew it was a question to which she knew the answer. "No, I don't think so; the dress looks new, that or very well kept, you know, washed and ironed." What he was saying was rather ridiculous for who cared if the dress was ironed, but he felt almost as if he had to keep saying things, anything, just as Phyllis had done with her question. To say something, anything, was to hold the poor child's reality at bay.

"Yes, you're right." The hem of her own dress was lying in a puddle of rain, and the rain's detritus. It had rained heavily an hour ago.

Jury pulled the dress out of the muddy water. It was a long green velvet gown. When she had left her car and come toward the scene, she had looked regal in that dress. Emerald earrings, green velvet — she had been paged in the Royal Albert

10

Hall and left immediately.

She had knelt beside him, on both knees, nothing to kneel on except the hard surface of the street itself. Her kneeling took almost the form of supplication. "I'll turn her over. Would you help me?"

He nodded. "Sure." She did not need help. Jury had seen her manipulate bodies bigger than his own, turn them this way and that as if they were feathers. She didn't, he supposed, want to see the ragged exit wound and where it had come from, the blood the little girl was lying in. They turned her, weightless. The bullet hole was very small, as if even the bullet had reduced itself to fit the story.

Jury said, "Probably a .22, at any rate, small caliber."

Phyllis Nancy said, "Richard, she can't be more than five or six years old. Who would shoot a child in the back?"

Jury didn't answer.

Around the two kneeling over the body there were the others: the uniforms cordoning off this part of the road with yellow crime scene tape; the police photographer; the other crime scene people and detectives from homicide; the couple who had been getting into their car when they found the body (she weeping, he with his arm around her); the mortuary van. Blue lights twirling and blinking everywhere. Police had fanned out to knock on every door in Hester Street, searching for someone who had heard or seen anything. Despite all of this activity, there was a strange hush, as if those who were moving were doing it on tiptoe, or talking, keeping it down to almost a whisper. The sort of hush one finds in early morning before the sleeping world becomes the waking one. Moving carefully, as if letting her sleep on.

Jury turned to Dr. Nancy again. "Can you estimate, Phyllis?" It could certainly not have been long. Even rolled halfway into the gutter, this was still a residential street, cars going back and forth or parked in the street, such as the one belonging to the couple.

"No more than a couple of hours," said Phyllis.

"Probably less, I'd think. She'd've been seen."

"I know. Really, how could she have been here for more than fifteen minutes without being discovered? In this little white dress?"

White, with bluebells, Jury thought, and blood soaked.

He would never have to see the little girl

again unless he chose to, unless he found it necessary. But Phyllis Nancy had no choice; she would have to perform the autopsy; she would have to split the child open. What was that line from Emily Dickinson about splitting a songbird and finding the music?

Phyllis rose. He had never seen Phyllis Nancy lose it, not over the years and all of the dead and mutilated bodies between them; he was afraid he was about to.

He was wrong. When she'd been walking toward the crime scene a little while ago, she'd looked regal in that dress and those emeralds. Now mud splattered and pale, she still looked regal.

She made a sign and the mortuary van pulled closer to the little girl.

*"Split the lark and you'll find the music."* That was it, the line from Dickinson. A fanciful idea for an autopsy. Jury looked down at this benighted child.

Bluebells and blood.

No music.

# 2

Wiggins was making tea, not an unusual thing except he was making it noisily: the canister rattling on the shelf, the spoon rattling against the cup, the pint of milk thumped down on the desk, the fresh packet of biscuits impatiently ripped open. He looked distraught. It was as if he were making this small commotion to cover this distress, or to signal it.

Jury had just walked in the door and took this minor commotion as a signal. "What's up, Wiggins? You look as if you'd seen a ghost. That or DCS Racer."

"I've some bad news, sir." He dropped two tea bags into the brown pot and didn't look at Jury.

The bad news was clearly for Jury. His mind fled immediately to Mrs. Wasserman, in her eighties now, and the only natural candidate for bad news. "What?"

Wiggins didn't answer immediately.

"Come on, Wiggins. I think I can take it."

Wiggins snapped off the electric water pot. "I'm afraid . . . well, it's your cousin, sir. Your cousin — she died."

For an insane moment, Jury didn't know what Wiggins was talking about. He stood there, just inside the door, with that announcement of death seeming to preclude any movement until the cousin flashed in his mind and the world started turning again. His cousin up north, in Newcastle-upon-Tyne.

"I'm sorry, sir. I'm fixing you a nice cup of tea."

As if this was not what Wiggins would do, death or no death. Jury almost smiled at this intrusion of Wigginsland. He sat down, still with his coat on, opened his mouth, but didn't say anything.

"It was her husband called, name of —"

"Brendan."

Wiggins was pouring milk into the mugs. "That's it. He said the funeral's to be on Saturday." To give himself something useful to do, he checked his desk calendar. "That'll be six March." He handed Jury his mug of tea.

"Thanks."

Probably trying to assess the measure of

Jury's grief, Wiggins said, "You didn't see her very often, did you? I mean all the way up there in Newcastle, well, you couldn't. But I got the impression you really didn't know her all that well."

Jury held the mug in both hands, warming them. "I didn't, no." He paused, thinking. "It was her dad, my uncle, who took me in finally after my mother died. He was a great person. The cousin's his daughter. She was never like him, and she's never really liked me —" Was that true, though? Brendan had gotten the exactly opposite impression, that she did indeed like him and was proud of Jury's being so high up in New Scotland Yard. He rubbed his forehead. Was he going to have to try to revise memory again?

"Jealous, I shouldn't wonder," said Wiggins, blowing on his mug. "Her dad taking you in and all. He must really have cared about you."

"He did." But his cousin hadn't, surely. Her talks with Jury were often barbed with sharp remarks and (Jury suspected) lies. He said, "The last time I saw her we were looking at pictures, snapshots and so forth, and she completely turned my memories on their heads. Things I thought had happened, hadn't, not according to her. I hon-

estly don't know what I can depend on now."

"She was winding you up, sounds like."

"Maybe. That occurred to me, or that's what Brendan said. We should be able to depend on our own memories, for God's sakes." He took a long drink of tea and set the mug down on Wiggins's desk. "I'm going out for a bit. I need some air."

He walked across Broadway to St. James's Park, which he wandered in for a few minutes and then sat down. He really felt it, her death. He hoped it hadn't been a bad one. He'd seen too many bad ones — gunshots, knives, the victims occasionally not dead yet and looking up with a look of dread. Jury hadn't known she was sick.

It was fine for him to say he saw his cousin seldom and that he wasn't close to her and that, actually, they had never liked each other. That could work in life; it didn't work in death. But then nothing did, he supposed. Death had a way of kicking out the props, of smashing one's carefully constructed defenses. Whatever comfortable conclusions he might have reached about Sarah were now as suspect as the events of his childhood. For maybe she hadn't been lying to him; maybe he had

17

really been but a baby when his mum died instead of the five-year-old kid who had tried to pull her out of the rubble of their bombed building.

How could he possibly have got that wrong? Impossible, surely. And what about watching the kids in their school uniforms treading off to school and wanting to be one of them? What about Elicia Deauville? She had to have danced in the room next door. Perhaps it was a different door, a different time.

No. Sarah must have been making things up. And wasn't it typical — ?

He left the bench and started walking the path again, his hands together behind his back, the stance of an old man. That was the way he felt. His cousin had been older, but not so much older he could dismiss her age as that of a vaguely "other generation."

Stop thinking of yourself, he told himself. There were Brendan and the children, grown up except the baby, that was the daughter's baby, she unwed, living with her mum and dad, mum taking care of the granddaughter while the tartish little daughter was out and about. Well, she'd better pull up her socks now, hadn't she? Do what she should've done in the first place —

Oh, Christ, this carping. What in hell was he on about other than to fill his mind with images and inoculate his thoughts against what all this meant?

It was this: there was an emptiness that he hadn't seen coming and that now he didn't see how he could fill. This, with the death of a cousin he had never really known. A demanding, bitter, mendacious woman who spread no happiness, and yet . . . She was the end, except for himself. She had been the last one, the only repository of memories, the last one who had been there as part of his childhood tapestry and, because she remembered, might keep it from unraveling. She was the last one he could check with and whether she lied (and she would call it teasing) seemed almost beside the point.

Jury stopped, thinking this strange. Perhaps it was beside the point because she knew the truth enough to lie about it. No one else did now except for him. For some reason that made him feel the truth had gone and taken the past with it.

He had walked to Green Park by now and sat down on another bench. At the end of it was part of a *Daily Express*. He pulled it over and looked at the date. The second of March. He shoved the paper aside, having no interest in the daily affairs of the country, no interest in the royals or in David Beckham, or in the turn of the century.

He should get back to the office and call Brendan: the poor man must be going nuts over this. What could he do with the baby? There were no grandparents, at least on her side of the family. Maybe on Brendan's there were, maybe in County Cork.

Jury knew he ought to get back to the office and call him. Yet he sat, leaning over, elbows on knees, poring over it, his last visit three months ago, his anger at her teasing contradictions and the pleasure she got from having the upper hand in memory. After all, Jury had been so young (she'd said) he really couldn't remember anything. But she could.

He looked out over the park and remembered a line of poetry: *Their greenness is a kind of grief.* It was a March bleakness he saw. That made him think of finding a florist's to send the family flowers, but he didn't know where to send them, to what funeral home. Not to the flat, Brendan was not much good on the domestic end, to say nothing of being preoccupied, and the flowers would sit out of water until he tossed them away. Perhaps they would even pain him.

The thing was, Jury felt a need to do something. He wanted to make up for something, though he didn't know what. Maybe for being the child his uncle really preferred, or maybe for giving Sarah a hard time when he was last there, before Christmas, or maybe for being the one still breathing when she wasn't.

It would be spring soon despite the austere and shrouded look of the day. He thought again of Larkin's poem: *The trees are coming into leaf/Like something almost being said.* He liked poetry. He preferred the plainspokenness of someone like Larkin or Robert Frost. But then poetry was never plainspoken; it gave only the appearance of it. *Like something almost being said.* He could never have put that into any other words, yet it came as close to truth as he could get, he knew.

He told himself again he hadn't even liked her. Then what was this tightness in his chest, this suffocating feeling (which he was glad Wiggins wasn't around to witness)?

What came to him all of a sudden was a memory of Jenny Kennington the first time he'd seen her, running down the steps of her house in Littlebourne, holding a badly injured cat. She didn't know Jury but she accepted a lift to the vet's. She talked about the cat, which wasn't hers, but a stray that must have gotten hit by a car. I don't even like that cat, she'd said, once he was safely in the vet's hands. Several times she'd assured Jury, I don't even like that cat.

Right, he thought. Sure.

He walked down Piccadilly and turned into Fortnum & Mason, which was always in a state of pleasurable havoc. Everyone (and when wasn't everyone in Fortnum's?) seemed to be staggering under the canopy over the display of foie gras and cheese and prosciutto sliced so thin you could see through it. The wonderful black-coated staff, the bright fruit, the collective swimming smells of tea and citrus and money.

Then into Hatchards, a bookshop that smelled like books — leather, wax, dark woodwork. An atmosphere, a sensual experience that the mammoth Waterstones up the street couldn't begin to match.

He walked on, stopping here and there, at a kiosk for a *Telegraph*, which he later tossed in a rubbish bin, unread. How had he got to Oxford Street? He looked in Selfridges' windows. The faceless manikins seemed to know the windows weren't much to look at, not a patch on Fortnum's.

In their lightweight summer-to-come clothes so insubstantial a breeze could blow them away, their heads were bowed or jutting forward as if searching for an exit. On the sidewalk, a Jamaican selling his unlicensed wares, sharp, but not so sharp that he picked up Jury's cop aura. Sticks of incense, tiny bottles of perfume so heady it would drop you in your tracks in a desert.

"You wife, you laddy fren, she like this, mahn. Women, they like this stuff."

Jury purchased a few sticks of incense and a little stone holder.

Every time — the newspaper, the manikins, the peddler — he'd forget for those moments and then turn away and it came back to consciousness that she was dead.

He had thought more about his cousin Sarah in the last couple of hours than he had in the last two decades. That's what it was, death's legacy — now there was plenty of time to think about the time wasted, the words unsaid, the history unshared, until it was too late. It's always too late, he remembered someone saying. One can never have done enough, said enough. It was like the lager you could never finish: jokes about the wooden leg, the hole in the pint. An unquenchable, alcoholic thirst.

You can never do enough for the dead. You search around for comfort but there is no comfort; there never was and never will be. There is only a gradual wearing away of the sharp edges, so that you don't feel ambushed at every turn, as if you saw the dead suddenly rounding the corner.

For a while he rode the Piccadilly Line, then switched over to the Northern Line at King's Cross. It was only in the underground he thought he saw such faces, no one looking happy, except for the teenagers banded noisily together, but even they, in an unguarded moment, looked pretty desperate.

While the antique Northern Line rattled the riders' teeth, he looked at the girl facing him across the aisle, who was beautiful, but wasn't taking comfort in it. She sat primly, knees together, hands clasping a small bag on her knees. Her hair was the kind you see in Clairol ads, long and shining. Above her in the parade of advertisements was one for a cold remedy depicting a skier happily taking a spill into a pile of snow. He was happy about it.

As the train clattered along, Jury studied an old Kit Kat wrapper on the floor, moving between high heels and scuffed boots. He watched it shift along, liking to think of themselves, he and Sarah, as kids going cheerily along to a sweet shop, but this image was his own concoction; he doubted they'd gone much of anywhere together.

I don't even like that cat.

Right.

He got up for his stop at the Angel.

Darkness had registered on him while he was walking along Regent Street, but the time hadn't. It was nearly ten o'clock. Where in God's name had he been all of this time?

The lights were on in Mrs. Wasserman's garden flat, and in a moment she was out and up the stairs in her old bathrobe.

"Mr. Jury, there was someone trying to get hold of you. Carole-anne said there were two messages on your answering machine and I was to tell you. From someone named Bernard."

"Brendan?"

"She said Bernard."

Jury smiled. "Carole-anne has trouble getting my messages straight." Boy, did she ever. Especially the messages from females. Carole-anne had always thought the only life Jury would ever spend away from hers

25

was an afterlife. "Thanks, Mrs. Wasserman." He turned toward the steps.

"Is everything all right, Mr. Jury? You look pale."

In the dead dark, how could she tell? Maybe he just sounded pale. "Yes . . . No. Actually I got a bit of bad news. My cousin died. Brendan's her husband. That's why he's trying to reach me. To tell me."

"I am so sorry. So sorry. To lose one's family, that is the worst thing."

It was as if, to her, all of the family were circumscribed in every member. To lose one was to lose all. "She was the last of the family. Except for me, I mean."

"Oh, my. My." She clutched the bathrobe tighter around her neck. "That is so dreadful. A person feels disconnected. I know I did. Like a balloon, that was how I felt. Drifting up farther and farther, a prisoner of gravity."

Jury was surprised. Mrs. Wasserman didn't often speak metaphorically. "That's a good way of putting it, Mrs. Wasserman. That's pretty much how I feel."

"Could I make you a cup of tea?"

"That's nice of you, but I think I'm too tired. I've been walking."

She shut her eyes and nodded, familiar

apparently with walking as anodyne.

"So I'll say good night. Thanks for giving me the message."

She turned away as he did and they went in.

As he put the key in the door of the first-floor flat, he heard a short bark, more of a woof. It was Stone, so Carole-anne must be out. She always looked after him when she was in. They all did, when they could. Sometimes Stan took the dog along, but not if there was to be a lot of traveling.

He plucked Stan's key from a hook inside the door, went up to the second floor and opened the door. Stone did not come bounding out, as most dogs would; Stone was as cool as Stan. The most excitement he ever displayed was some tail wagging. He followed Jury down the stairs, went inside and stood until it was disclosed to him what he should do. He had the patience and self-possession of one of those mummers wearing white clown suits, faces painted white. They stayed amazingly still, still as statues, which people passing took them to be.

Jury found the rawhide bone and set it at the foot of his chair. Stone lay down and started in chewing. "I'm putting the kettle on."

Stone stopped chewing and looked up at Jury.

"You want a cup? No? Okay. Want something to eat?" Stone woofed quietly. "That must mean yes. Okay."

He left Stone to his chew. He plugged in the kettle and rinsed out a mug and dropped in a tea bag. The kettle boiled as soon as he'd spooned a can of dog food into Stone's dish and called him. Then he poured water over the tea bag and let it steep while he watched Stone eat. That got boring, so he tossed the tea bag into the sink and went to his chair in the living room. He stared out of the window at blackness. In another minute he was up and rooting in his coat pocket, searching for the incense.

Jury fixed one stick in the rough stone holder and lit the tip. The dish in the kitchen clattered as if the dog were shoving it around with his nose. Stone must have smelled the incense, the strong fragrance of patchouli, for he left the bowl for this more interesting event in the living room. He sat beside the chair and watched the spindle of smoke rise toward the ceiling. He looked from the smoke to Jury and back again. His nose quivered a little, taking in the unfamiliar scent.

During that final visit to Newcastle last year, Sarah had retrieved her photo album and they had looked at snapshots of themselves as children, again throwing spanners in Jury's memory works, although she hadn't purposely done that; Jury had brought up the old days and her derisive mood had changed — she had simply wanted to look at the pictures. They had sat with the album on the table between them, turning pages. It was as if in this sharing of childhood pictures they were acknowledging something between them

You wife, mahn? You laddy fren?

No, it's for my cousin.

He watched the thin trail of smoke curling toward the ceiling, and listened to Stone's tail swish along the floor.

Like something almost being said.

# 3

The dead woman lay on a stone bench inside a stone enclosure that looked much like a shelter to ward off bad weather at a bus stop, as if she'd been waiting for one and simply fallen over, her torso on the bench, her legs off, feet dragging on the stone floor.

This shelter stood at the bottom of the large garden of Angel Gate. The garden had been neglected over the years and was now in the throes of refurbishment, being redesigned and reestablished. Thus, the first persons there in the early morning were the principal gardener and his daughter, a horticulturist. It was they who discovered the body. The next to arrive was the cook-housekeeper. She was busy giving tea to the father-daughter gardening team and any of the police who wanted it and who had arrived later from Launceston and Exeter.

Brian Macalvie, divisional commander

with the Devon and Cornwall police, stood with his hands in his coat pockets. Standing about were some two dozen crime scene and forensics people from Launceston police headquarters and Macalvie's people from Exeter. Brian Macalvie, motionless and silent, had been looking down at the dead woman for a good two minutes ("which you wouldn't think was a long time," one of his forensics team had said to a friend over a pint at the local, "but you just try it sometime; it's an eternity, is what it is").

No one standing right near Macalvie, then, was any more animated than the corpse. No one was allowed to touch anything until Macalvie was good and done. This irritated the doctor who'd been called to the scene (local and not indoctrinated to the divisional commander's odd ways). He had made a move toward the body and had been roughly pulled back by his coat sleeve by the chief crime scene officer, Gilly Thwaite.

"For God's sakes," said the uninitiated doctor, "it's a murder scene, not a funeral. I've got appointments."

The others, nine or ten, squinched their eyes as if over an onslaught of headache or sun and stared at the slate-gray sky as

Macalvie turned to the doctor. He was a general practitioner from Launceston, but adequate (everyone but Macalvie assumed) at least to do a preliminary examination in order to sign a death certificate. The Launceston M.D. whom Macalvie liked was unavailable.

"Let's at least turn her over," said the doctor. Then added, acerbically, "I think she's done on this side."

Gilly Thwaite made a noise in her throat. From here and there came a choked kind of laughter. Macalvie was not a fan of gallows humor.

Macalvie nodded to Gilly. "Go ahead." Gilly set up her camera, got evidence bags ready, started taking pictures.

In the "lovely silence" (as he often called it, when there was some) Macalvie returned his gaze to the body. The woman appeared to be in early middle age. But appearances are deceptive and she could have been younger or older. He put her in her late thirties on one end of the age spectrum, early fifties on the other. That was a very wide divergence and it made him wonder. She was quite plain, her face free of makeup, at least as far as he could tell. There might have been a little foundation or powder. But no eye makeup. Her hair was mushroom colored, dull, cut in a straight bob that would fall, were she upright, to just below her ears. Her suit was the color of her hair. It was well worn and not especially fashionable, perhaps a classic cut, undated, a rough tweed. Macalvie looked for another fifteen seconds and then turned to the doctor. "All yours." As the doctor grunted and stepped into the enclosure, Macalvie said, "And incidentally, for her, it really is a funeral."

He then turned from the stone enclosure to look back at the big house that belonged to the Scott family, what was left of them. Macalvie remembered Declan Scott, the only one of them living there now. Declan Scott was a man who'd had enough trouble in his life: three years ago his four-year-old daughter had vanished. His wife had died not long after.

Macalvie knew Declan Scott.

The man really didn't need a body in his garden.

# 4

When Jury got to New Scotland Yard the next morning, he called Brendan, rather ashamed of himself that he hadn't done it the day before. He knew at least that it hadn't been indifference.

"Are you all right, sir?" Wiggins was giving his mug of tea a thoughtful stir. Jury had declined tea, and in Wiggins's book, that pointed to something truly dire.

"I've been better." Jury half smiled as he punched in Brendan's number.

"You got a call from Dr. Nancy and one from a DI Blakeley. Over in West Central. Isn't he part of the pedophilia unit?"

"Right." Jury slumped in his chair.

"You look kind of pale." Wiggins would call up every anodyne he could muster. Of late he was into herbs and crystals, of which there were myriad combinations. (Rue that's for — What had Shakespeare said? Remembrance, maybe?) Depression, Jury was sure.

A girl answered and it was unnerving that he couldn't identify the voice. Which daughter was it? They were no longer girls, either, but young women. One of them was the mother of that baby who'd been handed over to grandmother Sarah. Christine? No. Christabel. Lavish names his cousin had picked. "Is this Christabel?"

"No. Jasmine. Chris ain't here." Thick Geordie accent.

"It's really your dad I'd like to speak to."

"Whyn't you say?" She turned away and called for Brendan.

"Yeah?" said Brendan.

Tired of it all already. No, more defeated by it. "It's Richard, Brendan. I'm so sorry. What can I do?"

"God, man, but I'm glad you called. I'm knackered." Relief spilled over into tears. His words came muffled. "You're coming to the funeral, right?"

"Of course. Saturday, isn't it?"

"Yeah. It's a bit longer than I'd like, but my brother's just getting out of hospital and he'll want to come, so we're waiting an extra day or two. Could I ask a favor of you, man?"

"You can. Anything."

"If you could just float me a wee loan — ?"

"Sure I can. I intended to take on some of the expenses anyway. So it's not a loan; it's me paying my share. She was the only relation I had left, you know. You shouldn't have to bear the whole expense of the funeral."

Wiggins (Jury saw) was listening avidly.

"Thanks," said Brendan. "Thanks."

"How much do you need?"

"Well . . . I was thinking maybe two hundred?"

The man would need more than that. "Are you sure that's enough?"

"Yeah. Should be."

"Doesn't sound like enough for funeral expenses. You know the way they are —" Jury would just send more.

Brendan said, "Yeah. I dunno. Another thing — I'm worried about Dickie. This manager where he works — this punter's giving him a hard time, as much as accused him of thievin'."

Dickie was the child Sarah had had late, that's all he remembered about him. "What's Dickie say about that?"

"Not much. But I'm afraid this guy's got it in for him." A sigh. "Kids. Especially that age. He just doesn't know where he's headed."

Who does?

36

"You know teenagers; they're hard to get to."

"I know they don't think like adults, but why should they?"

"Right. See, you know this; you understand this. Listen: the service is to be at three p.m. Saturday. I'll see you before if you can get up here from London."

"Okay, Brendan." Jury said good-bye and rang off. He felt somehow defeated again. He rooted around for an envelope and found one. Then he paused. "Hell, I forgot to get the street address —"

"I've got it right here." Wiggins twirled the Rolodex.

That's how much you've kept in touch, mate. Here's someone who's a perfect stranger to your relations and even he has the address. You don't. "Brilliant, Wiggins."

"It's the funeral, is it?"

Jury nodded. "As you said, on Saturday."

Wiggins nodded too, looking sorrowful. "I know how it feels. It's like your life being put on hold."

It's more like the caller just hung up, Jury thought. "Did we get forensics on the little girl?"

"Yeah." Wiggins passed over the report.

Jury looked at it. It confirmed what Dr. Nancy had said at the scene. There hadn't been twelve feet between the shooter and the victim. The angle of the shot was down.

"You'd expect that. She was only five. Small." Wiggins raised his hand, holding a gun of air. "Almost anybody would be taller than the child."

"Uh-huh." Jury pulled over a yellow pad and took a small metal ruler from the drawer of his desk. Using the criminalist's numbers, he drew a line from 0 to 12. Then he drew another line for the trajectory. He came up with the same diagram (not that he'd expected otherwise) and started moving the gun closer: nine feet, six feet. The tattooing of the skin would be slighter the farther away. He looked at the morgue shots. Hard to say. The exit wound was larger; probably struck bone and took it along. He thought about the trajectory. He picked up the phone and called Phyllis Nancy.

"She was sexually abused, Richard. Of course she was just too small for penetration, but there's still a lot of inflammation. But God only knows somebody tried. Five years old. Who'd do that? And it happened more than once. Who'd do that?" It sounded as if the words themselves were weeping.

"I don't know, Phyllis. But I'm going to find out."

Detective Inspector Johnny Blakeley headed up the pedophilia unit, but he himself was a one-man war. He found it difficult to hang about while proper procedure was put into place. He had had two near-career-ending inquiries, one because he'd roughed up a suspect and the other because he'd gone in without a search warrant. His dedication to his job was disputed by no one.

Jury remembered the five-minute answer to a question he had put to Blakeley about a case. You didn't ask Johnny a question about pedophiles and expect brevity. And if you walked away, Johnny would still be talking.

"These freaks really believe they're the normal ones and we're the abnormal. They declare their love for their little sweethearts as fervently as any Romeo. They go on and on and on representing themselves as the vanguard of enlightened love. They're educated, cultured. If once more I get referred to Socrates and his students, I'll drink the fucking hemlock myself. They're all so bloody self-referential it kills me." The telephone got slammed against the wall. At least, that's what it sounded like to Jury on the other end.

The phone at West Central was snatched up as if a hand had been hovering for hours just waiting; "Blakeley."

"Johnny. Richard Jury here. You called me?"

"I did. This unidentified child, the little girl shot in Hester Street. I can't ID her but I bet a year's salary — no bet worth winning, clearly — I know where she came from."

"Go on." Jury yanked the yellow pad around.

"There's a house in that street that's been operating for years as a haunt for pedophiles. The woman who takes care of the kids — meaning, makes sure they don't escape — is a piece of work named Irene Murchison. You remember I was, ah, hauled over by the inspectorate on the warrant charge? Well, that's where it happened. Murchison has as many as ten little girls — I know this from the street —"

(Meaning, Johnny's snitches — he paid them a bundle, that was the word out.)

"I tried until her solicitor slapped me with a harassment suit, which I acknowledged for a few weeks and then went back to harassing. Which got me in some trouble.

Anyway, this little girl; you haven't ID'd her, have you?"

"No. I've got people working the missing children list. We might get lucky."

"It'd be nice, but good luck in this case seems to be out for lunch. Don't get your hopes up."

"What makes you so sure about this house?"

"Well, for one thing, the comings and goings. The men don't live there. I stopped down the street several times and took pictures. Some days only a single client. I'm sure that's what they're called instead of sicko creeps. Some days one, some days six or seven. In and out, in and out. That's for one thing. The other thing is a man named Viktor Baumann. He's a sick creep, but he's a rich, well-connected creep, a silky bastard. He's a pedophile. The thing is Baumann has enough money to keep God knows how many plates in the air."

"And this is one of the plates?"

"Absolutely. These men are prominent businessmen. What the hell are they doing in North London in that house?"

"But wouldn't that amount to probable cause?"

"Nope. The Murchison woman is a coin collector. So are her customers. They come to buy-sell-trade. She does have a collection."

"You had someone pose as a visiting businessman and a collector?"

"He didn't get to first base. She knew something was wrong; Baumann hadn't vetted my guy. There must be a sign they make, a password or something."

"Tell me about Viktor Baumann."

"He's a big noise in finance in the City, that's in addition to being a piece of filth. But I can't touch him. There's no evidence he actually controls this Murchison operation. But there's another layer in all of this. In Cornwall, three years ago it happened: Baumann's daughter, his daughter by his ex-wife, went missing. Kidnapped was what the local police thought at first, naturally. But there was never any ransom demand. There were several possible explanations, the most popular of which was that Baumann himself abducted her. Or had her taken, that is. He doesn't do his own dirty work. The DCI who headed up this case put Baumann down as a prime suspect. The other possibilities were that some sociopath or sexual pervert grabbed her. But they couldn't get to first base with that, either. Then there's the possibility it was a deranged woman who'd lost a child and was pining for another one. None of these possibilities bore fruit. The kid's still missing. She was only four."

"Payback? Isn't that possible? A parent whose child this Baumann abused wanting revenge?"

"Possible. But if Devon and Cornwall police couldn't find anything, how could a citizen?"

"I don't know. Different resources, maybe. Why is Baumann their chief suspect?"

"Ah, because he lost custody of the child and he's been trying ever since to get it back. He couldn't even get visiting privileges. He's not one to accept failure. He wants what he wants and he'll take it if that's the only way. The police there could well be right."

"Who did you have dealings with?"

"Macalvie. He was the DCI. Now he's a commander, I think. He's tenacious, that's for sure."

Jury smiled. "I know him. Tenacity is only the tip of the iceberg. I don't think he knows what 'cold case' means. He never gives up."

"Cop after my own heart."

"I'll tell him you said that."

"Angel Gate," said Brian Macalvie, on the phone with Jury. "That's the name of

the house. She was found in the gardens."
He was speaking of the victim, the dead
woman they'd found lying on a stone
bench in a stone enclosure.

To Jury the name — Angel Gate —
sounded mythical. Gates of ivory, gates of
horn.

"We don't know who she is. She was
shot dead on with a .22. Chest. We haven't
found the weapon. By now it's probably at
the bottom of the Ex."

Jury made a small noose of the telephone cord. A .22. The little girl in Hester
Street was shot with a .22. Not that this
meant anything. He was in his flat, sitting
in the one comfortable chair in front of the
bookcase going over the autopsy report
again together with the findings of the
Hester Street house canvasing. "No leads
at all?"

"No. We're running her fingerprints.
DNA won't help unless we have something
to compare it with, obviously." He sounded
impatient. "Declan Scott did see this
woman once in the company of his wife.
This was in Brown's Hotel in Mayfair. She
was also seen by the Angel Gate cook. But
that was nearly three years ago."

Jury said, "Well, then, you do have some
sort of ID."

44

"Uh-uh, Jury. Scott has no idea why she was with his wife; the cook — who's no longer there — has no idea who she is, either. All she recalls is that the woman came to see Mary Scott. But neither cook nor Scott can ID her. No one in Brown's recognizes the face, either." Macalvie was silent for a moment. "This case needs your chronic melancholia, Jury."

Jury moved the receiver from his ear, looked at it and returned it. "What in hell are you talking about?"

"About Declan Scott."

"Go on."

It took Macalvie a few moments to go on. "It's hard to be around Scott for more than fifteen minutes. Have you ever known anyone like that?"

Jury reached round and pulled a volume of Emily Dickinson's poetry from the bookcase, thought for a moment as he thumbed through the preface of the Dickinson book. He said, "Thomas Wentworth Higginson."

"Who the hell's he?"

"Emily Dickinson's amanuensis, you could say. Her literary critic, editor, publisher — whatever. Anyway, that's exactly what he said about her, that he could hardly stay in the same room with her for more than fifteen minutes. That she was so intense, so emotionally needy, she over-whelmed him. Not surprising, considering her poetry. What about Declan Scott?"

"The little girl, her name was Flora. She wasn't his daughter, actually, but you'd never know it to hear him talk about her. About them. The wife died six months after the child disappeared."

A double blow. "How did she die?"

"Heart, apparently. Scott found her in the garden. A garden within a garden, a sort of secret garden. You know."

"No, I never had one of those. This is where you found the body this morning?"

"That was in another part of the garden, at the bottom."

"Still. Coincidence?"

"I don't know."

"Who else is there? In the house?"

"The only other full-time person is the housekeeper. A Rebecca Owen, the cook and housekeeper, but even she doesn't sleep there. He lives alone. There's little connection at all, he says, between him and the dead woman. He didn't really know her."

"The words 'little' and 'really' strike me as the operative terms. He did have some connection, right?"

"I told you, Scott had seen her once

having tea with his wife, Mary. The wife said she was an old school chum. Roedean."

"And obviously this dead woman wasn't the old school chum because you'd have Roedean nailed to the wall. And you'd know who she is by now." Silence. "So there's a connection between the old case and this one."

"Must be. The victim could have been involved, I think. It's been three years since the little girl disappeared. Probably you'd say Declan Scott should let go of it."

"Why in hell would I say that? Time passing could make it even worse."

No reply.

Macalvie really did not want to have to question this man. Jury thought about this.

Macalvie said, "That's the reason, see?"

"What is?"

"What you just said about time making it worse. Most people are of the 'time-heals-all-wounds' school. It's why you'd get on with him."

Jury smiled and shook his head. "Where was the daughter taken from? The house? Grounds? Where?"

"The Lost Gardens of Heligan."

Jury switched the receiver to the other shoulder, the other ear. "The Lost Gardens of Heligan? Sounds familiar. I've never seen it, but wasn't that the big restoration project going in Cornwall? That and — what's the other one?"

"The Eden Project."

"Heligan is a kind of restoration, isn't it? The gardens were there already, but had sunk into nothing, I mean, gone to seed."

"That's right," said Macalvie.

"Well, I've never known melancholy to solve a case. Lord knows, not mine."

"You wouldn't know, would you? In this case I'm not so sure. Declan Scott — well, you'll see what I mean. It's the past. He doesn't just remember it, he lives in it."

"Don't we all?"

# 5

Tall, thin, dressed in black, sleek as a seal, Baumann's secretary was on the telephone when Jury walked into the office. As he waited for her to ring off, he looked around this richly furnished room. Furniture as slick and angular as she was, black leather and glass. The wall to his left contained several glass-fronted shelves on which were displayed rows of coins against black velvet. Jury thought about what Johnny Blakeley had told him.

When she finally returned the phone (also sleek) to its cradle, he told her who he was and that he'd like to see Mr. Baumann.

"Mr. Baumann never sees anyone before ten." Elaborately she examined her watch.

"That's a shame because I have to catch a train at ten-thirty."

She looked at her appointments book with frowning deliberation. Finally, she raised her eyes and said, "I don't believe you have an appointment, in any event?" She registered this as a question in case he wanted to get into it with her.

"No, I don't" — Jury glanced at the metal nameplate on the desk — "Grace." First names generally brought them down a peg. Her eyebrows worked their way up, astonished at this liberty. "This is my appointment." He smiled winningly and shoved his warrant card toward her. "New Scotland Yard CID."

She pushed her secretary's chair back and got up. Still frosty, she said, "I'll just see if he can speak to you now."

"I suggest he does." It never quite worked when Jury tried to sound menacing. There was always that joke hiding behind it.

She went to a double door on her left, cherry and several inches thick; she pushed it open. He heard her mumble something to the occupant of the cushy inner office. Then she turned and pulled both doors open — both doors, dramatic entry. After she stepped inside, he heard her murmur something before she turned to wave him in.

Viktor Baumann rose and came around his desk to shake Jury's hand and say, "I'm glad the police haven't forgotten Flora. Especially Scotland Yard. She's been missing now three years. I want to help in any way I can, of course. Please sit down, Superintendent." Baumann reclaimed his desk chair, which looked like one of those German designs of aluminum and leather so lightweight it could have levitated.

Another office furnished with killer designer furniture, but this one was more spacious than the outer. Jury imagined the paintings were not only originals, but by contemporary painters he wouldn't know.

Jury said, "I'm with homicide, Mr. Baumann." Then, when Baumann fell back into his chair, Jury realized his error and quickly said, "No, not your daughter. I'm sorry. The murder is of a woman we can't seem to trace." He removed the police photograph and reached it across the space between their chairs.

Baumann glanced at it and looked away. "Sorry. I'm squeamish about the dead. And I don't understand what this has to do with me."

"Probably nothing. But she did have something to do with your former wife, from the look of it."

"Mary? How do you mean?"

Jury wanted to leave mention of Declan

Scott out of this meeting if possible. "They were seen together in Brown's Hotel having tea. According to your ex-wife, she was an old school chum." Jury kept his eyes on Baumann's, gauging his reaction. That was hard to do with this sort of man who had trained himself not to react in his business dealings if he didn't want to. Jury imagined business succeeded or failed thereby. It would be as hard to engage his involvement in the matter of this death as it would be the slickest of villains.

"But you say you can't find any connection between this woman and my ex-wife other than that?"

"We haven't so far. One would think the woman in this picture had appeared for this one purpose. Then disappeared." He had put the photo on the table, facing Baumann.

Baumann said, "I'm afraid I can't help you there, Superintendent."

"You're sure you've never seen her?"

Baumann's smile was a little unpleasant. "I'm sure. After all, the face isn't exactly memorable, would you say?"

That was cold-blooded enough, thought Jury. "Perhaps not."

"This was in the papers, wasn't it? I don't recall any photograph of the face, but I do recall the crime. It's rather lurid, isn't it? A dead body in the garden of a country estate?"

He seemed also to be avoiding Declan Scott's name. "Lurid, indeed. But so was the abduction of your daughter, who lived on that estate, and the death of her mother. Declan Scott's estate is figuring rather too often in disaster."

"Ah," said Baumann, relaxing a little, and picking up a paperweight. He apparently made the mistake that Jury was on his side. Or at least, not on Declan Scott's. "Then I suggest you look nearer home, Superintendent." He smiled archly.

"That's what I am doing, Mr. Baumann." To Baumann's quizzical look he said nothing.

"But you're suggesting Scott must figure in all of this."

"But of course he figures in it. That doesn't mean he orchestrated it. What reason would he have to kidnap your daughter, Flora?"

Baumann was silent.

Jury went on: "You, though, would be seen as having a motive. You'd been engaged in a custody battle with Flora's mother. Declan Scott wanted to adopt her —"

"Superintendent, Flora was — is — my

53

daughter. Is there anything at all ominous in my wanting to keep her as mine?"

"No, except that she disappeared. That's the point, isn't it? That you might have wanted her enough to steal her."

Baumann no longer looked relaxed. "So this isn't about this murdered woman at all. You're not here because of her. It's about Flora, again."

"My reason for coming wasn't Flora; it was this recent murder. But I think the two are connected, Mr. Baumann. It just seems to me that a stranger's murder in the same house as the one from which your daughter disappeared and the one in which her mother died might be related. Especially as this woman had actually gone to the house. She knew Mary Scott and she meant to cause trouble."

"And just how do you know that?"

"Because she was murdered."

"That's why you infer the connection between Mary and this woman?"

"I don't have to infer any connection. It's there. The two women knew each other."

"According to Declan Scott."

"He could be lying, yes, but I don't see why."

Baumann rose and went to a cabinet of

vaguely oriental design and painted a red so dark it was almost black. "Care for a drink, Superintendent?"

"No thanks. I've had at last count a dozen cups of tea." He hadn't done a good job of insinuating himself into Baumann's good graces; in fact, he'd come close to alienating him, so he said, "You're a numismatist, Mr. Baumann. Those coins look pretty valuable." He smiled and tilted his head toward the outer office.

Baumann poured a small gin into a Waterford tumbler. To Jury this was interesting. He would have expected whiskey. Gin before lunch. Jury believed that 75 percent of people walking around were alcoholics, perhaps including himself.

"Ah. Are you interested in coins, Superintendent?" He returned to the floating chair.

"I really don't know much about them. But I've been wondering what that one is you've been turning." It was an old coin encased in acrylic, serving as a paperweight.

Baumann smiled and held it out. "I suppose this is my favorite: a Greek tetradrachms, which means it's worth four drachma. That's Alexander the Great. One of my favorite coins. I've only seen two of them since I began collecting."

Jury took it. It didn't surprise him that Baumann might feel some affinity with Alexander. The coin showed him wearing a lion's head as a helmet. "Looks quite valuable," Jury said, handing it back.

"Not really. It's obviously extremely old, but that means little when it comes to value."

Jury, having returned himself at least in small measure to Baumann's good graces, said, "I got us off the subject. We were talking about Declan Scott."

Baumann drank, set down the heavy glass. "I simply thought that one reason for Scott to lie might be to steer the relationship between himself and this woman away from himself by saying she was a friend of Mary's. Then fabricating this story about having seen them together. There were no witnesses to this meeting, isn't that what you said?"

"We haven't found one, no. But Declan Scott isn't the only one who saw her —"

Baumann interrupted. "But you just said there were no witnesses."

"Not to the meeting at the hotel, but later, when she came to the house. And it wasn't Scott who saw her, it was the Scotts' cook."

The way Baumann turned his empty glass in his hands and regarded it, it looked as if he wanted another drink. "Well, is the woman one of those longtime retainers who'd do anything for the Scotts?"

"Are you saying she might be lying for him?"

Viktor Baumann shrugged and set down his glass. "It's possible, isn't it?"

"Highly improbable, though. I think this is an occurrence where Sherlock Holmes must be right: the most likely explanation is the simplest one."

"I couldn't disagree more. You don't seem to be open to all of the possibilities."

Jury said nothing, just waited for him to go on, which he clearly wanted to do.

"You've been taken in by him, Superintendent. Declan Scott is very plausible." Baumann slapped the arms of his chair as prelude to rising from it.

"I haven't met Mr. Scott."

"Well, if you do, you'll see what I mean. I'm sorry, but I have an appointment at ten." He moved to a cupboard, took out a coat.

Jury had also risen and watched him buttoning the coat. It was a black chesterfield, single breasted, velvet collar. Jury hadn't seen an overcoat like this in quite awhile, certainly not on his own back.

Still on the subject of Declan Scott, Viktor Baumann said, "He's too smooth for my tastes."

Jury laughed. "That's just what someone said about you. The word used was 'silky.' "

Viktor Baumann seemed to like that description of himself. But the man was so self-referential, Jury wasn't surprised. "I might want to see you again, Mr. Baumann, if you don't mind. I think you would want to know of any developments, in case this does have to do with your daughter."

"Absolutely, Superintendent."

Jury bowed a bit farther into diffidence. "Do you think I could have a closer look at your coin collection?"

Baumann frowned, then brightened. "Oh, you mean the ones out there? Of course. I'll just tell Grace" — he frowned — "no, on second thought . . ." He took a card from the small silver stand on his desk, then grabbed up the black pen in the holder, turned the card over and jotted a note. He handed it to Jury. "Grace tends to be a bit possessive. I'd rather not get into this with her. Just tell her what you want and give this to her. Otherwise she'll spend ten minutes thinking up reasons why she can't unlock the glass." Baumann opened the door. "I'll see you again, Superintendent. Grace will see to it." He nodded and walked out.

Grace's eyebrows did their little dance upward in question.

Jury handed her the card. "I just wanted to get a closer look at some of those coins."

The card having directed her to see to his wishes, she crimped her mouth, took keys out of a drawer, rose and went to the glass doors, which she unlocked. She handed him back the little card as if she had no interest in Jury's curiosity.

Jury had absolutely no interest in hers, or in the coins. He had simply wanted to leave Baumann on a friendly note. She stood at his elbow as he looked at the coins.

"I shouldn't pick those up if I were you," said Grace. "Mr. Baumann is extremely careful of his coins. They're quite valuable."

Given that the card had told her to give him every assistance, Jury considered taking her to task but decided it would be a waste of his time. "Thank you," he said, stepping back.

She locked the doors in a self-important manner. Then the keeper of the coins smiled thriftily and showed Jury the door.

# 6

The anonymity of train rides had always appealed to Jury. There were few other passengers in his car and he sat awhile just enjoying the emptiness of the Great Western experience.

He had brought along the Emily Dickinson book and as he read the poems he wondered what it must be like to have the kind of perception she had. It must hurt like hell; it must be intensely painful; it must be like cutting your teeth on glass. But at least you were awake. There had been too many times in the last few weeks he felt as if he were sleepwalking through life.

When the train stopped at Pewsey, a tired-looking woman with three small children got on and settled them down in the four seats with a table between. The youngest of the three clamped his huge eyes on Jury, across the aisle.

Jury closed his own eyes, having marked his place in the book with his plastic tea stirrer. He hoped to discourage the staring child. He leaned his head against the window. He did not want to connect with anyone. He was tired. He stayed this way for a minute, uncomfortable with his head on the cold glass, then righted himself and opened the book again.

Physically, he had recuperated from the shooting. It had been two months, after all. But mentally he found himself too often still lying on that dock on the Thames, wondering what in hell had brought him to that pass. He read: *"Of all the souls that stand create, I have elected one. When sense from spirit files away, And subterfuge is done."*

*"And subterfuge is done."* What a wonderful line. Who Emily elected would remain forever a mystery. Now, if he were to elect one, who would it be? His mind went blank. Then into this blankness came a face that took him utterly by surprise. A woman he had never considered and now he wondered how he could have missed it, a woman extricating herself from the shadows on numerous occasions, then drifting back into them. Why would she, of all the women he knew, come to mind? He nearly laughed aloud at this discovery. He

opened his eyes to find he was still the center of interest both to the boy and now the mother sitting across from him. He had never known such intransigent stares. And neither could be dissuaded by Jury's returning their adamantine looks. Their faces looked struck in marble.

He could move. Yet it embarrassed him to resort to moving.

He got a fresh cup of tea from the trolley server and tried to think about Macalvie's missing child, but he didn't have enough details to come up with anything. He could only think this child had been taken by someone, a woman, perhaps, who had lost a child herself and was desperate to replace hers. Either that or the ex-husband, Viktor Baumann. He hated to think of the alternatives. What better place to steal a child than an enormous, open series of gardens with plenty of places to hide?

He should stop speculating; he hadn't enough information even to do that.

Instead, he thought about Emily Dickinson. *"When sense from spirit files away, And subterfuge is done."* To take off the mask, to forgo pretense, to put your cards on the table. To have done with smoke and mirrors. . . . He rested his head against the back of the seat and fell asleep.

He must have slept through Exeter, for the next thing he knew the conductor was coming through announcing St. Austell. Jury gathered up his coat, paper and book. Now that he was leaving, the woman across from him finally closed her eyes; the little boy turned away.

Jury stepped down to the platform, looked around and saw a young man walking toward him, tallish, wiry, wearing dark glasses.

"I'm DS Platt, sir," said the detective and led Jury to a Ford Escort that, even in its lack of identification, seemed to scream *police police police!* Maybe Jury had simply ridden in too many Fords over the years.

"Commander Macalvie thought you should see the place where the little Baumann girl disappeared — Flora. The Lost Gardens of Heligan it's called. A fascinating place. The girl was taken somewhere around a part called the Crystal Grotto. Her mother had been ahead of her. She'd lost sight of her for only a few minutes."

"Fine with me, Sergeant Platt. Incidentally, what's your first name?"

"Cody." Then, as if it were a name to be explained, Platt said, "Mum was very fond of American westerns. 'Cody' was the

63

name of some cowboy or other. I used to play at being a cowboy, had a silver gun and fringed jacket and boots. The boss likes to call me that, 'cowboy,' I mean."

"Sounds like him." Jury laughed.

DS Platt seemed to like that response. "Anyway, I think Commander Macalvie wants you to get the whole picture of these events. Chronologically, that is. For the London train, St. Austell's a lot closer than anyplace else. And Heligan's near Mevagissey. Launceston's a good bit farther north. I'm to drive you; the boss said he'd be meeting you in a pub in South Petherwin. That's just this side of Launceston."

Jury did not take in this complicated geography, but he knew he would get here and there in good time. He pulled his door shut and Platt backed up and drove out of the car park, feeding the Ford Escort into one of St. Austell's twisted and hilly streets.

Jury said, "The whole picture, you said. So he thinks there is a whole picture?"

"The disappearance of little Flora and this murder? He does, yes."

"And what do you think?"

Platt seemed a little surprised at being consulted. "Do you mean, do I think it's all part of one case? Well, yes. This woman who was murdered had gone to Angel Gate — the Scott estate — before. Apparently, she was a friend of Mary Scott. Or an acquaintance. More likely, an acquaintance."

"Couldn't the husband sort that?"

"He doesn't — didn't — know the dead woman. Saw her once with his wife, he says, in London, but doesn't know who she was."

"Hm." Jury sat back and sleepily regarded the scenery, pleasant enough, but unimpressive. But then with Cornwall it was the coast, wasn't it? Not the interior.

They were soon pulling into the Heligan gardens' large car park, which was posted with signs directing cars and buses to their correct parking areas. Jury was glad that it wasn't summer. There'd be a mob. Tour buses, crowds. Platt parked beside a gray Plymouth. There were few cars.

They were out of the car now, standing there.

"The mother died soon after the daughter vanished?"

Sergeant Platt nodded. "Six months later. She was only thirty-nine."

"What killed her?"

Platt looked around the car park as if he

was hoping Mary Scott would step out of that old gray Plymouth over there, or the Morris Minor, or the sleek black BMW. "A broken heart, I shouldn't wonder." He looked at Jury, sadly. "Of course, they say you can't die of that, can you?"

His look was alarmingly sorrowful. Jury put his hand on Platt's shoulder. "Don't you believe it, Sergeant. You knew her, then?"

"Yes. I kept in touch, see. I knew Mary — Mrs. Scott, I mean — pretty well. And Flora, too."

Jury watched his face. "You were fond of them."

Platt nodded, looking off across the car park, merely nodding.

Jury said he'd like to see this Crystal Grotto on his own, if Platt didn't mind. On the contrary, the sergeant seemed relieved not to have to accompany him and told Jury he'd wait in the café near the gift shop. He could do with a cup of tea, he said, reminding Jury of Wiggins, who was supposed to follow Jury here the next day.

He walked up a path to the kiosk where the tickets were sold and where a youngish man was puttering about. Jury took out his ID and the fellow looked wide-eyed at him, impressed.

"I'll need a map of the gardens. I expect you have them here. I'm looking for the Crystal Grotto — I think that's the name."

The ticket seller handed one over and gave him brief directions. "And you've got your map . . ." He looked at Jury as if he couldn't quite believe he wouldn't be whisked there on some magic carpet, but instead was going to find his own way. Strange.

Jury saluted, touching his forehead with the map and walked on.

A mountainous rhododendron, ten times as tall as Jury, marked the entrance to the northern garden. In here, along the path, there was silence, deep silence, as if it too had been carved out of the garden ruins and restored. When he saw sunlight caught in the net of the branches he suddenly remembered the friend of his mother's, the watercolorist who'd gone blind. He remembered sitting with her in the little park across the street from her terraced house. On a little farther, through the latticed opening of intertwining branches, he spied a sculpture of a small girl up on her toes, who appeared to be caught executing one of those difficult moves in ballet and his mind flew immediately to Elicia Deauville — to her or to the false memory of her and her dancing on the other side of that wall of his terraced house, his childhood home. But his cousin had pretty much annihilated memories of his childhood, rendering them nugatory, or at best, suspect, memories to be taken out, exposed to the light of day to see how they held up. That war-time episode in Devon, the beach, the collapsed fences, the ginger-haired girl. Oh, but she had to have been real — the taunter, the teaser, the nemesis of all little boys — made, she must have been, for that purpose. And her hair, her flaming hair — surely, that had been real. He seemed to be going along in fits and starts, his mind stumbling, lurching in and out of these fretful scenes, trying to keep its balance. And he thought that's what life was — trying to keep one's balance.

Yet he hadn't stopped; he hadn't even slowed. His pace along the path was even. There was no one else; Jury's feet alone crunched on the gravel. There was no sound except for a bird somewhere above him.

All of this had taken less than five minutes when he came upon steps going down. They were moss covered, soft and a bit slippery. The Crystal Grotto was situated at the bottom of these steps. According to

Platt, Flora Scott had last been seen by her mother in front of this small cave. He wondered if Flora had gone inside the grotto to look, for the way the grotto was described made it sound quite romantic; pieces of crystal were embedded in the roof and back when the gardens flourished, the owners would set candles all about and the light from the candles would reflect on the crystals.

Mary Scott had apparently gone on ahead and around shrubberies that would have blocked her view of the grotto. But if it had been only a minute or two until she realized Flora was not behind her, whoever took the little girl had to have been following them and had to be very quick. Jury didn't see how this person could have been waiting in this spot, for Heligan's gardens were vast and she (Jury imagined it was a woman) wouldn't have known Mary and Flora would come this way.

He or she could have known, however, that they often visited here. If that was the case, it might not have been random. Which would seem to leave it at someone who knew them and meant to take Flora and not just any little girl. If it was Viktor Baumann, though, how could he have hidden the child for the three years since

69

her abduction? There was nothing more to be seen at the site of a three-year-old crime. If indeed it had been a crime.

His name was Marvin Griswold and he'd been working here in several capacities for more than four years. The ticket kiosk was only one of them.

"Well, it's hard to remember that far back, three years, I mean, remember exactly what the circumstances were," said Marvin Griswold in answer to Jury's question about the disappearance of Flora Scott. "Of course I remember the incident. I mean, it was in all the papers. It was very dramatic. For six months after you could hardly get near the Crystal Grotto. People can be such ghouls, can't they? But do I remember seeing them — her and her mother — on that particular day? No, I don't. It must have been someone else in the kiosk when they came."

He sounded a little resentful as if someone else was having all the fun.

Jury thought about the geography of the gardens. "Anyone entering comes by your kiosk to get a ticket?"

"Yes. It's not exactly a ticket; it's one of these pins." He held out a small metal tab that a visitor would affix to a jacket or coat.

"And leaving?"

Griswold shook his head. "Not unless they come back by the same way. More likely, they'd come out by way of one of the other paths, such as behind the gift shop over there" — he waved his hand in that direction, past Jury's back. "There are several ways that lead to here."

"And the Scott woman would have had a map."

Marvin blew out his cheeks in thoughtful contemplation. "I expect so. We always hand over a map with the pin. But she might not have bothered with one if she and the little girl visited often."

"When you didn't see her return, didn't you wonder?"

"No, because as I've just told you, there are a number of exits."

"Which also means there are a number of entrances. From the gardens to here, to the buildings, such as the gift shop. But there's only one exit back to the road. Through the car park."

"Yes, for the visitors. Of course there are other roads the workmen use. As to what you're calling a number of entrances, theoretically, yes. But people don't do that, do

71

they? Try to sneak in. I mean, not into a place such as Heligan. It's not a cinema or a Stones concert, is it?"

"No," said Jury, smiling.

Marvin sighed. "You know, I've already been questioned by police, and more than once."

"But not by me." Jury gestured in good-bye. "Thanks for your help."

Sergeant Platt was sitting on one of the wooden benches with a cup of tea when Jury walked into the café.

"You found it?" Platt said.

That made Jury smile for some reason. It was as if the grotto had a tendency to move around. "I did, yes. I can't say I'm much enlightened by the find, though."

"Yes, well, the boss just wanted to put you in the picture, you know. He was talking about atmosphere. Having a look round. You know." Platt frowned a little, seemingly pained by his not finding exactly the right words to describe what Macalvie had meant.

"And he was right. I should see it; I'm glad I did. Enlightenment, let's hope, will come some time down the way."

"You want some tea or something?"

"I could use some food. Maybe we can

just move along to Launceston."

"Right. South Petherwin, actually. A little village before Launceston. There's a pub there."

Good. A pub lunch. Jury was starving. Except for those dozen or so cups of tea, he'd had nothing all day. "Fine."

# 7

The Winds of Change was located in the village of South Petherwin and, given the size of the car park, was set up for a brisk business. The lack of it was probably owing to the time of year or the time of day. At the car park's far end, a large space was marked off for tour buses. Jury wondered what it was about the village that would attract tourists.

Brian Macalvie, who had driven there from Devon and Cornwall police headquarters, was sitting at the bar, drinking, smoking and watching the door. When Jury and Platt walked in, he waved them over as if picking them out over the heads of a crowd and as if he'd been sitting here for hours — days, even — waiting for the congenitally late.

Jury sat down and pulled out the menu. Cody ordered a club soda.

"What took you so long?" asked Macalvie.

Cody opened his mouth to answer, but

Jury got there ahead of him. "Most people say a simple 'Hello, how are you?' when greeting old friends. Your standard greeting has always been 'What took you so long?' "

Macalvie drank from his pint and stared at Jury, expressionless.

Jury repeated it: "Every time it's 'what took you so long?' "

Macalvie wiped a trace of foam from his mouth. "What did?"

Cody's snort of laughter got him club soda up the nose. Then he said, "My fault, boss; I let him go off."

"Me, the old pensioner leaning on his zimmer bar."

To Cody, Macalvie said, "You were supposed to show him the place, not let him go wandering all over."

Cody mumbled some half-baked apology and took his club soda into the room on the left with a billiard table.

Jury looked around for the barman. "I'm glad this is a pub. I'm starving."

"Lunch has gone off."

"Oh, terrific." When the barman came, Jury asked for a pint of Pride and tossed the menu aside, saying, "Let me get this straight. You discovered this dead woman is — was — an acquaintance of Scott's wife, Mary, according to the husband?"

"Declan Scott. The one I told you about. You'd wonder he could live there with so many memories." As if he knew the limit on memories, Macalvie looked away. "He wants to be where the memories are."

"Does anyone have a choice?"

There came a click of billiard balls from the room next door. The barman set down Jury's pint.

"Probably not. But don't some people feed on them?" said Macalvie.

Jury thought Macalvie might be one of them. "Perhaps. And this is the man you want me to talk to?"

"That's right."

"Didn't you say you didn't like him for this murder?"

Macalvie shook his head. "I don't. I don't think he did it, but I can't point to any hard evidence. He certainly doesn't have an alibi. He was alone, asleep."

"But you think this case is connected to the disappearance of the little girl. Flora?" Jury drank his beer, hoping it would fill him up.

Macalvie nodded, staring at the row of optics as if the name were so potent he had to find an antidote. When Macalvie didn't go on, Jury had to prompt him. "She was four? Five?"

"Four." Macalvie cleared his throat.

A brief answer, as if brevity could block out some part of this bleak scene. Again, Jury prompted him. "She was abducted from a point around this Crystal Grotto. Correct?" Jury was trying to coax him into responsiveness. Seldom did he have to do that.

Macalvie's eyes were now on the rings his glass was sweating onto the old bar. He pulled over a coaster advertising Johnnie Walker Black and slid it carefully beneath the pint. "Flora —" Again, Macalvie cleared his throat. "Flora and her mother liked to walk there. On this particular day — well, it was no different from the rest — at one point Flora got a little way behind her mother on the walk. Mum had gone round to look at some New Zealand plants for a few moments and then realized Flora wasn't right there. But she didn't panic; the girl was quite familiar with the layout and she was used to Flora's stopping along the way, just as she herself did. She called her name. No answer. She went on calling, retracing her steps and still no answer. Then she got anxious, then frightened. This had now been going on for a good ten minutes and of course those gardens are immense. She stopped people, asked them if they'd seen a little girl on her own, but no one had. Finally, she got hold of some of the staff and told them and they in turn got one of the administrators, who immediately called the local police. Before they came, the staff was searching, even some of the visitors were on the lookout. Cody can give you details about the search. This was three years ago. He was a DC then, detective constable.

"There were a lot of tourists, which made the search that much harder. Anyone could have come in, seen her alone and snatched her."

"She would have resisted — yelled, screamed, something."

"Probably. But how many times have you seen a parent pulling a crying, screaming child along. Last time you were in a Safeway, maybe? Mum looking stony, or maybe a dad trying to cajole the kid, and he or she keeps on yelling? I see you don't like that theory."

Jury had been shaking his head. "There has to be something seriously different about those instances and this one. Flora would have been yelling for help. I'm not saying a snatch wasn't possible, but it's probably more likely she was drugged, chloroformed, maybe. And then something got thrown around her — a coat, a shawl. Then she could have just been carted out like a sleeping child, head over the perp's shoulder."

Macalvie stirred his coffee. "You're good at this; maybe you should do it for a living."

"Thanks."

"There being no ransom demand finally made Mary Scott think it was the ex-husband, Viktor Baumann."

"I talked to him. I couldn't come to any conclusion. I mean other than that he's arrogant and a number of other things."

"Back then he looked like a dead cert. Another possibility was it was one of those snatches that happen when the perp, who's nine times out of ten a woman, wants the baby, not the money. So there wasn't much we could do. Hell, there wasn't anything we could do because the trail stopped.

"Mary Scott blamed herself for letting Flora out of her sight. Parents always seem to do that, don't they? I told her there's no way you can watch your child twenty-four hours a day. No way. If someone was determined to take Flora they would have found a dozen ways to do it."

Macalvie was silent for a moment, then he said, "The dead woman looked familiar

79

to Scott himself and that's when he remembered seeing her once with his wife in
London. He and Mary had driven up for
the day to do Christmas shopping. They
booked a room at Brown's. They returned
the next day. Scott had been visiting the
galleries, looking for a painting to give his
wife. He found one, probably set him back a
year's salary — I mean, for you, not me —"

"Very funny."

"— and when he walked into Brown's,
he saw Mary sitting in the lounge having
tea with a woman he didn't know. He
didn't want to intrude, and besides, he
didn't want her to see what he was carrying
— obviously a painting, given the shape
and size of the parcel — so he fixed it up
with one of the porters to wrap it in some
unrecognizable form and stash it in the
trunk of their car, which they hadn't been
using anyway. When he finally went back
to the lounge, they were gone. That was
near five o'clock. Mary must have gone out
again, for he didn't see her until after six;
she said she'd been at Fortnum's and in
Jermyn Street. She held up one of those
little Links bags. He asked her who her
friend was and she played dumb at first, as
if she didn't know what he was talking
about. When he said he'd seen her in the

lounge, having tea, well, then, she snapped her mental fingers and said, oh, yes. An old school chum she'd run into purely by accident. He asked her from where and she trotted out Roedean."

"What was her name?"

Macalvie shook his head. "Mary Scott didn't say. And her husband didn't ask. He said if she'd wanted to tell him she would have. Scott's got a real feeling for others' privacy."

"And the husband is the only one you've questioned who made any connection?"

Macalvie nodded. "The police photo didn't register with anyone at Roedean; no one remembered the woman. Why would she lie about that, something we could so easily check up on?"

"She didn't think there would be any reason to check up. She didn't know there would be a murder on her grounds."

"No, of course." Macalvie shrugged. "So where's Wiggins?"

"He'll be here." Macalvie had always liked Sergeant Wiggins, to Jury's great surprise.

Macalvie called to Cody and slapped down a tenner. While the bartender made change, he said, "Let's see how I relate, then, to the next one. A Dora Stout. She was the Scotts' cook for thirty years."

Platt had moved rather languidly to the bar and said, "You really want me to come, boss? I mean, three people, that might intimidate her."

"I'm sure. No, I want you to call her."

Cody nodded and pulled a cell phone from an inside pocket.

From his own pocket, Macalvie drew a crumpled bit of paper, smoothed it a little and handed it to Cody. "Tell her we'll be there in five minutes."

As Cody moved away to make the call, Macalvie and Jury headed for the door. "I don't like this case."

"I've never known you to like any case. I've never known me to like any case. This woman, this former cook, any particular reason you want to talk to her?"

"Background noise," Macalvie said as they got into the car.

Tiny Meadows was a clutch of houses in South Petherwin along the Launceston road and only a short distance from the pub. They could easily have walked; Jury said so.

"Does that set the right tone, Jury? Police arriving on foot?"

"Since when did you ever care about setting a tone?" said Jury as they got out of another police-issue blue Ford.

The house was small and trim. A dog barked when Macalvie tapped on the door with the brass dolphin knocker.

Dora Stout and her dog came to the door. Jury couldn't decide which of them was more eager to see police, given the wide smile and the tail wagging. Dora, true to her name, was a chubby woman, her round midsection set on her wide hips. Her thinning gray hair was brushed up in a cloud rather like a whipped custard. She did indeed make one think of food.

Both Macalvie and Jury pulled out identification, but Dora wouldn't fuss over trifles such as that; she waved them in merrily and directed them to easy chairs covered in a pattern of wildflower bouquets. On the back of the chairs were antimacassars. The dog, whom she called Horace, lay down in front of the little gas fire, but kept his eyes moving from Jury to Macalvie, back and forth.

"It was my arthritis, see," she said in answer to Macalvie's question, "made me give it up. I can't get around as I used to and my hands some mornings ache something fierce." She held them up as testimony. "So when they don't hurt so bad, I like to get my baking done. I've just popped some scones into the oven."

"I know," said Jury, "I can smell them; they smell wonderful." At this point, Horace's dinner would have smelled wonderful. "I hope they're done before we leave." In this hungry frame of mind, Jury could understand Wiggins's yearning after every Happy Eater they passed.

Macalvie just looked at him, but Dora was delighted.

"If you don't arrest me, I'll give you the lot." She laughed at her joke.

"I guarantee," said Jury, "you'll remain a free woman."

"Jury," said Macalvie, "do you mind?" He shifted to Dora Stout. "We're trying to identify this woman, Mrs. Stout." He slid the police photo out of the envelope. "She was, apparently, a friend or an acquaintance of Mary Scott." He handed her the picture.

Dora shook her head and looked pityingly at the victim. "Poor thing. Awful. Yes, I read about it. Shocking thing. You want to know if that's the woman who came that one day to see Mary Scott. Yes, this is her." Dora leaned back, holding the picture at arm's length, her glasses perched on her nose. "Not much on looks, was she?" Dora handed back the picture.

"You might tell Superintendent Jury what you know about her."

"It was over two years ago, no, nearer three, some months before Mary" — Dora took a handkerchief from some hidden place — "before she died. Right before then. The only reason I saw this person at all was because I thought it was Miss Owen — the new cook — who rang and I was just going along the hall to answer the door. But Mary Scott was there herself. I just got a glimpse of her" — she pointed to the photo — "before they turned and went out."

"Did they leave? I mean, drive off?"

"They could've done, but I paid no attention. Now I wish I had."

Hearing possible tears in his mistress's voice, the dog shifted his eyes to her and then abruptly back to Macalvie and Jury, looking as if he meant to fix the source of her trouble.

"That family," she went on, "had more tragedy than it needed, it did indeed. And now this."

"Flora, you're thinking of?" said Macalvie.

"The poor little girl. And them never to know why. That's an awful thing."

They were in the Winds of Change again, this time drinking coffee. Cody was once again in the billiards room. There was still no food, evening meals not being up yet. Jury was working on a bowl of pretzels. He was talking about the shooting in Hester Street and Johnny Blakeley's ongoing investigation.

"Shot in the back. A little kid. Christ."

"There seems to be a field day with little kids where this Baumann is concerned."

"Blakeley's a good cop. He's tenacious."

Jury laughed. "That's just what he said about you."

Macalvie was eating the pretzels.

"Leave some for me, damn it. I haven't eaten all day."

"Get Scott's housekeeper to rustle you up something. She's a hell of a cook."

"Yes, sure." Jury drained his coffee.

"Scott's a sad man but a great host."

"This is hardly host-guest stuff we're doing."

"Go talk to him." Macalvie looked at Jury. "I mean, as soon as you're finished with that pretzel."

# 8

Ten minutes later, Jury and Cody Platt were back on the A30. As they passed the Little Chef, he felt exactly as he imagined Wiggins must feel, taunted by the promise of cups of tea and beans on toast. Except for Wiggins, it was more of a soul hunger than an actual one. Jury wasn't about to split hairs over this; he told Cody Platt to stop at the next Little Chef or even one of those caravans set up by the side of the road.

Twenty miles later, Cody pulled into the car park of a Little Chef.

Inside, with a plate of nearly everything on the menu in front of him, Jury asked Cody about the investigation into the disappearance of Flora Scott.

Cody was drinking tea and occasionally taking a bite of toast. "Times I thought it was."

"Was what?"

"A disappearance. It was like she vanished into thin air. It was like a magic act." Cody had pushed his dark glasses up on his head. It was the first time Jury had actually seen his eyes. They were a disconcerting stone color, as if light had leached the color from them. Yet they were neither cold nor hard; it was as if the eyes felt this loss of color, as one might feel the loss of a person, and were saddened by it.

The waitress — Joanie, according to the name on the button on her collar — came with more tea and coffee. She smiled as if this were the greatest thing that had happened during her shift. Jury returned the smile. Walking away from the booth, she stumbled into a table.

Cody went on. "The Scott family must have had a lot of pull in the county. The grandmother, Alice Miers, lives in London, and she came straightaway. She was like a rock, you know, one of those people every family should have. I think Mary would have flown into little bits if her mum hadn't been there. Anyway, I've never seen so many police called to one scene. There must've been seventy-five, a hundred of us going over every inch of Heligan gardens and that grotto. We found sod-all, not a hair ribbon, not a kicked-off shoe lost in a struggle — there always seems to be a little shoe left behind in films, doesn't there? Or a little blue purse the mother said she was carrying. Not even that turned up. I would've thought she'd've dropped something like that."

"Your abductor would have picked it up."

"I expect so." He shoved the plate of toast to one side and was leaning over the shiny surface of the table, hands folded, working his fingers, as if this account were told in deepest confidence. "I concentrated on the grotto, thinking that would be a good spot to grab someone because it's not immediately visible. You remember — three or four steps going down —" Here he walked his fingers on the table, simulating the steps taken. "The grotto would have been the spot Mary Scott had just passed, maybe twenty, thirty feet behind her. I have my own theory about that, anyway."

"What?" Jury was polishing off the last of his eggs.

"Less than a couple of minutes had passed since Mary had been with Flora, had seen her, not more than that before she looked around, saw Flora wasn't with her and retraced her steps. What she said was she remembered last seeing Flora on the other side of the grotto, so, of course, she hurried back that way. I think the villain was inside the grotto with Flora, Flora either being chloroformed or his hand over her mouth to shut her up."

Jury frowned. "It's not deep enough, is it, to hide a person? What's Macalvie think about that?"

Cody sighed and sat back in the booth. "The boss would agree with you; he thinks they would've been seen. But not necessarily, I said to him, not if the mother was rushing by. It might have given this creep a better chance of disguising Flora, I mean, getting her into another coat, something different."

Jury put his fork down. He was still hungry. He pushed back his plate and considered ordering more. His coffee cup was nearly full. All he lacked now was a cigarette. He had never experienced the advantages of not smoking. To hear the propaganda, the lungs would expand, the scent of roses and violets become denser, the taste of peppermint sharper, the air clearer, the rain more crystalline and the bloody fields more Elysian. The clouds, he supposed, fluffier. The only benefit that he could testify to was that he could say he was no longer killing himself with nicotine. Not that this wasn't important; it was just abstract. And when, he wondered, had he become so obsessed with creaturely comforts?

"Do you smoke?"

"What? Smoke? No. I stopped a few years back."

Jury very nearly lunged forward. "Horrible, isn't it?"

Cody looked blankly at him. "Not really. After a few weeks, I hardly noticed." He shrugged. "Why?"

Jury leaned back in the booth, stymied. How could you trust a man who stopped smoking without a tremor, a man who could order a plain round of toast with his tea? You wouldn't catch Sergeant Wiggins nibbling on a piece of toast without beans on it. Never. Did Cody Platt spearhead a new race of men who could cut themselves and not bleed? Who could expunge their bad habits without any sense of loss whatever? He bet Cody showed up bright and early at the gym to do his hundred pushups and an hour on the treadmill, then bench-press (was that the word?) several hundred pounds while he balanced a ball on his toes with a dog sitting on it.

Come on, come on, come on, man, Jury chided himself. Jury asked, "Did you have much contact with the Scotts after this search was over?"

"With Mary — Mrs. Scott — yes, I guess I did. Keep up the contact, I mean."

Jury noticed the given name correction. Throughout this conversation, Cody had been calling her Mary. What was that about?

Cody went on. "I never saw a woman more destroyed. The thing is she blamed herself, as if she should have been holding her daughter's hand every second, but, well, you can't do that, can you? You can't hold your kid's hand every step of the way."

"No, you can't. What contact did you have with Mary Scott?"

"I was assigned to the house with some others. You know — the aftermath of a kidnapping with calls being monitored waiting for the bugger to call. I didn't man the phones. I was just general dogsbody, somebody to brew the coffee and run errands. Even the cook was put out of commission because of what had happened; even the *maid* was said to be prostrated because of it. She's not there anymore, the maid. For God's sakes, I always had the impression staff was supposed to carry on no matter what."

"A myth, I imagine. What about Declan Scott? Did he carry on?"

"He did, actually. He did." Cody sat back, frowning, as if he were trying to work out how the stepfather could possibly have the presence of mind to "carry on."

"Somebody had to, Cody. There had to be someone who could answer questions, who could take directions if and when this person called."

Cody thought for a moment. "I spent a lot of time in the kitchen, making coffee. She — Mary — came in. Their kitchen is huge; it's one of those that seem designed for a staff of fifty to do enormous dinner parties. Anyway, she'd sit down on a high stool and tell me stories about Flora: Flora at two, somersaulting in the gardens; Flora at four, insisting Declan take the goat out of the farmer's fenced-in acres. That sort of thing, on and on. Flora was so pretty. She had the bluest eyes I've ever seen. Cornflower blue, as blue as the dress she wore."

"You must have been a godsend, some-body for Mary Scott to talk to."

"But it wasn't, in a sense, real. Mary wasn't all there. She was living on another plane altogether."

"Denial, I suppose. Still, you seemed to feel you knew her."

"Yes." He fiddled with the menu, removing it from its chrome fixture. "She didn't talk only about Flora; she talked a lot about herself, too, and Declan Scott, how he really loved Flora. He wanted to adopt her, but the father — this Baumann — more or less told Scott to F-off." He repositioned the menu in its holder.

"Viktor Baumann?"

"You know about him?"

Jury nodded. "A colleague, a DI with the pedophilia unit's been after him for some time."

"What must it be like, to lose both your wife and your daughter? Declan Scott must have felt bankrupt."

"It's Fitzgerald who said that, wasn't it? The point at which one stops feeling because his feelings are spent. Emotionally bankrupt, that's how he described his characters. I don't believe it; there's always an account that you can draw on. Always. I'm not sure whether that's a blessing, though. Having despair be just around the corner."

Cody looked down at his uninviting empty cup and was silent for some moments. Finally, he said, "Maybe I should have got something to eat." He looked at Jury as if assessing whether the superintendent would fall in with this plan.

Jury almost laughed at the level of concentration Cody was applying to this matter. "Go ahead. I'm not in any hurry."

The waitress wandered over — wandering between tables and chairs was the only way to put it — and Jury noticed for the first time the ring on her finger. It was a diamond cut to its last facet, so tiny one might have thought the jeweler was splitting the atom. "I like your ring," he said. "I like the setting, too. It's beautiful."

Her blush was almost feverish. "I only just got it last night." She stretched her arm out for them to admire it from afar. "If I seem a bit dim, well, you know . . ." But her dimness went unembroidered with explanation.

"Not dim. Merely distracted, and you should be. Now, my friend here wants to order something else."

"Beans on toast, I think."

What else? Jury smiled.

"And more tea?" she asked, sunnily. As if the mere prospect of another cup were cause for celebration. Cody nodded and she thanked him. Then she was off, to stumble and nearly fall when one in a row of high chairs caught her foot.

Jury watched her cut a swath of near accidents across the room, then turned to Cody and said, "What was Flora like?

Was she a smart kid? Sweet?"

Cody's clear eyes grew troubled, like troubled water, a disturbance beneath their surface. "Oh, she was smart all right." He smiled. "But I don't know as you'd call her sweet. She was kind of stubborn."

"She was four years old. 'Stubborn' goes with the territory."

The waitress was setting down his plate of beans and toast with a flourish and a "Ta-*dah!*" She had apparently traded distraction for entertainment. Cody thanked her and she walked off, much more steady on her feet, like a sailor who'd finally learned the trick of it.

Jury watched Cody fork up the beans. So he did have his little indulgences. "You don't smoke. Do you drink?"

"No. I stopped that too." Cody shoved up his glasses and leaned toward Jury and said with an intense whisper. "I'm an alcoholic and believe me, it's hell, pure and simple. Never a day goes by I don't want it. It's sheer hell."

The corners of Jury's mouth wanted to creep upward, but he pulled them down.

Inwardly, he smiled. Cody redeemed.

# 9

Jury liked Detective Sergeant Platt, but he didn't want Cody with him when he visited the Angel Gate gardens any more than he had in the Heligan gardens. He wanted silence; he wanted to absorb whatever there might be in its sunken history, for he knew even without seeing the place where the body had lain that its history was going to hold some key to the solution. This was not his intuition, and it certainly wasn't a brilliant deduction. It was simple: either someone had wanted to make a "statement" (that overused concept!) by killing this woman here — thus the "here" was significant — or else the killer had little choice but to do it here, which might mean the killer probably had been in the house or the gardens to begin with.

It was okay with Cody if Jury wanted to walk about on his own. "I need to get some things done anyway. Over there" — he pointed to the white caravan off in the distance — "is our incidents room. We could have set up inside the house but the boss didn't want to do that." He turned to Jury. "And he told me to assist you in any way I can."

"You have done and I'll tell him that." Jury thought for a moment. "You know how he is about a crime scene — doesn't want anyone breathing on it?"

"Oh, *everyone* knows how *he* is." Cody smiled.

So did Jury. "I'm worse."

This was by no means true, but it acted as sufficient reason for Jury's wanting to go to the bottom of the garden alone and also made Platt feel relieved that he wouldn't have to run a Macalvie-style endurance test.

Cody had walked him from the front of the house around to the rear. He told Jury there'd been so many police about that it was hardly necessary to seek Declan Scott's permission; he wouldn't think anything of it if yet one more copper invaded his grounds. Then Cody left by way of a small door in the garden wall with black grillwork in the shape of an angel. Jury watched him disappear as if it were a magical effect; he couldn't help but think again of Alice in Wonderland. The gardens, the little door, the sudden disappearance as if Cody had fallen through it. He had disappearance on the mind, he supposed, but he still wondered what fictive element there was in all this, what childhood story.

The garden wall was a faded red brick like the house itself. It was lined by broad herbaceous borders. Two or three acres were undergoing restoration; that was clear from the parts torn up and from other sections freshly planted. It was nothing like Heligan, but still a big project. It had the look of a job being directed by a landscape designer or garden architect, laid out in squares and triangles and bisected by flagged paths and studded with the occasional piece of sculpture. In the middle of the garden was a fountain, a bronze rendering of two little boys with buckets, trying to douse each other with water. One was high above the other, so the one below would have gotten a thorough dousing. It made him smile; it seemed such a whimsical piece for gardens so formally landscaped. Yet it kept to a sort of unkempt wildness; there were masses of rhododendrons in pink and white, and several with large leaves and lemon-yellow flowers. It was very early March, but he imagined that the Cornwall climate could sustain early blooming. The rhododendrons enclosed a small area that Jury thought might be a garden within a garden, perhaps the secret garden Macalvie mentioned.

Mounds of box grew around the perimeter and edged the paths. Much of the area was torn up; still, there were plantings of luminous colors — buttercup, a green-needled, red-flowered plant that Jury couldn't identify, and a sheet of bluebells in the rhododendron garden. He thought of the little girl in Hester Street.

Jury observed all of this from the terrace, which was really the first terrace in three sloping downward; they were balustraded terraces with central steps leading down to the pool and the bronze boys. Still it was not immense, and because it was walled it seemed almost intimate. He walked down the steps and across and past the bronze boys with buckets to the bottom of the garden.

Yellow police tape served as a strange counterpoint to the tied-off plots that had been undergoing planting. And it was strange how the few steps down to the covered recess were so reminiscent of the grotto in the Lost Gardens. Jury crouched to go under the tape and went into the cold little room to see the stone bench on which the body had been found.

He looked back along the path which, in its middle part, curved around the sculpture of the boys. This covered niche was perfectly visible from the back of the house, although across a two-acre distance, but still not so far as to block a view. But since the shooting had happened after dark, whether it was visible in daylight hardly mattered.

Why had this woman come for the second time? Mary Scott was dead, so who was she meeting? It must have been for that purpose, so the someone must have a connection to the house, whether living in it or not. A strange meeting spot, in any event.

Jury walked back along the path, looking at the windows, having no sense of being watched. He walked around to the front of the house, where he saw an old man bent over a wheelbarrow into which he was throwing whatever he had uprooted from whatever bit of earth he was clearing.

A Sisyphean task the old man had before him, given the general state of the land in front of the house. It looked as if it hadn't been touched in years, and yet new shoots were still breaking through the earth, such as that iris forcing its way up through weeds. It must have been very hardy stock to begin with, hardy or so entrenched it couldn't be stopped by time or inattention or carelessness. Beside a dry pool a miasma of pink climbing roses covered a trellis, nearly closing off the flaking benches where the occupants had once sat to enjoy the perfumed air.

The arthritic-looking gardener (for Jury assumed him to be one) with his wheelbarrow couldn't have gotten this lot into shape in a million years. Jury supposed he was an old retainer, kept on so that he might feel useful, thus keeping at bay the end of his declining years. But he also might have been there as some sort of evidence of the past, the unchanging, changeless past.

The land here was thickly wooded. The branches of the trees on either side of what once had been a laburnum tunnel, or an avenue of chestnuts and laburnums and sycamores and oaks tangled together in so dense a canopy that the light of the afternoon sun could barely break their cover. It was inviting, at least to Jury, who liked his paths well shuttered. He walked for a short distance along this path, the path itself nearly obscured by rutted earth, tall grasses, weeds and fallen branches. Every once in a while he passed a tree whose trunk had been whitewashed with an *X* and Jury wondered if these trees were to be cut down, clearing the way a little. He picked at the whitewashed bark and found the paint to be old and flaking. Whoever had started the process of resurrecting this once-pretty path had forgotten it or decided not to bother.

And the avenue would have been pretty, inviting a stroll in fragrant air, the source of which Jury couldn't determine. He supposed it was a combination of scents. He turned and walked back, seeing the path as it once was. Jury had a divining eye, an eye trained to see outlines or patterns no longer adhered to but still there, like footprints in soft earth. The white crosses, the air of mystery and the tantalizing wish to find out what lay at the end of the path and if these trees were doomed. It was odd that the gardens behind the house were to be completely overhauled by some garden architect while the front of the house was, apparently, to be left untouched, seen to by the silent, elderly gardener. Declan Scott, he thought, must want to hang on to the past, or to his origins, or to keep whatever he could from changing.

A thankless job, Mr. Scott, a thankless job.

# 10

The door was opened by a woman of late middle age whose good looks were now fading and who appeared to be doing little to stop the progress. She wore no makeup except for a dab of lipstick and a boxy haircut that didn't serve her strong, squarish face. Had it not been for the white calf-length apron that bound her more like a winding sheet than an apron, Jury would have assumed she was a relation or friend of the owner rather than a member of staff. Indeed "staff," as he understood it, had been considerably reduced; the cook was standing in for a butler or valet, who once would have been a necessary adjunct to the house in its heyday of cars and carriages, when there was a full complement of valets, cooks, housemaids. There must once have been such staff, considering the size of the place and its obvious elegance, even though it might now not be "kept up" the way it once had been, very much like the woman who stood here now.

After he had identified himself — unnecessarily, for she knew who he was — the woman said she would let Mr. Scott know he was here and walked off. He waited.

To the left and right were long halls. She wore shoes with a medium heel, and Jury could hear the tap of her heels as she walked down the hall to his right and turned a corner. They were opulent, these halls, marble floored. Without her footsteps, they were also silent. He stood there hearing only the note of a thrush outside, and then he walked around the foyer. Furnishings, antique and valuable, if somewhat worn. There was a certain seediness to that wall hanging of a stalwart military figure, helmeted and upon a horse. Coin-size pieces of the velvet fabric of the tall furry helmet and of the horse's mane had rubbed off, as if the war had gone on too long, and soldier and horse were both fading. It hung above a secretaire of mahogany and stained maple and gilt, flecks of gold missing, some of the stain worn away. Nothing here wasted or wrecked, just suffering from the slow onslaught of time.

She returned and led Jury across the

foyer and along that same hall, where she stopped by the door of a large room, a library, apparently. Books lined three walls, the fourth occupied by a brownish-gold marble fireplace. A fire had been lit, fairly recently to judge from the size of the logs. She told him Mr. Scott would be here in a moment. This was accompanied by a rather tight little smile, enough of one for politeness' sake. His first impression was that she was hostile and trying to hide it, natural enough, he thought, with police invading the household.

Declan Scott walked in, handsome and haggard. He took everything over — the fire, the furnishings and Jury himself. Jury felt an immediate empathy; he liked Scott where he stood. Such empathy worried him for objectivity could go flying out the window; that kind of response to a witness could mean trouble. But he knew at a glance what Brian Macalvie had meant about the difficulty of staying in the same room with the man for more than a few minutes, although Jury thought he himself could last a good deal longer. He couldn't recall the last time he'd come up against someone in whom emotion was so visceral. And this despite Scott's strange air of insularity that could even pass as indifference if one hadn't spent a lot of years learning how to read people.

Declan Scott stood inside the room looking at Jury as if Jury were one more disappointment in a long list of them. Police, private investigators — all had failed to find the child Flora. Yet Jury suspected that Scott's manner was not fully explained by that dreadful event nor did it account for that look that said he knew Jury would miss everything by a mile.

Declan Scott reminded Jury of Angel Gate itself, its desolate gardens, echoing halls, opulent and frayed and nearly untenanted, as if its owner had already jettisoned part of himself and gone on with this remaindered half. He had a handkerchief in his breast pocket, and if it was there for show, it was doing a poor job of it, for the corner flopped over. But Declan Scott was not for show. Jury was sure of that.

Scott held out his hand. "I'm sorry you had to wait; I was in the rear gardens seeing to things. Well, that's what I call it. I'm sure my gardeners wouldn't agree. I saw you there before. I didn't want to disturb you."

Jury was reminded of the man's respect for privacy. He smiled. "Didn't you wonder who I was?"

107

"Oh, I knew who you were. Commander Macalvie rang me." He paused. "I must admit to some surprise that Scotland Yard would get involved, I mean, after all of this time. Why have you?"

"Let's say at the behest of Commander Macalvie."

"Okay. We'll say it." Scott smiled.

So did Jury. He had the feeling that Scott would cut through anything that struck him as not to the point. Jury went on. "I'm working on a case in London that might be tied to —" He hesitated over bringing up an issue so painful.

Declan Scott helped him. "My step-daughter, you mean. Flora."

"Yes, that's right. Flora. There could be a connection. There was a little girl we haven't yet identified —" Jury's mind seemed to widen, taking in vast possibilities. "It all seems to rest on identity, doesn't it?"

Declan raised his eyebrows. "Not sure I follow you, Superintendent."

"I'm just thinking out loud. The connection between this murdered child and Flora could be Flora's father."

"Viktor Baumann?" Declan, after motioning Jury into an armchair, sat down heavily on a sofa as if to take the weight of Baumann off his feet.

"Did you know him — I mean, had you met him?"

"Yes. Right after Mary and I were married. He reared his ugly head about custody of Flora. It was as if Mary's having married again would put Flora on the auction block or something." Declan looked off toward one of the high windows. "I wanted to adopt her and Baumann wouldn't agree to that. But — sorry, that isn't what you wanted to talk about." He reached into the fireplace with a poker, shunted burnt logs and coals about in there. On the fireplace mantel was the stone figure of an angel with a broken wing, his head bent, his hand above his eyes as if he were searching for something on the ground.

"On the contrary, it's just what I want to talk about. Do you mind telling me what happened that day? I mean, as far as you yourself know?"

Scott leaned forward, arms on knees; he seemed to be studying the faded figure in the carpet at his feet. "They went to Heligan — you know, the Lost Gardens — a number of times. It's a distance, so they took the whole day and had lunch sometimes in Mevagissey or St. Austell."

"Was there a pattern to these excursions

that somebody else might have known?"

Declan shook his head. "No, not really."

"How was your wife? I mean, did she seem, well, her usual self?"

Sitting back, he grew thoughtful. "The thing is, Mary hadn't been quite her usual self for a while. I don't mean she was moody or acting differently so that anyone would notice except for me. Anxious, I guess you'd call it. I thought it might be her heart problem — that's finally what killed her, though we neither of us thought it was immediately life threat—" He stopped. "Sorry."

"You don't have to apologize, Mr. Scott." Jury waited for a beat and then asked, "Do you think there's any chance at all she was afraid that Flora might be in danger?"

Scott looked at Jury, surprised. "I certainly wouldn't think so, no."

"We have to take into account even the most unlikely possibility. You understand. I'm sure the police questioned you pretty thoroughly."

Scott nodded. "Yes." He ran a hand through his dark hair, then brought the hand down to the back of his neck and rubbed, as if a muscle were cramped. Then he crossed his legs and smiled. He had one of those killer smiles, especially wrenching because he didn't often turn it on. Women must drop in their tracks when he smiled.

Jury had taken one of the police photos out of his coat pocket before removing his coat. He reached it across to Scott. "I don't think you've seen pictures of the body —"

"No, and I haven't missed them, either," he said dryly, taking glasses out of the same pocket the handkerchief drooped from. He looked at the photo without saying anything and then returned it to Jury.

"Have they identified her yet?"

"Not yet. You told police she was a friend of your wife's."

"That's not exactly what I said." As if weary of being misquoted or misunderstood, Scott slid down a little in the chair so as to rest his head against its back.

"An acquaintance, then?" Jury knew what the man had told police; he just wanted to hear him say it. Things that might have been missing in the first telling (or second, or third) might turn up in a later version. People recall different things at different times and, of course, for different reasons.

"I'm not sure; I'd definitely say acquaintance more than friend. But I had no way of knowing. I saw this woman" — he nodded toward the photo Jury was holding — "only once and that was in the lounge at Brown's Hotel. It's one of the most popular places in London for tea and is usually crowded. She was with my wife, Mary. They were sitting across the room, in a corner. At first I thought I'd go over and say hello, but then I didn't." He said this as if he wondered about his action — or inaction — and if it had made a difference, possibly even a fatal one.

Jury asked the question aloud. "Why didn't you?"

"I suppose I didn't want to barge in, you know."

"Not even on your wife?"

Declan smiled. "Especially on my wife. She liked her privacy and she got too little of it. But the other reason was purely practical; I'd bought a painting for her as a Christmas present and I didn't want her to know it." He went on. "Besides, they seemed to be so . . . engrossed, I guess I didn't want to disturb them." He ran his thumb over his forehead, moving it back and forth, as if he meant to press in some thought, or retrieve it. He looked up at Jury. "Perhaps that's the reason I didn't in-

112

terrupt. I read the situation as something a little odd. Mary did not look especially happy. I simply decided to wait until she told me."

"But according to what you told police, she didn't."

"No. She didn't even mention it; I was the one to bring it up. All Mary said was that the woman was an old acquaintance, an old school friend. Roedean, that's where Mary went to school. But she offered no name, and she said nothing else. Had I not said I'd seen them, I doubt she would've told me at all. It was disturbing because now it seemed furtive or secret, and that wasn't like her. She was always very open with me."

"This woman was a classmate?"

"I don't know. She didn't elaborate."

"The woman must have been important in your wife's life."

"Why?"

"Because she's been murdered." It was the same thing he'd said to Viktor Baumann.

"Yes. Of course." Declan looked chagrined, impatient with himself. "Mary's secretiveness about her should have made it obvious something about her was important. None of this makes any sense to me,

Superintendent." His eyes were sparked by the firelight. "The Devon and Cornwall police went through everything belonging to my wife, even the pockets of her silk dressing gown, looking for some link to the woman. All of her papers, her old correspondence — Mary kept everything. Once a little paper fluttered to the floor from the things she was carrying and I picked it up." He smiled and sat back, as if comforted by the memory. "It was an old note I'd written to her about a dinner party: 'Let's go. Gilbert is serving Dover sole.' Can you imagine holding on to such nonsense?"

It was clear the note itself might have been nonsense, but not the holding on to it. Jury smiled.

"I mean," said Scott, "it was hardly a love letter or a ticket to Aruba."

Jury liked the consequence of that. He smiled. "It might have been to her."

Scott looked over at the fireplace, either the fire or the photograph on the mantel.

Jury said, "Police found nothing?"

"Not as far as I know. They eventually found her diary, which I thought I'd hidden rather well. I stuck it in the airing cupboard. Who would look in there for such a book?"

"The CID."

Declan laughed and it seemed to draw him out of his melancholy mood, at least for now. "And I thought I was being so damned clever. See, I really couldn't stand their reading her diary. It seemed such an invasion of privacy."

"It is. But in a murder investigation, there really is no privacy. The diary didn't say anything about this woman? Not even about the chance meeting at the hotel?" If it was chance, thought Jury.

"Apparently not; the police didn't say."

"Didn't you read it?"

"No."

A man who was dead serious about privacy. "Did you consider leaving here — you know, finding yourself a house in London, that sort of thing? Because it must be painful, living here."

Declan looked at Jury as if the police must be dim. "Of course not. This is my family home. I couldn't stand leaving here and trying to live somewhere else. I hate change. It's like death, isn't it?"

It was not a rhetorical question. Jury didn't know how to answer, so he didn't. Scott's feelings about change accounted for the trees and paths and furnishings remaining in disrepair; it was why he kept all of his wife's things, Jury imagined. Declan

115

Scott was like his wife; if Jury asked him to produce the little note about Gilbert's Dover sole right now, he bet Scott could have done so on the spot.

Declan rose and went to the bureau and the soda siphon. Turning with the decanter held aloft he said, "Superintendent?"

"Yes, I think I will." While the drinks were being made, Jury looked at Scott and thought perhaps it was the way one comes to feel warm in freezing water. Or that Macalvie, for all this, was right and Jury had just hung on beyond that fifteen minutes, long enough to relax in the man's company.

"Tell me, who would get this place if you died?"

"Now? Flora, of course."

"But she's —"

"Please don't say she's dead, Mr. Jury. I know that's the most likely explanation. I hold out hope, which isn't unreasonable, is it?"

"No."

He handed Jury his drink. "I mean, it depends on why she was taken, doesn't it? For instance, if the villain here is Mary's ex, then Flora's somewhere safe and sound. It wouldn't be the first time we'd heard of that sort of thing." Declan returned to the sofa.

"Do you think that's what happened?"

He studied the fire for a moment. "No." He tossed back half his drink.

Jury was surprised Scott said that. Viktor Baumann had struck him as exactly like the sort who would be behind such a plot.

"Why not?"

"Baumann never wanted children in the first place according to Mary."

"It could have been power he wanted. I don't think the Baumanns of this world give up so easily." Jury wondered if Declan Scott had a clue about Johnny Blakeley's investigation of that house in Hester Street. Or knew anything about the pedophilia charge. He doubted it, and Jury certainly wasn't going to tell him.

"Do you have some pictures I could see of Flora?"

Declan said, smiling, "Only a few hundred." He rose and went around the sofa to the table behind it and opened a drawer. He took out a couple of dozen and spread them on the table between them. Then he picked out a snapshot. "This was the latest, I took on the day" — Declan cleared his throat — "she disappeared. She loved this blue dress; it was brand new and she was so afraid she'd get a spot on it she didn't even want to sit down." He laughed,

117

and picked out another snapshot. "Flora was three here. It was taken in Exeter at Debenhams where they had installed a Father Christmas for the kids."

Jury studied it. Her hair was golden and curly and she had that near-ethereal beauty which seems the provenance of tiny children, a beauty unmarked and uncorrupted. Father Christmas, of whose face one could see only the eyes above the billowy white beard, looked as if, at least at the moment, he shared in this too. Jury sat back with this picture and looked at it, trying to work out what it was that was so affecting. It was the essence of childhood, even his own, though his own had been so knocked about. But there had been moments, yes, he was sure there had been moments, and moments in everyone's life like this, a childhood distilled.

There were some with just Mary and Flora taken in the gardens of Heligan. Jury recognized the giant rhododendron. There were several with Declan and Flora. There was one larger one of Declan and a woman who was not his wife. It was taken in the street; behind them was the ornate art nouveau curve of one of the entrances to the Paris metro. He held it up. "Paris. Who's this?"

Declan looked surprised. "Oh. That's Georgina. A friend of mine. Georgina Fox."

"If you don't mind my saying so, she's gorgeous." She was. Tall, slender, with an airy blondness that seemed almost transparent. Jury wouldn't mind having such a "friend" himself. He smiled. "Good friend, right?"

Declan laughed. He was embarrassed. "That was a year after Mary died. I was still — anyway, I wanted to get away, so I went to Paris for a while." He took the picture from Jury. "Georgina. She was really — breathtaking, don't you think?"

It was as if Declan wanted Jury to reassure him he hadn't been a rotter for taking up with Georgina Fox after his wife had died. My God, who would blame him? "*I'd* certainly fall for her. What man wouldn't?"

"It didn't last long. A few weeks."

Jury looked up. "Have you got any more of Flora?"

Declan laughed. "Oh, I have plenty." He went back to the sideboard again. He pulled out a handful and passed them to Jury.

Flora at different times in her life. The baby, the two-, three- and four-year-old. Jury liked the way she stood in a couple of these, straight as a soldier at the entrance to that path he had just walked, the trees like sentinels, the white crosses. This (he thought she thought) is how you stand when you're posing for a picture. She wore a pale ruffled dress whose hem didn't reach her knees.

Declan sat, his elbow on a knee, chin in hand, watching the pictures move through Jury's hands as if they might spring to life again under the eyes of a stranger, a new person. "Mary used to call her 'Fleur' mostly to tease Flora." He smiled. "She hated 'Fleur.' " As if it were a new idea, he said, "You know, Flora was very down to earth, unpretentious — if you can say that about a four-year-old child." He sat back. "When I'm walking in London — anywhere, any town or city — and pass children on the pavement, I look at them and think how uncorrupted their world is and I grow appalled at what they'll have to face in a few years' time, what they'll come to know: drugs, pimps, charlatans, fools — the whole illicit world — and I have to stop to draw breath I'm so afraid and so appalled. How in God's name can they handle it? How can they shoulder the world?"

"Maybe mum and dad are there to take the weight."

Declan retrieved the photos, saying, "Some don't have a mum. Some don't have either. What then?"

"They deal with it."

"They shouldn't have to."

"I know," said Jury. He did.

At that moment, the same woman who had opened the door to Jury came unceremoniously to the doorway, pardoned herself and said, "Dinner will be ready in ten minutes, Mr. Scott."

"Good. Thanks, Rebecca. Mr. Jury will be joining me —" He turned to Jury. "You will, won't you? I can guarantee it'll be worth it."

"You bet."

She nodded and left.

The subject of his wife was one Declan Scott would never tire of. Thus, over a consommé, Jury asked him how they'd met.

"Quite by accident. In a pub in Belgravia. After she got away from Viktor she was living with her mother — Alice Miers, a lovely woman — in Belgravia. Alice has a house there, small but very nice."

Small house. Big price. These people knew how to live, didn't they?

"I still see Alice when I go up to London. I take — took — Flora, too." His voice trailed away. He held up the fluted glass into which the Chardonnay had been poured. "These glasses are from Prague. Mary loved glass. I don't much care; I'm more interested in what's in it."

"What's in it is very good stuff," said Jury.

Rebecca served the lobster with an excellent sauce (which leaned heavily on the same Chardonnay) and then withdrew.

Jury asked, "How good a look did you actually get of this woman in Brown's?"

Startled, Declan looked up from the food that had been transferred from serving platter to plate and said, "A fairly good one as I was trying to make out who she was. You think I might be wrong? I mean, in identifying her?"

Jury hadn't actually thought this through, but realized it could be true. He said so. "It just occurred to me; it was just a thought. It's been three years since you saw her."

"That's true. I don't know why she stuck in my mind. She wasn't attractive. But then if she wasn't the same woman, there'd be no connection between this murdered woman and Mary."

"Even so, there still might be. It's the fact it happened here, on your property. And there's Flora, too. That could be a connection."

Declan had been reaching for his glass and his hand stopped midair. Flora added to Mary, both losses must suddenly have washed over him. Mary, dying at such a young age, and Flora, a child whose last minutes — whose last months, possibly — might have been agony with no one to come to her aid — that must be unbearable.

Jury once again felt the weight of Declan Scott's despair. The air was heavy with it, and Jury felt as if he must do something. Perhaps that was what Macalvie couldn't tolerate. "I'm sorry" was all he could think to say.

Looking down, Declan shook his head and held out the palm of his hand as if resisting apologies or perhaps merely asking for time. Two seconds, three. "It's all right. I guess I still can't deal with it."

"Why should you be able to deal with it?"

He smiled slightly but bitterly. "You're right. Why should I?" Declan nodded and once again reached for his wineglass. "But as for this woman, yes, I'm quite sure it was the same woman. And remember, Dora Stout saw her, too. Dora was cook here for many years."

"I know. We've met. I saw her in South Petherwin."

"Dora left because it'd become too much of a job for her; also, Rebecca Owen had come. She'd been with Mary for some time when Mary was married to Baumann. There's no love lost there, I can tell you. Rebecca didn't like him."

Jury thought about this. "Dora Stout didn't get a very good look at her, but from what she said it could certainly have been the dead woman. You know the thing most memorable about her? Her extreme plainness. That's a funny thing to remember; one would think it would be utterly forgettable. I don't know why it isn't. Did Dora resent Mrs. Owen coming?"

"No, I don't think so. Indeed, I think she was glad of it; she wouldn't have wanted to leave Mary in the lurch." He stopped talking when Rebecca Owen came to clear the plates away. Jury told her it was delicious.

She thanked him and said that "the pud" would be up in a minute. Then she pushed through the swinging door.

Declan laughed. " 'The pud.' I love it."

She reappeared with tall, delicate glasses filled with custard, which she set before them, and then moved over to the sideboard to fuss with the accoutrements of coffee.

"What is this English predeliction for custard, Superintendent? You ever noticed it?"

"Of course. I'm a detective, after all." Jury had taken a spoonful and added, "But this isn't just any old custard."

Rebecca said, "It's sabayon. I'm afraid I put in too much Marsala wine."

"Is there such a thing as too much wine?" said Jury.

She smiled and asked Declan, "Should I serve coffee now or will you wait?"

"Oh, bring it on, Rebecca, please." He said to Jury, "Like some port?"

Jury shook his head. "I couldn't. I couldn't eat or drink one more thing."

"Then that's all. We're fine."

She poured coffee for them and went back again through the swinging door.

Jury said, "It galls me to say it, but I'd better root out the chap who brought me here. Or someone in that incidents room planted on your land. They'll collect me and drag me back to Launceston."

"Why do that? Stay here. As you can see

we're not overbooked for the night."

Jury was tired. And tomorrow was Friday and that meant getting back to London and then to Newcastle on Saturday.

He did not spend too much time thinking about the professionalism (rather, the lack of it) of accepting the hospitality of a witness or suspect. He was dead tired. Or perhaps the tiredness was the weight of Declan Scott's sadness that had come to rest on Jury's shoulders like a yoke. In any event, he accepted the offer of a room for the night and thanked him. He would call Cody to pick him up at Angel Gate instead of the White Hart in Launceston.

Jury looked out of the bedroom window at the night and thought Declan Scott did not discard the past easily. The countless reminders of what he had lost did not cripple him. Perhaps he was one of those people for whom reminiscence was an anodyne rather than anguish. He took comfort in having about him whatever she had touched or heard or worn or drunk from. Would someone think Scott of a morbid turn of mind, living in this house full of ghosts?

Jury didn't. If the past was pretty much

all you had, why would you want to discard it? Jury tried to picture him with a new flat and new friends. For there, he thought, was the illusion: to believe that one could start all over again and build a new life on the ruins of the old one. No wonder he had fallen for the beautiful Georgina Fox. But what are you supposed to use for building materials when all you have is burned wood and broken plaster?

The room had been cold, but the fire that had been laid and lit in the big fireplace soon drew the dampness and chill from the air. He thought of this later, in his room whose long window looked out over the woods in front and the avenue or what used to be now vanishing beneath leaves, grasses, ferns and beleaguered hedges. He thought of the white crosses. He must ask Declan Scott what they meant.

He was tired enough that he was sure he could fall into a black mine of sleep, but he didn't. He lay for a long time with eyes shut, eyes open, letting scenes he had fashioned of the lives of Mary and Flora and Declan Scott unreel like a film in his mind.

And the mystery woman. The reel stuck on the mystery woman, the dead woman lying on the stone bench. A statement, a message, perhaps even a warning. But he had no idea what that could mean and while he was trying to make sense of it, he slept.

# 11

The next morning they went out through French doors that opened onto the terrace and walked down the steps, not in the best repair, to the path and the bronze sculpture of the little boys. The path ran all the way from the stone steps to the rear of the garden.

"Temperamentally, I suppose I'd rather leave things as they are."

"Then why change it? It's a massive amount of work."

"Because Mary wanted the gardens restored," Declan answered, as if this should explain everything, not just a wild acre or two. "I've commissioned Warburton and the Macmillans — that's the father down there" — he gestured toward a short, squarish figure digging in one of the beds midway along — "to bring the place back to life, its old life. That's what Mary wanted. Those steps we just went down — ?"

Declan looked over his shoulder.

"From the terraces, you mean?"

"Yes. They're a little mossy and slippery now. But those steps were once turf covered. It was cut to fit. They were covered with grass. Perhaps it's ridiculous, but I'd like that."

Jury looked behind him at the steps, four of them on each terrace. "What you could do is just get some sod, couldn't you? The kind builders use to cover up bare land around new houses?"

"No, my landscape chap told me it takes a particular kind. I need someone with, as he put it, 'an intimate knowledge of turf.' You wouldn't happen to have it? Or know someone who does? Frankly, I can't imagine anyone with so esoteric a bent."

Jury smiled. "You seem to enjoy the refurbishment, though."

"Hm. Here we are," Declan said as they came upon a man in a gray coverall, flat leather cap and garden gloves so stiff they could have stood by themselves with the boots in some corner. "Mr. Macmillan, this is Mr. Jury, a friend of mine." He turned to Jury. "The Macmillans are the most sought-after gardeners in Cornwall. And Cornwall, being as it is full of gardens, that's saying something."

Macmillan bathed in this compliment as if he'd expected no less a one. Waving his hand over the area immediately surrounding the fountain, four beds bisected by narrow paths, he said, "What we're plannin' on doin' here, Mr. Scott, is take it all down to seed and — if you want me to follow the old plan to the letter" — emphasis indicating he would rather do anything but, for he stopped long enough for Declan to allow him some freedom, which Declan didn't — "we'll put in the tulips, just as before, but ah would like t' try t' break out the breeder tulips, an' ah can tell you the colors would be most astonishin' an' well worth the effort."

Declan said, quite seriously, "All right, Mr. Macmillan, I'll follow your greater wisdom here."

Macmillan blinked his sandy lashes, and his tan eyes looked happier. "And as for the begonias, ah would strongly suggest Dragon Wing if we can get enough heat in your glass house; we could have flowers this year if that was the case."

Declan looked over at two small glass buildings at the side of the wall, strangely unobtrusive. "I don't know; that is, I don't know about the heat. We'll talk about that later."

"But Millie was askin' about the turf. You know what a perfectionist she is. And there's the enameled mead thing, too. Ah don't have much truck wi' tartin' up the place but —" He shrugged aside the tartish notion of enameling.

"Tell Millie not to worry. I'm sure someone will come along, like the winter solstice."

Macmillan didn't appear to believe this and gave Jury a sour look as if he might be having a hand in the garden business. "Another thing, could ya' please have old Abbot just stick t' the front. He's about here all the time, givin' his advice."

Declan smiled. "No, Mr. Macmillan, I won't tell Abbot that. He's been here forever, long before any of us. These grounds were his once. So you'll just have to bear up, won't you?"

Macmillan turned a shade of purple at being told off, then went back to his work.

Declan and Jury continued on the path. "What did you mean by the winter solstice?"

"Nothing. I thought it must have something to do with the alchemy of gardening. I like to say things like that to pretend I'm not a complete dud in this line."

Jury laughed. "I see you're not."

"Then you're blind. I am a complete dud."

They were nearing the end of the garden and the yellow crime scene tape and coming up on a young woman who Jury assumed must be the daughter. Same sandy eyes and eyelashes, same gingerish (not ginger, not brown) hair, same coverall. The resemblance was quite amazing.

Declan introduced Jury again.

Millie said, "Mr. Scott" — looking away at the wall that surrounded the two acres of garden — "you'll want the grapes back, I expect." Shading her eyes, she peered off into the distance as if the grapes had made their escape through the crumbled brick to freedom. "There's the two vineries in perfectly good order, so that's no problem." Then she set about scattering Latin terms and other references to her work, words that Jury was sure he knew when she started, but had no idea of when she'd finished.

"That's fine, Millie. When will the rest of the crew be here to help clear some of this stuff?"

"They'll be along," she said, telling him nothing, but merrily.

He accepted this laissez-faire attitude and continued on with Jury.

"It seems ominous, that tape, that smiling bright yellow," said Declan.

Then, hearing his name called out, he turned.

A man was standing on the terrace steps waving his arms to gain attention. He came down the steps toward them. Every so often, he raised his arm as he walked, as if he would prevent them turning away as long as he could keep himself in motion and in their sights. Or at least in Scott's.

"Marcus Warburton. He's the landscape chap. Does a lot of gardens around here."

Jury was a little surprised there were enough gardens around here to do. Warburton was a tall fellow with sharp good looks, a face that was more angles than planes — thin, rather Grecian nose, a model's cheekbones. And well dressed. The cut of the suit was of the ample Italian style — Armani, Fendi, Zegna — its material a shade somewhere between the silver and the brown of the birches. Clotheswise Marc Warburton was not standing still, as was Declan Scott, whose tweed jacket was probably from a tailor on Jermyn Street or Savile Row, but tailored a decade ago.

When Warburton heard that Jury was a Scotland Yard superintendent, Jury fully expected him to say, "Oh. Yes. You."

He smiled at Jury — the smile sharp as the rest of him — and said what Jury was sure brought him down here to the gardens, "It's a hell of a thing, isn't it, Superintendent, that woman found there." He nodded in the direction of the stone alcove.

Jury thought it was as if the body didn't fit in with the landscaping plans, but Warburton was stuck with it.

"It must be serious if the Devon and Cornwall police are calling you in."

Jury's face was blank as he said, "Not really. I just happened along."

Abruptly, Warburton laughed. "Why don't I believe that?"

Jury smiled. "I don't know. Why don't you? You knew Mrs. Scott, then?"

"Yes, of course."

Jury couldn't determine if that settling in of a mournful look on Warburton's face was real or feigned. Yet why would the man want to pretend? Mary Scott had been dead for over two years. Her husband might still mourn her, but the hired help could put off the trappings of woe, surely.

Warburton began, "She was —" But something in Jury's face stopped him from saying what she was.

Declan Scott had turned away.

"I wonder if I could speak with you sometime," said Jury.

Marc Warburton showed no particular discomfort at this request. He folded his arms and said, "Police already have. You might want to check with them."

Even Scott raised his eyebrows at this thick-headedness.

Jury merely said, "I already have, Mr. Warburton, as it's the Devon and Cornwall constabulary's case. But details can go missing sometimes from one account to the next. Memory changes."

Warburton was all smiles, yet his face was neither open nor friendly. "Of course, Superintendent. Anytime. Now, if you like."

Scott said, "No, not now. I'm showing the superintendent round the garden."

Warburton nodded. "Well, anytime, then. I'm always available. Declan knows how to reach me." He turned and walked up the path.

"Marc's very good at what he does, but he wants to control everything — even you."

"Especially me." Jury laughed. "He didn't like me talking to you. At least, not on your own."

They passed through a stand of birch

trees, silver and pinkish-brown bark. "These were Mary's favorite trees."

Together, they looked at the enclosure with its stone bench. Jury said, "This place could only be opportune if you live on this property."

Declan looked surprised and then laughed. "Then it's down to me. I'm the only one living here."

"I didn't mean it in that way. Anyone connected with the place, staff —"

"Ah! Then it's down to Rebecca Owen. That's a pity. She's such a good cook."

"Staff doesn't include your gardeners? I'm talking about people who are well acquainted with Angel Gate."

Declan frowned. "That could be anyone here — well, it's beyond belief."

"It's even harder to believe that someone outside of Angel Gate would choose to meet the victim here. It's hardly a convenient setup for a shooting. Which is what I said before: it's not exactly opportune."

"I find that extremely difficult —"

"To believe. Right. It's always difficult, Mr. Scott."

They walked in silence toward the terrace until Jury said, "You're not extending this project around to the front of the house, apparently."

"No. That's Abbot's country. But I guess the real reason is that the woods there have been like this as long as I can remember. Well, as I said" — Declan shrugged — "I hate change."

"I was wondering about the white crosses. Then you don't mean to take down those trees?"

Declan stopped and looked at him. "That's Flora's handiwork." He smiled. "There was an itinerant tree surgeon — or so he called himself — stopped at my door and asked if we wanted them cut down."

"Can a surgeon be itinerant?" Jury laughed. "And you said?"

"I said no, that wasn't the meaning of the white crosses."

"What was Flora's purpose in marking them?"

"She said it was a way to keep from getting lost. You just follow the white crosses."

"Getting lost on her own grounds?"

They'd continued walking.

"Oh, I expect she thought you could get lost anywhere."

When they reached the terrace steps, Declan stopped, hands behind his back, and looked down. "What, I'd like to know, constitutes an 'intimate knowledge of turf'? I know there are different kinds of soil — acid and less acidic and so forth — but how could the subject be so extensive as to require a serious study all on its own?"

Jury's hands were behind his back, too. Thoughtfully, he said, "Oddly enough, I know someone who's quite an expert in gardening arcana. I mean, he seems to have acquired an intimate knowledge of the oddities of medieval and eighteenth-century gardening. I think I've even heard him talk about —"

At that moment, Rebecca Owen came out through the French doors to tell Jury that Sergeant Cody had come to pick him up. Jury said he'd be there straightaway. Then he turned back to Declan. "I think I've heard this person talk about enameling — is that it?"

"Enameled or flowering mead, yes."

"So he might know about both that and the turf business."

"That would be very helpful. Give me his name and I'll ring him."

"Oh, I'll ring him." Jury smiled. "I'd be happy to."

# 12

While Jury was walking in the garden with Declan Scott, Melrose Plant was sitting in his living room with Agatha, a different thing altogether.

A new hermit had been installed, the previous one having taken a job with Theo Wrenn Browne. He had been hired in the hope that he would scare off Agatha, that or at least cut down on the number of her visits. It would have done, only Mr. Bramwell was so insufferable that Melrose had suggested he might be happier working with Theo Wrenn Browne (who was no stranger to insufferability).

"He absolutely gives me the creeps," said Agatha as she piled more thick cream on her scone. She was speaking this time of the new hermit, who had been vetted by Marshall Trueblood and found acceptable. Mr. Blodgett had experience; he had put in a year as hermit on the estate of Lord

Thewis and could furnish references. Trueblood had sent him along to Ardry End.

Melrose immediately liked his looks — a bit small, a bit bent — and asked him what he did.

"Wot ah do? Well, wiff all due respec', sir, ah does wot 'ermits do. As you know."

"Well, the point is, my last hermit was always down in the pub, when he wasn't complaining about the hermitage."

It was outside of this structure that they were standing. Mr. Blodgett had inspected it and found it quite the best hermitage he had ever seen. "You musta got one o' them rum ones. Give us all a bad name. Pubs is out, sir; ah sits mostly."

"But you can walk about, can't you?"

"If you requires it, sir, ah be happy to." He bowed, deferentially.

Melrose especially liked the way he kneaded the flat cap he held in his hands.

"Now, can you lower?"

Mr. Blodgett frowned. "Lower? Ah don't believe ah know wot you're meanin', sir."

"It's just looking sort of fierce. And wild."

"Mebbe you want one of them actor fellows?"

"No, no. See, all I want you to do is

141

creep about when my aunt is here, especially at the drawing-room windows."

"Ah expec' ah could, on'y me eyes ain't
too good. How would ah know it's her?"

"Because it's always her; she's the only
regular visitor I have, and she's over here
every day. It's damned tiring."

That had been several weeks ago, and
Melrose was quite satisfied with Mr.
Blodgett's efforts. Unfortunately, with his
bad eyesight, Mr. Blodgett had fallen into
the duck pond one cold February morning
and was still recuperating and Agatha still
making her daily visits.

Melrose was at the moment contemplating his goat, which was eating breakfast
(or brunch, as it was near eleven ) outside
the drawing-room window where he had
found some tasty grass or young leaves. It
was not the same as Blodgett's being there,
for the goat (if Agatha saw him at all)
merely ruminated beyond the windowpane
and did not present a fearsome picture.
Melrose found the goat displayed rather
remarkable tranquillity. Or acceptance, acceptance of its lot in life subject to the
whim of any passing stranger, of being
bought and sold, of being transplanted
from Farmer Brown's (or whatever his
name was) meadows to the Ardry End

stable as companion to Melrose's horse. Melrose liked the goat's face and the ruminative way it had of chewing, as if it were concerned with broader things, not food.

It had been Diane Demorney's conviction that Melrose had to get a goat to keep the horse happy. "You can tell by looking at that horse he's pining for company."

"You saw Aggrieved exactly once, Diane, from twenty feet away during the cocktail hour. At five o'clock you couldn't recognize your own hands, so don't tell me how Aggrieved looked."

Diane didn't care a whit for his opinion and just plowed on. "A goat or a cat. Genuine Risk had a cat in her stall that went with her to all the races out of town. A horse needs company."

These comments had been offered in the Jack and Hammer back in January, during the time Richard Jury was still among them, also recuperating. The six of them — Diane, Trueblood, Vivian, Jury, Theo Wrenn Browne, and Melrose — crowded about the table in the window. Seven of them, if Mrs. Withersby insisted on standing by their table with her mop and bucket.

"What's his name?" asked Marshall Trueblood, meaning the name of the goat.

"Doesn't have one. I can't settle on one. I was thinking maybe Provok'd."

"We should have a contest," said Theo Wrenn Browne, who had just returned from two weeks in Ibiza, looking like he'd popped out of a toaster (and with about as much élan as a slice of bread).

"Winner gets a fifth of vodka!" said Diane.

Mrs. Withersby, pounding her mop a few times on the floor as if it were a gavel or divining rod, exclaimed, "Gin! Or mebbe brandy, or else that twelve-year-old whiskey Dick's got." She leaned on her mop.

"Whatever," said Trueblood. "We've got to have rules, though. We've got to narrow it down or we'll just waste time running through stupid names like Bubbles or Yellow Teeth."

"Funnily enough," said Jury, "I don't think I'd ever have come up with Bubbles. Yellow Teeth, maybe, but never Bubbles." He was sitting in the window seat next to Vivian. He had taken up the chewing gum habit and his jaw sometimes worked overtime.

Melrose said, "Okay, the horse is Aggrieved, so let's limit ourselves to some name that goes with it. Like Agitated, or

144

something. We could really limit it by insisting the first two letters must be 'A' and 'G.' As I just said — 'Agitated.' "

"Aggravated," said Vivian.

"Is that your official entry?" asked Theo.

"So come on, everyone, put on your thinking caps!" said Trueblood.

Diane, who had left her thinking cap in Oddbins, sighed.

"There should also be the rule that you have to stick with your first choice," said Theo Wrenn Browne. He gave them his crimped smile.

"We should write it down," said Jury, between chomps on his Juicy Fruit.

"Good suggestion," said Trueblood, who rose to grab a half-dozen coasters advertising Adnam's and started dealing them out. "You can write your name on the back. That way nobody will know whose name it is."

Vivian looked mystified. "What earthly difference would that make?"

"It's the way it's done."

Theo Wrenn Browne said, "There should be a time limit."

Mrs. Withersby cackled. "Time fer a drink, that's y'r time limit."

"I'd say five minutes?" Vivian suggested this. "Who's going to time us?"

"I shall," said Theo Wrenn Browne.

They sat quietly sipping their drinks and looking at their coasters. Vivian chewed her lip.

"Three minutes you've got. Three minutes." Theo wrote on his coaster.

Jury was first to finish and tossed his coaster on the table. Now the rest of them wrote their choices and Theo Wrenn Browne brought down his hand. "Time's up!"

Trueblood collected the coasters, shuffled them and handed them to Melrose. "You should do the honors. It's your goat."

Melrose set down his pint. "Right. I'll just read them out, but any that don't follow the rules are out of the running."

"What rules?" said Diane, languidly smoking.

Melrose sighed. "Come on. The name has to begin with the two letters of Aggrieved's name: 'A' and 'G.' "

"Oh, that," said Diane.

Melrose cleared his throat: "First one, Agatha — very funny —"

"Let's not have a commentary," said Trueblood. "Just read."

"Okay. Agatha."

"Agro.

"Agape.

"*AG*-a-pey, not A-*Gape*," Theo said testily.

Trueblood sighed. "Please shut up and let him get on with it! Start again."

"Right: Agatha.

"Agro.

"Agape.

"Aglow.

"Agoat. —"

Melrose stopped, looked round the table with narrowed eyes. "A*goat?* Okay, whose is this?"

Jury chewed his gum.

"Well, if you're not going to take this matter seriously, there's no point, is there?" said Theo, even more testily.

"I can tell you who's not taking it seriously," said Jury, "and that's your damned goat."

So the goat remained nameless as Agatha jammed up her scone.

Melrose liked the goat's calm manner. The only thing he'd ever seen as peacefully disposed to its surroundings was a manatee. If goats and manatees took over the world, they would render it slumbrous. How restful to rouse oneself only for a cabbage or a lettuce.

"I don't see," said Agatha, "why you

need a goat; you've already got a horse."

"Your logic is impeccable. The reason I've got a goat is because I've got a horse. Horses need pals."

"You're turning this beautiful house into a barnyard!"

"It's an idea." Melrose rattled back another page of his *Times*.

"Your poor mother would be aghast!"

Melrose stared at her, then bolted from his chair like Secretariat out of the starting gate. "That's it!"

Agatha fell back as if she'd just been punched. "What in the world are you doing? What's the matter with you?" To his departing back she called, "Where are you going?"

"To see my goat!"

# 13

"Soil?" said Miss Broadstairs, later that afternoon to Melrose, who was stopped at her gate and looking into a garden which, even in the first days of March, was heady with scent, although he couldn't locate its source. Something in that shrub? That vine? Emanating from the little greenhouse? In her winter garden were still vestiges of her summer — plants wrapped and staked or wearing straw collars, skeletal remains of borders and hedge, brown stems or sinister-looking black ones reaching out their twiggy fingers.

"Soil?" Alice Broadstairs said again.

Melrose had just that morning received a telephone call from Richard Jury, which had left him (but only after fifteen minutes of argument) committing himself to going to this place in Cornwall called Angel Food or something.

"Angel Gate, for God's sakes. Try to

keep that straight, at least." This, from Richard Jury.

"Why, yes, Mr. Plant, I can certainly tell you how to determine the condition of your soil." This, from Miss Broadstairs, who then launched into talk about clumping and alkalinity and acidity in a stiff wind of words that pushed Melrose back a few steps. Why was it, he wondered, that gardeners, unlike publicans or butchers or mechanics — in other words, a large part of the population — why was it that gardeners had to fly their answers at you with the dedication of kamikaze pilots? He cared nothing at all for clay and clumping, and as to shoving his fist in the earth down to his elbow? Melrose snorted.

"I really don't want to do that, Miss Broadstairs."

Her laugh woke the cat Desperado, which hissed at Melrose (who would have hissed back had the cat's mistress not been right there) and turned and turned as cats do, circling until they drop from sheer boredom. "But, Mr. Plant, if you want to garden, you must get your hands dirty." Gently, she whisked a lock of gray hair back to the bun from which it had escaped.

"No, you see I'm thinking more along the lines of telling somebody else to do it."

The utter stupidity of this remark caused even Desperado to look round again. The obvious question here would have been *My dear man, how in the world can you tell somebody else if you know sod-all yourself? Eh?* Only Alice Broadstairs didn't use expressions such as "sod-all" and, in her unrelenting kindness, would not ask a question that might embarrass Melrose, no matter how richly he deserved it.

"I was thinking more of sod." Why was he continuing with these ridiculous questions? Was he even sure he meant sod? Jury had said "turf," but wasn't that different from sod?

"Oh, well, that's quite another matter."

He waited for her to go on, but she didn't. "Yes, isn't it?" He thought for a moment. "Have you ever come across a turf expert?"

She laughed. "No, I'm afraid that my garden doesn't run to things so exotic." She clicked her shears several times as she looked around. "I don't know anyone with such an encyclopedic knowledge of the subject."

That gave him a brief chill. "Encyclopedic? There's that much to know, is there?"

"My goodness, yes. Have to go to school for that kind of expertise." She laughed her small laugh as she applied the shears to a bushy shrub of some sort wearing a straw collar that he supposed was there to protect it from frost.

"Of some sort" was the sum and substance of Melrose's shrub acquaintance, even though he had spent some time as undergardener at the Ryland house just this past December. A fat lot of good it had done him. His mind was like a sieve. "Perhaps the library . . . ?"

"I should try that if I were you. And there's the Royal Horticultural Society. You could try there, too."

Melrose stood around a few moments more. He looked at the brute of a cat, sprawled atop the stone plinth. "Desperado appears to have lost more parts of his person."

"Oh, yes, if you mean that bit of ear . . . He will fight with Ada Crisp's little dog. And how's your goat, Mr. Plant? Is he getting on all right?"

"Fine, just fine." Did he really want to be the sort of person who was asked How's your goat?

"They're quite wonderful creatures, aren't they?" she said. "So intelligent."

"Do you think it might know something about turf?"

Miss Broadstairs laughed until she was bent in the middle, not difficult for her as she was quite thin. She finally stopped and ran a finger under a watery eye. "Well, they're wonderful company for horses, I hear. How's your horse?"

That was better. How's your horse? suggested all sorts of colorful things about an owner. Riding through woods on a misty morn, show jumping four and five hurdles, galloping across fields — that sort of thing. "Aggrieved couldn't be better. He doesn't seem to mind it at all, not racing. He is a racehorse, you know."

"Why, no, I didn't." Miss Broadstairs shoved more loosened hair back from her nice, plain face, a face like a pancake. "And are you going to enter him in one?"

It always made Melrose feel puffed up to talk about his horse and horseracing. He added the scene to his repertoire, this time seeing himself on Aggrieved at Newmarket or Newbury, lengths ahead of the others, an image dimmed by the fact that Melrose was six feet tall. "No, I don't think so, at least not at the moment. But Aggrieved seems quite content just having me ride him around, or just grazing."

"How nice. Now, this friend of yours —"
What friend?

"Tell him that he must test the soil for alkalinity and —"

Oh, that friend.

On and on her words were coming straight at him, *zzzzzzzOOOOOOOMMM* — ! Got him in one!

"Many thanks, Miss Broadstairs. I'm off to the library."

# 14

The librarian, Miss Twinney, was helpful, suggesting various gardening books, although gardening as such was too broad a subject. Miss Twinney couldn't help him much when it came to soil, she said. That was perhaps too narrow a subject. Soil, sod and loam. "Loam" was a favorite word of his and he mouthed the word silently as he read about its rich properties.

It occurred to him that the rudiments of soil behavior might be found in the children's section. Melrose knew this to be true: if you wanted the basics, look in children's books.

Back in that section, at the rear of the library, he pulled out and perused *Dirty Debbie*, whose book jacket showed a small, black-haired girl with a spade, watched by an assortment of barnyard animals in much the same way he was being watched at that moment by a little girl of perhaps seven or eight with bobbed mouse-colored hair, wearing pink dungarees. She was folded into one of the overstuffed chairs, in one of those acrobatic positions only children can manage.

Pretty soon she got up and, under the pretext of selecting another book, came to stand beside Melrose and run her finger over the spines of the ones nearest him.

Melrose had never been able to pin down any reason for his effect upon children. It was not Richard Jury's effect. No, for Jury children would rush into burning buildings. For Melrose they wouldn't bother to blow out a match. He seemed to bring out their combative spirit. They couldn't do enough for Jury; they couldn't do enough *to* Melrose.

The child with skin like cotton candy and very large brown eyes pulled on his sleeve and said, "You've got my book, I think."

He looked down at her. "Your book? I believe this" — and he turned it face out — "is the library's book. Not yours. You do not have exclusive rights to it."

"I only meant I was reading it."

"Oh, *really?* How much have you read?"

"Half."

"Half?" Melrose consulted a page near

the beginning that showed Debbie digging a hole with her dog, Boots. "What's her dog's name?"

She screwed her mouth around, thinking. "There wasn't any dog in the part I read."

"You said *half*, didn't you?" He started to sneer, but decided he should act like a grown man.

"That's right. Just not that half. I read up to the dog and then after the dog. But I didn't read the dog part."

Miffed, he asked her, "What's your name?"

She slewed her eyes from him to the book. "Debbie."

He sighed. Naturally.

"It's my birthday."

"Is it? My. How old are you?"

"Seven and a half."

"You can't be because birthdays don't come in halves."

She scoured his face with a bristly look. "I have one every half of a year."

"Oh, don't be ridiculous."

"It's true. It's because I got really sick once, so I had my birthday early, in case I died."

"You'll stop at nothing to get this book, will you? I expect if I continue to refuse, you'll drop down in a heap on the floor?"

Clearly, she was entertaining this suggestion.

"No, don't bother. Here, you can have it." He thrust it at her, for he had spied another copy of *Dirty Debbie* and slid it from the shelf. "And I'll have this one." He turned and marched off to the library's little coffee room with Debbie at his heels. At the entrance, he looked round. "Where are you going?"

"I'd like a bun."

"And you think I'm going to buy you one?"

She nodded. "Like I said, it's my birthday and I didn't even have my tea today."

"And is that *my* fault? Go complain to your mum."

"I can't."

Now, Melrose was aware of a rule barristers followed when questioning witnesses: never ask a question to which you do not know the answer. Brushing off this sage advice, Melrose asked, "Why can't you?"

"Mum's — dying."

Melrose shut his eyes and wondered why he had to be here (speaking of death) when he could be spending a pleasant hour rowing across the River Styx. He had noticed Debbie's hesitation in reporting this sad fact. She sniffed, but he knew it wasn't a prelude to tears. He doubted this child would stoop to such cheap emotionalism as that. She'd much rather lie.

"Oh, all right, come along." He heaved a great sigh as they made their way to the counter and the pleasant elderly lady who served up coffee and pastries. Mrs. Kimble, he thought her name was. He greeted her and ordered a latte. Then he said to the girl, "You'll have a double espresso?"

"No. I'd like a lemonade, please."

"All right, Polly."

Aha! He'd caught her this time! "*Polly* is it? Funny, Mrs. Kimble, but she told me her name was Debbie." He looked down at her with a bit of a leer.

"Debbie's my middle name. I'd like a jam doughnut please. And a cream bun." Her eyes just about reached over the counter.

Did the child have an answer for everything? Well, Mrs. Kimble here would surely know her mother. "It's such a shame, isn't it, Mrs. Kimble, about Polly's mother?"

"Oh? And why's that, Lord Ardry?" She was foaming up the milk and stood wreathed in a steamy smile.

"That she's at death's door."

This did not disturb Mrs. Kimble at all, seeing it wasn't true. "I hardly think so, Lord Ardry. I just saw her pass by on the other side of the street with her cousin."

Melrose looked down at Polly. "Dying, is she?"

"It's been taking a long time. Anyway, you can walk around, can't you, as long as you're not completely dead?" She left him and took her lemonade, doughnut and bun over to one of the tables.

They ate for a few moments in silence. Silence except for the kicking of the rungs of the chair. Jam doughnuts were better than talking any day. He said, "I have a good friend by the name of Polly." He was thinking of Polly Praed, whom he hadn't seen in some time. "She lives in a place called Littlebourne."

This stirred no interest. Finally, she was finished with eating and drinking and would now perhaps reenter the world.

When Melrose rose to leave, Polly slid from her chair and put on her coat. It was, Melrose thought, not very substantial for a winter garment. And she was wearing sandals, which struck him as hardly sturdy enough for this time of year.

"Oh, are you leaving, too?"

"Yes."

Polly padded along behind him. He could hear the small plop of her sandals hitting the cobbled pavement.

He turned and walked backward for a bit. "Why aren't you wearing proper shoes? It's wintertime, you know. Ice, snow, all that."

"It's not snowing."

"Well, it's not snowing *now*, but it has been." He waved his hand toward the green, where gray ruffles of snow were melting round the little pond. "You can smell snow coming, you can smell it in the air."

"It doesn't smell, snow doesn't. It's only white rain."

He noticed how she had declaimed this without so much as a sniff to test her theory.

Melrose, now walking forward, asked over his shoulder, "Is your purpose here on earth just to contradict others?"

"I don't have any purpose."

As he looked back at her, in her sandals and thin coat and without mittens, he could have believed it, had it not been for her diabolical cleverness in talking her way

161

out of black holes. "Come along, come along, I can't talk to you if I have to walk backward."

She came a few steps nearer, but still stayed close behind him.

"Have you been to the bookshop before?"

"No." She shook her head.

"I'm surprised. I thought everyone in Long Piddleton has had the pleasure of sussing out its charismatic owner."

"I'm not from here."

That rather stunned him and he stopped. "What do you mean?"

"I mean, I'm not from here."

If he picked her up by her heels and shook her, he wondered if the postmistress — he and Polly were standing in front of the post office — would report him to the authorities. Had he ever known a child both as fanciful and literal as this one?

"Yes, I *know*. You already said it. Then where are you from?"

"Sidbury." Here she pointed to what she apparently thought was the Sidbury Way.

This brought to mind, only God knew why, *The Guermantes Way*. It would be interesting if Polly were to come along in *Time Regained*. What would Proust make of her? He could well imagine Polly herself being spit up by involuntary memory. "So if you're from there, why are you here?"

They were near to Ada Crisp's used-furniture emporium. Her Jack Russell terrier, sitting on its regular stool outside of the shop, started barking, as it always did, no matter who or what strolled by. Dog paradise could descend and he'd still bark.

"Mum's got a friend here she came to visit."

"So why aren't you with your mum instead of following me around?"

"I wanted to see things."

"Well, you've — oh, shut *up!*" said Melrose to the barking dog. "You've been gone well over an hour, probably a lot longer. Don't you think your mother wonders where you are?"

"No. I'm to be back by four and it's not near that yet. We've got a lot of time."

Melrose gave a fake guffaw. "Oh, we do, do *we?* And must I be back by four, too?"

They'd by now come to the door of the Wrenn's Nest Bookshop and Melrose had to admit he was curious to see what Polly would make of Theo Wrenn Browne. And what he would make of her. "Here's the bookshop. Come on."

"Well, Mr. Plant. It's been some time since you've graced our shop. Have you been visiting the new Waterstone's in Sidbury, then?" He waggled a bony finger at Melrose, then looked down at Polly. The smarmy tone changed to an instructive one. "I don't believe I know you, dear —"

No response from Polly. Just a look.

"— but we will observe all of the rules in the children's corner, won't we? We wouldn't want to damage our beautiful books, would we?"

Polly kept on staring at him until he grew uncomfortable and shifted his gaze to Melrose. "You were looking for books on American racehorses back in January. I've got in one or two; I think you'll find —"

To shut him up, Melrose interrupted. "Soil, Mr. Browne. Sod and soil. Formal gardens. And my friend here will no doubt find something worthwhile in the children's corner."

This was a section of the store Theo had decided to allot to the kiddies. This was not because he liked them (he didn't), but because he now had to compete with the very library he had tried so hard to close awhile back. The library, pumped up with new money, as a result of the café, had moved from almost closing to a roaring success. Miss Twinney had supervised the expansion, the adding of a children's room.

It was largely owing to Marshall Trueblood's saving the day with his idea of Latte and the Library that had made the place so hugely popular. Here was another reason for Theo Wrenn Browne to hate Trueblood. Indeed, Theo was so enraged, he blistered. Trueblood was always trumping him, most brilliantly in the chamber pot affair. That was a legend in Long Piddleton; people were still talking about it.

"Just as long as you're careful," he said to Polly, who was in no way attending, but whose big brown eyes were scouring all of the shelves.

Polly liked books, thought Melrose.

To Melrose he said, "Gardening, well of course, we've plenty of books on that." He lifted the hinged top of the counter and stepped through.

Polly, in the meantime, had taken off for the children's section.

"Not gardening as such, but turf, sod, soil. And enameled mead."

"That might be harder. It's so special-ized. Enameled mead, my goodness."

Melrose followed him to the shelves at the rear of the shop, where Theo pulled out one after another of gardening books, two of them great tomes that Melrose thought would serve far better as places to rest one's knees while digging and planting than they would as reference books. Melrose looked at and rejected them. His eye went to one titled *The Serene Gardener*. He pulled that out and leafed through it.

Theo smirked. "I'd hardly think that's the one for you. You certainly don't strike me as being into one of those Eastern faiths."

As long as Theo was against it, Melrose was for it. "I'll have it, I think."

"Well, it's certainly not about soil alone." He pushed his metal-rimmed glasses up on his nose. "May I ask what your interest is in sod?"

"You may."

There was a silence during which Theo waited for an explanation. None was forthcoming. Theo cleared his throat. Melrose just kept turning pages of *The Serene Gardener*. He very much liked the approach; it was inactive.

Theo expressed his doubt once again that Melrose would find a whole book on turf. "What you need is to find an expert on that."

"What I need is to *be* an expert on that."

A voice piped up from a distance. "I found one!" Then here came Polly, running up to them and holding a book. Two

166

books, for another one was under her arm.

Melrose took it, saying, "*Tillie Lays Turf.* Interesting." It sounded to Melrose rather pornographic.

"It's a child's book," said Theo, master of the obvious. "Whatever good would it do you?"

"An *old* child's book. An elderly child. Tillie is actually putting down sod. What's this other?" He nodded from Tillie to the bright blue book under Polly's arm.

She showed him.

"My goodness, one of my favorite books, a Long Pidd bestseller, *Patrick the Painted Pig.*"

"I want to buy it except someone's gone and messed it up."

Theo sucked in breath. "What? How? It's a brand-new book."

Polly opened it to the offending pages. "You should sell it for half."

Irritably, he opened the book to the pages she'd marked. It looked as if dirt, perhaps potting soil, had been spilled and even rubbed in. "This is disgraceful!" He looked at Melrose as if Melrose himself were the agent of destruction here. "It's that Sally, or her brother did this — !"

"Sally and Bub were warned off, remember? Did you take out a restraining order against them?"

"Don't be ridiculous. It was you, Mr. Plant, that let 'em get off so easy. You purchased this book, I mean one just like it, and gave it to them. That's putting them on the high road to a life of crime, that is."

"Well, Mr. Browne, I'll have this Tillie book."

They started walking toward the front of the shop.

"And I want this one," said Polly. "Only you can't charge the whole seven pounds fifty p for it."

"I most certainly can!"

"Nobody'll buy it for that."

"She's got a point, you know."

Theo lifted the counter's hinged lid and moved to his cash register. Glumly, he said, "I'll take a pound off the price."

Polly shook her head vigorously.

"Better take what you can get, Mr. Browne. Half off is a good offer."

"Oh, *very* well." He brought his fingers down on the cash register keys as swiftly as if he were conducting the London Symphony Orchestra. "That'll be three pounds seventy-five."

Melrose went to reach for his wallet when Polly took a five-pound note from her pocket and handed it over. "Well, my goodness," said Melrose. "Your mum certainly set you up for the day!"

"No. I earned it."

"Doing what, if I may ask?"

She looked down at *Patrick the Painted Pig.* "Painting."

"Really. Are you having a show at the Royal Academy?" Across the street, Trueblood went into his antiques shop. "Ah, there's a friend of mine; I must speak to him. It's time you joined your mother, isn't it?"

Polly didn't look as if she agreed it was time to do anything that she didn't want to. "No," she said.

"Well, I've got to be going."

"Good-bye."

When he reached the shop into which Trueblood had just gone, Melrose turned. She was still over there, standing where he'd left her, as if he *had* left her all on her own. He had, after all, spent upward of an hour with her and refused to feel guilty. Where was the mother? He plunged into the shop, which was cool, shadowy and crowded with handsome pieces of furniture. Trueblood had impeccable taste.

"I need something on enameling," said Melrose to Trueblood's back.

The back turned. "Did anyone win the contest?"

Melrose sighed. "Are you still back there with that silly goat-naming business?"

"Silly? As I recall you were dead serious. You didn't want anyone amusing himself at your goat's expense." Here he chortled and held a fine piece of crystal up to the dusty sunlight. "Enameling, yes. I've got a book on it." Trueblood moved over to a stack of books on the floor (as there was no more room on the shelves), pulled one out and handed it to Melrose.

Melrose leafed through the large book as Polly had leafed through her *Patrick Pig* book, and probably to just as much enlightenment. "This is jewelry."

"Yes? Enameling. Little bits and pieces of colored enamel in some setting or other."

"No, what I need is to do with gardening."

"You've got me there, old bean. Don't think I have anything; actually, I don't know what it is."

Melrose groaned. "I'm to go to Cornwall tomorrow to act like an expert in it, it and turfing up some steps."

Trueblood made a blubbery sound with his lips, his reaction to Melrose's being "expert" in any field at all. "Take that."

"*This?* But didn't I just say —"

"If you're messing round with this enameled garden or whatever, you'll impress people as knowing so much about the subject that you can afford to go about it in this eccentric fashion."

"Marshall, you don't know what you're talking about."

"Of course not." He was holding a small silver crucifix set with precious stones. "That's by way of being the point, isn't it? Since you don't know a damned thing about the garden or flower variety of enameling, you pretend to know so much that your knowledge simply bleeds over into actual enamel."

Melrose considered. It was just the sort of weird notion they'd come up with sitting around in the Jack and Hammer. Which wasn't a bad idea. "Let's have a drink."

"Twist my arm." Trueblood dropped the crucifix on the table and they walked out.

She was not there, Melrose was relieved to see, looking across the street. But he did wonder where she was.

# 15

The church was dim and almost absent of ornament, except for the rose window at their backs, and the gathered candles and a few somber statues.

Jury had been very surprised to find that Sarah had kept to her Scots Presbyterian birthright and not converted to Brendan's Roman Catholicism; he admired her for sticking to her guns, which must have caused a family war, not with Brendan himself (one of the most easygoing men Jury had ever known) but with Brendan's family, who would have tried every tactic at their disposal to get her to switch.

It was one of the moments of prayer, this one following a hymn he wasn't familiar with (well, that counted for most of them), and with his head bent, he thought about Sarah's ability to stonewall the in-laws, in spite of her having no one in her own family to take her side. That must have been hard.

The moment of prayer was over and the procession to the grave site begun. There were a fair number of people, most no doubt Brendan's friends. He looked somehow burnt — his face dark and waxen and his heart in a million pieces. You could tell that was so.

The girls, Christabel and Jasmine and the youngest, Chastity, all clustered together. The boy, Dickie, sixteen, stood a little apart. All of them had been raised remarkably in that small flat with a partitioned-off dining room brought into play as an extra bedroom. Brendan had expressed gratitude for the flat, considering they hadn't been tossed out by the landlord.

Jury heard little of the grave-side service, his mind escaping into childhood, as much as he could remember after his uncle took him from that orphanage. His aunt and uncle had lived in Suffolk, or that part of it a raft of older boys had christened "Fuck-up." One of the boys had been another cousin — Jury wondered now what had happened to him — a much-older brother who paid little attention to him; he just nodded now and then, looking at Jury as if trying to place him. Where had he gone? He might be dead, too.

* * *

The reception (Jury was glad to see)
wasn't held in Noonan's, but in a dim old
hotel close to the church. Brendan's flat
was of course out of the question for a
crowd of this kind. He had chosen this
hotel. The room in which they had gathered was probably a ballroom now used for
functions such as this, or wedding recep-
tions (that strange other side of the coin to
this), conventions, reunions. He wondered
who or what in Newcastle one would want
to reunite with.

Newcastle. He supposed it might be a
pleasant enough city if one were to look at
it without the blinders on of death and the
dole. To him it had always been a cold gray
pile of rocks that most people would be
gladly shut of. Sarah certainly would have.

"Oh! You're the one she kept talking
about!" He turned to see a chubby woman
wearing a straw hat with a paper flower on
its brim. The flower bounced when she
talked.

"I'm the policeman, if that's what you
mean." He tried to smile, then gave up on
it.

"I certainly do. My, she did set such
great store by you. Even put your picture
up" — the woman nodded toward the end

of the buffet table, where a large collage of photos and snapshots rested on an easel — "and reports of your cases. You should have a look." As if some mission had been accomplished, she plucked up a little cake and munched. "Of course, she was only your cousin. It could have been worse." With that chilling pronouncement, she turned and left.

They'd been standing by the buffet where sandwiches and small cakes were arranged. He was drinking punch that someone had thankfully pumped a quart of Jamison into. Baby pictures, wedding pictures, pictures of a holiday by the sea when the kids were little. Birthdays, anniversaries, even newspaper clippings, these surprisingly about Jury himself, his picture at the top. Inspector, chief inspector. Some years ago. Brendan had been telling the truth, then: she must have been proud of him and his job.

Brendan came up to put a hand on Jury's shoulder. He was drunk or on his way to being.

Jury said to him, "It's quite a crowd, Brendan. All of us should be so well remembered. But, you know, I was a bit surprised Sarah hadn't become a Catholic."

Brendan laughed. "Not my Sarah, no

175

way. She always said she'd live up here in godforsaken Newcastle, but she was damned if she'd change her religion."

Brendan was pointing at the picture collage. "She clipped all that stuff, sometimes the same story from two different papers. She had a shoebox full of newspaper clippings."

Absurdly, Jury found himself getting angry with Sarah. "Our memories didn't seem to mesh. She seemed to enjoy making a point of it."

"Ah, for God's sakes, man. I told you last time you were here she's just takin' the piss out, is all. Look at you. You'd never have got to the top of your job without being able to sort people. Why couldn't you her?"

Jury hardly knew what to say.

Brendan went on: "She thought you let her down, Richard. See, she depended on you for the news. That's what she said."

Stupidly, Jury said, "What news?"

Brendan laughed. "Any news. From London, maybe. She put it that way: 'I wish Richard would come and bring the news.' I don't know what she meant, exactly."

"Neither do I," said Jury, sadly.

His train didn't leave until six, so he thought he'd grab a taxi and go across the river to the Baltic, a place he'd never been in — well, that was true enough. Where had he been in Newcastle, except to the pub with Brendan or taking the kids Christmas shopping that one year? A long time ago. That was a visit he would never forget, not the part with the kids, but the part before that — Old Washington and Washington Old Hall. Helen Minton and the most adolescent love at first sight, it still made him blush to remember. Well, that hadn't lasted, had it, mate? Old Hall. It struck him as ironic that George Washington's forebears would come from a little village slap up against another little one like Washington and its half dozen pubs on its single street. Where they liked to joke and say that wasn't sawdust on the pub's floor, but the furniture left from last night's brawl. Fighting seemed to be a cottage industry; they fought out of frustration and anger at their unemployed plight.

Jury was in the taxi now, looking out over the Tyne and the incredible bridges that spanned it. He bet they could compete with New York and those bridges that linked Manhattan and Brooklyn and the rest.

The driver, reading his mind said, "See that new Millennium Bridge is being built.

Oh, that's goin' t' be a corker when it's done." He nodded toward the middle distance where huge cranes appeared to be floating on the river. "Knock y'r eye out, that will. You'll be able to spit at any other bridge in the world. You know how it's going to work?" The driver was trying to herd Jury's eyes in the rearview mirror.

"No. I don't know anything about it."

"Like an eyelid, like an eyelid comin' slowly up."

Jury smiled. "I can't picture that."

"See, it tilts; the whole bridge tilts so the ships can get through. The blinking eye is what they call it."

Jury wondered at his accent. "You from the south?"

The driver thought this was funny. "Not on your life. County Durham, that's me. You been there? To Durham?"

Jury closed his eyes. Back with Helen Minton. Here came another memory rushing toward him faster than the end of the bridge. Jerusalem Inn. He wondered how it was two people. . . . Jury shook his head. Was any chapter of one's life ever irrecoverably closed? Or written off?

"Here you are, mate."

"Big place," said Jury, getting out.

"It's big all right. Me, I never been. But I

figure people that live in a place are the last to see around it."

"You're right." He handed over the cab fare and a big tip.

It raised the driver's eyebrows much like Jury now imagined the Millennium Bridge would rise. "Listen, how far's Newcastle Station from here?"

"Newcastle Central? Ah, you can walk it in fifteen minutes. Signs all along. Y' can't miss it."

Jury was surprised by the Baltic, by the scope of it. It was divided, according to the map, into "levels" rather than floors, and all in all the place housed several restaurants, a cinema, artists' studios and, most prominently, of course, art.

Jury felt he moved clumsily among the paintings, abstract and indescribable, and strange installations. He felt old hat in his preference for Millais and Rossetti, whose content you could hunger after and feed upon. He wondered, though, if it was the present art's emptiness or his own he was feeling and excused himself from looking any longer at the paintings. He went up another level to catch a view of Newcastle from the observation room. The enclosure, all windows nearly, jutted out from the west wall of the Baltic and allowed a panoramic look over Newcastle, the Tyne and Gateshead. Night was falling, and the lights across the Tyne had switched on. Jury was slightly stunned by the view of the Newcastle skyline. It was sensational; it was better than any view of Southwark across the Thames, with the fairy lights of the National Theatre complex, Tower Bridge and the docks and quays. Along with most people, he had long identified Newcastle as a scruffy, down-at-the-heel, doleful place — Lord knows, hardly a destination city. But from up here it was anything but; this made Jury feel better about Brendan's lot; he wasn't after all living in an environment of unrelenting drabness.

He had to go; he had to catch his train.

Near the exit was a bookshop. He went in and looked through a bin of prints, thinking he might buy one. He came upon one that he was sure wasn't in the Baltic's collection. It showed a cartoonish family around a table set for a meal. Their eyes were so dark they looked masked. The dinner table was set in deep grass, swamp or mire, probably, with water in the background. On their plates or in their hands were butterflies. It was called *The Butterfly Eaters*. He thought about this surreal picture for a moment and wondered if they were feeding on illusion or ambiguity. He returned the print to the bin.

He left the Baltic and began his fifteen-minute walk to Newcastle Central. The driver was right: the way was clearly marked, a trail of signs directing him to the station. One couldn't take a wrong turn or lose one's way.

Jury stopped and for a moment, in his mind's eye, he saw the row of old alders in front of Angel Gate. He saw the white crosses.

He bought a coffee and a dried-out sausage roll from a kiosk at the train station. He hadn't been able to eat at the reception. He was catching the 6:10 train to King's Cross. He read a local newspaper and tossed it aside, not wanting to read anymore about the depressed North.

He sat on a bench and after a few sips of coffee — bitter and metallic — fitted the top back over the cup and dropped it in the refuse bin along with the rest of the sausage roll. Then he walked along the platform. He had been in this station several times and found it pretty depressing. But weren't most railway stations, even those with the bustle and business of King's Cross or Victoria? They were places to say good-bye; rarely did he witness people saying hello, and he wondered why.

He went back to his bench and watched a nondescript dog without a collar moving around, snuffling the dust bin, and Jury wondered if he smelled the sausage roll in there. It was still lying on top. He reached in and got it and separated sausage from bread (although who's to say the dog didn't like bread?). Jury broke the sausage into a couple of pieces and put it down in its paper container in front of the dog. The dog vacuumed it up inside of five seconds. Well, he said to the dog, more or less said to him, That won't do, will it? He returned to the kiosk and bought another sausage roll, which he waved back and forth a few times to cool it off. Then he again broke it up and put down the pieces. Again, the dog gobbled it up.

Jury sighed, ran his hand along the dog's bony back and asked him, Will we ever be full, any of us? Because what he felt was a huge emptiness that was only confirmed by the cavernous station, the dog, the endless tracks.

His train came. He wished the dog well, walked along the nearly empty platform and boarded, feeling like a man who had nothing for anyone, a man who never brought the news.

# *The* Child Thief

# 16

Melrose got out of his rental car — he had decided the Bentley was too showy — and stood on the gravel looking at Angel Gate. It was an impressive great pile of red brick mellowed with age to pink. Georgian, by the look of it. No less impressive was the avenue of beeches along that winding drive up to the house.

He gathered up his pigskin suitcase and made his way to the door.

This was opened rather quickly by a little girl of undetermined age. That is, the age might be a certainty for her, but not for him. He could never tell. She was just very young, with hair of such a dark brown it looked black. She was wearing unflattering eyeglasses. This welcoming committee was swelled by her dog. Which, Melrose was glad to see, was not in automatic-bark position, one of those dogs that barked and barked whenever something was opened —

185

door, window, package, no matter whether or not someone dangerous was on the other side.

"Have you come about the gardens?"

"Yes, I have. I like your little dog."

"His name's Roy."

"Peculiar name for a dog."

"It's not the 'Roy' you're thinking of."

"Had I been thinking of one?"

"It means 'king' or 'your highness' and it's spelled R-o-i. It's French, but nobody says it right, so I just changed it to plain Roy."

The temperature seemed to have dropped ten degrees since he'd been standing here, but perhaps that was simply the effect of a Melrose-child encounter. He hoped she wasn't another Debbie-Polly, or he could be stranded here by the door for a week. "Look, could we continue this discussion inside? Before we take up the French Revolution?"

Reluctantly (it seemed to him) she held the door wide.

"Ta, very much." He kept telling himself sarcasm should not be wasted on children. "I'll say one thing for your dog — he doesn't bark."

"He doesn't need to."

Melrose frowned over this inscrutable explanation.

"You're to come to the kitchen. Aunt Rebecca's making lunch."

He followed his guide from the lovely marble hall into an equally lovely dining room. Lovely to Melrose because it looked used, comfortably used. The family portraits (if that's what they were) were not as imposing as portraits usually are. The subjects here all seemed to have been caught doing something and the painter captured the spontaneity, except for the military-looking one up on the horse.

"Who is Aunt Rebecca?"

"My aunt."

"I gathered that. Is she anything else?"

"She takes care of me since my mum and dad died."

(Oh, dear. This was sounding familiar. Would he have to walk softly now?)

"She's housekeeper here."

She had pushed through a swinging door and he quickly raised his hand to keep it from thumping back in his face.

It was a vast kitchen, one of the biggest Melrose had ever seen outside of a hotel. Along one wall ran a row of windows that lent the room a greenhouse effect. Light poured through across a long deal table set with three places.

"He's here," said the girl. "This is him."

Having done her duty, she went to sit at the table.

The woman who turned at this announcement Melrose supposed was Rebecca Owen. She looked surprised. "Lulu, I told you you were to come and get me when Mr. Plant arrived!" She wiped her hands on a kitchen towel and said, "I'm so sorry. I'm Rebecca Owen, Mr. Scott's housekeeper. He was called away and asked me to be sure you were comfortable. He'll be back later this afternoon, around teatime."

Melrose was glad to know he would be staying in a house where tea was still a ritual. It warmed him to know this.

She turned and picked up a platter of sandwiches. "I thought you'd like some lunch."

"That's kind of you. You know, what I'd really like is some coffee."

"We've got that, too. If you'll just have a seat." She nodded toward the long table where Lulu was already ensconced, sitting with her back to the window through which a dazzle of sunlight made her straight dark hair look like licorice.

Melrose took the seat opposite her, the better to survey the grounds beyond. The platter of sandwiches appeared and Lulu

188

helped herself to one from which she took one slow bite after another, handing down little bits to Roy — at least Melrose assumed she wasn't just throwing them down on the floor.

Rebecca Owen poured Melrose coffee and Lulu what looked like lemonade. She then sat down.

Melrose said, "I have a question about your dog."

They both looked at him, Rebecca Owen more surprised by this question than Lulu, who probably had a question about everything on God's green earth.

"At night, if a robber came in, how would you know, seeing that Roy doesn't bark at strangers?"

Lulu looked thoughtful and pushed her glasses up on the bridge of her nose. "I expect Roy would think of something." She drank her lemonade, watching Melrose over the rim of the glass.

Definitely a Polly type. He turned to Rebecca Owen. "It looks as if Mr. Scott is having extensive work done." He nodded toward the wall of windows, which he was facing.

"He is. Everything had pretty much gone to seed over the last few years, and now he's decided it wants sprucing up."

Melrose took umbrage. Was he to be no better than a sprucer? He said, "Has he someone overseeing it? Or just the gardeners working?"

"He has a landscape fellow. I think he's called a garden architect. It seems everything these days has its specialist, doesn't it?"

"Yes. It's hard to find a general practitioner anymore. They're all specialists. And specialists within the specialty. The whole thing's going to hell. Oh, pardon me —"

Lulu smiled.

He said to Miss Owen, "And you, do you specialize?"

"Lord, no. I'm general dogsbody: cook, housekeeper, doorbell answerer — that is, except when Lulu decides to be the welcoming committee herself."

Rebecca Owen was an attractive woman who didn't spend a lot of time in front of a mirror. He put her in her late forties or early fifties.

Lulu, who looked as if her weight could be measured by quantities of air, was now eating a watercress sandwich. Roy had come out from under the table to sit stiffly by Melrose's chair. Why was it that other people made dogs want to frolic, whereas all he provoked in them was this blind staring?

190

He drank off the rest of his coffee, finished his cheese sandwich, pushed back and said, "Tell me where I'm to stay and I'll be off."

"Of course. Lulu can show you to the cottage; it's just over there." She pointed across the gardens.

"Okay," said Lulu. "I can carry your suitcase if you like."

"Certainly not. I'm much bigger than you." Melrose picked up his case and they went out.

The kitchen was in, or perhaps constituted, the short left wing of the house. They crossed a patio and walked down several wide, shallow terraces that gave a sunken garden effect to the land beyond. They passed a bronze statue of two boys with buckets, one lad holding his bucket higher than Melrose's head and could have doused him had there been water running and had the boy, of course, been animated. Melrose thought this sculpture amusing and a pleasant respite from draped and armless maidens.

Lulu pointed off to the bottom of the gardens. "We had a murder here."

Triumph or pride registered in her tone, as if the place had done something wizard.

He expressed surprise. "Good lord, who was murdered?"

"Nobody knows, not even the police."

They were walking a path that was out-lined in yew hedges and crisscrossed with other paths. "Your gardens are beautiful."

"I like it when it snows. When the snow tops the hedges and shadows move back and forth."

"Do you get snow in Cornwall?"

"Sometimes we get a lot."

Melrose seriously doubted it. Down to-ward the bottom of the garden he saw two figures, a man and a woman, planting or hoeing or whatever people did in that world which he would prefer not to mess about in. None of the Ryland experience as (so-called) undergardener seemed to stick ex-cept filling and emptying wheelbarrows full of dirt.

"That's the Macmillans. He's her father. They have a big garden shop outside Launceston. Here's the cottage."

Architecturally, the cottage bore no re-semblance to the main house. It was built of stone and knapped flint in a checker-board design, with a thatched roof, and even a thatched porch overhanging a wide step flanked by two narrow columns. It was surrounded by a hedge out of which had been carved a topiary to hang over the pebble walk. Only a one-up, one-down, it was the fussiest little place Melrose had ever seen. The fuss continued on the inside with the curtains patterned in blue and pink hydrangeas and sofa and two armchairs covered in a cretonne full of pansies, roses and lilies — a regular flower garden of furniture.

No wonder Lulu liked it. "I'm going to live in this someday. How long are you staying?"

"Five, ten minutes and then I'll clear out and leave you to it."

"The kitchen's in here. Come on!" she demanded. Melrose was not allowed to linger. "See, there's everything you need, like a teakettle." She pointed out the mismatched, but very colorful crockery on the open shelves; the pots and pans; the various appliances, small, but clearly big enough for the one or two (at most) people who'd be occupying it.

"You should be a tour guide. Blenheim Palace would suit you."

"I don't know if I'd care for a palace." She had a way, when she was thoughtful, of wrapping a strand of hair round her finger, which was an unsuccessful maneuver, since her dark hair was so straight.

"The Churchills will be inconsolable to hear it. Well, if you'll excuse me, I'll get settled in —"

"Okay." And she was through the cottage door quicker than a rabbit.

Here was someone who made up her mind and acted on it immediately.

Melrose decided the first order of business was to go upstairs and take a nap.

# 17

"You're to come for drinks." Lulu intercepted Melrose at the cottage door as he was standing in the doorway contemplating food. Sleeping always made him hungry.

"I am?" He looked at his watch. It was five o'clock, he was surprised to see. "And by that, do you mean tea with you and unidentified others?"

She squinted in thought, as if the decision were hers to make. "Mr. Scott said maybe you'd like whiskey."

"Mr. Scott couldn't be righter. So he's home, is he?"

She nodded. "I'm supposed to tell you and bring you."

"Right. Hold on while I get my jacket and we'll go."

He did this as she hopped from one foot to the other in one of those energy-wasting displays that kids seemed to favor. Following her along the pebble path, he said,

"My name, incidentally, is Melrose Plant."

Now, she was walking backward to talk: "My name's really Louise, but I don't like that name. I want people to call me Lulu."

"I don't care too much for mine all that much, either. But I don't want people to call me Lulu."

"You can use your middle name."

"I don't have one."

"Oh." Interest in his name went completely south and probably interest in him, too. She hopscotched her way now on the wider path to the terrace and the house.

It tired Melrose to watch her expending all of that energy. He took solace in the wild growth around him. Solace? Why should he need it? He must; otherwise it wouldn't have sprung to mind. Although a goodly part of the gardens had come under the purview of the landscape designer and the horticulturists, there was still this wild space around the cottage and its wintry flowers — drifts of snowdrops against the far wall, shoots of narcissus, a handful here and there, the dry fountain, the path from cottage to house in patches slick with moss or covered in bramble, ivy rampaging up the perimeter wall, the white birches at the back, their trunks looking too delicate to withstand any heavy wind (but which were protected by the brick garden wall), bare coppery stems of Rubus grass, thick brown tangles of clematis — it was, he supposed, what any serious gardener would call a right mess, but for him it had a strange charm.

Ahead of him now, and his meandering thoughts, Lulu was calling. He wondered which steps were the ones to be "turfed." He sighed. Must he really talk about it over drinks, when he'd much rather talk about the past? His past, Scott's past, any past.

He walked up the steps to the French doors Lulu had disappeared through. She was nowhere to be seen. Probably just getting him on his feet and moving was her understanding of the word "bring" and delivering him to wherever the whiskey was being put into play.

Melrose looked around this octagon-shaped room — at the high windows and the portraits hung between them, at the deep gold walls that might have been paint or might have been damask, with the last of the wan light showing in faint oblongs on the floor. The room's only furniture consisted of two French settees facing each other but out of easy conversational range.

He walked from here down a long gallery that led to a room at the end whose pocket doors were halfway open. Farther along this gallery were the entrance hall and the front of the house.

Tentatively, Melrose presented himself at the door of this room, a library, judging from all of the books. A dark-haired man stood by the fireplace mantel, upon which sat a glass of whiskey. There was also a woman whom Melrose didn't see immediately because she was sitting in a wing chair with its back to the door. The man himself was impressive, the woman plain as junket. Declan Scott, a handsome and (probably to many) tragic figure, a widower and filthy rich, must have had women lined up all the way down that avenue of trees. Melrose doubted that the woman here would have been in the running, though.

Look at Melrose himself, not quite as tall or as handsome but just as filthy rich, and he wasn't peeling women like grape skins from his person. So it had to do with a way (unconscious, Melrose was sure) of isolating one's self. Declan Scott would have far more reason to do this than Melrose. His wife dies, his only child disappears, and now he's got a body in his garden. Lucky man.

"Mr. Plant!" Declan Scott had looked

up from talking to the seated woman and seen him. He advanced toward Melrose, hand out. He introduced the woman as Hermione Hobbs.

Melrose shook Declan's hand, saying, "I'm glad to be here. Your house is beautiful."

"Isn't it just?" said Hermione Hobbs, with a curdled smile. She was a person, Melrose guessed, who was always ingratiating herself to others, and sometimes got a bit sick of it.

Scott held up the whiskey decanter in invitation and Melrose nodded (he hoped not too eagerly). "When I was walking from the cottage, I had the feeling of being caught in a time warp," Melrose said as he accepted the drink Scott handed him. "It was a very seductive feeling, I mean the temptation to do nothing but just contemplate it."

Hermione said, "You know, I've often felt the same way."

Which Melrose was sure she hadn't.

"But I must be going." She placed her glass on the small table beside the chair and rose.

Declan Scott made no attempt to detain her. "Thanks for stopping by, Hermione."

As he made to accompany her to the

door, she said, "Oh, I can find my own way out. Nice to meet you," she said, and walked out.

"An old friend," said Scott as he gestured for Melrose to sit down. Melrose felt he was sinking into the small deep sofa, rather than merely sitting on it. Declan Scott sat in an armchair across from him. But unlike the settees in the octagon room, these were placed for conversation.

"You're suggesting," said Declan Scott, smiling, "if you were I, you wouldn't change it?"

Melrose wondered for a moment what he meant, then said, "You mean the time warp business?" The man certainly listened.

Declan nodded and went on. "I'm restoring the gardens out there as an act of will. Or maybe I should say an act of faith."

"In what?"

"I don't know. Maybe that's the faith part. It's because my wife wanted it. And I've waited too long as it is." He held up his glass — his own was empty — to see the reflection of the fire, or perhaps the emptiness of the glass. Then he rose and went to the drinks table, a handsome gilt-and-brass-mounted commode, whose twin sat on the other side of the fireplace. Melrose knew enough about antiques (hanging around Marshall Trueblood did that) to know those pieces, taken together, would be in the thousands of pounds. Family heirlooms, probably, but it made him reassess his own filthy rich factor.

Declan poured his drink and went on. "I like that section around the cottage. I like it that snowdrops grow no matter what you do or don't do. They were my wife's favorite. Mary was one of those people it was relaxing to be around. There aren't very many of them, people with whom you can kick off your shoes, sit back and sort of sink into the ground. Like that garden out there, sunk in desuetude."

"Well, if it reminds you of your wife, no wonder you don't want to change it."

Declan looked up from his drink, whose cut-glass surface he'd been tracing with his finger. "Perhaps you're right." He returned to his chair. "According to Superintendent Jury, you're quite the expert gardener."

"Not at all, not at all. My line is turf, pure and simple. Oh, and enameling, too, of course."

"And why did you choose to concentrate on those two aspects of gardening?"

Melrose's mind went blank (not for the

first time). He might have expected the "what" but certainly not the "why." Why indeed would anyone care *why* Melrose was interested in turf? "Well, turf was a favorite subject of my father. Many's the time I'd hear him holding forth on the beauty of soil. I guess I was just indoctrinated from an early age." Let's get off this subject in a quick hurry. He deliberately downed his whiskey, and then held up his glass. "I wonder — ?"

"Oh, sorry." Declan took it to the drinks table. "Well, you mustn't mind the Macmillans, the father especially thinks if he doesn't know about it, it isn't worth knowing."

It probably isn't, thought Melrose, as Declan handed back his glass and sat down.

"Anyway, don't let Macmillan get in your hair. The old guy can be extremely bossy."

"I'm surprised the Macmillans don't do it themselves — the turfing."

"They never have, and the old man calls it 'flighty pretty,' which goes for the enameled mead, too."

Melrose laughed. "I'm sure he'll find me 'flighty pretty,' too."

"I hope you live up to that description;

it'll furnish me enough entertainment to eke out my days."

Melrose laughed again. Declan Scott was rather entertaining himself; indeed for all the gloom and doom that dogged him, Declan himself hardly lived up to the notion of the tragic figure. But he would have to eschew the entertainment if they were to get to the subject of murder. He'd started to work his way round to it, when Scott brought it up himself.

"I'm sure after you'd been here for ten minutes, Lulu told you about the murder."

"That's about how long it took her, yes. This must be awfully unpleasant — a murder in your garden."

Declan smiled. "Not for Lulu. What surprises me is that police can't identify this woman. You'd think that with all of the sophisticated equipment they have, and that with fingerprints, DNA and teeth and so forth, they'd have got it in one, wouldn't you?"

"Well, first there has to be something to compare fingerprints with. About all it says is that she'd never been arrested."

"They've got Scotland Yard in on it: your friend." Declan smiled. "He's a very pleasant fellow. After five minutes, you forget he's a detective."

"I'd suppose that manner's put any number of villains away."

Declan's smile broadened. "I see what you mean. But this woman. It's so extraordinary. It seems there's nothing to tie her to, well, anything. It seems so strange when we live in a world where you can scarcely breathe without proof of identity and where people seem to know more about you than you do yourself, yes, it's very strange. It's almost as if she appeared for a single purpose — and then vanished. Or would have done, if she hadn't been murdered. Appeared and disappeared — that whoever she was, she was that person for that purpose only."

Melrose considered this.

Declan shook his head. "For a purpose we may never know, but one in which I, for some reason, appear to be involved. That part of it, I really don't like." He set his empty glass on the rosewood table beside his chair. Then he looked at the portrait over the mantel for a moment and said, "She was so very plain, one couldn't help but notice. Strange."

Clearly he was not referring to his wife, if this was her portrait. She stood in a black velvet evening gown, her hand up on that same mantel. Anything but plain.

"In Brown's Hotel, she seemed out of place."

"Brown's?" said Melrose. "You mean the Mayfair hotel?"

"Yes, sorry. All of this has been gone over so much I forget not everybody knows about it. I saw her there, having tea with my wife. The woman seemed old, somehow. I'm not talking about years, I mean, I suppose, old-fashioned. Well, that's not it, either. Something clung to her, like dust, as if she were done in sepia tones, you know, like those old photographs."

"Perhaps what did happen was what was supposed to happen. Except the end of it, of course; that is, from her point of view, she didn't see *that*."

Declan said, "You've lost me."

"I'm just wondering if it was an act for your benefit." Melrose shrugged and sipped his drink. It was very good whiskey.

Declan said, "Well, enough of murder. Let's get back to the gardens."

Oh, let's not. He sighed. "Miss Owen mentioned an architect or landscape designer."

"That's Marc Warburton. The gardeners, they're the Macmillans. They have a big nursery just outside Launceston."

Warburton. Melrose loved that. He visualized all of the Touchetts and Isabel Archer spread out across the grassy terrace having tea. He said, "But if Mr. Macmillan owns a whole nursery, can't he supply the turf for the steps?"

"I asked him. He was unsure as to exactly what was needed."

Good. "Well, it merely depends on the acidity and alkalinity (could that be a noun?) of your soil, but your gardeners would know that with all the planting they've been doing."

"They said they'd heard of it but never actually seen it."

That makes four of us — or five if you count Lord Warburton. "That's odd. I would have thought your landscape architect would know all about it."

"Oh, he knows about it; he just hasn't used it. Maybe he thinks it's the wrong thing to do. I'm afraid you're on your own here."

Thank God.

Melrose wanted to steer the conversation around to little Flora Baumann, but he didn't want to bring it up himself. He stared at his glass, rejecting one opener after another. Lulu. "Lulu is your housekeeper's niece, I understand."

"Great-niece. Her parents were killed in

a road accident. She's a bit shy until she gets to know you."

Melrose nearly choked on his whiskey. *Shy?* He said, "You must be used to extremely forward children, then. I found her to be far from shy. I think she's cagey."

"Cagey?"

"Sure. Well, not being used to children, I could be dead wrong. I've never had any children." He glanced at Declan. It was as if Melrose had wounded him.

"I had. Well, a stepchild, but she felt like my own. She disappeared."

"What?"

"At first, we thought she'd been kidnapped. I still think she was. But in theory, unless there's a ransom demand . . ." Declan's voice trailed off.

"Why? There are other reasons for taking a child. We're always hearing about a baby's being stolen from a hospital ward or from a stroller while the mother's in a shop. No ransom demand there."

"I know. What bothered me most was I was afraid that the police wouldn't pursue a so-called abduction as vigorously as a kidnapping. But I think they did all they could; they tried awfully hard. Flora and Mary were visiting Heligan — the Lost Gardens, you've probably heard of them.

Flora was abducted. That was three years ago. We never saw her again."

The world might as well have switched off a light in the man, for everything about him seemed suddenly to dim so that it was like looking at a photograph developing in reverse, going back to a lack of image, going back to nothing.

# 18

The following day dawned clear and cold. Not that Melrose was up in it. He wondered sometimes what an up-at-dawn experience would be like, but he never wondered enough to try it.

But here in another man's house and on another man's payroll (at least metaphorically speaking), he knew he'd have to be up before ten (his usual fall-out-of-bed time) and was prepared to make that sacrifice. Especially this first morning, when he wanted to be out "going over the ground" before the Macmillans arrived. For after they arrived, he planned on going into St. Austell for "supplies."

He was up, wearing his flat cap and a suede jacket with a fleece-lined collar he had purchased in Sidbury and which he had asked Ruthven to beat up a little so that it looked old and worn. Ruthven had claimed the jacket was already beat up, if that described a garment so poorly tailored that no man of any taste would wear the thing. But at Melrose's insistence he had done a fair job with it: creased, cracked, oil spotted and with a few bits missing from the fleecy collar.

Melrose opened the cottage door to be surprised by Lulu with her dog, bearing a little tray. They both stared up at him, Lulu and Roy. "Good morning, Lulu."

"Here's your tea." She thrust the tray at him with all of the good will of the *Man in the Iron Mask*'s jailer as he slipped the tray through the slot.

She ran off and he watched her go, wondering if Jury had talked to her. Then he gulped down his tea and with his pipe in a breast pocket proceeded toward the garden. They were already there, Macmillan and his daughter, tamping down earth, pulling up weeds, whatever one did in these cases. (Melrose now wished he'd paid more attention to Miss Broadstairs.) He decided to be hearty.

"Mr. Macmillan!" he exclaimed. Macmillan rose from his kneeling position. He was a small man, but strong looking, his nerves probably semiconductors of electricity. One could say that too for the daughter, who stopped working in order to lean on her hoe like a figure out of a Whistler painting, only not as graceful.

"I'm Melrose Plant!" he announced, glad that he could use his own name. This turf expertise was, after all, only a hobby. "I'm here about the steps and the turf." Could such a person call himself a "turfer"? Better just stick with "turf." He left off the enameled mead job, not wanting to allow too much opportunity for questions.

"Nice t' meet ya."

"And I, you."

Thank God Jury had introduced him to Scott as educated, and he didn't have to drag out his execrable North London accent that people would believe even less than they'd believe Melrose sang with whales.

"Millie!" called Macmillan, unnecessarily, since Millie was already there. "So when d' you start on them steps?" He nodded toward the several short flights of terrace steps leading from the stone patio down the grassy plateaus to the fountain.

"Oh, soon. First I need to pick up a few things, you know, a certain kind of fertilizer (better not be too specific, as if he could be) and a couple of other items."

"Su'prised you didn't get Warburton to

211

get it for ya. He knows the right places."

Warburton, landscape architect. Shift gears. He looked at some as yet unplanted rhododendrons. "Are you much bothered by voles, Mr. Macmillan? I'd suggest that you wrap those roots in bark just up to ground level." This was one of the four pieces of gardening arcana that Melrose had mastered. Diane Demorney thought that four was overdoing it. He needn't learn the specifics of all four.

But Melrose didn't agree. The more he could get specific about, the more comfortable he felt.

*"Just don't get into roses. Once that starts, you're a dead man,"* said Diane in the Jack and Hammer two days before. *"Indeed, insist that you not be consulted in any way about roses or anything connected to roses. If roses come up at all — and what gardener doesn't bring them up? — say it's always been your tenet the less known the better. That will sound so weird that they'll immediately conclude you must be a font of wisdom when it comes to roses. But I'm warning you, once you mention black spot you're done for."*

Macmillan scratched his neck. "Well, ah could have a vole or two abo't."

Millie said, "I've seen no evidence of voles, Dad." She looked Melrose up and

212

down as if the evidence might just be standing before her.

Melrose took his pipe from his pocket and was considering lighting it but pipes were tricky things to light, so he hit the bowl on the heel of his shoe, knocking out the bit of tobacco that remained. He did this while sizing up Millie, who might be the bright one of the two. "I didn't say there *were* voles, Miss Macmillan. I merely asked." He smiled. He had read up on voles because they were smaller than mice and he'd liked the drawing of them scampering up a tree and chewing the bark with teeth "like scissors" *Country Life* had said. He went on, "You might want to protect that young holly over there with tree tubes." He was making himself unpopular. He smiled. There was a salutary side to this: they wouldn't want to talk to him, most certainly would not attempt to instruct such an arrogant gardener, and would leave him alone to his nonwork. Not having caught anyone's fancy with his bark wrapping or vole, Melrose brought out his third morsel. "Well, where shall I put my little plot of enameled mead?" He looked about as if it were a rhetorical question. Who would give a damn, except some medieval poet who could go on at great lengths? "I have always loved a medieval garden, haven't you? They're so romantic." How delightful. They were both looking at him from squinty brown eyes.

"Maybe in there?" said Millie, pointing toward a deeply hedged-in allotment. "There's a pond. It's quite pretty."

"Really?" Melrose walked over to the opening in the hedge and looked in. "Yes. A kind of secret garden, isn't it? That should do nicely. One can, of course, get elaborate in one's design, but I myself prefer a simpler one. I've always liked the effect. Ordinarily, one doesn't do this until spring; that's in order to cut the grass first. In the 1600s, gardeners were known to cut around each flower with shears to make the blooms stand out."

Millie said, "It's like in jewelry, Dad. Tiny bits of colored gemstones arranged to make —"

They were interrupted by the approach of a third person, who, judging from Millie's expression, was of particular interest to her. "Marc!" she called out, waving.

Melrose didn't see why the call and the wave were necessary given they were the only ones there.

Marc Warburton was a good-looking man and nobody's fool, an impression

Melrose could have done without. If anyone here could see through him, it would probably be Warburton. Macmillan and daughter quickly chose up sides. She said, "Mr. Plant, here, is looking for the right spot to put in his enameled mead."

Melrose didn't much care for the "his" in that statement, as if Declan Scott were merely humoring some eccentric relation.

"Yes, I know, but I don't see any reason to do it." Warburton smiled. The smile was rather twinkly.

"It's an effect I've always thought very pretty," said Melrose, standing his ground. Don't back down from any position, no matter how weak or laughable. *Never, never, never, never back down.* Diane sounded like Winston Churchill at the top of his game. "I've always thought it a charming pre-Raphaelite thing. Of course, as I was just saying, it works best in spring, given one has to cut the grass to accommodate the flowers. But I thought I'd try just a bit of a pattern to see how Mr. Scott likes it."

This time Warburton squinted. He was not, Melrose decided, as sure of himself as he made out to be. "What sorts of flowers would you use for this?"

"Periwinkles? Violets, pansies . . ." Good God, in early March would a pansy even know its name? Don't back down don't back down . . . It was becoming a mantra. "Set off against, oh, *Helleborus agitatious*." He would like to have washed that down with a glass of whiskey.

Warburton had taken out a pipe; now Melrose wished he had his in his mouth, too, puffing away.

"That's a new one on me," said Warburton, himself about to puff away when he got the thing lit.

"Yes, it's rather hard to come by. But I could have my man send some from Ardry End." Not only was he possessor of this rare helleborus plant, his man was in on it, too.

Macmillan put in his two pence. "Wot's it look like, then?"

Melrose took the stance (the coward's stance, Diane would have said) of hedging his bets by getting closer to reality as these people knew it and looked at the distant clumps of hellebore of whatever Latin names, white or a pale something. "Like that, except deeper and rather chummy."

" 'Chummy'?" They looked at him, round eyed and startled.

Oh, hell, he should have said "chubby." Well, too late now. This is what came of barely digested stuff from *Country Life*. "Yes, it's just a word I use to describe a plant that gets on well with others. Helle-bores that like shade, for example. Though the *agitatious* prefers filtered sunlight, it's quite friendly with shade, too." Melrose smiled. There were times when all he wanted to do was pat himself on the back. The other three didn't look as though they had that in mind, however. Or four, if one counted Roy, who had run along the walk to sit and look at Melrose with curled lip. Roy was the only one whose nonsense limit was working full throttle.

Marc Warburton had now taken a lighter from a pocket, one of those flamethrowers that could be used to caramelize a crème brûlée. Melrose could not now rescue his own pipe, nearly empty of tobacco, and be-sides it would appear to give Warburton an edge. No, he would have to look rumina-tive without the advantage of peering through soothing spirals of smoke. But he better speak first now. "I —"

Warburton stepped all over his "I." "Mr. Plant, I'm interested in what brought you here."

(Murder and disappearance?) Melrose smacked down "here" as if it were a bad-minton bird. "The turfing, you mean? Yes, Mr. Scott wants to restore the gardens to their original —"

Smack. (The game got testy.) "I'm well aware of that. I'm the designer."

*Smack.* "I'm a little unclear about this designing business. Where does the design come in if you're following the original?"

Big *smack* from Millie, who quickly came to the defense of Warburton. "He has to find it out, doesn't he? He has to rediscover it, see?"

Melrose would have loved to step on "rediscover," but he held his tongue.

Roy, however, was glad to make his feelings known. He turned and turned in circles. Although that could have merely indicated confusion as to what the hell was being said.

Bigger *smack* from Melrose. "But surely the footprint (excellent term!) is here. We can make out the old beds, borders, paths, can't we?" He smiled winningly.

Well, perhaps not winningly, for no one appeared to be won, except Roy, who came from Warburton to Melrose, who had just expressed the sharpest insight of the morning. Even Roy could have found the footprint.

Warburton was searching for a counter*smack* to the footprint notion. "The original plan isn't all that clear —"

(Oh, what a lame rejoinder! Warburton

should take a lesson from Diane.)

Said Millie: "What plants and shrubs are in the original have to be redesigned." Rediscover, redesign, Millie Macmillan was really gung-ho on doing things over again.

Melrose frowned. He wondered if Warburton was a necessary adjunct to this garden restoration. He certainly was as far as Millie was concerned, but . . . He also bet there were original architectural drawings of Angel Gate and its land. He decided to extricate himself from the party. He glanced at his watch and exclaimed, "Wow! I'd better get going! I've got a date with some fertilizer in St. Austell!"

"St. Austell?" said Millie. "But wouldn't it be easier to get it round here someplace? St. Austell's a distance. We hardly ever go there."

Precisely. Melrose smiled.

# 19

In St. Austell — quite a charming town had Melrose been in the mood for charm — he found a garden supply store where he purchased two bags of fertilizer called Turf 'n' Grow because he thought the play on words ("touch-and-go") was very imaginative for someone in the fertilizer business. The other reason he bought it was that the gentleman who waited on him said it was a very unusual type of fertilizer, containing numerous ingredients — a chemical bombardment — to enrich the soil. Yes, it was expensive, "but I think you'll find it's worth it." Melrose had always believed the more a thing cost, the better it was — wine, clothes, cars, Brown's Hotel and the Ritz. This did not extend, however, to beer and animals, excepting racehorses. Aggrieved had cost him a pretty penny; he'd bought the horse from the Ryland Stables. But his goat Aghast he'd bought for a song. Well, you couldn't race a goat, after all.

And turf, of course he'd need the turf. It was his plan to buy any old turf as long as it bore some resemblance to grass; or even if it didn't, he could say it too was a most unusual brand. No, turf didn't come in brands, did it? An unusual *cut*, yes, he doubted anyone would want to get into that with him. The garden shop manager said, yes, they could get him some and deliver it if he could just give them instruction. (*"Ha!"* Melrose had said in what he hoped was a good-natured, farmerlike voice. "Better the instruction should come from you!" The manager had just offered a dim sort of smile.)

As Melrose whistled his way along the pavement, he pictured a goat race. If Newmarket would just put one in between the horse races, it would probably do a lot toward relaxing the race goers. Rather like bringing on cheerleaders in American sports at halftime. He was carrying a bag of fertilizer over his shoulder, feeling like a character out of Thomas Hardy (as he was also wearing his flat cap), thinking he must make a good show of a man consumed with his trade, hard worker, no slacker. It felt good, but not so good he would want to continue with it outside of the demands of his present job. His car was parked along the street and he dumped the fertilizer into the trunk.

In the small jam of people at the crosswalk, he recognized the woman he'd met at Angel Gate, Hermione Hobbs. This could be a golden opportunity to get some information. He followed her for a few minutes, waiting to see whether she stopped at one of the shops. He hoped she wasn't going into the church across the way to do brass rubbings. She passed a tearoom (good choice) and was coming up on a pub on the corner.

He hurried and caught her up. "Miss Hobbs," he said, with far more enthusiasm than he felt.

She turned. "Oh, *hal-* lo." These horsey types always seemed to lean on the "e" until it became an "ah." "It's Mr. —"

"Plant. Melrose Plant. I'm doing that bit of work for Declan Scott."

She shielded her eyes as if from his bright self and said, "What brings you to St. Austell?"

Well, good grief, it wasn't exactly Aruba, was it? All manner of people were spilling into St. Austell. But she seemed to want to make something of it merely by virtue of her presence here.

"Supplies. I've just been buying fertilizer

at the shop down there." He nodded in the direction from which he'd come.

"Fertilizer?"

"Yes. Your garden supply shop is well stocked with the stuff."

"It is?"

"I began an interest in turf and flowering mead when I was at Oxford."

"Oxford?"

She was having a hard time taking anything in, wasn't she? "I read medieval history there and turfing and enameled mead; well, I had always wanted to do that at Ardry End."

"Ardry End?" Her eyes lit up.

"Yes, my home. It's been in the family for — look, would you care for a drink (pointing toward the pub) or a cup of tea (pointing toward the tearoom)?" That he had kindled an interest in himself and fanned the sparks with Ardry End was clear.

"Why . . . yes, that would be pleasant. Tea, I think."

Probably one of those women who thought drinking in pubs was a man's job and felt she would be better complemented by flower-bedecked cushions and cakes and scones.

It was crowded, but two women were

putting on their coats and Melrose nabbed the table they were leaving. The floor was uneven (de rigueur for a tearoom), causing the table to rock slightly. Instead of table-cloths, there were paper place mats, but one could hardly expect a total adherence to graciousness in these pushy times.

A thin woman in her sixties with lips that seemed permanently pursed in disapproval took their order for tea and toasted tea cakes, all — Melrose was sure — straight out of the bag and the packet.

"Tell me more," said Hermione, leaning toward him, all eyes and ears.

Melrose had forgotten what he'd been telling her less of. "About what?"

"Your family seat. It must be lovely. Is it in Cornwall?"

"No. In Northamptonshire."

"Oh."

He noted the disappointment. Was that because Northamptonshire was not a destination county? Or was it the distance from Cornwall? "The country around there is beautiful. Not as beautiful as Yorkshire. There's a place for you! The North York Moors." Well, that was a bit wide, but it was a way into murder. "Yes, it's too bad Yorkshire has so many bad associations for us, isn't it?"

"Pardon?" She looked vacant.

He had segued quite smoothly to the subject of murder. "You know — the Yorkshire Ripper, the Moors Murderers."

The tea and cakes had arrived. "Th'nk you," said the purse-lipped matron as she put the cups and plates down.

Hell, did she have to bust in on the murder? Now he'd have to rev the subject up again, for he had decided Hermione had a fifteen-second attention span.

"This looks lovely," she said, pouring tea.

This was clearly her favorite word. "Um. One wonders about crime these days."

"Why?" She operated on her tea cake with a surgical precision.

Why? He'd sooner talk to Lulu. "Well, we have so much more of it."

She smiled and ate her tea cake. "I expect it's better not to think about it, don't you?"

"No, actually. I mean, you surely must be curious about this murdered woman at Angel Gate?"

"That was most peculiar. This is quite nice," she said of the tea cake.

The tea cake was receiving as much attention as the murder. *It would have been deep air,/The heaving speech of air . . .*

Melrose was suddenly reminded of Wallace Stevens's poem. He decided he was sitting across the table from the heaving speech of air. Hermione could hardly be in the running for Declan Scott.

He felt in this one-sided conversation as if he were dogsledding, pulled along by a laconic pack of huskies. He said, "It's quite dreadful what Mr. Scott has had to suffer. His wife dead, the daughter abducted. I don't see how he manages to keep his balance."

Her little finger was cocked above her teacup as she sipped. "That was awful! Poor Declan."

He waited. When she said no more, Melrose heaved a little air himself and whipped the huskies on. "It must have been dreadful for the child's mother, too. I mean to think she should have been watching —"

In an uncharacteristic little outburst, Hermione said, chinking the teacup back in its saucer, "She should have been, shouldn't she? Well, Mary was never the most careful person. She was so absent-minded."

Absentmindedness would hardly cover the situation. "But he didn't blame her, did he? And, of course, the little girl was his stepdaughter, not his daughter." That could have been better put, but it probably made no difference with Hermione.

She chewed and thought this over. "I don't think Declan blamed Mary, no, but you know one does want *someone* to blame."

Drily, Melrose said, "I should think the kidnapper might be good for a start." She missed the sarcasm. He went on. "There must have been a lot of speculation. I mean as to why the child was taken?"

"Declan's got mountains of money, of course."

"But there was never a ransom demand."

"That was peculiar. There was some talk about its being done for revenge, but I can't credit that."

"Why would anyone want revenge? Where did that idea come from?"

"The Hardcastle girl."

Melrose was for once in this conversation taken aback. "Why would this Hardcastle girl want revenge?"

Hermione shook her head. "No, no. Elsie Hardcastle was the victim." She went on sipping her tea.

Melrose nearly reached over and took the cup. At last, a morsel of information, although it sounded as if it might be more than just a morsel — and then she stopped. "What . . . how was she a victim? Of what?"

"Why, Mary Scott. You see, it was raining and the traffic light was malfunctioning. This was in Meva. It was several months before Flora's disappearance."

God, at last she was saying something, but excising the bits that would have made clear what she was talking about. "Back up for a moment. First of all, where's Meva?"

"Mevagissey, a fishing village not far from Heligan. It was dead dark and the light wouldn't change. Mary had no choice but to go through it, finally. Elsie was crossing the street and had her umbrella up. Mary" — Hermione shrugged — "hit her. Worse, though, Mary didn't stop. It was a hit-and-run. But she managed to make the coroner believe that she honestly thought she'd hit something in the road. She didn't think for a minute it was a person. It was raining so hard, coming down in torrents, and she thought that affected her ability to judge. And everyone knows that narrow street that goes down through the village is hell to drive in the best of circumstances.

"Well, she didn't hit Elsie squarely on, and she certainly didn't run over her.

When she got back to Angel Gate, she was extremely upset and she told Declan she was afraid she'd hit either an animal or a person. Immediately, he called the police and gave them the information. So it was certainly not a hit-and-run, I mean, not in the real sense of one. The coroner was surprised that the blow had, actually, killed the girl."

"She was charged, though?"

"Yes. But the coroner's court didn't convict her." Hermione paused. "Some people thought it was her husband's money that saved her, as much as the story she told. I'm rather surprised you haven't heard this. Declan told me you're a friend of that Scotland Yard superintendent." She smiled.

Surely, he was not now about to find that Hermione Hobbs was clever, was he? An altogether different cup of tea?

Hermione went on. "You can imagine how the Hardcastles felt when Mary got off."

"The court found her innocent?"

"Yes. The Hardcastles, the father and mother, were pretty restrained about the outcome. It certainly was a dreadful accident, and Mary was so torn up, well, it was hard to hate her."

If he'd been the parent, Melrose wouldn't find it hard to hate her or kill her. Or worse.

"It's quite possible that Declan —" She stopped and fiddled nervously with her spoon.

"Declan?"

"I shouldn't say anything."

Oh, do, dear lady, and I'll buy you another pot of tea, another plate of scones, all the stuff in the window you've been coveting. Hell, I'll buy you the tearoom! You've finally come through! "What shouldn't you say?"

Now she was busy pleating her paper napkin.

"More tea!" said Melrose, and motioned to the proprietress, who sulked over.

Hermione laughed a little. "Oh, well, if you —"

Melrose asked the woman for another pot of tea and a selection of the cakes in the window.

The woman picked up the empty tea-muffin plate, went to the window and plopped four of the cakes on the plate and returned it to the table. She picked up the pot and moved off.

"She does everything with so much élan, doesn't she? Now, you were saying about Declan Scott — ?"

She still looked doubtful.

Don't dumb out on me now, for God's sakes. "You were about to say that Declan Scott could have done something with relation to the Hardcastles."

"Yes, well, I don't know if I should say it, but Declan might have given the Hardcastles a large sum of money not to make a fuss."

A "fuss." Your child is killed and the most Hermione could come up with was "fuss." This paying off, if he had, sounded cold-blooded not so much of Scott, but of the Hardcastles. Melrose wondered how much money had changed hands.

He wondered if Jury knew about this accident. A few months between Elsie's death and Flora's disappearance might have police connecting the two. And Declan must have been under the impression that the Hardcastles were satisfied — broken-hearted, but satisfied — that Mary Scott really hadn't known what she'd done. And Scott had, after all, called the police; they'd admitted she'd done it.

Back with a fresh pot of tea, their churlish server deposited it on the table and then took herself off.

Hermione said, "Police questioned people, Mary's friends. I thought they

231

might want to establish something about her character. The police who questioned me wanted to know what sort of person Mary Scott was and as to her character. I said it was unimpeachable. I didn't mention her absentmindedness, the way she sometimes walked around with her head in a cloud. I was afraid that would make them wonder whether she'd been paying attention to the road. And if it was anyone's fault, it was the town's, I think. The light had been stuck that way for hours; several people attested to that. Well, it seemed to me it was down to them, to the town — the police or someone."

"When Flora Scott disappeared, was there any talk about the Hardcastles' possibly being behind it?"

She frowned. "Well, I expect so. But the Hardcastles are such an unassuming couple. I could not begin to imagine they might have been lying in wait for an opportunity to harm the Scotts. That's diabolical, don't you think?"

"Yes, but then people can be diabolical."

"Well, there's the other child. A son. Elsie wasn't the one and only."

So the one wouldn't be missed so much? Parents didn't divvy up their love. Melrose thought they loved each of their children completely. If one died it was not a half of the whole who died; it was the whole. He had no experience in this, but he imagined that's how it was. He wondered if Hermione had children — probably not.

"Then who might have done it? I imagine you asked yourself this."

Hermione gave this what she had of her share of serious thought. "A stranger, it must have been. Although I hate to even think it — a pedophile, perhaps? Or a thwarted woman, one who couldn't have children. Or what about the murdered woman?"

Surprised, Melrose looked up. "Why do you say that?"

"I don't know, perhaps just because the two seem related." She glanced at her watch. "Oh, my goodness. We've been sitting here over an hour. I really must be getting on home."

Melrose signaled the proprietress again. "Shall I drop you off? I'd be glad to."

"Thanks, but I have my little Morris Minor. You should see it. They're delightful cars."

People were always so proud of their Morris Minors, they always seemed to want to introduce them to whomever they were talking to. "I've enjoyed this discussion very much," said Melrose.

"I, too. And thank you for the tea."

The proprietress was doing double time at the cash register (no computers here!), and Melrose wondered if she was also cook and cleaner-up.

They thanked each other again and walked off to their separate car parks.

# 20

The ground floor of Angel Gate was a blaze of light. As he got out of his car, Melrose wondered if Declan Scott was throwing a party.

He had taken the pebble path around the side of the house and was on his way to the cottage when Lulu appeared.

"Mr. Scott wants me to tell you you're to go in." She hooked her thumb over her shoulder toward "in."

"Any room in particular? Or am I just to wander round the dining room like Banquo's ghost?"

Lulu, literal to a fault, considered this question. She pushed her glasses up on her nose and appeared to be deciding upon the answer. "I guess the library. That's where the others are. Who's Banquo? Did he really have a ghost or are you making it up?"

"Mr. B was a king murdered by

Macbeth." No. "Macduff?" No. Good lord, had he even forgotten the plot of *Macbeth*? "Well, one of the Macs, anyway. And he came back to haunt — whoever. Shakespeare is responsible yet again for traitorous doings and bloody revenge."

"Were there a lot of them?"

"What?"

"A lot of Macs?"

"You bet there were. Macs all over the place. Never mind. It's only a story." He turned and started for the house.

"Flora wasn't," said Lulu, as if calling him back to storyland.

Surprised, Melrose quickly turned to her. "You mean Flora wasn't just a story?"

Lulu nodded. "She really got stolen."

"Did you know her well, then?" He thought they might have been much the same age.

She nodded. "We used to play. Nobody knows where she went. Or who took her."

Melrose detected in this, not surprisingly, some anxiety.

"But I know," said Lulu. She had a piece of string round her finger, which she wound and unwound.

He stared at her. "You do? Who, then?"

"The Child Thief."

Here was a new wrinkle, a new record in

childhood imagination. "Is that *a* or *the* Child Thief?" Now that was a comforting question! "I mean, is there just one, or are there several?" Another brilliant question. Why wasn't Jury here? Where was the man when you needed him? Melrose felt at a loss, although he hated to admit it.

But he wasn't confusing Lulu; she remained firm in her belief. "Only one. There's just the one Child Thief."

"Oh. Well, uh, what does he look like?"

"Like anybody. Like you."

"*Me?* I assure you, I'm *not* the Child Thief. It wouldn't occur to me to steal a child!"

"That's just what he'd say."

She was standing with her feet rolled in, a favorite child posture.

"You don't *seriously* think it's me, do you?"

"No."

That was a relief.

"You wouldn't know how," she added. "All I'm saying is he could be anyone. He could be a lady, too."

"Look, why do you think Flora was taken by this person?" The whole plot was making Melrose nervous.

Lulu looked off into the distance. "Because he's a Child Thief. If you *were* him, isn't that what you'd do?"

"But this is going around in circles!" He came at it from another direction. "Did you tell the police this?" Macalvie would be delighted to hear this theory promulgated.

She shrugged. "They never asked."

"Oddly enough, I don't expect they would."

Head bent, Lulu was tying knots in the string. "I could've told them." She spun the string in the air and round her finger.

"Told them what?"

"Where he lives."

Melrose sighed. He would be stopping on this path all night listening to her spin out this fantasy in a pattern as twisty as the string. "Just as long as he doesn't take up residence in my cottage, I don't care."

She was winding the string again. "He lives in different places. Sometimes in London, and sometimes around here, and other times in" — she was thinking — "Scotland. And sometimes in —"

"I'm sorry I can't follow this Child Thief on his rambles, but I must go into the house now if Mr. Scott is expecting me. So let's walk. I imagine your aunt is waiting for you in the kitchen, isn't she?"

That went unanswered, but Lulu did

trudge along toward the house. She said, "You better be careful."

"Careful of what?"

"Of *who*, you mean."

It sounded as if her mind was hosting the Salem witch hunts. "*I* don't mean anything. You're the one with all the ideas."

As if he had not spoken, she said, "There's a lady in there you don't know." Now she was bouncing what looked like a button on her hand.

"What lady?"

Lulu gave him a look reserved for fools and little children. "The one in there —"

Her pointed finger reminded Melrose of Marley's ghost.

"— with Mr. Scott. Her name's Patricia."

"You're entirely too familiar with the goings-on around here. Do you spy and listen at doors and look through keyholes?"

She ignored that as they walked along to the patio. He said, "Thank you very much for giving me the message. I've enjoyed our little talk. Are you going to the kitchen?"

She nodded and ran off in that general direction.

Peculiar child. Well, he was certainly out of his depth with her. He walked through the octagon room to the library.

This, thought Melrose, is more like it! When Declan Scott introduced him to Patricia Quint, Melrose made a swift comparison between Ms. Quint and Hermione Hobbs. Not only was Patricia Quint in the library, with a drink in her hand, but so was Marc Warburton, with a drink in his.

Melrose wondered — in a shamelessly chauvinistic turn of mind — if she belonged to Declan or Marcus. Or, indeed, some husband somewhere. It was hard to believe that a woman who looked like Patricia Quint did not have some man hovering in the background, if not the foreground, here in front of the fireplace.

The slim white hand not holding a drink reached perfectly straight out and shook Melrose's. "I've never known an expert on turf and enameled mead. When you're finished here, perhaps you could come to me?"

Melrose made a short bow. "A pleasure. What problems do you have?"

Patricia laughed. "I can't grow anything."

"That does present an obstacle."

Pat Quint, in her cream-colored suit, looked as if she'd come straight from the mint. She looked moneyed, true, but it was her clarity — of skin, of eyes — and precision — the perfectly fitted suit, the perfectly cut hair — that gave her this newly minted look. The enameled lips, the diffuse blush — all of this might have looked "turned-out" in an artificial way. And though artifice was evident in each lash and silky eyebrow, still she did not look artificial. It was strange, he thought, that she managed to avoid it.

Marc Warburton was smiling (though not heartily) at this talk of Melrose's speciality, and added, "I'm not sure there's enough in turf to take up much of one's time, though, is there?"

"Well, not until you're dead, no," said Melrose.

They all liked that, especially Pat Quint.

But Warburton didn't want to let go of it. "You went into St. Austell for some sort of fertilizer? I can't imagine you'd find anything you couldn't get at Macmillan's own nurseries."

"Perhaps. Much of the mixture is straightforward enough, but there are one or two things I mix with it that only the place in St. Austell carries."

Warburton frowned. "Really? What's that?"

Melrose smiled. "Even in fertilizer we have our secrets. Can't expect me to give them all up, can you?"

"Dirt isn't always merely dirt, right?" said Pat Quint, with a laugh.

But Marc was back, objecting again, this time to Declan. "I could probably have done this for you, Declan, if you'd told me you wanted it."

"It came about accidentally, Marc. When I was talking to this Scotland Yard — well, you met him. Mr. Plant here is a friend of his."

Melrose objected. "An acquaintance, not a friend. I was doing a job near Northampton, an Italian water garden sort of thing (he was thinking of Watermeadows, which really was Italianate, and with a sad history). Superintendent Jury was conducting an investigation —"

"But why's he here?" asked Pat with some alarm.

Melrose thought that should be obvious.

It was. She went on, "I mean, this murder's a job for the Devon and Cornwall police to sort, isn't it?"

"Apparently not," said Declan. "Why? Do you object to Scotland Yard on your doorstep?"

"Not *my* doorstep."

He shrugged. "Our doorstep, I mean. Our corner of Cornwall."

"I don't object. Scotland Yard just suggests the case is more dramatic."

Declan said, again in that somewhat instructive tone masked by a smile, "I'd say a body found on my grounds is pretty dramatic, Pat, with or without Scotland Yard."

"It must be painful for you; it must seem like living it all over again. I mean, Flor—"

"I know what you mean, Pat."

As if the man could forget, thought Melrose.

Patricia Quint recovered a little ground by saying, "I'm sorry. At times I can be rather thick."

Declan smiled. "I know."

Warburton said, "What have the police found out? Anything new?"

"Don't know. The police don't confide in me." There were times he wished that was true.

Patricia said to Declan, "It's as if someone had a vendetta against you."

"I didn't know the woman," Declan said. "Why would the killer relate her to me?"

"Ah, well, that's the thing, isn't it?"

"Or not," Declan answered.

"Speaking of gardens," said Melrose, trying to make up for his "footprint" argument earlier, "I find your design of this one quite lovely, Mr. Warburton."

Marc's eyes widened, as if surprised to hear a compliment from Plant.

"Thanks. But most of the credit goes to the Macmillans."

"Yes, but it's the architecture that starts it on the right path." Melrose shifted the subject. "Have you lived here long, Miss Quint?"

"Pat, please. All my life, really. I don't live here year-round, though; I go up to London quite often. I've got a place in Knightsbridge. Pont Street."

Pont Street was not a cheap address, but then Pat Quint was not a cheap person. Consider the Upper Sloane Street clothes — Ferragamo, Armani, Max Mara, one of those. "And your house here?"

"Halfway between here and Mevagissey."

Mevagissey. A place Melrose had barely heard of before was now turning up everywhere, it seemed. He would have liked to hear more about the fate of Elsie Hardcastle, but that would have to wait.

Pat went on. "It's a popular village with tourists. You know, fishing village on the coast. It's near Heligan, indeed, right round the corner. The Lost Gardens have become a significant tourist draw. Well, they are beautiful, aren't they?"

Here was a subject best served cold, like

revenge. The Lost Gardens of Heligan.

Declan said, "British troops were bivouacked at Heligan in the Second World War. It was quite interesting, what they did. At one point they decided to mimic the class system, the upstairs-downstairs syndrome, you could say. So they took on different roles."

"How did they decide who was to be whom? Lord whoever on the one hand, and the underbutler on the other?"

"That's what's so fascinating. They did it by rank. So the highest ranking would perform as family and the lower ranks as staff. Then within those categories, there was further ranking: master sergeant, say, as butler; plain sergeant as underbutler. Captain or lieutenant as the titled owner, lieutenant as his son, the earl of whatever."

Pat laughed. "That's charming, but what was the point of it all?"

"Something to do, I guess. Maybe we never lack the desire to dress up and be somebody else. You know, the trunk in the attic we looted as children?"

Pat Quint said, "I can remember doing that; dress-up appeals to all kiddies, doesn't it?" Then, clearly feeling she'd strayed once again too close to little Flora Baumann, she quickly put in, "This enameled mead stuff — what is it exactly?"

"It's quite simple." What followed here was much the same information he'd given Jury, such as it was. But then if you were completely unfamiliar with the subject, it probably sounded quite esoteric. Except to Marc Warburton, who didn't mind taking a backseat to Melrose for the moment.

"What a pleasant effect that must be," said Pat.

"I hope so."

Declan Scott was smiling slightly, but he looked far away and unhappy. He was leaning forward in his armchair, watching Melrose, but not really seeing him.

It was at that point that Rebecca Owen came to the door and announced dinner.

"You'll join us, won't you?" said Declan as he set his half-finished drink down.

"Thank you, but I'm meeting someone" — Melrose looked at his watch — "right now, actually. I'm late."

# 21

Jury was sitting at the bar of the Winds of Change with Sergeant Wiggins, who had come with him from London that afternoon. They'd been met at the station by DS Platt, who appeared to have immediately forged a bond with Wiggins. Perhaps it was their mutual rank. Right now they moved down the bar to continue whatever they had going.

Jury was drinking lager.

"Sissy drink." Melrose asked the barman for an Old Peculier.

"Sorry, sir, we're outta that. How about a Guinness?"

"They're not the same." He sighed, gestured toward Jury's drink. "Give me one of those."

"Sissy."

The barman smiled, enjoying this little cabaret performed by coppers. "Yes, sir." He went off.

"So what do you think of Declan Scott?"

"He's so charming I'd like to kick him around his garden."

"Ha!" Jury set down his pint and looked at Melrose with a smug grin. "Just what I said about Vernon Rice, remember?"

"It's not the same thing at all." Actually, it was. "What about our victim? Haven't police ID'd her yet? It's been a week, hasn't it?"

Jury shook his head. "You'd think someone had wiped the slate clean on her. You'd think she had no past."

"Or that she'd shared — Thanks," said Melrose when his pint was set before him. "Shared someone else's. It's hard to believe anyone could slip through the net. The only thing you know about her is that she met Mary Scott in the lounge of Brown's Hotel and you don't even know *that* for sure."

"Why would Declan Scott invent her? The cook Dora Stout saw her, too."

Melrose thought for a moment. "Here's something: a woman named Hermione Hobbs told me about an accident Mary Scott was involved in."

"I know. Hit-and-run in Mevagissey three and a half years ago. She killed a girl named Elsie Hardcastle. Macalvie was all over the father; Hardcastle was at the point of claiming police harassment." Jury looked down the counter to where the barman was shoveling crisps into bowls. When the barman looked up, Jury raised his pint and tapped it.

The barman came along and took the empty glass.

Melrose lit up a cigarette and dropped the book of matches on the bar. He did a double take when he saw Jury staring at him. "What? *What?* For God's sakes, it's been *years* since you quit; am I to throw myself on the reformed smoker's pyre every time I light up?"

"It has not been 'years.' It's been one year and thirteen months —"

"In other words, years —"

"— which is no time at all to a smoker. We should institute the smoke-free restaurant rule."

"You're the worst kind of reformed smoker. You're the take-all-the-fun-out-of-it kind." Melrose exhaled a stream of smoke, not precisely in Jury's face, but not precisely out of it, either.

Jury waved it away and coughed artificially. "Secondhand smoke is as bad for your lungs —"

"Oh, *puleeze.*" Melrose stabbed out the cigarette. "All right, Macalvie more or less assigned himself to Flora Baumann's case, and consequently paid a lot of attention to the hit-and-run. Anything to do with the Scotts he would have paid attention to."

"Right." Jury turned to look across the bar and saw Cody Platt and Wiggins in the other room at the snooker table. Wiggins was racking the balls. Wiggins playing snooker? God had to be kidding around. No, apparently not, for now Wiggins was chalking a cue. Jury called over to Cody Platt.

"Sir?"

Jury motioned him over.

Platt leaned his cue against the table as Wiggins gave Jury almost exactly the same look that Melrose had. Talk about your killjoys.

"Yes, sir?" said Cody.

"Do you remember a hit-and-run case involving Mary Scott?"

Cody nodded. "In Mevagissey. 'Bout three and a half years ago, that was. She ran a red light and hit a girl named Elsie Hardcastle."

"She got off with a suspended sentence, right?"

"Right. For one thing, she didn't exactly 'run' the light. It wasn't working right. If she'd waited for the green, she'd have been there all night. Several people attested to it being out of commission. Rain flapping around like sheets in the wind. And the girl Elsie was wearing dark clothes and had her head hidden by her umbrella. Mary Scott would have needed second sight to avoid her. The thing that told against Mary was that she fled the scene."

"Thanks. Back to your snooker. How'd you ever get Wiggins to play?"

"Me get him?" Cody smiled. "No, it's the other way round. He got me to. He's champion, Al is." Cody walked off.

Melrose said, "Al?" He was eating vinegar crisps.

"I have never heard Wiggins talk about snooker, never."

"Well, Sergeant Wiggins may be leading other lives."

"I've never been sure whether he's leading this one."

Wiggins was just about to make a shot when Jury called to Cody Platt again. The cue slipped off the ball and Wiggins, clinging to his shooting position, shifted his gaze and gave Jury an uncharacteristic black look.

"Sorry," called Jury.

Cody snickered and walked to the bar. "Thanks. I'm losing."

"A hit-and-run in any event is a serious matter. I'd've thought an inquest would have come up with something — depraved indifference, perhaps — that would have landed her in the nick, no question."

Again Cody spread his hands and shrugged. "Declan Scott has a lot of influence around here."

"Declan Scott is also a man of some character and conscience. I don't see him trying to buy his way out of manslaughter."

Cody said, "His way, perhaps. But *her* way, that's different. He would have jumped through hoops of fire for Mary Scott. I don't think he'd have thought twice about buying off the local constabulary, or magistrate, or the Hardcastles."

"Can you be bought?" said Melrose.

"Probably."

Wiggins, cue stick still in hand, came up behind them. "May we go on with our game?"

"Absolutely go on with it," said Jury. "According to Cody you're quite the lad when it comes to snooker. I've never heard you as much as mention it, though."

"No, well, you don't play, do you?"

"No, Wiggins, and I don't drink green gunk or eat black biscuits, either. But you're always more than happy to satisfy my curiosity in that regard."

Wiggins curled his lip. "Ha ha." He walked off with Cody.

Melrose caught beer in his windpipe from an aborted laugh.

Jury slapped him on the back. "I'm not sure Sergeant Platt's a good influence."

Melrose gave a strangled answer. "Oh, I think just the opposite."

Jury plucked menus from little aluminum holders, handed one to Melrose.

They looked, trying to decide between the fish, the beef, and the curry. One of each fish and beef made it easier, especially since they didn't intend to order one of the five different curries listed.

Jury shook his head. "This menu makes me nostalgic for the Blue Parrot."

"I'll tell Trevor Sly." Trevor Sly owned the Blue Parrot. "He'll be thrilled."

"Trevor Sly is always thrilled." Jury closed his menu. "Thrilldom is his métier."

"I'm having the plaice and chips."

"And peas, for a change. Yes, that's a creative choice, isn't it? I think I'll have that, too. So will Wiggins and Cody." Jury called over to them. "Fish and chips all right for a meal?" This earned him another scowl from Wiggins, whose shot Jury had once again ruined. But they both agreed to the fish and chips.

When the barman came along, they put in four orders for the fish and chips. "Less work for the cook." He laughed and said the food would be right up and then got them fresh drinks.

Jury thought for a moment and then washed his hands down over his face. "I don't get it."

Melrose looked at him. "What? This case?"

Jury nodded. "Here's a little girl abducted and no demand for ransom of any kind ever made. It's been three years. If I'd been Mary Scott, I'd have slid completely off the rails."

The pub fell quiet. All they heard was the occasional crisp click of the billiard balls.

"Listen, I'm sorry about your cousin," said Melrose. "Was it hard? The funeral?"

"The funeral wasn't, but, yes, her death was hard. Does someone have to die before you sort things out?"

"Yes."

Jury looked from Melrose to his watch. He paused to see if Wiggins was about to hit anything and then called over to Cody. "What's happened to your boss? He should've been here an hour ago."

Cody leaned his cue against the table and took out his cell phone. While he waited he seemed to be studying the table. He spoke into the cell, nodded, slapped it shut. "He's on his way, be here in twenty minutes."

The twenty minutes was taken up with the fish and chips, surprisingly good. Wiggins stated his preference for mushy peas, a preference none of the others shared. They all drank more beer, except for Wiggins, and Cody, who sipped club soda.

Melrose asked their barman if he could locate a Puligny Montrachet '64 in his cellars and the barman (to his everlasting credit, thought Jury) turned this over in his mind and said, "The '66 and '70, but not the '64. Sorry." He walked off.

"Rotten luck," said Melrose.

"Some days are like that," said Jury.

The door opened and rain and Macalvie swept in. He stood by their table and shook some beads of water from his coat. He didn't take it off; he rarely did.

"You're getting water on my fish," Jury said.

"It's used to it." He moved off to the bar.

"They're out of the Puligny Montrachet '64," Melrose called after him.

In a couple of minutes Macalvie was back carrying a glass of whiskey. "Christ, what a night."

"Where've you come from?" asked Wiggins, still plowing away at his plate. "You seem a bit . . . out of sorts, if you don't mind my saying."

"I'm always out of sorts, Wiggins. Glad to see you, though." He sat back, took out a cigar. "I was at Angel Gate."

Melrose was surprised. "I just came from there a couple of hours ago. Have I missed something?"

"I wanted to talk to Declan Scott."

Now Jury was surprised; he was about to say he thought Macalvie was leaving Declan Scott to him, but didn't.

Melrose said, "When I left they were about to sit down to dinner."

"I know. I interrupted them. While they were having dinner, I went to the kitchen to talk to Rebecca Owen. She gave me a cup of tea. Nice woman. She came to Angel Gate on the same day that our mystery woman did. I was hoping she might have remembered something about the victim. Which she didn't. I went back. Same thing. No sign of anyone around. She wasn't around when the mystery lady came to the house. So she had nothing to say about whether Scott had seen her or not."

"Why would he lie about having seen this woman with his wife?"

"Yeah. Rebecca Owen said the same thing: 'My goodness, why would Mr. Scott lie about her?' Then this niece of hers —"

"Lulu," said Melrose.

"Lulu says 'Because people like to lie,' as she sat munching a cookie. All eyes, she is. So's that crazy mutt of hers."

" 'Because people like to lie.' " Melrose said, "It sounds like one of her mysterious pronouncements. They don't mean anything."

"Oh, right?" Macalvie hooked a thumb toward Melrose as he looked at the others. "Our expert on childhood behavior has spoken."

"I'm only making the point that Lulu has a flair for drama. She likes to make you blink."

Macalvie said, "She asked me if I was ever going to find Flora." He looked around the pub. "I said I just didn't know. To which she then says, 'Why? Aren't the police smart enough?' "

"Good question," said Cody with a snicker.

Macalvie's mouth formed a small circle

through which he puffed smoke. "Yeah, so after I slapped her up the side of the head, I modestly confessed, 'No, I guess we aren't.' "

" 'That's too bad,' she says as if I hadn't been kidding." He drew in on his cigar again.

A dozen or so customers had come in while they'd been sitting at the table. It was an indifferent pub night. If there really was such a thing.

Macalvie went on. "So then I asked Lulu if she missed Flora. 'No,' she said."

"Her aunt gets a little upset by this. 'Lulu, you don't know what you're talking about. You and Flora had good times together.' Lulu would only admit to *some* good times. This kid would drive me nuts inside five minutes. She's so contrary."

Wiggins looked up from his few remaining chips (it took him an eon to finish a meal), his eyebrows raised.

"So Lulu stood — or rather jumped — from one leg to another like she had to pee while that dog was bouncing off the walls like he needed a fix. I got up from the table, thanked Miss Owen and turned to go. Then Lulu said, 'I know who took her.' "

"Ah," said Melrose.

"Ah, what?" When Melrose merely shrugged, Macalvie went on. "Well, this stopped me in my tracks. I looked at her looking at me, looking at and stirring her tea and waiting for me to ask. Okay. I gave up and asked: 'Who?'

" 'The Child Thief.'

"I opened my mouth to ask what in hell she meant and she said, 'That's all I'm telling you.'

"Ordering my hands not to strangle her, I asked why? Why wouldn't she tell me more?

" 'Because I don't know any more than that. It's just the Child Thief.' That's what I mean." He paused. "No wonder I hate talking to kids."

Melrose knew it wasn't for that reason. "Lulu's not one of your ordinary children."

"There are no ordinary children." Macalvie turned to Jury. "What do you think?"

"About Lulu? I don't know. I haven't talked to her."

"You could get something out of her, I bet."

Jury drained his pint, set it down. "I don't know if you can talk to kids if your purpose is to get something out of them." He shrugged. "Maybe you can't talk to anyone if that's your purpose." He looked round the table to see all of them looking at him, perplexed. "Sorry." He added, "I'm going over there in the morning. I'll talk to her." He felt vaguely ashamed, without knowing why. He picked up his pint, remembered it was empty and got up. "I'm in the chair; who wants another? Before Wiggins and I toddle along to Mevagissey."

Wiggins looked up, surprised, and none too happy. "Sir?"

"A family by the name of Hardcastle. The mum said they'd be happy to see us."

Wiggins looked with something akin to longing at the other room with the billiard table.

"I'm sorry we can't take it with us, Wiggins."

Melrose said, "Well, I've got to get back to my digs or I'll never rouse myself in the morning. I wish I had Ruthven here."

"Yeah, that'd help your case," said Macalvie. "A gardener with his valet."

"It'll take forever," said Melrose. "All I have is this rented car, made for midgets. Good night."

Jury and Macalvie said good night to him. Jury set down his pint and asked Cody for the keys to the Ford.

Macalvie asked him to hang on for a minute.

Cody gave the keys to Wiggins and they both rose and announced they were going to finish their game. They returned to the snooker table.

"What?"

Macalvie said, "Do you think it's possible this woman can't be traced because she actually wasn't this woman?"

Jury looked down into his empty glass. "Yes, that's exactly what I think."

"Maybe she was masquerading as somebody else and that's why it's been such a damned problem identifying her. Look, we've circulated this morgue shot; we've run everything we could possibly run. The pathologist has found nada as far as the body is concerned. But if she doesn't look like that in real life? Except for staff at Brown's Hotel — assuming Scott's story is true — who might recognize her as the woman with Mary Scott, and when she was here, well, what if all the rest of the time she looked entirely different?"

"Why would she have disguised herself to present herself to Mary Scott?" said Jury.

"I don't know. Unless . . ."

"What?"

"Unless the disguise wasn't necessarily for Mary. Maybe it was for Declan."

261

# 22

The car was pointed toward Mevagissey. "Pointed" was the right word, since Wiggins had found a road thin as a string and was driving as if the car were a missile. It was still raining.

"Try to miss that wagon up ahead, will you, especially the two people in it?"

"I see it, sir." Wiggins sighed in exasperation. "Of course I see it." He cut the wheel and raced past it, never caring what could have been coming toward them, and thank God nothing was.

"I've never known you to drive like a maniac, Wiggins."

"It's probably getting out of London, all that filth, and breathing clean air and feeling freer, you know."

"You'll certainly be feeling deader."

The rain poured. Wiggins drove.

"We're coming into Mevagissey, I think."

Which was, Jury was sorry to see, at the

bottom of this impossibly narrow road. The sign at the top suggested one park in one of the car parks at the top. Fortunately, there were lights, lights coming from tea-rooms and small souvenir shops. It was now dead dark. Wiggins started down.

Jury said, "You've noticed this road is walled on each side?" He pointed left and right like a flight attendant pointing out exits. Of which they'd none. "They're very unforgiving, these stone walls."

"Haven't hit anything yet," Wiggins said in a chirrupy voice.

"You're a police detective, and you're satisfied with the logic of that statement? Is it your recent association with demons or with Cody Platt that's opened up this devil-may-care side of you?"

"I'd hardly say that, sir."

"I know. That's why I'm saying it."

Jury shined a small torch on the map of the town and directed Wiggins to the left, then the right, then the left again and they ascended another street.

"Seems to be all cliffside." Wiggins urged the car on, as if it were an unyielding donkey.

"Doesn't it just?"

It was dead dark. Jury preferred not to look out of the passenger's window.

"Strange how the night just shuts down so quick," said Wiggins.

"Quick as a coffin lid."

The road finally straightened out.

"What else did Cody tell you about the Hardcastles?"

"They're lower middle class, that the death of the girl Elsie is probably the most that's ever happened to them."

"It would be, wouldn't it? The loss of a child would be the most that happened to anyone. Certainly to Mary Scott. To Declan Scott, too, even though Flora wasn't his." Jury was checking numbers and names on the houses.

"Yes. I didn't put it right. Cody meant that he thought the parents were pretty much making a meal of it. It sounds terrible put that way; he meant that he didn't believe all of the histrionics. They — or the mum, at least — were overplaying their hand."

Jury frowned. "That's interesting."

"She seemed to Cody to be delighted to have the attention of the police."

"It's nice to be wanted, isn't it? Here it is. On the left there." There was space for another car on the concrete apron next to the little sign that said HARDCASTLE HAVEN.

"Hardcastle. Wasn't that the name of a character in one of those Restoration comedies?" said Jury, opening the car door and getting out. He looked at the pebble dashing of the front of the house, its dim porch light barely showing in the darkness. "*She Stoops to Conquer,* that's it. Goldsmith, I think."

"Pardon?"

"The play. Early-eighteenth-century stuff. Restoration comedy. That's it."

They were walking by way of a path made up of evenly spaced circles of stone. The path looked fake. "What are their first names?"

"Hers is Maeve; his is William. Then there's the remaining child, Peter, who's around twelve. Mental, he is."

Jury was about to correct Wiggins when the door opened and there was Maeve (Jury assumed) in a bright flowered dress, a whole garden of flowers against a light blue background that looked a bit too summery for March. She had a pasty complexion and a quick bright little Cupid's bow mouth, full of talk, Jury was sure.

"Are you the men from Scotland Yard, then?" She asked this even as Jury and Wiggins were getting out their warrant cards. "William! They're here!"

It sounded so much what one might call out, announcing relations who'd turned up for a celebration or an eagerly anticipated sporting evening.

He called back the answer: "Well, bring 'em in, love!"

"Come on in. Just go on through — that's right — to the back parlor."

In the wavering watery light cast by wall sconces and the street lamp in the rain slipping through the open door, the hallway made Jury think of a rainy alley.

With William in the back parlor was a sodden-faced lad with the small, closely set eyes and puttylike countenance of a child cursed by Down syndrome.

"Sit down, sit down," said Maeve. "Our Petey's made tea!"

Petey did not respond to this and Jury imagined his connection with tea making had to do with putting the sugar on the tray, no more. Petey immediately attached himself to Sergeant Wiggins, going to stand close by his chair and planting a hand on Wiggins's arm. Wiggins did not want to appear to be shaking off the hand, but shake it off he did under cover of reaching for something — his notebook, his pen — in a side pocket of his coat, which he still wore. He did not return forearm to chair arm, either, seeing Petey was still fixed to the spot.

His mother chimed, "Now, Petey, that gentleman's a police officer and he could arrest you if you don't behave." She thought that quite amusing.

Nobody else did.

Said William Hardcastle, "It's three and a half years since that woman run down our Elsie. Now they're sendin' Scotland Yard around. Bit late in the day, I'd say." He pinched ash from his cigarette, smoked down to a stub. He looked uncomfortable in his clothes, as if donning a fresh white shirt was too much of an effort. He'd sooner be in his vest, as usual, for sitting around drinking a cup of tea and watching the telly.

Jury had not removed his coat. He could see Macalvie's point here. Wiggins, though, now took his off as an act of self-defense and draped it across the arm of the chair where Petey stood to form a kind of barrier between them. The child was undeterred. His hand crept along the coat.

"This is in relation to a new case, Mr. Hardcastle. You've probably heard about the murder of a woman on the Scotts' estate." He wished immediately he could call back that word, with its suggestions of wealth and privilege and (to William Hardcastle) indolence and lack of moral fiber.

Hardcastle said, sententiously, "What goes around comes around, I says to meself when I read about that." He stabbed a forefinger at Jury.

It wearied Jury to hear such claptrap cliché. "What do you mean? That Mr. Scott somehow deserves misfortune?"

"It's a curse, I say. Those people are cursed."

Soberly, Jury said, "I expect Declan Scott would agree, considering he's lost both his wife and daughter. And now there's the murder of a stranger on his property."

With another finger pointing, Hardcastle said, "Where there's smoke, remember? And I can tell you we didn't appreciate you lot comin' round hintin' maybe I'd somethin' to do with that little girl's disappearance. Right, Maeve?"

Was it a signal for tears? Maeve didn't actually shed any, but she was quick with her handkerchief, pressing it hard against her eyes. "Our poor Elsie. Dreadful. Criminal that was. And that Scott woman gets off with no more'n a slap on the wrist.

That's what money'll do for you. You can run a child down in the street and nothing happens to you. Criminal."

"El-suh," said Petey, trying a word on for size, it made no difference what word. "El-suh."

"Poor Petey feels it more'n us, I shouldn't wonder."

Petey smiled broadly at the room before returning his gaze to Wiggins.

The room seemed to be misting over with cheap emotion. "Given the disappearance of Flora Baumann occurred not very long after your daughter was killed, I think it reasonable you might have come under suspicion, Mr. Hardcastle. Anyone in your position would, and they were considering all possibilities. Of course, I can understand your dismay." And other shibboleths, thought Jury, falling into the cliché rut.

"I expect you can imagine how my William felt," Maeve opined, "with him as much as accused of making off with that little girl?"

"What," said Mr. Hardcastle, "was I supposed to be doing all those months after our Elsie was run down? Was I supposed to be plotting my revenge on the Scotts?"

"I doubt anyone would blame you if you had been."

Jury's tone was so mild and conciliatory, Hardcastle was having a difficult time holding on to his anger. He lit a fresh cigarette. Jury looked around. It would appear the Hardcastles were not having financial difficulties. "That's some telly you have there." It was mammoth, at least a thousand quid, that'd set them back. The car parked on the concrete standing beside the police Ford was a BMW. These were not Bimmer people. The furniture was well worn, but then Maeve and William would not bother changing anything that required a total redecoration. They'd go for the flash stuff, if they had a windfall; they'd spend it on showy things — cars, TVs. And Jury didn't doubt there had been a windfall, most likely from Declan Scott. That would have done a lot to lessen their resentment of Mary Scott's being let off so easily.

"The conditions," Jury could not help pointing out, "were all against Mrs. Scott that night: traffic light not functioning properly; the dark; the rain; Elsie's black clothes."

"Drink, that's what I'd put it down to," said Maeve. "There was that pub down the way."

Even patience-on-a-monument Wiggins

winced at this. "There's always a pub down the way." He was leaning to the far side of the armchair. Petey had his thick arms folded across the overcoat.

"Petey," said Jury, "come over here and do something for me, would you? There's something I'd like to see."

Petey looked wide eyed and doubtful that there'd be anything better to see than Sergeant Wiggins.

"Come on." Jury made a beckoning motion with his hand.

Petey finally gave up his position by the chair and went to Jury. Wiggins looked as if he might weep with relief.

"Over there on the mantel" — Jury pointed to the fireplace — "bring me one of those photos of Elsie, would you?"

Petey walked over to the fireplace, reached up and took one of the pictures, which he then handed to Jury.

"Thanks."

"Aren't you the *clever* boy, Petey," said his mother. She had a way of addressing the boy as if he were a waltzing pig.

Jury looked down at the face recognizably like her brother's only better defined. She was not pretty, nor would she catch up to prettiness as an adult. But the poor child should have had the chance, at least.

Jury looked squarely into Maeve's small eyes, which darted away even as he looked. He wanted to catch her in an unguarded moment, but he wondered if that was even possible. "You must miss her very much."

The eyes, prepared with a tear, swept back to his own. "Well, of course we do."

Jury rose, and so did Wiggins, with obvious relief. "We've taken enough of your time."

"Here, though, you've not touched your tea." The cups remained on the tray.

Jury didn't bother answering that. "You've been very helpful, and we appreciate it."

Petey detected signs of leaving and didn't like it. "Nah nah nah," he cried, dragging down Wiggins's coat.

It was all Wiggins could do to keep from smacking him away.

"I can't say much for the mum and dad," said Wiggins, as they both climbed into the car. "You'd've thought they'd do something about that boy, wouldn't you? Him hanging all over my chair."

"I don't think they really like him, Wiggins. I don't think they pay much attention to him. Cody Platt was probably right. There's not much real feeling regarding either of the kids. No, I can't see William Hardcastle as a man who would go to such lengths to repay the Scotts as to take Flora Baumann."

They drove back up the steep street through Mevagissey in silence, then through countryside.

"It leaves us, doesn't it, pretty much in the same dark with Flora's case?" said Wiggins.

Jury was silent for a moment, watching the rain on the windscreen, watching the wipers clear it. Wiggins was driving at a fairly normal speed. Jury found the rain restful. He laid his head against the headrest.

"Are you all right, sir?"

"Hm? Yeah. Fine. You know there's one thing that hasn't been mentioned although it's a perfectly obvious alternative: Did Flora know her?"

" 'Her'? You think it was a woman, then?"

"Could be. A woman is far less threatening than a man. And if Flora knew her, well, not threatening at all, perhaps. There was no noise, none at all, according to Mary Scott, who couldn't have been more than twenty feet away."

"What if she'd gone farther than that

and was ashamed to admit she was careless, that she really hadn't been watching Flora properly?"

"You're right. There's no way of knowing. But I'm going to assume Mary Scott was telling the truth. She doesn't sound like a careless mother, not at all. Indeed, given the first marriage to Viktor Baumann, I'd think carelessness is the last thing she'd be guilty of."

"All right, then. Flora wouldn't have raised a fuss when she first encountered this person, but would she have gotten into a car with her?"

"Unlikely, I suppose, unless the kidnapper had one hell of a convincing story."

"But her mum was still in the gardens. Flora wouldn't have gone away with somebody else."

"Unless, as I said, this person could convince her."

"Wait, though. An exchange like that would take *time*. The kidnapper wouldn't have had the time to convince the little girl of anything, not with Mary Scott likely to turn back and look for Flora."

"Also, I keep forgetting Flora was only four years old," said Jury. "You can't reason with a four-year-old very easily."

"I think she'd have to have been overpowered. Chloroform, something."

"Probably." After a longish silence, Jury said, "I'm going back to London in the morning. You carry on."

Wiggins took his eyes off the road long enough to miss the dry stone wall they were passing by a few feet. "A good idea. You've been looking peaky these last couple of days. A rest'll do you good."

"Maybe, but that's not why I'm going. I'm going to talk to Mary Scott's mother. And I want to see Viktor Baumann again." He tapped the window. "There's a cow up there." Jury nodded toward the road.

Wiggins started to brake. "What in hell's a cow doing out this late?"

"Beats me. I'll have a word with its mum."

Seeing the headlights, the cow lumbered off. They drove on.

Wiggins said, later, "What's he like, this Baumann?"

"Very, very slick."

"I don't know what else to think except either it was the father or someone else who just wanted the girl. Do you think there's much chance of — Do you think she's dead?"

"Yes."

"Does Commander Macalvie?"

"No."

Wiggins sighed. "If one of you has to be wrong, I hope it's you."

Jury looked out the window at blackness. "So do I."

There was silence for a little while. Jury was thinking about the play. "In Goldsmith's play, the hero — if you can call him that — was so shy around women of society that he couldn't court them. The squire's daughter pretended to be a parlor maid. He had no trouble going after her at all in that guise."

Wiggins looked over at him when he stopped talking. "And what, then?"

"Just that nearly all of Restoration drama turned on mistaken identity. Everything issued from that central point."

"You're thinking of the dead woman?"

"Yes, I am."

"But we don't know who she is; her identity isn't exactly mistaken, is it?"

Jury looked out at the ragged edge of the anonymous field flying past. "No. But it will be."

Wiggins wondered what he meant and kept on driving.

# 23

Jury set his mug on a rickety, uneven table and leaned over to inspect the fertilizer bag. " 'Turf 'n' Grow.' Odd name."

They were drinking tea in the cottage the next morning.

"A special kind of fertilizer."

"What's special?"

"I don't know. At this garden shop in St. Austell, I just asked for something not generally used around here. So they lugged this stuff out of a back room. He said he very rarely sold it; it's too expensive. It's fabulously rich stuff. It'll grow anything."

"Good. Maybe it'll grow me a brain." Jury sat back and reclaimed his mug.

"I wanted to get something Marcus Warburton wasn't familiar with. I actually believe he's convinced I know what I'm doing." Melrose rubbed his pale gold hair into a froth. "But I'm not sure about Declan Scott. I think he can see through walls; he's very perceptive."

"You're good at impersonating rarefied intellectuals. I don't know where you get it."

Melrose studied Jury and chewed his lip. "That wasn't really a compliment, was it?"

"That's why I use you."

"I'd rather hear 'That's why I pay you.'"

"Oh, come on. You're too rich already."

Melrose sighed and dropped his head against the back of his flowery chair. "Sometimes I wish I weren't."

"Rich?"

"Yes."

"No, you don't."

"You're right; I don't."

Jury set his mug on the table and gave Plant's leg a little prod. "Let's find Lulu."

The small face at the kitchen window disappeared as Jury and Plant approached along the stone path lined by bright pink rhododendron. March was cold, but these gardens were showing vibrant color.

Jury said, "Can these make it through the end of winter?"

"If the Macmillans have anything to say about it, they'll make it through the rest of the century. They like a lot of splash.

Splash, as if colors were rain and left pools behind."

Roy came dashing toward them, running in circles, then veering off the path and running a straight line.

"He's herding. He thinks we're sheep. Border collies are very intelligent."

"Roy's not a border collie, for God's sakes; he's a mutt."

Melrose turned at a shout from the bottom of the garden off to the right.

"That's Millie Macmillan. I'd better go see what she wants. I'm sure Lulu will be along straightaway, after Roy."

Melrose left and Jury stood there in the path. Now Roy, with Plant gone, sat dog still, in the ordinary way, tongue lolling. He looked at Jury and yawned. It was as if he could finally relax. Perhaps Plant presented some challenge, some source of sport that Jury lacked. Yet the dog looked expectant, as in a holding pattern, waiting for this man to make his move. Jury looked around for a ball or stick to toss and saw a braided piece of rope, a chew toy, lying in the hedge. He picked it up and when he straightened, a little girl was standing there as if she'd just materialized.

"Oh. You've got to be Lulu." He said this with one of his best smiles.

She hitched a strand of straight black hair behind her ear. "That's right." She stood gazing at him. "That's Roy." She pointed toward the dog. "It's really French, r-o-i, for king, but we just call him Roy."

"My name's Richard." Then, with what he thought was quite a good wind-up, he pitched the rope across the hedge. Roy took off like a missile. He was a black and white blur. "That's the fastest dog I've ever seen."

Hands behind her back, Lulu rocked on her heels, as if waiting for something.

Dark hair with a fringe that hid her brow, and her somber blue eyes seemed swamped by the big, unbecoming glasses. But neither the glasses nor the fringe could totally hide the shape of her face, heart shaped and delicate.

There was a white iron bench behind them. Jury sat down and stretched out his legs. "Your dog makes me tired just watching him."

"I guess you're a policeman." She moved a little closer to the bench.

"That's right. How did you know?"

"Because that's who keeps coming."

"Why don't you sit down?"

"Okay." She sat at a slant so she could

see his face, which she appeared to be regarding with a lot of interest. "I guess you're here about the murder."

He nodded. "Police have just about reached — well, we're stumped."

"I know." She sighed heavily (stagily), shaking her head. "It's really too bad." Which, of course, it wasn't. "One of the policemen was here last night, one of the Macs, asking questions. He didn't know much."

One of the Macs? Jury did not pursue this.

"My mum and dad were in a car accident. They both died. I wasn't there."

Her voice was smaller, her tone worried as if she had missed something cataclysmic by bare seconds and that the car might have rammed the tree even as she had turned her head away. There was something inherently frightening about this, almost as if she thought had she been there, had she not turned away, her mother might still be alive.

He looked at her pale face. It was what a child might terribly think: if you fail in your watching of someone (mum, dad), he or she might disappear. But it was more than that; the disappearance could be your fault because you looked away. He felt a hand on his arm.

Lulu said, "What's wrong? What are you thinking about? Did you know her?"

"The woman who was shot? No."

"I thought maybe you did — but that's silly. If you knew her, then the police would know who she was. Unless you didn't really know her, that maybe she was someone who looked like . . ."

Jury listened while she rattled on with this convoluted story of identity like a kid's mixed-up version of what Macalvie had said. Finally, she wound down when Roy came over to settle down and watch. He said, "I was thinking of my mother." He noticed she stopped patting the dog and grew very still. "She died when I was two or three or maybe six (Jury being no longer sure after his cousin had talked about it). She was killed by a bomb that dropped in our square in London. In the war they sent us kids out to places in the country because London was so dangerous. So I wasn't there when it happened." He had thought he was, but then the cousin had corrected this memory.

There was a stillness.

"You weren't watching."

He shook his head. Why were children saddled with the burden of magical thinking? He could feel it even now.

"But you couldn't have stopped a bomb," she said.

"No, I couldn't. But sometimes kids believe just thinking something will cause it to happen. Well, we know that's not so — we know now. But when you're a child, it gets mixed up in your mind."

"I know. Like not watching someone."

"That's right." Jury thought for a moment. "Once I had a friend named Jimmy Poole who stole geese. They caught Jimmy Poole when he was stealing goose number three." Jury smiled. He rather enjoyed that image.

She didn't. "Anyone can steal a goose. They're not smart like dogs and cats. I just don't see why a person would bother with a goose." There was a silence as she thought over her problem. "Anyway, it's not nearly as bad as stealing children."

"Children? No, of course not, but I don't know anybody who would go around stealing children."

"I do." Her voice grew smaller again as if it were trying to squeeze itself into a tiny place. "It's who took Flora. It's the Child Thief." She turned her head slowly to look Jury in the eye. "He only takes children."

Jury frowned. "Are you afraid he could take you?"

She looked at Roy and then reached down to pet him. It was a way of keeping her face hidden. "I don't know. I think he takes only pretty ones."

Jury closed his eyes against the sadness of that stratagem. When he opened them she was turned to him, adjusting her glasses, brushing the fringe up out of her eyes. These two movements he knew were meant to give him a better look at her face, to judge the danger she might be in.

Not much of a choice for him: if you're pretty you get stolen; if you aren't . . . well, where's the consolation in that? He turned this over. "If you keep the glasses on at all times and let the fringe hide your eyes, you'll probably be safe."

When the implications of this came clear, she nodded. She even smiled a little.

Jury asked, "But this Child Thief. What does he do with the children he steals?"

"He takes them home and . . . either he locks them up in the cellar where the rats are, or he shoves them in the attic that's always dark or sometimes he chains them to a post in the back garden and they have to stand in the snow." She paused. "Or he lets them live in the house and even gives them their own room. But then he doesn't talk to them, and if they talk to him" — she looked at Jury again — "he doesn't answer."

Her skirt had been twisted more tightly than Roy's bit of rope. "And she has to go all her life never talking to anyone. Never."

Jury noticed it had changed from "them" to "she." It was the silent treatment that she would have to endure if the Child Thief got her.

She felt guilty. Jury was sure, but about what? Had she done something to Flora in those visits Mary Scott had paid to Little Comfort? Had she told someone about their visits to Heligan?

"Did you like Flora?"

"Kind of. A bit." She slid farther down on the bench, her legs out.

Jury waited.

"There were times I couldn't stand her."

"Times I can't stand him, either." Jury nodded toward the path along which Melrose Plant was approaching.

Lulu giggled. It was an authentic child-delighted giggle. Her eyes sparked; she covered her mouth with her hand. "But he's your friend." Here was a testing of the friendship waters in general.

"Well? Do friends like each other all of the time?"

She shook her head vigorously, swinging

her lank hair. Jury wondered why her aunt didn't have something done to it so that it set off her face to more advantage.

Melrose stood there, looking from one to the other. "You two have been sitting here doing nothing while I've been bedding and weeding — and so forth."

"No, you haven't. You've been talking to the Macmillan girl," said Jury.

"Lulu!" Rebecca Owen's voice came from the door of the kitchen. She was motioning for Lulu to come in.

Lulu looked less than pleased. "I'm supposed to go in for lunch." With little enthusiasm, she got up; she said good-bye.

Watching her run off, Melrose said, "Where does she get her energy?"

"She didn't get it from me." Jury slapped the bench and got up. "I'm off to London. I need to talk to Viktor Baumann again. Viktor's got his finger in a lot of pies, I think."

"I can barely keep a finger in one. Couldn't we have found a ruse for my being here that's better than a turf expert?"

"I expect I could've. That's just what came to mind."

Melrose gave him a look. "Richard, that's not the first thing that comes to anybody's mind."

"When they think of you it is."

# 24

Alice Miers sat in the living room of her fine house in Belgravia looking intently, even squinting, through her narrow reading glasses at the photograph, then handed it back to Richard Jury with a shake of her head. "I don't know, Superintendent; I've never to my knowledge seen her before."

Jury took back the photo. He had always wondered what that qualifying "to my knowledge" meant. It suggested to him a hesitancy, as if the person being questioned felt some outside agency, some broader "knowledge" would explain it.

"You're sure?"

"No. But only because I'm not absolutely sure of anything." She smiled.

Jury's smile answered her own, except that his wasn't wan.

"She has something to do with my daughter?"

"It would appear so."

"Declan doesn't have any idea?"

"No. She might have come out of the past."

"That's reasonable." She sat chin in hand, looking wide eyed.

Again he smiled. She was having a joke at his expense, but he hardly cared. He told her the circumstances surrounding this dead woman's appearance.

Alice Miers sat back. "It's not strange that Mary might have come across an old acquaintance, but it certainly is strange she would have lied to Declan. Roedean. That's such an idiotic lie. Too easy to check, as you already know."

"To credit your daughter with some sense, though, she'd have no reason to believe anyone would check. Not her husband, certainly. He's a man with a great respect for privacy. And she wouldn't be anticipating any investigation. So 'old school chum' would seem to be an easy explanation."

"You're right about Declan. It's one of his great qualities. And he has many of those." She sat back, hands folded in her lap. "Perhaps because of that, he's a person one shouldn't want to practice subterfuge upon." She turned her face toward the window and the garden beyond it. "Our own lives appear to us as so discontinuous — one thing ends, another begins, it's broken off and something else comes along — marriage, divorce, remarriage, a child . . . death." Here she paused and looked at the fire. "And nothing seems to run through it. But with family, something does run through it, something does cohere. A family is ballast."

"But if you don't get along with other members of it?"

She rolled her eyes, fine gray eyes set deep in her head, making the cheekbones even more pronounced. "You're not going to say 'dysfunctional'? We used to say 'unhappy.' Tolstoy certainly did. But none of those good old words are invited to the party anymore. They're vague, abstract. But 'dysfunctional' is so concrete, isn't it? It sounds like something gone wrong in a car's electrical system, or a hangover. When applied to such a protean concept as family, though, it means nothing more than 'unhappy.' At any rate, my harangue here means simply that family is important. It astonishes me that people expect the members of a family to get along and when they don't get along, they've let us down. I always think of a family as being greater than the sum of its parts. Something runs through it, as I said, like the pattern in this carpet." Here she looked down and traced its feathery green fronds with her shoe.

Jury rested his head against the back of his chair. "Wouldn't some say that what runs through the family is simply blood?"

"Perhaps. But Declan isn't a blood relative, and I feel tied to him." She rose. "No, don't get up; I'm just going to get the coffee. You'll have some?"

"I certainly will."

She smiled and left the room.

In her absence Jury rose and walked around. Across from the fireplace was a wall of photographs. When he saw such incontrovertible evidence of what she'd been talking about — family — it left him feeling bereft again, for there had been no family other than his cousin in Yorkshire, and no photos other than the two he'd taken away with him of his mother and father. Here was Alice with dozens, each framed and in its place, all up and probably in some kind of order. There were many pictures of her daughter Mary and of Mary and Declan. Then came half a dozen with Flora taken with several different people. He sighed. Incontrovertible evidence, true. But what Alice Miers had forgotten was that some people had families, but some people didn't.

The house was narrow, but deep. At the other end French doors led out to a garden that looked green now with winter plants. Beside the fireplace a longcase clock decorated in green and gold chinoiserie had been furnishing a soft tick of background music. Over the pale marble mantel hung a large oval mirror. He looked at himself thinking he looked pretty much as usual.

Alice returned carrying a humble black tin tray that held a Thermos of coffee, mugs, sugar and milk. Jury rather liked this presentation, liked it more than a silver coffee service, which made him feel he must learn the art of drinking all over again. They reseated themselves.

"Why are you smiling? Do not laugh at my Thermos. Either don't or go and get a tea cozy. They're next to worthless." She held the jug aloft. "Milk? Sugar?"

"Yes, thanks, a lot of both." He leaned forward to take the mug. He said, "Look, I know this is a painful subject, but you must have given a lot of thought to what happened to your granddaughter."

She held his eyes as if glancing away might make him vanish, much in the way of what he thought Lulu feared, and she'd be left with only the Thermos for comfort. "Yes. I thought about it. I think about it. All the time."

"This woman's murder is tied to Flora's disappearance, at least I think so."

The police photo was still lying on the table, beside the tray. Alice picked it up again. "She doesn't look the type to be leaving broken hearts in her wake. But perhaps that's shallow. Just because she wasn't pretty." She shrugged. "Strange, isn't it?"

"To say the least. What do you make of Mary's secrecy?"

"Well, certainly she didn't want Declan to know something and perhaps that 'something' caused this woman's murder. Or was related to it somehow."

"She visited Angel Gate, too. The cook, Dora Stout, saw her. Caught a glimpse, anyway."

Alice was yet more surprised. "I didn't know that. And did she tell Declan?"

Jury shook his head. "No. He found out only when Mrs. Stout told the Devon and Cornwall police."

Shaking her head, she looked again at the pattern in the carpet. "That makes me feel extremely sad. Here's Declan, probably the most trustworthy and generous hearted of anyone I know, and whatever it was, that was kept from him. This woman turns up a second time and Declan *still* didn't know about her?"

Jury changed course. "Did you see your granddaughter often?"

"Not as often as I'd've liked. I can't travel; doctor's orders. I did, of course, when Flora . . ." Her voice trailed off, came back. "Mary and Declan were very good about bringing Flora to me. Declan still is. I mean . . . was."

"You knew Rebecca Owen, didn't you, when she was working for your daughter and Viktor Baumann?"

"She's a grand person; she really is. I thought it was lucky she was there when Mary was married to him. Rebecca seemed to give Mary some strength, something like that. With Viktor, one would need it." Alice sipped from her mug.

"Not the most popular person in this account."

She made a noise in her throat. "He was awful. I've never known anyone so cold but who seems quite charming. God, but I was relieved when she got out of that marriage." She looked back at the garden. "But people like Viktor cast a long shadow. They can reach out wherever they are and grab you. And keep hold. Declan wanted to adopt Flora but I knew Viktor would never agree to that." Alice rested her chin in her hand, cupping it. "She'd be seven now. Any knock on the door when I'm not expecting anyone, any phone call where I hear a stranger's voice . . . my heart stops. I think it will be news of Flora." She sighed. "Hope isn't realistic, neither is faith, but you still have it. How could I possibly stop hoping, especially since I don't know why she disappeared in the first place? One possible explanation is that someone took her to raise as their own. I can see by your expression you don't agree." She smiled.

"I must go." It was already darkening. He could see the gathering shadows through the French doors at the rear of the house. For some reason he couldn't have explained, he had a yearning to see this space. Now, with his coat on, he nodded toward it. "Could I see the garden?"

Surprised, she said, "Why, of course." Alice rose from the sofa and they walked down the narrow hall. She took a heavy sweater from a row of wooden pegs by the French doors. She then opened the door, stepped out and waited for Jury.

# 25

Carole-anne sat in Jury's flat, slathering shrimp-pink varnish on her toes. Her chin was on her knee and for one swift second she reminded Jury of Lulu, when the two couldn't have been more different, and not just agewise. Carole-anne's hair was ginger, although that hardly described it: Santa Fe sunset colored was better, and her eyes were a ferocious blue, burning turquoise right now as she revved up again with her complaint that Richard Jury was lately too much among the seldom seen.

"And poor Mrs. W —"

This was Mrs. Wasserman, in the garden flat, whose every breath, to hear Carole-anne tell it, depended on Jury's presence here in Islington.

"— has really been having an awful bad time with her bronchitis and all."

"She's always had bronchitis. She's nearly eighty, after all. One would expect one or two bad days now and then."

Finished with her toenails, Carole-anne plunked the tiny brush back into its bottle, crossed her arms over her breasts and stretched out her legs and looked at the effect.

From his vantage point, the effect was sensational. With her arms crossed that way, the neckline of her dress virtually disappeared. She was wearing a shrimp-colored jersey. It was simple; it was clingy; it was scarce. Pink skin, pink nails, pink dress, hot red-gold hair.

"We could be sitting in a sauna. Only not as naked." He looked again at the dissolving neckline, the short skirt. "I take that back."

They sat in silence, two seconds of which was too much when she could be complaining instead. "I expect I'll go down to the Nine-One-Nine."

Jury was surprised. "Is Stan back?" He looked at the ceiling, which was also Stan Keeler's floor. Since Stone wasn't with Carole-anne, he deduced that the dog was with Stan.

"Oh, *he's* been back. I'm certainly glad *he* is, as others *aren't* except the odd night now and again." This was to make Jury jealous, as well as guilty, which it did, a little, to Jury's dismay. Fatuous idiot, he thought.

She said, "I've been to the Nine-One-Nine a lot."

The Nine-One-Nine was the club where Stan played when he was in London. The smug way she said this made Jury want to laugh. "You're a groupie." He smiled.

Her pink-pearled lips opened in astonishment. Even her toes drew back, insulted. "I most certainly am *not!* I should think I'm better than that!" Steam seemed to rise from her hot pink surface.

"You're better than everything," he said, throwing her completely off. "Stan must have groupies, though. Stan's hot. His group's always had a huge cult following. If he'd come up from underground, he'd be the most popular musician in London. Hell, even his venue is in a basement." The Nine-One-Nine was down some stairs on a little side street.

Somewhat heartened by "better than everything," Carole-anne lifted her hair away from her neck, a move Jury could get used to but better hadn't. She plucked out her dress at the neckline and fanned it away from her. Another move he could get used to.

"I'll go with you," he said, pulling his

297

shoes around. To keep her toes company he'd taken them off and was sitting in stocking feet.

She was again astonished. *"You?"*

"Hell, yes, me. The one and only." He went about tying his shoes.

She stood up and adjusted what there was of her dress. Another good move, thought Jury. Hands on hips, she said, snootily, "Well, if you're sure you're up to it."

Don't kid me, thought Jury. He knew she wanted him to go.

"I can't stick with you all night, you know."

"Oh, don't worry about me." He swung his jacket up and stuck an arm through. "I've got my groupies, too."

# 26

"Baumann has never been arrested — cor rection: he was cited once for drunk driving. Wouldn't you know?"

Jury heard rustling on the other end of the phone, background voices, and then Johnny's voice returned, went on about Viktor Baumann. "He's like sand — runs right through your fingers. He's got a girl-friend — or maybe I should say a partner in pathology — named Lena Banks, beau-tiful and psychopathic. Like my old mum says, put 'em in a bag and shake it and see which falls out first."

"Lena Banks." Jury stuck the receiver between shoulder and ear, looked for a pen, found one, said, "Address?"

"The Culross. It's in Culross Street, off Park Lane."

"Good address." Jury sat back. "Tell me about her."

"She's been with Baumann for at least a

decade. Never married, but never without a man. Traveled extensively, lived in Lisbon several years, Berlin, Paris, London, Rome, New York, name it. Does she work? Not really. A bit of an actress, a bit of modeling. Viktor takes care of her for the most part. The last ten years or so she's been either with him or near him. Bit of a wide lass is Lena, bit of a crook, bit of a dabbler in art fraud. Different things."

"Where do you come by your information?"

"Eyes and ears always on the street, Rich." Johnny had more snitches than all the rest of them put together.

"Is she high class, low class, what?"

"She's cultured, educated, well connected."

Jury stared out of the window that gave on to nothing but limitless space.

"Are you thinking, Richard? Or did you hang up?"

Jury wouldn't mind getting into that flat in Culross Street. But he obviously didn't have cause for a search warrant. "Isn't the Culross one of those time-share arrangements?"

"Right. Except they don't call it that. It's popular with people who do a lot of traveling. Expensive as hell, what you pay for it, and the flat doesn't actually belong to you. It's probably a great convenience for people who travel, but me, I want my own place even though it is a third floor no lift in Hammersmith."

"Do me a favor and send round what you've got on her."

"Will do."

"Thanks, Johnny. I think I'll pay the Culross a visit."

"You won't get into that flat, Rich."

"I know."

"Miss Banks, sir?" said the nattily uniformed porter behind the black marble counter to whom Jury had just shown his ID. He had to hand it to the Culross, a visit from New Scotland Yard didn't rattle them at all. "Miss Banks isn't currently in residence. We're expecting her to return" — he looked at a big black register — "next week."

"Then if the flat's empty, perhaps I could see it?" No he couldn't, but he thought he might as well try.

The porter was shaking his head. "I'm afraid not; it's occupied at the moment."

"This is a time-share arrangement, then?"

The porter registered a bit of irritation

at this, offended the residences here were described as something so crass as "time-share."

"No, no. There's no restriction on time. One is guaranteed a residence anytime; the difference is that it isn't always the same residence. Therefore, one might occupy different places at different times. And, anyway, a look round wouldn't do you any good as there is nothing personal left in the residence itself. Personal effects you wish to keep here would be left with our concierge to be put in your flat before you arrive."

"By personal effects you mean what?"

"Photographs, laptop computers, things one might bring along to make the residence more like home."

Jury thought for a moment. "And where are these personal effects kept?"

"Our concierge sees to all of that."

"So let me talk to him."

"He's not here at the moment, sir, as he had a small emergency."

"I have a small emergency, too. I have a homicide emergency. So you're elected to show me where these items are stored."

The porter's face flushed. But his manner was impeccable. "I believe I can do that for you."

He led Jury through a lobby richly appointed with velvet and satin curtains, antiques, marble, mahogany and relaxing color combinations. It was a feast for the senses, a taste of opulence. Perhaps this sensual picnic made up for the fact that that hundred thousand quid you were shelling out was for space, not place.

They finally arrived at a storage room on the downstairs level.

"Who keeps the keys?"

"I have one; the concierge, of course; and since our owners' goods have to be accessible at all times, there are several other keys. Of course, we strongly recommend not leaving valuables, such as jewels or money, here. We have a safe for that sort of thing."

"Meaning one is accessible and the other isn't?"

He nodded.

"Any member of your staff can, theoretically, access Miss Banks's things?"

"But no one would, I mean, other than to place items in her residence before she arrives."

"How do you know that if there are numerous keys and someone just wanted a look round?"

"I assure you, Superintendent, every

member of staff is carefully chosen and vetted."

"Yes, of course. But that still doesn't answer the question, which is that *theoretically* your owners' things could be gotten at by just about any one of your staff."

The porter shrugged. "If you insist."

"I do. Right now I insist on seeing whatever Miss Banks left behind."

"With all due respect, sir, I believe for that you need a search warrant."

"No, I don't. This stuff is in the public domain as you describe it. Anyone can get to it. So let me see her things."

The man took out a set of keys, moved them about and found the one he wanted. "I don't see what you expect to find."

"I don't, either. Thank you."

They entered the room in which locked bins took up most of the space. "I'll find her things for you, but I really must insist that I remain while you examine them."

Jury wanted to laugh. "Of course, stay."

Scant offerings, certainly, the articles that he brought and set on the table.

"As you see, there's very little here."

A laptop computer, a leather briefcase and a zippered leather portfolio, and perhaps a half dozen toilet articles — lotions, perfumes. "Would you open these for me, please, since you probably prefer I don't do it myself?"

The porter unzipped the portfolio, which contained a legal-size pad and a pen. Then the briefcase, which held a small calfskin photo album, the sort that one can carry in a pocket or purse.

"May I see that, please?" The album was handed over. Jury undid the clasp, revealing a little waterfall of snapshots. There were several plastic windows for the pictures, pictures of Viktor Baumann and, he assumed, Lena Banks.

Jury stared at these for a moment and then showed them to the porter. "Is this Lena Banks?"

The porter took his time drawing out his glasses from their case and adjusting the earpieces. He looked at the pictures. "Yes, it is."

Jury wasn't sure what he'd expected, perhaps to find Lena Banks was the woman in Declan Scott's garden.

But he certainly hadn't expected to find Lena Banks was Georgina Fox.

Fiona had delivered the folder from Blakeley to Jury's office with a little note saying "DI Blakeley wants this back ASAP."

He opened it. The glossy photograph was a glamour shot, the filamented light weaving through her blond hair. Lena Banks was beautiful, no doubt of it, even more so than Declan Scott's Paris snapshots had shown her to be. Yet the beauty struck him as ephemeral, an arrangement of light and shadow merely. Simply put, Lena Banks was extraordinarily photogenic.

He rang Johnny again, thanked him for the file.

"Paris?" asked Johnny. "Yeah, Lena Banks was in Paris about — let's see" — papers rustled — "a year and a half ago. Why?"

"A detail. If it's important I'll let you know. Do you have anything on her activities in Paris during that time?"

A brief silence as Johnny seemed to be searching his desk, as if a Parisian Lena Banks might turn up in a drawer.

Jury laughed. "It's okay, Johnny; you can't be expected to know everything."

"Why not?"

"Declan Scott was in Paris then. It was after Mary Scott died and Flora disappeared. He was, understandably, pretty depressed. During that time he met a woman who called herself Georgina Fox. Their relationship lasted a few weeks, I think he said. Point being that Georgina Fox is Lena Banks."

At the other end of the phone Jury thought he heard something fall — a chair, a man. "Johnny?"

"Back with you. What in hell was she up to, do you think?"

"Getting herself involved with Declan Scott, by the look of it."

"Interesting. But her *chief* involvement was with Viktor Baumann. He's always been her chief involvement. Let me know what you find out."

"I will."

After he hung up, Jury looked at the photo album. He would just take this along with him when he saw Viktor Baumann in the morning.

# 27

Jury drank his first mug of morning tea and stared out his living-room window at the oblong of park across the way that he had always wanted to loaf in, just sit on a bench and stare at nothing, but had never found time to do. He moved around the flat, picking up a book here, a magazine there, thinking about Viktor Baumann and the snapshots he had recovered from the Culross storage area. With his second mug of tea he was back to standing in front of the window, thinking about it, trying to sort out some better, more ingratiating, way to approach Viktor Baumann and feeling distinctly unclever.

Third mug of tea. He got into his coat, stuffed the snaps in an inside pocket and left the flat.

Jury walked along Ludgate Hill toward Cheapside. He rather liked this marriage of tall modern buildings of glass and stone to the murky, twisted little streets. The small businesses — Indian takeaway, cleaners — and others extremely pricey — Penhaligan's (skin care and cologne); Halcyon Days (where you could buy a little enameled box for a hundred quid a toss). How the narrow streets could coexist with the sleek office blocks Jury wondered at.

He came to the coffee bar where he and Mickey Haggerty had sat and talked. He went in. As if he needed another cup of tea or coffee. The pretty waitress was there behind the bar as if she hadn't moved an inch since last he saw her, as if she'd been standing like that for weeks, months. Time was like some drunken homeless person, tilting toward him and away.

He ordered a cappuccino. "Haven't seen you in a while," said the waitress after she'd come back to place it before him.

"No. I just had some business in the City to attend to. I'm not a regular."

She looked disappointed to hear this. He thanked her and she went off again.

As he drank he thought not about Viktor Baumann, but about Mickey. He turned from the counter, letting his eyes travel over the metal tables and chairs, seeking the one they'd shared. He would never be able to come into the City without remembering. *"In answer to something that troubles the blood and the bone."*

Poor Mickey.

Jury walked out.


Grace was perhaps more forthcoming, but just as frosty when Jury presented himself that late morning. "And this time, Grace —"

She flinched.

"— I do have an appointment." He stood in front of her desk, reached out and tapped the big leather book.

She pushed a button and informed Mr. Baumann that Superintendent Jury was here to see him.

Viktor Baumann walked around his desk as self-possessed as ever and held out his hand. "Nice to see you again, Superintendent." He gestured toward the same leather chair and Jury sat down. "Have you made any progress?"

Jury smiled. "Progress is hard to measure in this job. We have come up with some new information, though, and I have one or two questions for you."

Baumann nodded, sat down and closed his hand over the glass weight with the Greek coin.

Make a good weapon, that would, thought Jury. "We've come across a woman who appears to be germane to this case, and I wonder if you might have any knowledge of her. Her name is Georgina Fox."

To give him credit, Baumann didn't even blink.

"When they were both in Paris, she had an affair — a rather intense one, at least on his side — with Declan Scott." Here Jury passed over one of the snapshots of Lena Banks. One without Baumann in it, of course. Jury felt almost detached from this transaction, wondering if Viktor Baumann would deny any knowledge of the woman in the picture, and sensed he wouldn't. He was too smart. He certainly would consider that if the police had found a snapshot of Lena Banks, it could have been among several, some of which included Viktor himself.

Baumann killed a little time opening a case and taking out glasses that Jury bet he didn't need. He wrapped the thin pliable stems round his ears and looked at the picture. His reaction was one of astonishment. It was fairly convincing, Jury thought. Baumann was a good actor.

"I know this woman, Superintendent, either that or someone who could be her twin."

"And this someone is Georgina Fox?"

"No, no. That's just it. The woman I know is Lena Banks."

"Lena Banks?"

"Yes. I don't understand this." He did not return the snapshot to Jury, but laid it carefully on the corner of his desk and looked bemused. "You say she and Declan Scott were lovers?"

"Lovers, yes, for a short time. I'm sorry, but is this Banks woman a particular friend of yours?" He watched Baumann's expression. How much to tell? How much to hide? Baumann was quick.

"I, uh, thought so." He smiled, as if whatever the relationship, it wouldn't stand up to this. "But what I can't get over is this Fox woman. If this is indeed Lena Banks, why would she present herself to Scott under a false name?"

Jury wanted to say, Why would she present herself at all? "Good question. How well do you know her?"

"Lena Banks? She's a good friend of mine . . . well, we're lovers, actually. I've known her for years."

Jury reached for the picture. "Assuming she is passing herself off as Georgina Fox, does she have form, Mr. Baumann?"

"Pardon?"

"A police record."

Baumann's laugh was short. "Good lord, I hope not. But how did you come by her picture?" He inclined his head toward the snapshot.

"Chance." Jury reclaimed it, put it in his pocket. "One of my colleagues had a file on her. She must have something to do with the pedophilia unit. It's DI Blakeley who had it."

"Yes, I believe I've met Inspector Blakeley."

"He heads up the unit." Jury shrugged. "Better him than me, I say. It makes me tired — all of the time and manpower spent on something that's simply a matter of taste."

Baumann paused in the act of lighting a cigar and gave an abrupt laugh. "That's damned peculiar coming from a policeman."

"Sorry if it offends you." Jury smiled; it took a lot out of him to do it.

Cigar lit, Baumann sat back, rocked a little in his chair and said, "No. It's not offensive. Then you don't consider it aberrant behavior?"

"No more than being gay is." Jury knew

he was being studied, being assessed as Baumann's eyes measured him.

Baumann leaned forward, spoke in a confidential tone. "What people like Inspector Blakeley can't understand is that it's about love, not abuse. We've all had experience hugging children, cuddling them, kissing them and that's deemed perfectly natural. So why is it unnatural to take this affection — to extend this affection?"

Jury kept his face as blank as possible, cleared his mind as if he were shoving images, like furniture, about so he wouldn't fall over them, so he wouldn't reach over, grab this guy by his necktie and choke him. What amazed him was that Baumann, a shrewd businessman, didn't seem to realize that he was as good as admitting to being a pedophile. Or if he was not a pedophile himself, not one of them, he was certainly espousing their propaganda. Why else would he want to justify it? Nor did he seem to care Jury was there for an entirely different purpose than Flora's abduction. Which had been Jury's intention. He said, "Now obviously, if a child is taken against his or her will, no, that shouldn't happen."

"I couldn't agree more. And if the bastard who took Flora is ever found, I'll kill him myself." Baumann made little jabs

314

toward Jury with his cigar by way of punctuating what he said.

Jury drew out his small notebook and thumbed up a few pages and came to a blank one that he pretended to read. "A chief inspector with the Devon and Cornwall police, Macalvie —"

"Macalvie? I had a stomach full of that one."

"We always look, you understand, at family members first, especially when there's been a custody battle."

"I wouldn't refer to it as a 'battle,' Superintendent. On Mary's side, it was. But she was being utterly unreasonable."

"Sympathy goes out to the mother always in such circumstances."

"Mary has always been able to elicit sympathy."

"When Flora disappeared, did you go to Cornwall?"

"Police contacted me hours after she was abducted. City police turned up on my doorstep, said the Devon and Cornwall police asked them to come round to see me. They questioned me for an hour, asking pretty much the same thing in fifty different ways: how I felt about the custody hearing and about my wife's remarrying." He sat back, pulled down his waistcoat and looked, for some reason, pleased with himself, as if simply putting up with the police was some cause for self-satisfaction. "No, I didn't go to Cornwall. Couldn't see the purpose in doing it."

No, thought Jury, he wouldn't, since the only thing of importance was himself and not the desperate plight of a woman he had once professed to love.

Baumann puffed at his cigar. "This Scott — I take it he's landed gentry? What does he do? Nothing, probably."

"I expect he doesn't have to. Not like us poor sods who have to work for a living."

Apparently liking the description of himself — of them — as poor sods, Baumann laughed. "I can see you're a man after my own heart."

Jury nearly bit his tongue. But it must have been this inference on the part of Viktor Baumann that Jury was on his wavelength that made him forget he was talking, after all, to a CID detective.

"Mr. Baumann, thanks very much for letting me take up your time. I appreciate it."

Baumann walked him to the door. "Anytime, Superintendent. Anytime."

Jury was directed to the rest room by the

secretary, surprised he had kept Viktor Baumann from his appointments this long, rather like a gladiator waiting for a thumbs-up.

# 28

On his way back to Tower Hill and the tube Jury turned off Fenchurch Street and walked toward Lower Thames Street. In one of the little streets he passed he saw the new office block that had been built on the site where the Blue Last had stood before a bomb wiped it out in the war. He thought the pub was as embedded in his consciousness now as it was in the members of the family who had owned it. Some had died in the blast; some were still alive.

He was taking the same route he'd taken on those few occasions he'd gone to the Snow Hill station of the City police. That had been to see Mickey. And then he was thinking about Liza and the kids and knew it was not a good route to take.

Better to bypass the Liberty Bounds too for the same reason. But he didn't. It was noon and he wanted a drink and maybe a meal the same as anyone.

The Liberty Bounds was a very large pub and at lunchtime crowded, though it was on the early side for lunch. Jury took a place at the bar and ordered a bottle of Adnam's. He got the bottle instead of draft for a change, mostly because he liked to pick labels off beer bottles.

He drank and thought and picked at the Adnam's label. He took out the police photo of this still nameless woman and knew that she didn't exist. Oh, she was flesh and blood — dead flesh — but she had existed really as someone else, a someone certainly missing. They'd been looking for the wrong woman. Except for Mary Scott and Dora Stout, she had appeared to few people in the guise of this woman in the picture. Staff at Brown's — the concierge, perhaps; the waiter who'd brought the drinks — but hardly anyone else. For she looked so unremarkable, who would remember?

Smoke and mirrors. Right now, he looked in the one above the bar. Same face, same expression he saw in his bathroom mirror. Same eyes, same hair, same —

He looked at the photo of the dead woman again. So unremarkable, who would remember? But everybody had who had seen her. What was so memorable was

319

that she wasn't. What was so memorable was her astonishing plainness.

That, on the other side of the coin — he yanked out the album and Lena Banks's picture. On the other side of the coin might be astonishing beauty.

Jury took out his cell phone. Dead. He had forgotten to recharge it again. He asked the bartender where the phone was and was pointed upstairs. He climbed the stairs, feeling a slowness come to him that hadn't been there yesterday . . . oh, for God's sakes, *move,* and he took the remaining steps two at a time.

The final *brr-brr* of his telephone sounded just as Brian Macalvie unlocked the front door. He picked up the receiver. Dead. He tossed his keys onto the small table by the entrance and went to his kitchen, where he pulled a bottle of beer from the pristine environment of the frig (there being nothing else in it except milk for his tea) and continued on his way to the bedroom.

He flopped on the bed, drank the beer and tried both to think about and not think about the case. It had been bad enough the first time with the disappearance of little Flora; now it was worse because he would also have to feel the failure of the first time and that the failure had brought murder with it this time.

He took another pull at the bottle of beer and thought about Declan Scott. He would have to go to Angel Gate. The more he thought about what he believed, the more he believed it. It made sense. The first person one suspects is a family member.

Macalvie lay there, drinking his beer, looking at the ceiling. Now he thought of Cassie. When he got to that godforsaken cottage in the Fleet Valley, he found she had been shot such a little time before that the milk in her cereal bowl was bright with cold. Nor had the shooter even granted her the mercy of not seeing it coming. No, she had to watch the gun come up and point. But the lack of mercy was not really directed at her. It was aimed at Macalvie and it was such a brilliant stroke of revenge, shooting the little girl and having him find her — he couldn't summon up anything worse. It was because of him she had been stolen, because of him she had been shot.

At least (and it was certainly the very least, and no comfort) her mother knew what had happened.

The phone started in ringing again. He

should answer it. He didn't.

He pulled his arm up over his eyes and tried not to think of Cassie and found Cassie was all he could think of, sitting there with a bullet in her and in her eyes that look of fright.

# 29

On that cold night, Declan Scott looked up from the little photo album. He said nothing, but seemed to be waiting for Jury to explain what he could never explain himself: that Georgina Fox was not Georgina Fox. That she was Lena Banks.

"I'm sorry," said Jury. "There's not much worse than finding someone you loved is a lie. I don't know any other way to put it."

Declan almost laughed. He moved from the fireplace where he'd been standing, looking at the album, to the wing chair opposite Jury. He tossed the album on the table between them, drank his whiskey and looked across the blue-green sea of carpet. He shook his head, again in disbelief. "Don't feel bad, Superintendent. I'm not hurt; I'm just amazed. This murdered woman is Georgina?"

"Lena Banks."

Declan shook his head, then ran the heel of his hand across his forehead. "I was never really in love with her, it was feeling so empty after Mary's death, if you know what I mean. You look as if you do." He smiled. "I don't think anyone can take Mary's place. I really loved her."

It was such a simple declaration. And Jury supposed it was bad news for Patricia Quint. "No woman has to take her place. You just carve out another place."

Declan smiled. "Of course, you're right." He leaned over and flipped the album open. "What did you say her name really is?"

"Lena Banks."

"Lena Banks." Declan rested his head on the back of the chair. "Paris. I guess it's dangerous to go to Paris in the state of mind I was in."

"Anyplace would have been dangerous."

"Lena Banks." As if repeating it often enough might dispel the smoke. "It was all the effect of depression, emptiness, hopelessness. Failure. I really felt I'd failed Mary in not being able to get Flora back."

"How could you possibly? You didn't know why she was taken and there wasn't a footprint to lead anyone anywhere, to point anyone in any direction. No calls, no ransom demands. Nothing. If it was failure, then failure was inevitable." Jury leaned toward him, this man had gone through enough without being a pawn in one of Baumann's games. "Listen: I want you to tell me whatever you told Lena Banks — or Georgina Fox. You talked to her about Mary and Flora, you must have."

Declan nodded, his hand shading his eyes as if he were ashamed of the memory.

Jury said, "Why wouldn't you? Talking about it probably eased the pain a little. It usually does."

"Ordinarily I'm reticent about my feelings. Sometimes I think I'm stuck in the past because of that. Or it's the other way round: I don't want to let the feelings go, so I hang on to the past."

Jury looked around the room, its outer edges in near darkness. The angel on the mantel with shaded eyes looked composed but almost desperately so, like Declan Scott.

"My mother used to tell me I'm the youngest old fuddy-duddy she knows. But I think she appreciated that Mary didn't want to make any big changes to the house. She had the nursery painted yellow for Flora and that was the extent of any sort of transformation."

Jury leaned toward him. "What did you tell Lena Banks about Flora?"

Declan sat back. "I talked a lot about her. Georgina — I mean, Lena — listened. She was, she said, appalled by what had happened and asked if I suspected anyone. I said, yes. Flora's father. He was a man with a lot of power and used to getting his own way — a megalomaniac, from what I'd heard — and he was the most likely person to have done it, or had it done. She thought it strange that there was no ransom demand. I agreed, but not if the father was the guilty party. 'If he was,' she said, 'wouldn't he have been clever enough to ask for money?' I admitted there was truth in that. Or of course it could have been some complete stranger, someone who wanted a child. We talked about this off and on for the weeks I knew her. You're right, it did help a little. I wondered, though, why she was so very interested in Flora's kidnapping. I hardly know what to call it anymore. Yes, I did wonder. Anyway, then she was gone, without a word."

"She was gone because you convinced her you didn't know what had happened to Flora."

Declan looked puzzled.

"She was sent by Baumann to find out what you knew."

"You mean he thought *I* had her?"

"Or knew where she was. That he had Lena Banks strike up a relationship with you certainly indicates that. Remember, with Flora's mother gone, he'd have custody."

"I see what you mean." Wearily, Declan leaned his head against the back of the wing chair. The fire had died down and his face was half in shadow. "Now we're left with the unknown person who might have taken Flora for any number of reasons. I don't want to think about that. I wish it had been for money; I almost wish Viktor Baumann had taken her."

"Believe me, you don't."

Declan sat up and looked at Jury, eyebrows raised.

"Viktor Baumann, among other things, caters for pedophiles."

Declan was almost out of his chair. "What?"

"A colleague of mine has been keeping Baumann in his sights for a long time. He — Baumann — has set up house in North London where he traffics in little kids. Girls anywhere from four years old into their early teens. There are never fewer than ten little girls there."

The blood drained from Declan's face. "You're not suggesting Flora —" He stopped.

"Probably not, but anyone who's such a moral blank card as Viktor wouldn't stick at using his own child."

"But when they — Mary and Flora — were living with him —" Again he stopped as if words were hardly up to carrying this sort of meaning and weight.

"Oh, not then. I very much doubt it. Her mother was there, after all. And Flora would have been too young." If there was, thought Jury, such a thing as "too young" for these people.

"Wait a minute, though." Declan shifted to the edge of his chair. "Awhile ago you said that Lena Banks was trying to find out Flora's whereabouts and if that was so, it indicates Baumann didn't do it. 'Indicates,' doesn't mean 'proves.' Can you be sure he doesn't have her?"

"No, not absolutely."

Declan set his head in his hands as if he were examining his own skull. "Don't tell me this; don't tell me this."

"I'm not; I'm not telling you this. I think there's very little chance that Viktor

Baumann has Flora. He wouldn't have set Lena Banks on you if he had." Jury wished he was convinced of this.

"If that was the reason for her attaching herself to me."

"Possibly. Or it could be simpler; it could be she was really in love with you. In case you saw her now, though, she wouldn't want you to recognize her."

Declan did not look up. He said through his interwoven fingers, "Mary and I had been married such a short time, but even so, I really felt Flora was like my own child."

"I know." Jury rose. "I need to stop at the police van."

Declan got up, too, but rather slowly, as if the conversation had aged him. "You'll want to go out by the French doors behind us and through the gardens. It's quicker. Thanks for coming here first, Superintendent. It was very kind of you."

"I just wish what I had to say could have been kinder."

As he walked Jury to the doors, Declan said, "No, in one way it helped, finding out the truth usually does, doesn't it?"

Jury stopped on the dark patio, looked up at the stars and wanted to say No, give me lies any day, just let me get through one day without bad news. "Yes, I guess it does, Mr. Scott. Good night." He raised his hand in a good-bye gesture and walked off into the garden.

Cody Platt was sitting in front of one of the computers. When Jury appeared, suddenly, Cody made a hurried attempt to turn it off.

"What was that racket?" Jury asked

"Just checking my e-mail."

"You must have a lot of e-mailers trying to bump you off. I thought I heard gunfire."

Jury wondered about these subterranean night skills of Cody. But considering him, there were a dozen nonincriminating reasons. Behind one of the three desks, Jury picked up a file of crime scene photos and leaned back in the old wooden swivel chair. "Where's your boss? I've got some information for him."

"Went to his flat earlier, but he said he'd be back. He got your message. I'm here manning the equipment."

"Sergeant Wiggins, where's he?"

"To his digs in Launceston. Said he needed rest, said he was coming down with a cold."

"Same one?"

Cody's eyebrows shot up. "Pardon?"

"Nothing." Jury smiled.

"Got anything new? I've never worked such a case. How can anyone like this vic have left not even a footprint? Forensics has gone over the whole bloody lot and come up with —" He made a circle with his thumb and forefinger. "It's maddening."

"Not anymore, at least not that part of it." Jury took out the album and passed it over.

Cody looked at the snapshots of Lena Banks. "She's gorgeous. Who is she?"

"Look again."

"I could look for a long time, but, still, who is she?"

"She doesn't look familiar?" Jury pulled over the file of police photographs lying on another desk, opened it and shoved it toward Cody.

Cody looked. Cody frowned. He bent closer. He shook his head.

Jury told him.

"I'll be damned! But doesn't that mean that Viktor Baumann must not be the one who snatched Flora?"

"It appears so."

"Why would they begin looking for her again?"

"I doubt Viktor Baumann ever stopped looking for her."

# 30

The little square cream-washed house at the end of a rutted lane still looked to Jury more functional than livable.

"It looks exactly the same," said Jury. "I'm glad I'm alive to see it. You drove like a maniac; is there something about Cornwall that brings out this desire to go faster? Especially along narrow roads between drywall fences?"

Macalvie did not respond to this, but to what he was thinking about at the moment. "I swear I can't believe this masquerade."

"*Everyone*, Brian, is masquerading. That's what I said to Wiggins. It's like a Restoration comedy. The whole thing turns on identity."

"It looks like it — why doesn't someone answer? He knows we're coming." When Macalvie raised his fist to do some pounding, the door swung open. The squinty-eyed housekeeper, who opened the small, thick door and who Jury seemed to remember was named Minerva, was there largely to discourage callers.

"Hello, Minerva. Where is he?" said Macalvie.

Minerva frowned but stood back so that they could go into the room where Dr. Dench was seated at a table. "I'm just having a late-night snack." He waved them into the room. "Come in, come in."

The little house was some sentimental tourist dream of an English cottage — beamed ceilings, whitewashed walls, uneven floors. Forget the cold and the damp, the ancient plumbing, the lack of garden front or back.

A table had been laid near the fireplace and a plate with the remains of several portions of cheese, cut from the several rounds on the table, were on Dench's plate.

"Sit down." Dench gestured toward the chairs opposite his own. He poured red wine into two more glasses. "Have some cheese. There's some delicious Neal's Yard cheddar, Wensleydale, Roquefort, apricot Stilton. Help yourself."

The rounds and triangles of cheeses looked as if they'd been cut by a precision instrument, barely a crumb on the plate, except for the Wensleydale, which would crumble if you looked at it. As far as Jury was concerned, cheese in any circumstances tasted good, but cheese when one was really hungry was an onslaught of the senses.

Smoking a cigar, Denny Dench gave a ragged little laugh. "My God, when was the last time you ate, Mr. Jury?"

"When I was six." Holding a heavily laden biscuit in one hand, with the other Jury pulled the album holding Lena Banks's snapshots and put it on the table.

"He's been snacking," said Macalvie, "ever since he got to Cornwall."

Jury said, between bites, "Yes, well, I haven't seen Exeter police so lavish in their offers of snacks." Jury drank his wine.

"I'm glad you brought along the brains of the outfit, Brian."

"Look at these, Denny," said Macalvie, who set the morgue shot beside the snapshots.

Dench took Lena Banks's little album. "Hmm. Beautiful woman. Is this someone I know?"

Macalvie handed over the police photo of Lena Banks.

Denny held the picture at arm's length and looked from it to the smaller picture.

He studied the two for a moment. "Interesting. Other than that they're the same woman, or is that the point?"

"That is, yes. How can you be sure?"

"How? Because that's what you came here for." Denny Dench snorted and got up. "Obviously, they're the same. Bones. It's all in the bones, Brian. You can muck about with anything else: hair, eyes, lips, weight, age. But you depend on the bones. Come on, see my new computer program."

They went down the cellar staircase. Jury loved the Georgia O'Keeffe print hanging at the top of the stairs: one of a skull. At the bottom of the stairs stood a white, glass-fronted cabinet, holding a number of unidentifiable objects, including ropy-looking things that Jury sincerely hoped were not fingers; and sinister looking jars.

With all of the bones lying around, or parked on benches with little tags that had something to do with identification, the laboratory might have been an archaeological dig. But that's what Dench was, wasn't he? A forensic anthropologist. It might have been a graveyard that had turned out its bones, for bones were everywhere. There was a small skeleton that looked as if it had belonged to a child of twelve or thirteen.

Dennis Dench moved one of these bones a tiny bit to the right and regarded this fresh design.

"Anyone I know?" asked Macalvie.

"Possibly, if you happened to be in Sidmouth in the late sixties." He had snapped a folded sheet open and was covering the bones as if he worried they might get cold. "These are the bones of a boy uncovered when a building contractor laid waste to an old pub called the Serpent's Tooth."

Jury was reminded again of the Blue Last. Sometimes he wondered if he'd be thinking about it on his deathbed, as if there were something he'd failed to do that would have made it turn out differently. Of course there was. Of course there wasn't. Solutions don't present themselves any sooner because it would save a vast amount of tears and bloodshed.

"This reminds me of that boy," said Denny, "we found buried along the coast. We had a problem with that identification, didn't we?"

"You did, I didn't," said Macalvie, generously.

It was true, though, that he and Dench had disagreed totally about those bones, and Macalvie had been right.

Dench went to his computer. "Hand me that folder."

Macalvie did so.

"Now look." Dench placed the snapshot of Lena Banks below a video camera that digitized the image and transferred it to the computer screen. From the folder he took one of the police photos of the woman who'd been shot. He transferred that to the screen, wiped out the right side of the face and the left side of Lena Banks's and after adjusting the focal to enlarge the snapshot, moved the half face of one to the half of the other.

"Bingo! Same woman. And to make it even better —" The computer generated an image of Lena Banks's abundant hair on the other half of the image, replacing her poorly cut and drab hairdo. "It's always amazed me that such superficial things as hairstyle and makeup can change a face so dramatically. But bones — the cheekbones of both, the mandibles — I should have seen it immediately. Look at those cheekbones. I've been looking at skulls too long. Where does this leave you?"

"Ahead, I hope. And back to Viktor Baumann."

"Who's he?" Dench had returned his

gaze to manipulating the images on the computer screen.

"Her lover, for one thing. He was Mary Scott's first husband and it very much looks like something has changed now."

Dench was now sliding the snapshot under a viewer and didn't seem too interested in the context of these pictures.

While Denny Dench fooled with his computer, Jury walked around the lab. He imagined the two photos that concerned them at the moment were fairly boring to Dench no matter how fine the cheekbones.

He went back to the child's skeleton from the construction site in Sidmouth. He felt a wave of sadness wash over him, standing there, looking down at the boy's articulated bones, wondering how old he'd been. Ten? Twelve? The skeleton seemed so small and thin and insubstantial one might wonder how it supported a boy who rode a bike, played football. Jury tried to see through the eyes of this lad: being seduced from the playground or pavement with a promise of something sweet, new, shiny, and then having it slowly dawn on you that you might never ever go back, that you might never see your parents or your house again. How long could a child hold out hope? One moment you're standing in a garden, the next you're being dragged into a car or into the bushes or an alley, your voice muffled by the rough hands of a total stranger. And the next moment? A gun, a knife, a dirty mattress on a concrete floor?

For if this boy had lived, if he'd been found by the police or anyone, and been returned as flesh and blood to his home, he would never again entirely belong to it. No, a person abducts a child and something of the child stays behind. How could it not?

The child would always be bound to the devil who did it.

Jury stood staring down at the skeleton. "The Child Thief."

"What?" asked Denny Dench.

"Nothing."

# 31

It was late, nearly eleven, when Macalvie pulled the car to the curb in front of the White Hart Hotel. "We've got time for one glass before the booze is shut down."

Around closing time pubs always seemed to get more crowded, only because they got noisier and more anxious. The open-all-hours London law seemed not to have reached all the pubs in the provinces. The White Hart was serving last orders to a lively clientele.

For a few minutes Jury and Macalvie drank in silence. Jury turned around on the bar stool with his pint in his hands and looked the room over. He liked the way pubs combined the ordinary old stuff, such as hunting prints, with the crasser new stuff of jukeboxes. He remembered years ago, at a pub in Dartmoor, Macalvie putting his foot through one that had been playing some old song he couldn't bear hearing. Loss. Loss and guilt. "Plant told me," Jury said it without intending to. "Something happened to you in Scotland. He didn't tell me what."

Macalvie nodded. "It did."

Jury watched a man feeding the jukebox.

Macalvie pushed his pint around on the bar, making wet circles. "That was in Kircudbright. You know, that place in Dumfriesshire that artists love. I was living with a woman who had a six-year-old daughter. She was snatched right out of her bed, out of our house. This was payback for what happened in a drug bust we made in Glasgow when the villain's twelve-year-old daughter was shot in crossfire. I didn't shoot her, but I was heading up the unit. I'd run up against the father several times, so he held me responsible. I got instructions to go to an old house in the Fleet Valley. I did. I found Cassie sitting at a table, a cereal bowl and a plate of toast before her. She was shot in the head. Her body was still warm; it couldn't have happened more than five or ten minutes before I got there. You see, the milk was still cold." He stopped. "How do you deal with something like that?"

"The way you're dealing. The way you collared the person who killed those two

341

poor kids near Lamorna. Trying to nail the villain who took Flora —"

"I didn't."

"You will. That's how you deal with it. There's no other way I can see."

Another silence. Then Macalvie said, "It's these little kids. It's what happens to them. They haven't done a damned thing. They're innocent. Why should they have to pay for what we do? They can't stand up for themselves; some of them are so little they can't even speak yet." He closed his eyes. "What I do, what I try to do, is put myself in that place, in their place, you know? Feel what they must feel. Terror. Like that."

"Maybe you shouldn't go there, Macalvie."

Macalvie looked down at the dregs of his drink. "Neither should they."

There was a silence while both of them stared in the mirror, but not at themselves and not at each other.

Jury said, "When I was in Newcastle I saw a painting called *The Butterfly Eaters.*"

Macalvie turned.

"It shows a family seated and standing round a dinner table set in tall grass or mire. Each has a butterfly, either on his plate or holding it up in the air. Their eyes are dark and shadowed, all the same, staring out of the painting." Jury took a sip of his lager. "What does the painter mean? They're trying to steal beauty for themselves, but they can't? Are they dining on illusion, falling for something unreal?"

Silence again.

"Why are you bringing up this painting?"

"It just seems relevant. As if that's what we're doing, trying to dine on butterflies, falling for illusions."

"You mean that we can't see past them?"

"Past them or through them. Yes."

They were silent again, drinking.

Macalvie said, "What about Declan Scott?"

"Oh, he's fallen further than we have."


A streak of light shone under Wiggins's door. Why was he still up?

"Chesty" was the reason given. He lay there under the white sheet with his book splayed across his chest, answering Jury's question.

"The temperature in here might be comfortable for camels, Wiggins, but not for humans. No wonder you're 'chesty.'" Jury yawned and sat down on the end of the bed.

"How was London? What happened?"

Jury told him. "Not only is Lena Banks Georgina, but she's also our mystery woman. She's our dead lady. It was Lena Banks who was murdered."

Wiggins was stunned. "So now we know who she is, who has a motive?"

"Everyone." Jury yawned again.

"Pardon?"

"I'll explain tomorrow, or do you plan on sticking to your bed?"

"I should be up and about."

"Good." Jury lifted the book from the turned-down sheet over Wiggins's chest. "Another Eighty-seventh Precinct novel?"

"It's an early one. I find it's best to go back to the beginning and get to know the characters."

Jury had thumbed to the page that listed all of the books in the series. "Christ, he's written hundreds of them. To work your way up from the beginning you'd have to be born again." Looking at Wiggins's pale, reproachful face and soulful eyes, he thought maybe he already was.

"It doesn't hurt to understand the way the police over there work."

"With all due respect to Mr. McBain's cop shop, we're not over there. We're over here."

Wiggins said, sententiously, "A narrow

mind never got a person anywhere."

"It would have helped Hamlet no end. Why is it, Wiggins, when you come down with something, you get preachy?"

"I hardly think I preach. I guess it's that I have more time to think. It would do you good, you know."

"What? To think?" Jury was half sitting, half lying on the bed, shoulders against the footboard, one more of Wiggins's remarks away from sleep.

"No, of course not. You think quite enough. No, it wouldn't hurt you to relax. And maybe to read more. It's calming. A good book has a warmth to it."

He had his hands crossed over Ed McBain in an almost holy manner.

"The last book I read was Emily Dickinson. She's anything but calming. I think she spent her entire life dying."

Wiggins frowned. "Then why did she bother?"

"With what?"

"Writing poems. I mean, why upset yourself?"

Jury searched around for a good answer to this and found none. But, as Wiggins had just said, Why bother? "Did you read Emily Dickinson in school? I seem to re-member doing it."

"No. We hadn't time for things like that. The impractical things."

"She created a persona, a pose so that she could say what she wanted to say. A favorite pose was the innocent, uninoculated child."

"You mean who hadn't got its shots?"

Jury had developed the art of not processing a lot of Wiggins's remarks. "It's the child asking questions or being unaware. 'Will there ever be a morning?' Like that. Children can ask what adults don't dare to because we don't want to admit we're scared and we don't really want to hear the answers."

"Well, not us. We're first of all policemen and of course we want to hear the answers. At least, I certainly do." Implying that Jury might not be up to snuff when it came to truths' being spoken.

"The world is seen as that much more dangerous a place." Jury was now lying across the bottom of the bed (Wiggins having had to move his feet, which he hadn't wanted to do), his head propped in his hand. " 'If I shouldn't be alive/When the Robins come,/Give the one in Red Cravat,/A Memorial crumb.' God, but that's sad. It's what I mean: she's always dying."

"You've developed a markedly morbid turn of mind since that shooting —"

Perhaps I have, thought Jury. Impractical Emily.

The phone's persistent ringing Jury mistook for the lark Emily Dickinson suggested splitting open to find its music. Instead of the usual *brr-brr*ing, the phone warbled.

Clumsily his hand searched out the receiver and lifted it. "Yeah?"

"Up, up, up, Jury."

"Hullo, Macalvie. What time is it? Four a.m.?"

"No, nine. I've been talking to Wiggins."

"He's up this morning?"

"Of course. The only layabout is you. Me, I've been up for hours. I don't begrudge you a little extra sleep."

"Decent of you."

"Get dressed. I'll treat you to breakfast." Macalvie hung up as Jury was shoving his shirt into his pants.

A shining plate of bacon and eggs was just being set down at the table in the corner when Jury walked into the lounge.

"They do breakfast here? I'm surprised."

"They do for Devon and Cornwall police. Probably think it's wise." Macalvie plucked a piece of toast from the porcelain rack. "Tell me this: why is it we can build a bloody tunnel under the Channel, but we can't serve hot toast?"

Jury bit into a piece of bacon. "I can't work out why I'm always hungry. Starving."

"You been eating?"

Jury thought of last night's cheese and biscuits. "No, not really."

"There's a valuable clue."

Macalvie held up the toast rack and looked around for the girl.

"If I believed in curses — and maybe I do — Declan Scott is under one."

The girl had returned to the bar and now Macalvie, having got her attention, was stabbing a finger at the toast rack. She scuffed over in her thick-soled shoes.

"Hot toast, love. The way you do that is the second it pops up, you grab it and bring it in immediately. That's the reason it's called 'toast.' "

She stood with her hands on her hips, her wad of gum working from back to front and round to the other side. Wordlessly, she took the rack.

Macalvie raised his mug of coffee in both hands, then lowered it. "What was her purpose in talking to Mary Scott? The only reason I can see is Flora again. Baumann thinks Mary knows something, or they both do, Mary and Declan. Or it could be Lena Banks acting on her own."

Jury shook his head. "No. Going against Baumann could be hazardous." Jury stopped for a moment. "She might have had information. She might have found out something about Flora."

"What, though? That she was dead?"

"Would she have made the trip for that reason? Incidentally, one of the detectives in the pedophilia unit has been following Viktor Baumann's doings for a long time."

"That makes me love the guy even less. 'Following' how? What's he been up to? Internet porn?"

"No. Worse than that, I mean really worse, he keeps a house in North London, set up precisely for this reason. We think that's where the little girl came from who was shot in the street a week ago."

"Christ. And you can't link him to the shooting? Or the house?"

Jury shook his head. "So far, no physical evidence."

They were silent, thinking. Then Macalvie said, "Lena Banks comes to Angel Gate, but not to talk to Declan Scott."

"If we can go by what he says. But it's possible she contacted him and said 'Meet me outside.' Or he contacted her, same message."

"With intent?"

"I don't know. You still don't have the murder weapon," said Jury.

"It's also possible she didn't come for the same reason as she did the first time. I'd say she knew where Flora was — say, in a convent in Italy — and she's willing to trade this information for a great deal of money."

"After three years of Flora's being gone? Three years ago she told what to Mary Scott? What was the reason for meeting her in Brown's Hotel in London?"

"Then maybe it was to get information."

Macalvie pushed his barely touched plate to the side. "There's one person I don't think I've paid enough attention to: Alice Miers."

"I talked to her. Nice woman."

"She knew about Viktor Baumann."

"Oh, she knew more than just 'about' him; she had firsthand knowledge, and, like the others, hated the man."

"She has no alibi for the time in question. She says her doctor doesn't want her traveling."

"Is it likely she'd have shot Lena Banks and left Declan to face the police? She loves him."

Just then the girl was back with the hot toast. She plunked the toast rack on the table.

Jury took a piece, eyed Macalvie's bacon. "You going to eat that?"

# 32

"And what," asked Melrose, in no hurry to hear the answer, "don't you like about the way I'm doing this?"

He was addressing Lulu, who stood near the pond with Roy beside her, questioning the design of the little patch of ground that she had already taken issue with more than once. "We don't plant flowers so early in March."

Melrose was kneeling over a square of grass between boxed hedge and the white bench. "Maybe you don't, but I do and so does Mr. Macmillan and I'd presume so do most other gardeners." Since he didn't know what he was doing anyway, he hardly needed to haggle over when he was doing it. He was engaged in planting a sample of his specialty just to see how it looked. He had chosen to do this in the little interior garden, as it had a nice patch of grass that he had already cut for a smooth surface.

He had Trueblood's big book beside him as a design reference, and he had made a drawing. It was to this that Lulu was pointing now.

"Those little squares need to be closer together. And the grass is too high to see the flowers."

Roy barked once. Melrose had to admire his closely guarded barks. *I'm a slave with too many masters. Even Roy is getting in on it.* He used his trowel to dig up a bit more earth. He was doing all of this for show; he thought it was time he got his hands dirty. With his gloves on and his canvas hat he thought he looked pretty much the part.

"You could do some snowdrops or those other things." She pointed to the ones growing by the hedgerow.

"Those are aconites and, behind them, hellebores. We don't need any more. They wouldn't look right in any event." Lulu was now sitting on the grass in one of those impossible reverse-yoga positions that not even the Buddha could master. Her legs and feet jutted outward, hands grasping ankles. "You'd be a smash in the circus."

Lulu did not reply to this, relegating the remark to the conversational quicksand in which Melrose was generally sunk. "You need more colors. You can't have only bluish pansies. See —" Here she held up the page from Trueblood's prodigious book, which showed an enameled pin of a bird in flight nearly collapsing with color from all of the bits and bobs of porcelain. "See these bits; they're all different colors, green and yellow and red and blue sprinkled about."

"Really? Me, I'd like to be sprinkled about with gin, whiskey and rum."

Into the quicksand. *Thunk, suck.*

"Anyway, that's a brooch you're looking at. It's jewelry."

Roy, present during all this, was lying flat, head on paws, eye trained on Melrose and trowel. Perhaps Roy thought all of this spade work was about digging up his store of bones.

"Roy doesn't mind if it's all blue."

Roy gave a bark that broke off in the dead middle. Really stingy or not wanting to waste the other half of a good bark on Melrose. Now, however, the bark came just before the calling of Lulu's name. "Ah! Your aunt wants you."

But Lulu didn't look around. She chewed her lip as she looked at the questionable blue flowers. His garden design was lying beside him, one he believed to be pretty decent, as he had been guided by Warburton's intricately architectural design of the whole works.

Her aunt, having given up on Lulu to come get the tray, walked toward them with the tea mugs. She did not seem too perturbed by her niece's lack of response. She was a good-natured woman, and very patient.

"Here we are, Mr. Plant. I thought you might need some tea. It's nippy out here. Lulu, you shouldn't bother Mr. Plant."

"I'm not. I'm helping."

Roy panted heavily, probably to indicate the extent to which he was helping also.

Melrose called on his own good-natured self — the smaller part of body and soul — and said, "She's keeping me company. Roy, too."

Rebecca Owen wrapped her cardigan tighter round her. It was an unbecoming russet color. "That's very nice of you. There's not much around for Lulu to do." She shoved her fists into the cardigan pockets.

Not much to *do?* Was the woman *blind?* Lulu was doing everything. "I see what you mean. There are no children round at all for her to play with." Excepting me, of course.

Lulu said, "There used to be Flora." She was squatting, examining Melrose's tiny flowers.

Her aunt caught her breath, as if this was a dangerous subject for anyone to broach.

Melrose was delighted; he'd been trying to work around to the subject of Flora. "Yes. That's a tragedy."

"Indeed it was."

"We used to play all the time," said Lulu.

That, thought Melrose, must be wishful remembrance, from what he'd heard.

"When she came to our house for tea," Lulu went on, "she was really pretty. She was prettier than —"

Rebecca Owen stepped on this. "Let's not talk about her, Lulu. It makes us all feel terrible."

It didn't make Melrose feel terrible, nor did it Lulu.

"Well, I'll leave you to it," she said and walked off back to the house.

Lulu immediately started in on something else: the murder site. "Over there —" She pointed in a direction beyond the small garden to the larger. "That was where this lady was murdered."

"I guess you must have been pretty

scared when you heard about it."

She ignored this. "Mr. Macmillan found her. There was *lots* of blood."

Children were such ghouls. "I don't know about that."

He didn't have to. She went on. "She was shot right here." She pointed in the region of her heart.

Melrose tamped down another set of tiny blue flowers. "It's very strange. Very terrible."

"Probably someone followed her here."

He was somewhat surprised by this theorizing. She appeared to have given it some thought. Of course, any child would want to explain it to herself since the grown-ups didn't seem to be doing a slap-up job of it. "That could be right, but the question would still remain, why here? Why at Angel Gate?"

"Maybe to talk to Mr. Scott." She pulled at a small clump of weeds.

"If she was visiting, wouldn't she have just gone to the front door?"

"Not if it was a secret."

"You mean she didn't want anyone to know they were meeting? But look here. There's only Mr. Scott living here."

She had picked up an acorn and was batting it up in the air with her palm. "There's us!" she gaily called out. "And he has guests sometimes."

That wasn't much of a reason. Scott would know if he was or wasn't playing host. Then it occurred to Melrose: cell phones. Those damned contraptions! But of course they'd be handy for a sudden meeting or an assignation or stealth. Hello, darling. Look out over the terrace; here I am!

"Well, did he have guests?"

Lulu was still jumping the acorn up and down. "Mr. Warburton was staying. We were playing Cluedo."

"You and Mr. Warburton?"

"And Mr. Scott. And that lady. I was Niece Rhoda."

"What lady?" She must mean Pat Quint.

Lulu shrugged.

Yes, "that lady" was too much competition for Lulu. He wondered how much competition Flora had been.

"It was right before tea. We like to play games, me and Mr. Scott. We play cards sometimes."

This sounded so much like what she'd said about Flora and herself. We used to play all the time. Melrose was suddenly swamped with sadness for this child who had been left high and dry when it came to playmates and had to entertain herself. And these adults were all she knew. Not even school chums, it seemed, visited here.

"Well, then, you must be quite fond of Mr. Scott."

She studied the ground and gave a nod so small he wouldn't have seen it if he hadn't been looking for it. It was as if she needed to keep how much she liked Declan Scott a secret. Then she said, "He's protecting me. You know. From the Child Thief."

Melrose thought for a moment. He knew there was no point in simply pooh-poohing what she said. "The Child Thief didn't come here, though. Flora vanished from the Lost Gardens."

He was suddenly struck by what he'd just said, by the dimension of fantasy in it.

*Vanished from the Lost Gardens . . .*

By its Alice in Wonderland-ish nature. He couldn't work out what he meant by this. What did he mean?

She was looking at him now, curling a strand of hair whose straight ends her fingers couldn't quite wind. Waiting for him to banish the Child Thief to perdition. Perhaps he should never have mentioned Flora, should have left the name unspoken.

She said, "Maybe he likes gardens."

"No. He likes places he can get into and out of easily. This house and grounds are walled. Just look at them!" He extended his arms, taking in the whole garden, the whole world if he could have done.

"I've looked." Her tone was acerbic. Message: You fool.

The impenetrability of the gardens where they were now was a lie. The Child Thief, like any dark creature — under the bed, in the closet, creaking overhead in the attic — could walk through walls.

Melrose said, "Well, one thing's clear: if he ever tried to get in here, Roy would chase him until he dropped." This mightn't have been the best time to make this point as the dog was stretched out in the sun, napping.

Lulu looked at Roy, dubiously.

"The Child Thief's probably not afraid of dogs anyway."

Another dubious look at the napping dog.

"Anyway, as you said, Mr. Scott will protect you."

"What if he's not here that time?"

Melrose slapped his palms against his chest. "Then *I'll* protect you."

Lulu looked at Melrose far more dubiously than she ever had at Roy.

# 33

Rebecca Owen was talking about Lulu.

Melrose had returned the tray to the kitchen for this express purpose: to get her talking, preferably about Mary Scott, but if she wanted to talk about Lulu, let her talk. They were having another cup of tea. He laughed. "Believe me, I can see she's very imaginative. What's this obsession with the Child Thief?"

"Oh, she's been on about that to you? You mustn't pay any attention to her, Mr. Plant. The things she goes on about!"

"The Child Thief might be a more complicated concept than we think."

"How do you mean?"

"I'm not sure." He picked up his teacup, set it down. "It makes me uncomfortable."

Rebecca laughed and rose with the empty biscuit plate. "I expect Lulu loves that."

"What?"

"To make you uncomfortable."

Melrose felt a sudden coldness around him; he watched as she put the plate in the sink. "It must make you feel really down that both Mrs. Scott and Flora are gone."

"Oh, indeed it does, indeed it does." She looked away, out over the garden.

Melrose thought it might be better not to question her more about the Scotts unless he sounded a little curious. "Well, I'd better see to my work. Thanks for the tea and biscuits."

"Did Sergeant Wiggins hear someone say tea?"

It was Jury standing in the doorway, Wiggins behind him. "I wouldn't say no to a cup myself."

Rebecca rose, a bit flustered. "Oh my, yes. Of course." She felt the pot. "It's still hot, but I can make a fresh —"

"No, this will be fine."

As if the day's mission were none other than drinking tea at this table, Wiggins divested himself of his coat and sat down, all smiles.

"I'm glad to see you've recovered, Sergeant," said Melrose. "You did look a bit peaked yesterday."

"Must've been one of those twenty-four-hour bugs. Three sugars, please, Miss Owen, if you don't mind."

She lifted out three lumps with the little tongs and plinked each into his cup. "And I expect you'd like a biscuit."

Wiggins nodded as if sickness had never encroached upon his rather spindly frame. "I would, yes."

In this onslaught of teaness, Jury was left to wield the little tongs for himself. He said as he sat down, "You're carrying on, then, Mr. Plant?"

Melrose favored him with his most insincere smile and started to speak when Lulu suddenly appeared before them, dispersing herself around Jury like dew or dandelion filaments.

"*Hel*-lo, Lulu; how are you-loo?"

Melrose winced. You-loo? That was about as funny as a canker sore.

But Lulu liked it. She giggled, pleased as punch. "Here's a present," she said to Jury. She held out a purple pansy, returned to its soil-filled container.

The nerve! "Just hold on!" commanded Melrose. "That's one of my pansies."

"It's an extra one; you don't need it." She returned her gaze to Jury.

Who said, "That makes sense, if it's extra."

"Who *says* it's extra? I mean besides Lulu? I had them counted out, measured and planted."

Lulu said, "If you'd lined them up properly, you'd see it's one too many."

Roy barked once and Jury reached down and scratched his head. Roy's tail went slapping away like a beaver's.

"You're messing with my enameling." He rose in high dudgeon before he reminded himself he didn't care a fig about his enameling.

Lulu was gripping Jury's arm as if it were a rope thrown into quicksand.

He said, "Perhaps we should all go out and have a look, see if it's okay. For you must realize, Lulu, that Mr. Plant here is an expert and you shouldn't bother his project when he's not around."

"Okay," she said, handing Melrose a smile like a penny to the homeless. He'd known smiles that didn't reach the eyes. But a smile that hardly reached the lips? She was jumping up and down in her enthusiasm, her brave brown hair jumping, too. For some reason, that's how she struck him, as brave.

"Wiggins, you stay here and finish your tea."

The earth that Melrose had tamped down so nicely had been disturbed. "You moved them, Lulu!" The line of purple-blue pansies was straight.

"Only a little. It looks better; it's even."

Jury disengaged the hand Lulu was hanging on with both of hers, again for what seemed dear life. He knelt. "Let's see here."

Oh, for God's *sakes,* thought Melrose. As if Jury knew anything about it! Then again he reminded himself that he himself didn't know anything about it.

"I think," said Jury, "it's meant to have the colors mixed. See, you've got all these purple ones together. You should put some white and yellow in there."

He sounded just like Lulu. Melrose glared. "Since when do you know anything about the art of enameling?"

"Well, I don't, do I? But I've seen enameled jewelry." He tapped Trueblood's book. "You've got this whole book here, for reasons known only to yourself, on enameled jewelry." Jury leafed through it. "The colors are mixed together."

Oh, the triumph on Lulu's face! "I told you, didn't I?"

Now that Jury had taken up her argument, she was playing some sort of jumping around game with Roy. Her aunt came out on the path and called for her to come in.

"Good-bye, good-bye," she called to them over her shoulder.

"Good-bye," muttered Melrose.

Jury smiled and set off across the path that led to the cottage. "Come on, I have a few things to tell you."

"They better be good."

Jury tossed his coat on one chair and sat down in a wicker rocker, adjusting the pillow behind him. "The reason we were having such a time identifying our victim was because she didn't exist."

"Oh, well, nonexistence does rather put a crimp in recognition. What are you talking about?" Melrose sat down and took out his cigarettes, then thought better of it and returned the pack to his pocket.

"She was, in the first instance, Georgina Fox, Scott's old girlfriend. Except Georgina didn't exist, either. There was no Georgina. The victim's name was Lena Banks." Jury told him about his visit to the Culross.

"Lena Banks," said Melrose, as if tasting the name. "Where does she fit in?"

"By way of Viktor Baumann. Miss Banks is, or rather was, his longstanding mistress. She picked up with Declan Scott when he was in Paris after his wife died. Since Lena

Banks is no longer speaking, except perhaps in eloquent silence, I can only specu-
late that she was getting information for
Viktor Baumann."

Melrose said, "They thought Declan
Scott knew where Flora was, which means
they *didn't* know. Which further means the
child was taken by somebody else."

"Right." Jury leaned back against the
cushion and closed his eyes. "The Child
Thief."

"Don't you start that." Melrose decided
this time in favor of a cigarette. A cigarette
was a thinking prop.

"I wasn't actually trying to be funny."

"Flora was abducted three years ago."

"And six months after that Mary Scott
dies. And a year after that, Declan Scott
meets up with Lena Banks, aka Georgina
Fox."

"What if he's lying?"

"Declan?" Jury watched the thin smoke
rise from his friend's cigarette. "I don't
think so."

"But that's a purely subjective judgment."

"Yes, well, I'm not in St. James's, so I
can be as subjective as I like." He flashed a
smile, on-off, quick as a light switch.

"You're sure of this ID on the victim?"

"Yes. We took it to Denny Dench. He's one of Macalvie's favorite experts. Bones. If Declan Scott didn't recognize this woman as Georgina, probably nobody would, except for Dench. He looked at photos of the two women and said they were the same person. He used a piece of equipment that can compare images."

"Okay, so this Lena Banks is the victim. Now, with that all cleared up, who in hell killed her? Patricia Quint? Lord Warburton?"

Jury opened his eyes. "That name sounds familiar."

"Henry James. I just call him that for a laugh."

"Isn't he the one who wanted to marry the heiress? What's her name?"

"Isabel Archer. Everyone wanted to marry Isabel Archer."

"To choose a suspect from your list, what would Warburton's motive be?"

"I've no idea. Patricia Quint might have a motive if this is Georgina come back. I get the impression she wants Declan Scott for herself."

"Does she? I imagine any woman would."

Melrose nodded.

"But the murdered woman didn't look

like Georgina, so why would Patricia Quint kill her?" Jury asked.

"Perhaps she knew somehow who this woman was."

"That's pretty weak, if Scott himself didn't suspect anything."

Melrose thought for a moment. "Could the Banks woman have been acting on her own?"

"That's possible, I guess. Macalvie suggested the same thing. But it would be dangerous."

Stubbing out his cigarette, Melrose said, "There are too damned many people walking around with other people's faces in this case."

" 'Nobody knows who anybody is.' I think Melville said that — *The Confidence Man*. It's a frightening thought. You can't get a toehold and certainly not a finger hold, yet you're expected to climb the mountain. All the labels are wrong and all the names missing. We go on acting our roles."

"If that's the case, you can never come up with a solution."

"No, probably not." Jury paused. "But I do think Viktor Baumann's behind all of this."

"Then did he murder her?"

"I doubt it; he's far more likely to get someone else to do his work. One of the guys in what we used to call the Dirty Squad has been after Baumann for a long time."

"Really? What for?"

"He's got a little operation going that caters to pedophiles."

"My God. And he wanted custody of Flora Baumann?"

Jury nodded.

"Then does this pedophile thing have to do with your child who was shot in North London?"

"Yes, I think so. I'm going back tomorrow."

"You just *left* the place. You look tired."

Jury shrugged.

Melrose said, "Who in the name of God would shoot a little child in the back? What kind of person could do such a thing?"

"Another child?"

Jury was on his way to the police van when he saw Patricia Quint coming into the bottom of the garden through the iron angel door in the stone wall. She was wearing an old coat, hugging her arms around it as if she were cold.

"Miss Quint," Jury said, nodding.

"Oh, hello. Your work is never done, is it?"

"It seems so. Could we sit down for a moment? There are one or two questions I'd like to ask you."

"Yes, certainly. Only not there, if you don't mind." She nodded toward the stone bench.

"No, of course not." The crime scene tape had been taken down. Perhaps she thought that was an open invitation to use it. Instead they moved to one of the white iron benches.

"Incidentally, what were you doing just now?"

"Doing?"

"I merely wondered why you'd be out here."

"Taking a walk."

"Around the grounds of Angel Gate?"

"Yes, why not? Did you think — do you think I should be put off by the murder?"

Jury smiled. "No, I wasn't thinking that."

Puzzled, she looked at him. "Then what?"

"It's just that you don't, you know, live here."

"I'm an old friend of Declan's." She

looked at him in some astonishment. "I hardly think he'd mind."

"Oh, he wouldn't *mind*." Jury left the emphasis hanging.

"Superintendent, is this what you wanted to ask me?"

"No." Jury paused. "How well did you know Mary Scott?"

"Quite well."

"I'm not sure what that means. A good acquaintance? A confidante?"

"Well, I don't know that she divulged any secrets to me, so, no, I guess she didn't confide. People can be friends short of that, can't they?"

"You did consider her a friend, though?"

"Of course. I knew Mary before. I mean before she married Declan. When she lived in London, when her name was Baumann."

Jury was surprised now. "Then you must have known her husband."

"I did, yes. Actually, I knew him before he met Mary."

Macalvie hadn't said anything about this; perhaps he didn't know. "What did you think of the marriage?"

She frowned, thinking. "Well, I got the impression he loved her. He was extremely attentive."

"That sort of behavior doesn't always spring from love."

"Of what, then?" She smiled. "Or is this just a rush of police cynicism?"

Jury smiled. "I'm not a cynic, Miss Quint."

"How could you help but be with what you must see on an almost daily basis? You're a homicide detective, after all."

She seemed to want some cynicism here. Jury said, "True. But to answer your question about attentiveness, it could be that her first husband wanted to control her. Seeing to her comfort would also prevent anyone else from seeing to it. Often, the most seemingly devoted people are really suffocating the object of their devotion. Love means breathing room, and a lot of it."

"I see what you mean. But it's hard to think of Viktor as suffocating Mary."

"She left him, didn't she?"

Patricia Quint looked out over the gardens. "Yes. She did."

"What do you know about Viktor Baumann?"

Her gaze returned to Jury. "Not much, really. He was a hard man to know."

"How was he with Flora?"

She thought for a moment. "You know I

don't ever recall seeing Viktor with Flora. Well, she was only a baby then. It's hard to think of Viktor with a child."

Jury looked the question at her.

"He's just not a bedtime-story, naptime, zoo-visiting sort of person."

"Yet he'd tried very hard to get custody of Flora before she disappeared."

"You think he did that? Kidnapped her?"

"It's always a possibility. Are you still in touch?"

"With Viktor? No. I did see him some time ago when I was in London. We had a drink and some chat."

"How was he?"

"Fine, as far as I could tell."

"You couldn't have had much of a friendly feeling for Mary Scott."

She sighed. "You do jump around in your conversation. Why would I not have felt friendly toward Mary?"

"Because she'd nabbed not only one man you favored, but two of them. How could you be anything but resentful?"

She smiled a little and turned away. "What makes you think I was interested in Viktor?"

"He's rich, intelligent, handsome and, from what I've heard, quite charming, although I admit I didn't find him so."

She turned and looked at him, the smile still on her lips. "Neither did I."

Jury was a little surprised. "I gathered you did from your description. Declan Scott, then. He's all of those things and more. He's a nice guy."

Her smile broadened. "Aren't we going to get to the 'where were you on the night of so-and-so?' "

Jury smiled. "I understand that you were here for dinner, along with Marc Warburton."

"That's true. Are you going to ask if I took any solitary walks round the grounds then?"

"Did you?"

"No." She looked at him, puzzled. "Is it your idea that whoever killed this woman was someone from the house, then?"

"Not necessarily." Jury turned to nod toward the iron angel gate. "Both the victim and the perpetrator could have come in through any one of these gates, or even from around the front of the house. No, the possibilities are nearly endless, I'm afraid."

She got up. "I'm cold, Mr. Jury. If you don't need me anymore, I think I'll go in." As if she could see through the wall behind them, out into the grove, she said, "It's strange having that police van parked out there."

"Yes. Very disconcerting."

Pat Quint looked up at the trees, still dripping from an hour's-old rain. She sighed. "I didn't answer your question altogether, you know, about Declan." She leaned down a little, as if to inspect the violets. "I really love him."

The admission was so heartfelt, Jury felt almost sad that she might never get him. Finally he said, "Good."

" 'Good'?" She'd turned her head to look up at him.

"Yes. He needs that kind of support."

Now she hesitated. "Even if he doesn't know it?"

"He knows it. On some level, one always knows it."

When she didn't speak, he said, "It was photographs Mary Scott found of these gardens, the way they were a long time ago, that inspired her to have them restored. So it's really changing things back."

"You think Declan lives in the past?"

Jury nodded.

"Why?"

"He hasn't had all that much luck in the present, has he?"

★ ★ ★

Cody Platt and two other detectives Jury had seen but didn't know were in the big van doubling as an incidents room, both on their cell phones. They both nodded to Jury. When Cody saw Jury, he started to rise until Jury motioned him down and sat down himself on the other side of the desk.

"At least now we know the name of the victim. That's a break," he added. He went on, "If you don't mind me saying it, that was a good job of police work."

Jury smiled. "I don't mind, but it was really my colleague's police work."

"Who's that, then?"

He was so damned literal. "Detective in SO5 who has a particular loathing for Viktor Baumann. His name's John Blakeley."

Cody tipped back his chair, crossed his hands behind his head and studied the ceiling of the van, thoughtfully. He shook his head and said (as if this were the point), "No, sir, I don't know him."

"No. Anyway, Blakeley told me about the victim, a woman named Lena Banks." Jury told Cody about the Hester Street operation.

"My God. *This* is the man who'd get custody of Flora?"

"I'm afraid so."

377

Cody slowly shook his head, then said, "The boss said that forensic anthropologist, Dench, took one look at the photo and knew — like that." He snapped his fingers.

"It's probably the focus. Dench is focused on bone structure, on skeletal remains. He can't help himself. When he eats fish, he leaves behind on his plate all of the little bones perfectly aligned."

"That's kind of creepy."

"Yes. Well, Dr. Dench may be a bit creepy, but he's a focused creep. Makes all the difference, doesn't it?"

"I don't know; maybe."

Never a rhetorical question Cody didn't find worthy of investigation. Where had Macalvie found this orphan intellect? Under what toadstool or little stone bridge? Jury smiled. Cody had a mind like quicksand.

"This Hester Street operation, why in hell doesn't Blakeley raid the place?"

"Ah. There's a thing called probable cause, remember? What with the shooting, he can probably get it, but that would mean every house on Hester Street and possibly even houses along the cross street. It's hard to be certain. There's no way of knowing exactly where she came from. That makes it very hard to get a warrant."

"Yes, but I don't get it. He says there are ten kids in that house at any given time and he can't come up with probable cause? Surely they've been watching the house? If not the kids themselves are going in and out, the villains are. The so-called customers? Just collar one of them."

"He has. Perfectly respectable businessmen. Who then issued a complaint against Blakeley. He tried passing himself off as a customer, another coin collector, but didn't get to first base."

Cody grunted. "Why not? How much of a numismatist do you have to be?"

"I don't think it's that. I think only men Viktor Baumann gives a pass can get to first base. So it's knowing — something. I'm not sure what. Anyway, Blakeley and his group were slapped down for harassing the poor woman."

"Makes me want to weep, that does." Cody's expression darkened. "I had a little sister once. One day I was minding her when Ma went to the shops. I resented it because I was supposed to meet my mates to fool around and who wants a kid tagging along, know what I mean? So we were walking along the pavement in Slough, me trying to pretend I didn't know who she was, for I was in for a razzing having to babysit her, and her calling me *'Cody wait up, wait up.'* And me, paying no attention. It wasn't until I met up with my friends and we were talking I realized I didn't hear her; I looked around and didn't see her, either. I guessed she'd gone into the sweet shop and I told them we'd got to look for her. That's what we did. All of us, everywhere. I was scared. I've never been so scared. Long and short of it is, we never saw her again. I could hardly face Ma with this. Betsy was seven."

Jury was stunned. "Then when this happened to Flora, it was having to live it all over again for you."

Cody nodded and sat looking down at the papers on his desk. With a whiplash motion he scraped them off, sent them flying, and with the papers anything else that happened to be within his line of vision.

It was the suddenness, the abruptness of the display as well as the intensity of the rage that got Jury. Completely gone were the sanguine manner and scattered attention. If Jury wanted focus, here was focus. Cody was volcanic.

"I'm sorry, Cody. Then little Flora's disappearance must have been twice as awful for you as for the others."

Except for Macalvie, he didn't add.

# 34

The turf had filled the back of a pickup truck and been breezily delivered that morning by one of the young men from the garden supply place in St. Austell.

Having just unrolled a length of it, Melrose stood with his hands on his hips wondering what in hell he was supposed to do with it. He had spent precious little research time on this. He stood staring at this stuff, and then around at grass growing in the normal way of things and wondered at some of the idiocies landscaping had fostered. Besides himself, that is.

He draped the turf down the shallow steps leading from the grassy shelves above one of the several terraces to the gardens below. One length was not nearly enough to run all the way to the bottom. It would take at least one per terrace. Since he didn't know anything about this particular kind of turfing, he would have to pretend he knew it so well that he completely disdained his turf — its quality, its practicality, everything.

He saw Macmillan coming. At least it wasn't Lulu, who would not accept anything Melrose said without a battle. Mr. Macmillan, though, being a true expert, was therefore aware of his own limitations and was much more willing to take Melrose's expertise at face value. Right now Melrose took up a stance, shaking his head emphatically and, for Macmillan's sake, *tsk-tsk*ing.

"Trouble, Mr. Plant?"

Melrose threw up his hands. "Trouble, Mr. Macmillan. As you can no doubt see."

Macmillan looked, scratched his head. "Can't say as ah do. Looks pretty good stuff to me."

"Well, it isn't good enough. Rather hopeless, isn't it? Look at that color, for one thing."

Macmillan bent over, hands on knees. "Looks green." He looked up at Melrose for confirmation.

"Oh, it's green, all right. It's green. But much too rough a green."

Again, Macmillan, still bent toward the turf, looked over his shoulder. "Rough?"

"The seed was most likely burnt. You know, sunburned when it was sown."

Macmillan frowned, comfortable in his ignorance, but happy to learn a thing or two. "Well, ah do know seed can get burnt, Mr. Plant, but . . ."

Melrose stepped on "but" seeing there might be an involvement in something else. "And not liberally enough sown. Yes, a stingy hand was at work here, Mr. Macmillan, a stingy hand, indeed." He clapped his own unstingy hand on the old man's shoulder.

"That a fact? Well, ah never knew there was such a thing." Macmillan then looked more closely at the grass beneath his feet. "How 'bout this lot, then?"

"Oh, this?" Melrose rubbed his shoe over a patch of perfect green. "For its purpose, it's fine, absolutely." He was sorry to see Lulu and Roy coming their way.

Mr. Macmillan wiped his neck with a big handkerchief. "Well, truth be told, ah can hardly tell any difference. It kinda matches up, don't ya think?" He turned to Lulu. "Mr. Plant here's saying this" — he pointed to the as yet unrolled up turf — "here's a bit dodgy."

Lulu considered. "I think it looks the same as the other." She kicked the incline wherein the steps rested.

"Oh, well, to the untrained eye, I expect it does." Melrose smirked. "Nothing for it, then, but to roll it up and take it back." What a happy solution! Only now here came — of all people — Declan Scott, who seldom hung about to oversee the work.

"How are you getting on, Mr. Plant? I can see you've got some help." Declan smiled.

Lulu looked up at him with the most intense admiration. "He says it looks dodgy."

Melrose had on an old feed hat he'd found in the cupboard of the cottage and thought he looked very much the humble gardener. "I question the quality of the grass."

Ignorance can defer to knowledge or just manage on its own. Declan said, "I wouldn't worry about it. I don't think anyone without your eye would ever notice, right, Mr. Macmillan?"

"It's what ah was just sayin'."

No, he hadn't been, had he? But that was hardly the point. Melrose was glad the hat shaded his eyes. "If you think it's all right, then, I'll just go ahead . . ." And what? Trim it up, he supposed. "Unfortunately" — he was rooting through his basket of potluck tools — "I don't seem to

384

see my shears in here. That's odd." It would serve her right if he turned on Lulu. "You haven't borrowed them?"

She frowned. "No. Whatever would I want them for?"

The enigmatic Roy chose, from his wardrobe of barks, a snuffling one, through his nose. As if he hadn't enough people hanging about, now here came Millie strolling over to the party from the clump of Rubus grass and Jury from the angel gate. Melrose felt like a pileup on the A30. He sighed at his tools. "I must have the shears to work on this lot."

"What kind d'ya need?" asked Macmillan. "Millie," he called, "just go get my shears, girl."

"Oh, but I'm afraid that won't do."

Millie had started, stopped, started toward them again.

Melrose went on, wishing that Jury would go stand somewhere else. "Unless, of course, you have the number thirteen Black Diamond secateurs? They're somewhat difficult to find. I bought mine in London, that shop near the British Museum."

Millie frowned. "Never heard of that kind, I haven't. Black Diamond? You, Dad?"

Macmillan frowned and shook his head.

"Never mind. I expect the thing to do is call my man at home and have him send them."

Jury interrupted. "No need for that. I'll pick them up for you. I'm going to London. Be back tomorrow. Faster than any post." He clicked his small Biro into place over his small notebook. "Where's this shop, now?"

If Melrose had had the Black Diamond shears in his hand right then, they'd've been in Jury's heart. He could have whipped Jury with the thorn branch Lulu was using to hector Roy, but instead he rattled off a street and number. Any street within barking distance of the British Museum, what difference did it make? And any number.

They had finally all walked away from their sideshow, Jury off to collect Cody, who would drive him to the train. Only Roy remained, he having decided to stick with Melrose as a dependable source of entertainment. He had followed him into the kitchen, where Melrose now sat. After all that, Melrose thought himself worthy of a banquet, but had settled for cozying up to the teapot and some of Rebecca

Owen's superior tea breads.

She had poured tea for both of them and said, "How are you getting on with your turf, Mr. Plant?"

He winced, wishing people would stay away from that, as if it mattered anyway, as if it were painting frescoes on the walls of the Brancacci Chapel; he wasn't Masaccio, turfing the Garden of Eden, for God's sakes. Oh, to be in Florence! "It takes time. No, these things can't be rushed. Ah, thank you."

She was passing him the cake — Madeira, cherry, poppy seed — and he took a slice of the Madeira. He welcomed the quiet after the production outside.

"Most things can't, really," she said.

"Pardon?" What was she talking about?

"Be rushed. As you were saying."

"Oh."

"I expect that Scotland Yard superintendent knows that better than most." She sipped her tea. "They have to be so meticulous, don't they?"

She sounded — tentative, probing. As if she wondered at the wisdom of asking — or perhaps telling — him something. "He's very good at his job. I've known him quite some time." This was no secret, so Melrose didn't mind saying it.

"Mr. Scott said he was the one who recommended you."

Was she suspicious? He couldn't tell. She struck him as an astute woman. All he said to this was, "Yes, he did." He waited for her to go on, but she merely drank her tea in silence. Finally, he said, "How long have you been with the Scotts? Or, rather, with Mrs. Scott?"

"Since Flora was a baby. When Mary was married to Viktor Baumann. She needed help. Oddly, they had no servants at all. They lived in this huge flat at St. Katharine's Dock, very luxurious it was, yet they had no maid, no cook, nothing. They ate out all the time. Mary wasn't much of a cook." Remembering this made her smile until the smile saddened. Then she picked up again. "She said she was tired of supporting half the restaurants in London. But after Flora was born, she put her foot down about having help. I was taken on as some sort of housekeeper, nanny. It was quite pleasant.

"One night when her husband was away I cooked dinner for Mary. She was impressed enough to double my salary if I'd cook two or three nights a week. Viktor Baumann was an inveterate restaurant goer, but even he agreed to sit still three nights a week."

"I'm not surprised. Your cooking is nothing short of fabulous."

She chuckled. "Thanks. I'm a chef, actually. Many years of training, had my own restaurant in London for a few years. Then I tired of the hectic pace of it and sold up. I didn't really need a job. I didn't go in search of that one; a mutual friend recommended me as someone who's good with children. I always have been for some reason, even though I have none of my own. Flora — " Here she propped her chin in her hand and turned away. Too painful to speak of.

So Melrose took another tack. "Why did his wife have to insist on having help?"

"Viktor Baumann didn't like having strangers in the house. That was one reason. I think he felt women belonged in the kitchen and the nursery."

Melrose frowned the deeper. He was thinking of Ruthven and his cook, Martha. But then of course that was completely different; they'd been around all of Melrose's life. "But all staff, unless you've got old family retainers on it, are strangers to begin with. Actually, Mr. Baumann sounds paranoid."

She gave him a frank look. "Oh, he is. He's completely untrusting. I've always found, you know, that a person like that can't be trusted himself. In the same way that liars find it hard to believe anybody else. And of course there's the belief that women are pretty much chattel. Mary should've been able to do all that herself, kids, housekeeping, cooking, according to him."

Melrose ventured a comment: "You don't care for him much, do you?"

"Does anyone? Oh, except for the ones who don't really know him and are charmed. I think another reason he didn't want staff around is that he's extraordinarily jealous. He was of anyone Mary was fond of, man or woman. He was of me, I know that, but also of her women friends. Not to mention any men friends. The poor girl had very little company, mostly acquaintances because of this. Patricia Quint kept up; she's a very loyal person."

"She knew Mrs. Scott back then?"

"Yes."

"You were close to her, weren't you?"

"Yes." She looked off. "She insisted I come along here. Marrying Declan Scott was the best thing that ever happened to her. Outside of Flora, that is. He's as different from Viktor Baumann as a man could be. He doesn't deserve what's happened to him." Her arms were folded on the table and she looked down into her empty cup, scattered with tea leaves as if she meant to read them. "Viktor used Flora as a weapon, either that or a chess piece. He thought it was all one of his games."

"Do you think she's dead?"

Rebecca Owen seemed to shiver at the very thought of it. She rubbed her arms as if she'd caught a chill. "I really can't stand to think that."

"I don't doubt it. Only, you know, there are worse scenarios."

"And better," she quickly said. "It might not have been someone who meant her harm."

A pedophile, thought Melrose, is probably convinced he means no harm. He did not say this. "Then you believe it was a person who simply wanted a child for herself?"

"Yes, I expect I do. It happens all the time, doesn't it? Women who snatch babies out of prams in front of Waitrose, things like that?"

Melrose thought she was being truthful in this instance and that she did believe it, or at least wanted to believe it so much she'd convinced herself. It was possible, he thought: wanting to believe a thing so much you finally did. "You're probably right. But then you must not think this woman's murder has anything to do with Flora."

"You're right. I don't."

"Then . . . what?"

She shook her head. "Perhaps it was the wrong person shot."

Now, *that* was novel. "The wrong person? Well, but why?"

She leaned toward him, as if her physical presence could better convince him. "What if they had a meeting planned, an assignation? And the wrong woman turns up? It would have been too dark to tell straightaway."

"But wouldn't a rendezvous —"

"I doubt it was that."

"— point to Declan Scott?"

As if Melrose were a trifle slow, she gave a short laugh. "Doesn't it point to him anyway?"

Melrose's eyes widened in surprise as she rose abruptly and took her teacup off to the counter. He could understand she might believe it was Scott who'd shot this woman. But that the woman who was shot was not the one he planned to meet? That was preposterous: a woman he knew —

this Georgina Fox (as far as he's concerned) — simply strays into the garden even though she had no plan to meet him or anyone? No, Rebecca Owen didn't believe that; she was too intelligent. "Do you — ?" But he was being too curious. "I suppose anyone would wonder. I don't mean to be intrusive." He smiled, he hoped, sheepishly.

"Yes, you'd hardly expect this sort of thing out here in the country, especially this country, Cornwall. It seems so far removed from everything." She paused. "What does this Scotland Yard man think?"

She was back to it again. "I'm afraid you'll have to ask him. These policemen don't talk much."

"Really? Well, I'll be sure to tell Cody Platt. He never stops talking."

Again, Melrose was surprised. He frowned. "You know him, then? I mean aside from this awful business?"

"Oh, yes. Cody was here even before Flora disappeared. Declan called in the police to report a break-in — we'd had a few things stolen. Cody came. He was a constable then. For some reason, Flora took to him and he to Flora. And he also to Mary. I know his presence after what happened to Flora was a comfort to her. He's a detective, after all, and perhaps a — symbol? Proof that they hadn't stopped looking for Flora. And, of course, that's what he told her, that this Commander Macalvie never stopped. He wasn't commander then; I think he was a detective chief inspector. But all the same. Yes, Cody Platt was a comfort."

Through the window, Melrose watched Lulu throwing something for Roy to run after. He asked, "What happened to Lulu's parents, Mrs. Owen?"

"They're both dead. Both in an auto accident a few years ago. It was absolutely terrible, Ben and Sara were on their way to St. Ives for a little holiday. At a roundabout near Camborne, a lorry plowed right into them. Ben had piled up so much in the backseat, he couldn't see out the rear window. At least that was what I thought might have happened." She rose and went to the sideboard and pulled out a drawer. From this she took out a newspaper clipping she brought to Melrose. It gave the details of the accident.

"They'd left Lulu with me for the time they'd be gone. Otherwise, well, she'd be gone, too."

Rebecca Owen looked so sad that

Melrose didn't know what to say except something banal: "I'm sorry. What a horrible loss."

"I wonder if her being so young made it easier on her? She didn't seem that disturbed."

"Throwing up a front, I expect," he said. Everything about this case seemed to be "throwing up a front," where the victim was as hard to identify as the murderer.

"She seems to be by herself most of the day. Doesn't she have school chums?"

"Oh, yes, of course. She goes to a very good school; Mr. Scott sees to that. He's extremely generous. They're on holiday at the moment. Something to do with staffing problems. I believe two of the teachers had to leave — well, some kind of scandal, and I expect the less said the better, as far as the children were concerned."

Melrose wanted to laugh. No, the more said, the better, as far as Lulu was concerned.

"But she gets on well with adults, doesn't she?" said Rebecca. "You certainly have an effect upon her, and a very good one. I think you light a fire in her." Smiling, she took the cake plate to the sideboard.

What? He fired Lulu up? He didn't know

if he believed in this fire-lighting business, but still he felt warmed by it.

At that moment Lulu walked in with Roy and they stood there. "You've been having tea for ages. You were supposed to come out . . ."

Nag, nag. Bark. Fire extinguished.

Lulu was stopped from following him out by her aunt and made to "have a lie down or you won't be able to last out the evening."

Ha! thought Melrose, as he walked to the secret garden. Lulu could outlast the Pleistocene. He studied his enameled mead design. Well, "design" might be too fine a word, but it did look rather good. The snowdrops were a nice accent. What he hadn't boned up on was exactly how to cut round the enameled patches. That's why the grass was cut before the little flowers were planted; otherwise one had to do it by hand.

"That's quite pretty, Mr. Plant."

Melrose turned at the sound of Warburton's voice and his tweedy, tobacco-y smell. Warburton was pointing with his pipe. "Snowdrops. Now that is original. Never seen that before. Rather white, wouldn't you say?"

"I used a similar design first in my own garden in Northants. Indeed I designed one entire slope in silver and gold. Used marigolds for the gold (that was a bit too obvious wasn't it?), but only for a band running down the center."

Warburton's usual sunny expression deepened into a frown. "But wouldn't the marigolds be too large for achieving this jewellike effect?"

Drat! How stupid of him. He might as well try to plant shoes. "Oh, yes, but this was your dwarf marigold."

"Dwarf?"

"It's a hybrid, isn't it? I happened on it by chance. A chap I know who's very much into hybridization — you wouldn't believe his greenhouse! At any rate, I don't expect he's put the dwarfs on the market yet. I'll send you a sample, shall I?"

"I'd like that, yes. You're really on the cutting edge, Mr. Plant. Ah! No pun intended!" Warburton laughed.

So did Melrose, just to stay on the good side of him. "One tries to keep abreast."

Warburton sucked on his pipe and mused.

What, wondered Melrose, could he possibly be thinking about? The snowdrop situation? The murder? Given Warburton, who generally had his drawings with him. Warburton without his drawings could think of nothing, could advance no theory, could come to no conclusion. The comment about snowdrops — "rather white, wouldn't you say?" — had pretty much exhausted his conversation.

Melrose wondered if Henry James's Lord Warburton had been as shallow. No, he was sure James's character was a man with some depth. Lord Warburton's life had simply appeared to Isabel as lacking the freedom she craved and which she thought she had found in Osmond. Deluded girl! Good lord, had he taken to admonishing fictional characters? Anyway, this Warburton was easily as shallow as the brass dish of the fountain nearby and in constant need of replenishment by the boys with the buckets. When the water was turned on, Melrose imagined that sculpture would be even more delightful. He could use a blast of cool water.

But why in heaven's name had Declan Scott engaged Warburton, then? Must be because the design was pretty damned good.

Millie, however, clearly disagreed. For her, it was the man himself. Melrose had a little insight about her, too: Millie tended to brood, unlike her father. She mistook this broodiness for smoldering passion and mistook Warburton's lack of conversation in the same way — a Heathcliff to her Cathy. His black eyes like coals put Melrose more in mind of a snowman than a Heathcliff. He wouldn't have been at all surprised to have Warburton melt at his feet.

Warburton was still standing there, contemplating Melrose's work. Finally, he poked his pipe stem toward the tiny flower faces. "Oughtn't that purple one sitting there be put in that line? It seems to need one more." This was the single plant that Lulu had removed and left sitting by the bed.

Oh, who the bloody hell cares, man (he wanted to yell), with wars and starvation and the world in tatters? Rarely did Melrose consider the tattered world and was now being forced to contemplate his own shallowness.

You want the trivial, lad, well here it is. And God set about thrashing him with a snowdrop.

Embarrassed, Melrose pursed his lips and studied the weight of the steely looking sky. You must be more forbearing about others, said one of his chorus of ever-remonstrating voices. Really? Why? said the voice sitting in the wing chair eating a biscuit. *Really, why?* was pretty much its entire repertoire and the voice was pleased as punch with that response. Good. Melrose was back on track.

"Do you think symmetry is needed here?" he asked Warburton.

Pipe returned to mouth and a few puffs later, Warburton admitted probably not, and that he was always probing with his architect's eye. "Can't help myself."

"Tell me, Lord — I mean, Mr. Warburton, what prompted this whole restoration project?"

"Mary Scott, poor woman. Maybe under the influence of Heligan. That's an enormous project." He knocked his pipe against the fountain to loosen the tobacco. "It certainly wasn't Declan. I mean, Declan is always happy with the way things are, but he's having this done as a kind of — well, he's doing it for her." Warburton seemed to like that reason. "Declan could go forever without changing things inside or out."

Melrose had gone down on one knee, resetting the deep purple-blue pansy in its former hole. "It was Lulu who messed the line about. She pulled this one up and set the others farther apart. I doubt she'd try that with Macmillan's planting."

"Ha! Better not. Macmillan would have her hide. That child's into everything. Bossy little thing. She's always after an argument."

An argument? Well, something.

Melrose stood and gazed down at his pansy relocation. It looked no better than it had before, but neither had Lulu's realignment looked better than before.

Well, that was gardening for you. He pulled off his gloves and tossed them down beside the trowel. No wonder he didn't do it.

# 35

Jury went through the wrought iron gate with the angel and back to the pond garden to sit on the same bench he had left not long ago. This garden within a garden was so private and secluded one wouldn't know there was a lot of work proceeding elsewhere. On the other side of the high yew hedge he could hear the Macmillans' voices.

Flowers were beginning to bloom here, banks of blue flowers in front of the hedges — dark delphiniums, some silvery blue bush he couldn't identify, cornflowers, feathery blue grasses. The pansies in Melrose Plant's little square of grass looked startled as if this were neither the time nor place for their appearance.

Not April yet, so a little early for restoration, rebirth, reclamation. If you believed that sort of thing. Jury passed his hand over his face and with the gesture had a sudden chill, thinking that was the way one closed the eyes of the dead. He wondered what it was he felt had left him for good. Was it a rough belief that things really did add up in the end? He felt less and less sure of that these days.

From the other side of the hedge came the voices — words, laughter — as if a parallel world of sound were passing him by. He wanted to give up on the whole bloody mess; he was tired. But he supposed nearly dying would have anyone rearranging his list of priorities. Only he found he had no list. Everything that might have made it up seemed equal, equally important or unimportant.

His mind was clouded, going nowhere. Come on, you're a smart fellow, a good detective. You can work it out. The facts again: Three years ago, Flora Baumann disappeared from the Lost Gardens of Heligan. Six months afterward, Mary Scott dies. A year after that, Declan Scott meets Georgina Fox, aka Lena Banks, who is probably working in the interests of Viktor Baumann.

Jury was leaning over, arms on legs, looking at the edge of the pond and some tiny flowers that were being lightly buffeted by the breeze. Leaning forward, head down, he felt rather than saw a presence on the other side of the lily pond. He thought: It's either the killer with a gun pointed at me or some old Angel Gate ghost. It is certainly something that is not announcing its presence. He raised his head and looked. Neither. It was Roy. Roy sitting on a white bench, twin of Jury's, now flailing the bench with his tail, *whamwham*. He did not bark; he had something in his mouth.

Jury thought: Okay, Roy, bring it here — the key to the strongbox, the accusing letter, the monogrammed handkerchief, the wax seal, the glasses, the lipstick, the ring, the bit of chiffon torn from a dress that I will immediately recognize.

He knew it was none of these things, though it should have been. Dogs were always dragging important things in from the woods or out of the drainpipe. He could make out even at this distance Roy had a blue flower, hardly surprising, given the whole range of blue flowers here, banks of them in front of the hedge, beds of them near the pond. He wasn't sure what they were, being fairly flower blind. Cornflowers, blue grass, delphiniums.

Come on, you dumb dog. Give us a clue, make yourself useful. At least a silver cigarette lighter or a lion-headed cane. Jury stopped. Cornflower. They weren't always blue, but when they were blue they were very, very —

He had said it, hadn't he? Cody? When they'd been in the Little Chef. "Her eyes were the bluest I've ever seen. As blue as her dress."

Roy still sat there on the far bench, flower in mouth, head cocked. Righteous. Jury whistled. Roy jumped down from the bench, trot more of a swagger.

Righteous. Devil may care.

The dog followed Jury to the van, both of them slogging through the wet grass, both feeling as if they'd finally got hold of something with meat on its bones.

"Cody."

Surprised, Cody looked up from his cell phone, said, "Sir?"

"Sign off."

Cody did so, hand still clutching the phone as if he might need help.

Jury sat down in the same chair he'd inhabited earlier. He knew he could be wrong, and it would be easy enough to check, but he also knew he was most probably right. He leveled a look at Cody. "You said her eyes were the same shade as the dress she was wearing: cornflower blue."

Cody nodded. An expression of dread

like a shadow moved over his face.

"I'm wondering how you knew that."

The expression changed. He looked relieved and gave an abrupt laugh. "It was in the papers, wasn't it? There had to be a description; how else would anyone recognize her if they saw her?" A small triumph, his smile said.

Jury shook his head. "Blue eyes, blue dress, yes. But then you must have seen her."

"I knew what color her eyes were, and I must've seen the dress, too. Or I'd never have said it."

"That's the point. You couldn't have seen the dress because it was new. She'd never worn it before is what Declan Scott said. So it was that day you saw it, Cody, the day she disappeared."

He was out of his chair. "You're not saying *I* had anything to do with it!"

"Not yet, I'm not. Sit down. Tell me how you came to see her."

Cody sat back, said nothing.

"You were following Mary and Flora, weren't you? And probably not for the first time —"

With a poor imitation of a laugh, Cody said, "A stalker, is that it? That's what you're saying?"

"No, that isn't it. A protector is more like it. You worried little Flora might come to harm. And the horrible irony is, she did, because for a moment you must've looked away. You didn't see the person who took her because you would never in a million years have withheld that information. Just suddenly, Flora wasn't there. Like your little sister. It must have been like reliving it; it must have been hell. You must have felt — and still feel — you failed yet again. You told me it worried you her parents didn't keep a tight enough hold on her."

Cody nodded. "She'd be out in the front, wandering in the trees; she liked the little path between them. I drove in a couple of times and saw her. I mean, I know it's private property, this, but anyone could get in. It just didn't seem safe. Mary" — he paused, suggesting his feelings for Mary were more than he wanted to feel — "I can't say I was an actual *friend*, of course, just more of a good acquaintance. After the break-in here I'd stop by once in a while. You know, just to see how things were." Involved with his story now, as if he'd only been waiting for someone to tell it to, someone who'd get it, who'd understand, Cody leaned forward, arms on desk, hands clasped. He went on: "Believe me I searched my mind afterward remembering exactly what I'd seen and I hadn't seen a stranger. I searched the spot, the very spot that day when other police came. You're right, I lost sight of her for a minute. I had binoculars — I hate how that makes me sound like a voyeur, but that's what I was doing, how I was watching.

"You see, Declan Scott just didn't seem to do a good job of watching over her. He's just too laissez-faire, you know, easy come easy go."

Jury broke into laughter. "That's the last way I'd describe Declan Scott. Easygoing? The man's a cauldron of intensity. You're describing what you were yourself. You were only a kid, Cody; what happened wasn't your fault. Your mum sometimes took your sister shopping. Do you imagine she had an eye on her every minute? Of course not."

There was a silence. Then Cody said, "Shall you be telling the boss?" From under lowered lids he looked up darkly at Jury.

"No. I shall not. That's strictly up to you."

"He'll have my badge."

Jury shook his head. "No. I think he'll understand. Commander Macalvie has good reason to, believe me."

"He'll understand I'm a head case."

"Because you want little kids taken care of, right? That makes you a nutter? No." Jury rose, gave Roy a little "get up" boot with his toe. "Cody, you're a regular Holden Caulfield."

Jury left, Roy quick by his side.

Devil may care.

# 36

As Melrose was walking the pebble path, he saw Jury coming from the gardens. He waited for him in front of the cottage door, and when Jury drew abreast, he said, "Are you really going back to London or was all that just eyewash?"

"Yes, I'm going back —"

Melrose opened the door.

"— making a special trip to get your Black Diamond secateurs."

"Oh, very amusing, ta very much," Melrose tossed his cap on the chair and Jury stepped inside. "You were a huge help back there."

"I thought your way of stonewalling was, actually, brilliant."

Melrose was in the small kitchen, shaking the kettle. He stuck it under the cold tap. "Well, it wasn't my quick thinking. It was Diane Demorney's tutelage. Never, never, never back down from anything you've stated as fact. Diane's worse than General MacArthur. 'I shall return' is bollocks to her; 'I shall never leave' is more like it."

Jury laughed. "The kettle's boiling."

As he measured out the tea and poured the water over it, Melrose went on to recap the talk in the kitchen with Rebecca Owen. "It's clear she loved Mary and Flora and hated Baumann. He sounds an awful chauvinist, and paranoid, to boot."

"Jealous, was he? That goes along with the paranoia."

"She was especially interested in what you thought. She asked me more than once."

Jury sat back and stretched out his legs. "That's not too surprising, is it? She'd wonder what was so arresting about this murder that Scotland Yard would get into it."

"Yes, I expect so." Melrose had sat down and was taking out his cigarettes when he looked at Jury. "What?"

Jury frowned.

Melrose paid no attention and lit up.

"What were you doing out there with your flowering mead and Warburton?"

"He was advising me on the arrangement."

"Oh, that's cool. Isn't that tea up on its

feet yet? Been steeping long enough."

Melrose went to the kitchen and clattered cups and saucers around. He went on about Warburton. "His advice about the number of pansies came after Lulu's advice. They didn't agree. These people who claimed to know nothing about enameled mead advising me . . . How many sugars?"

"One."

Melrose spooned in sugar, added milk and carried in the cups, sloshing a bit of liquid into Jury's saucer.

"Mugs are easier."

"I do not like mugs," said Melrose. "Indeed, I hate them. Mugs suggest drinking while you're wandering around doing stuff; you should be sitting down over tea and certainly not doing anything else, except reading. But definitely sitting down. Like most other things," he added thoughtfully.

Jury shook his head. "You've been too long in the Nitwits Club."

"I beg your pardon?"

"The Jack and Hammer branch of Bedlam. Our friends."

Melrose mustered some phony indignation. "Are you aware that one of these nitwits — Diane — saved my *life* once? And don't you recall that if it hadn't been for that bloody Masaccio triptych Trueblood was on about, we might never have solved that case? And how about Trueblood's brilliant defense in the chamber pot affair?"

"Oh, well, the Nitwits have had their moments, yes. No one would deny that."

Melrose stirred his tea with the little spoon. The spoon made him think of Lulu. "Lulu's rather sad, I think."

"I don't."

Melrose winced. "God, but it takes a lot to get you to trot out the sympathy."

"I don't mean her situation isn't sad. It is. I mean I don't see any particular sadness in Lulu herself." He smiled. "She seems to be enjoying things."

"How could she not be sad? Losing both her parents at once?"

"She was what? Four? Five? How much would she have understood?"

This irritated Melrose no end. "Come on, Richard, you're just being thick."

"Maybe. Did you ever read *A Death in the Family*?"

"No. Who wrote it?"

"James Agee. The father's car skids off the road and he hits his forehead in an especially vulnerable point — it's really a freak accident — and dies instantly. What I remember, though, is the reaction of the little kids, a boy and girl, probably five and seven. They're not really all that upset and wonder if they should be."

"Denial."

Jury shrugged. "Possibly. But we all depend on that term overmuch. We're confronted with an event that calls for a certain reaction, we think. We expect that a child would be inconsolable, heartbroken, weeping and lamenting if the parents die. And I suppose a lot of children are. But there's this other possibility. Lulu's pretty happy, it seems to me. You don't think she's enjoying a body being found on the grounds?"

"Oh, well, *that*. But that's different. It wasn't *her* body or the body of anyone she cares about. It's not the same thing at all."

"Maybe." Jury looked at the thin rain beyond the window. "Macalvie told me about the daughter of his lover and what happened. Can you imagine? What a weight to bear. That probably explains a lot about him: the mind-bending meticulousness. How careful he is, how demanding. My guess is he feels he could have saved her, this little girl, if he'd been careful, if he'd been more exacting. God, the things we expect of ourselves."

"There's nothing on earth he could have done. The child was doomed from the moment they took her."

"But he'll always blame himself for the kidnapping in the first place."

Melrose nodded. "It was utterly merciless."

Jury nodded and rose. "And this murder does remind him that the fate of Flora Baumann might be the same. He didn't find Flora the first time around. He thinks of it as another failure, as failing all over again. Of leaving Flora's mother in the lurch." Jury set down his cup. "I've got to be going. Thanks for the tea."

"Why? I mean why are you going to London this time?"

"Unfinished business."

"That tells me a lot."

Jury smiled, gave Melrose a short good-bye salute.

Cody Platt was standing in front of Beaminster's desk, talking to him and Swayle, who looked as if he'd settled into that swivel chair for life, chair back tilted as far as it would go, his arms hanging loose outside the chair arms. He was laughing.

Jury was surprised a detective as louche

as Swayle could survive under Macalvie. But maybe he was different around Macalvie, and his boss could hardly do bed checks.

Beaminster stopped midlaugh when he saw Jury. Swayle creaked the chair forward and Cody turned round. Only Cody smiled.

"Cody, can I talk to you for a minute?" He watched Cody's eyes widen, his complexion turn a little ashen; probably he was thinking it was yet more about his following Mary Scott and Flora.

"Sure." He moved up to the front of the van.

The other two watched with faces that said Go, why don't you? Just go. Jury did not return the looks or absorb the hostility. He sat down at the small table serving as a desk, facing away from the two other detectives. They'd have to listen hard to pick up Jury's end. Cody took the chair across the table.

Jury kept his voice low. "There's something I need to take care of in London. Your boss thinks you might want to take care of it with me."

Relief and curiosity replaced the anxious expression. "What?"

"It's related to Viktor Baumann."

"Baumann." He looked by turn angry, sad, hopeless, vengeful. "That bastard."

"How much do you know about him?"

"I know he made Mary's life a misery at the end; I know that he had Flora abducted."

"You don't actually know that, Cody."

"Yes I do," he said, simply.

"But we've got no proof, and worse, we're no nearer to finding her" — as if they would or could — "to finding out what happened to her."

Cody's eyes flashed. There was something electric about the boy — Jury didn't know why he thought of him as a boy . . . yes, perhaps he did. He could see Cody all those years ago, in his fringed vest and chaps, snapping those two toy silver guns out of his double holster and looking for any available place to let loose with a fusillade of clicks: stuffed lion or rabbit, maybe? The poster of Queen, whose guitars looked as dangerous as rifles? He let them have it, anyway, and the wall, too, for good measure. This little western unreeled in Jury's mind as Cody was talking in terrible earnest about Flora and the endless possibilities as to what happened. That's the word Cody used: "endless." He seemed to have worked up little scenes, cameos that she could be in Dulwich, she could be in Devon or Dorset or another country, for that matter.

"She could be, yes." Like your sister. Only, Jury didn't believe it. "You haven't asked me just what it is I want to do or want you to do."

"If it means putting Baumann away or even causing Baumann trouble —" He shrugged, raising his forearms, palms flat in a gesture of I should care?

# 37

Brian Macalvie stood in Declan Scott's living room, still wearing his coat.

"Let me take your coat, Commander."

"I'll keep it, thanks. I won't be here long. Where is she, Mr. Scott?"

Declan dropped the arm that he had reached out to take the coat. "I beg your pardon?"

"Flora. Where is she?"

Declan came closer, as if some physical proximity would allow him better to understand Macalvie's meaning. "I'm sorry, you'll have to explain —"

Macalvie didn't explain. He kept his coat on and went on talking. "Why it took me so long to work this out, I don't know. Wait. Yes, I do know. I was taking this case too personally. Still am, probably. A third motive didn't even occur to me. I mean besides money or a warped desire for a child. Flora was abducted in order to keep her

419

out of harm's way. Harm in this case meaning Viktor Baumann, who's relentless when he wants something. Then, when Mary died, the threat doubled — quadrupled, even — because you hadn't a legal leg to stand on when it came to keeping Flora with you. Baumann, as her father, would have gotten custody. So where is she? France? Italy? In Florence? Venice? In a boarding school, maybe? A convent?"

Without waiting for an invitation, Macalvie sat down while Declan still stood, his face blank as a plate. Now Macalvie did the inviting: "Sit down, why don't you?"

"Thank you. I'm beyond sitting down." He walked over to the fireplace and leaned on the mantel, arms folded. "Let's assume you're right —"

"Let's."

"What about Mary?"

"Oh, your wife would have been in on it. You might even have done it for her sake."

"Then there'd be no crime in it, would there?"

"Probably not. Except for sending police all over the damned place on a wild-goose chase."

"Then — ?" Declan shrugged.

"Well, *then* there's still Lena Banks lying

on a slab in the morgue. Murder — that *is* a crime, Mr. Scott."

"Why would I murder this woman?"

" 'This woman'? That's a bit standoffish of you, considering you had an affair with her. Why would you kill her? Presumably she meant a world of trouble."

"Such as?"

"You say she was talking to your wife at Brown's. We have only your word about that."

"Why would I lie about it?"

"Perhaps to establish it was Mary and not you she came here to see."

"But it *was* Mary. Dora Stout saw them. And why would she disguise herself?"

"So you wouldn't recognize her?"

Declan's laugh was unbelieving. "Commander Macalvie, I didn't even *know* her at that point."

"But I believe she thought — or they thought, Lena Banks and Viktor Baumann — that you very possibly would later on, at some point. And would they want someone as memorable as Georgina coming here? I know I'm speculating, but this action wasn't taken suddenly; it was a long-term plan. There was a threat involved. And the threat, I'd guess, was something like 'If you don't hand over Flora, Viktor will get her

421

anyway and that would be far more traumatic for Flora.' "

"And that's what he did: he took her."

"No, he didn't, Mr. Scott. Viktor Baumann is still looking for her. That's what the whole Lena Banks affair in Paris was about. They both believed you'd talk, given the right person to talk to. But you didn't."

Declan's laugh again registered disbelief. "I didn't talk because I had nothing to say, for God's sakes. And in the hotel over three years ago — could we just assume for the moment I'm telling the truth?"

"Okay. She was there on Viktor's behalf, again. As I said, she threatened Mary."

"Perhaps you're right. But as Mary didn't tell me what they talked about, I can't say yes or no."

"Why *wouldn't* she have told you? You were her husband."

"Because Mary was paranoid when it came to Flora. And that's not a figure of speech. Baumann had always had her tied in knots over that little girl. If she thought telling me might somehow jeopardize Flora's safety, she wouldn't have."

Macalvie was shaking his head. "I don't believe that. If it had happened, she'd have told you. That's one reason I don't think it happened."

"Look, Commander Macalvie, no one knows. You're wrong, I can tell you that." Declan did sit down then, looking at Macalvie and then looking away. "I'm afraid Flora's dead."

"Parents don't usually relinquish hope as long as there's a tiny chance a child is still alive."

"I'm not really Flora's father. I think faith has a lot to do with blood. It's like a sixth sense, like intuition. When you know something beyond all reason. Mary had it. I don't mean I didn't love Flora, for I certainly did. But I was only around her for a short time. All right, I can understand your coming to the conclusion you did, that I might have staged Flora's abduction. But that still doesn't explain why I'd kill Lena Banks."

"Several possibilities there. Rage at Georgina for betraying you —"

Declan laughed. "Oh, really? Well, one problem there is that I'd have had to know Lena Banks was Georgina."

Macalvie shrugged. "Who says you didn't? Number two, Lena Banks found out you had Flora, had her somewhere."

"If that's the case, Viktor Baumann also knows."

"Probably."

"Then he'll come for her — look, are you going to charge me? It would put paid to at least part of this business." His voice sounded very tired.

Macalvie gave him a long look. "No. I can't charge you, not without more evidence. We haven't even found the weapon yet."

"Then why are you telling me all this?"

"I want to know where Flora is."

"She's dead." Declan was resting his arms on his knees, his head down, looking at whatever figure in the carpet might disclose something.

"You said that before." But Macalvie thought the finality and despair in the words sounded genuine and a doubt crept into his mind. Or was it simply pity? Or was it — much more likely — identification? Remembering the little girl sitting at the table with a bullet in her forehead? He should not be working this case; he was too close to it. "Did your wife know she was going to die?"

"Yes. But not when. Until the end. Within the space of a few months her heart grew so weak she could hardly breathe at times." He looked away.

"I'm sorry. I really am."

"Yes. Thank you."

Declan Scott rose and Macalvie, who was just under six feet, still felt Scott towered over him. "I'll walk you to the door," said Scott.

Macalvie looked at the French doors. "If you don't mind, I'll just go out through the gardens. I want to talk to my men in the van."

Declan nodded. As Macalvie opened the door, Declan said, "You're wrong, Commander. Dead wrong."

Beaminster and Wiggins were in the van, which was cold. Something had happened to the small portable heater. The bars looked anemic. Wiggins, who looked more dreamy than pale, was on the phone, and nodded by way of hello.

Beaminster, who'd been on the phone himself, laughing at something, quickly put it down, as if laughter, in the service or not of this investigation, was prohibited.

Wiggins hung up and said, "I've checked every convent, every school within a twenty-five-mile radius of Paris and Florence. No sign of her. One sister" — he looked at his page of notes — "Sister Anne made it quite clear to me they didn't welcome the intrusion of police as their convent was a sanctuary and did I really think she'd tell me if such a child was there? Didn't sound very godly to me, if you know what I mean."

Macalvie sighed and sat down at Swayle's desk. "Keep looking. Go another twenty-five miles out. He knows where she is." Macalvie was almost certain of this, but "almost" was a long way from a dead cert. "I think if Declan Scott confessed, he'd get a pretty light sentence . . . ."

"Yes, probably he would."

"Viktor Baumann. Lena Banks and Viktor Baumann. If they had my kid I'd kill them myself." He looked at Wiggins and added, "I hope your guv'nor nails the bastard."

# 38

Cody parked the car at the curb in front of the Islington house. Jury had offered to put him up overnight — or, rather, Stan Keeler would put him up. Stan had gone to Germany again, "where they appreciate us." That had made Jury smile. So there was a chink in the old Keeler armor, the only self-pitying thing Jury had ever heard Stan say. Anyway, Stone would be delighted to have someone in the flat. Cody was a dog person. (Later, after a look at Carole-anne, he made it clear to Jury that he was also a girl person.)

Mrs. Wasserman recognized Jury's tread and was suddenly there on her steps (the ones to the garden flat), illuminated by a sliver of light from the moon coming from behind a slate-colored cloud. "Mr. Jury, Mr. Jury." She shook her head sadly as if it were indeed all Mr. Jury's fault, whatever it was.

"Mrs. Wasserman. Is something wrong?"

She was looking at Cody. *He* was clearly wrong, this stranger, until Jury introduced him as Detective Platt of the Devon and Cornwall police.

"Ah, another policeman! I am glad of that. There can't be too many. There is a prowler, Superintendent. He was on these steps not ten minutes ago."

Mrs. Wasserman's paranoia came in waves, the biggest ones hitting the shore when Jury was absent for more than a day or two. He was her ballast. There might have been someone here, but it could as easily have been the milkman or the postman or the delivery boy from the Chinese restaurant on Upper Street. Caroleanne was fond of shrimp fried rice.

"Did you see him at all?"

"No, of course not; it was too dark, wasn't it?"

Jury had his little notebook out and his pen. "Anything at all you remember?"

She pinched her lower lip, pleating it. "Only that he was tall. And thin." Everyone was to Mrs. Wasserman, who was herself short and chubby. She said this, looking at Cody. Cody was indeed a rail. "I couldn't see well. I told you —"

Jury packed notebook and pen away and

smiled. "Not to worry; if he comes back, we'll know it. But it might simply have been someone looking for an address." Someone, more likely no one.

Carole-anne, who was equally adept at picking up signs of Jury's return, was rushing down the stairs from her third-floor flat as Jury was trudging up to the first floor. "Super!" she cried, launching herself at him like a missile. If he hadn't caught her in a hug, she'd have flown down the stairs, headfirst.

"You lead a complicated life, Mr. Jury," Cody said, gazing at Carole-anne as if the sun had risen at midnight.

Carole-anne left Jury's embrace and might just have flown into Cody's if he'd had his arms open. Unlocking his door, Jury introduced them, saying, "I thought maybe he could stay in Stan's flat."

Nominal resident manager, Carole-anne held extra keys to all the flats. There were only Jury, Mrs. Wasserman and Stan Keeler, who was seldom there. So right away, Carole-anne pulled at Cody's hand and marched him up to the second floor. Jury watched her departing back. How was she dressed tonight? Some vibrant shade of lavender that had never seen the inside of an old lady's clothes cupboard. Luscious silk top and short, short skirt.

Jury stood catching a sight of this before he turned into his living room and levered himself, like an old arthritis sufferer, into his armchair. He sighed. He had been out of hospital for two months and had to admit to a wistfulness to return, even if it did mean Nurse Bell. He tired too easily now. Too easily for what, for God's sakes? The center court at Wimbledon? Riding point to point at Newmarket? Poor you.

Clatter on the stairs. It could have been a herd of zebra but was instead Carole-anne returned from orienting Cody to Stan's place — "Guitar here, piano there, anything else you need?" — to orient Jury to his life. What did she think of Cody? He was someone to go down the pub with, which is what she said.

"Cody'll be down in a minute. Thought we'd go to the Angel. You?" She raised her eyebrows in question as she sat down on the sofa.

"Me?"

"Oh, pardon me for asking." She picked up one of the beauty magazines that she kept on Jury's coffee table in case she got bored — at least that was always the impression — and sat flicking through it and swinging her foot.

It was the shoes that made the clatter. Why did women wear wooden blocks? It looked as if they'd shopped in a lumber-yard instead of a shoe store. Jury looked at the magazine. "Why do you bother with those?"

"To get beauty tips, you know" — here she lifted a handful of copper-colored hair that would have had the fire brigade here if the hair had any more highlights, pointed to her skin, her eyes — "makeup and clothes, of course." She lifted one corner of the lavender skirt.

Jury laughed. "Carole-anne, you should be giving tips, not getting them. Coals to Newcastle, that is."

She looked round the room as if to discover the source of this alien voice, as if the very air were clogged with suspicion. "Is that one of your compliments?"

"Not mine. God's. How's work?"

She was still frowning over the Jury compliment. Then she stopped and started flipping through *Beauty Secrets*, vol. 1,000,000. "Andrew's up on a bit of a high horse."

This was Andrew Starr, a man not given to high horses; too much patience might have been his problem. He owned a shop in Covent Garden called the Starrdust. It

431

sold horoscopes, magic effects, dreams (all the same, in other words). It was a fascinating little place that catered as much to kids (such as Wiggins) as to grown-ups (Jury tried to think of one).

"High horsing about what?"

"You know, that Lady Chalmers, the short one with the loud voice. We can't even hear our stereo over her. Well, she's blind deaf, ain't she? You know who I mean."

"Actually, no."

"So she had Andrew do her horoscope, and that's really complicated at best and near impossible at least if you haven't got your dates sorted. Anyway, he told her eighty —"

(Andrew did not come cheap.)

"— and she claimed he'd told her twenty. Twenty pounds, that's just ridiculous, that's just cheek, you ask me. For one of *his* horoscopes. And he gives all of his customers a price list. This one is the most detailed horoscope —" She made a big circle with her arms, as if embracing sky, planets, stars. "And all the work that goes into it, well, he's a perfectionist —"

Was there an emphasis on the *"he's,"* as though she had one of the nonperfectionists seated opposite her?

"You know, maybe that's what you need!" She snapped the magazine shut, having found a topic — Jury — who was even more interesting than the application of eyeliner. "If Andrew'd done you one before, I bet you could have avoided getting shot."

Jury just smiled slightly at her brightening eyes. "I don't want to know the future. I don't want to know what woman — or women, plural — is going to knock me up the side of the head and drag me off to the registry office."

"Oh, don't be daft!"

"Daft? And why's that?"

"You'll be here until you're old and crotchety."

"I'm already old and crotchety."

He heard the *click click click* of a dog's toes and the quick *thump* of a pair of feet. In a moment Cody entered with Stone.

"Nice digs you got here!" Cody said with more enthusiasm than the digs called for. It was meant, of course, for the digs' tenants, one tenant in particular. "Ready?" he asked in a general way.

Stone woofed a couple of times. He always seemed to be making sounds through a soft medium, cotton or clouds or something. He was ready.

"You coming, then?" Cody tried to sound as if he wanted Jury to.

Jury shook his head, smiled. "No, I don't think so." He looked from Cody to Carole-anne. Not a chance, son.

When they'd gone, he sat for a while. But he grew increasingly restless, staring up at a dark stain on the ceiling, old water damage, he supposed. He reached behind him and picked up a book. He didn't want the book, but what was beneath it: the autopsy report Phyllis Nancy had sent round to his office.

Where had this child come from? He was occupying his mind with unanswerable questions to avoid reading the report. He pulled the lamp behind him to the right of the table so that it shone on the pages.

The bullet had entered the back between the fifth and sixth thoracic vertebrae. The bullet had struck bone, which made the exit wound larger. There were more details, cold and clinical, as they should be. Only they didn't erase the crime scene from Jury's mind. The toes of her black patent shoes turned inward in one of those awkward stances little children manage to make graceful. She was six years old, as nearly as they could put it.

There was no doubt whatever in Johnny Blakeley's mind that the child had come from Number 13, Hester Street. But Johnny's mind wasn't enough to get them a warrant. The law, Jury reflected, seemed to many people to protect the villain, the crook, the killer.

Police had swarmed on that street, gone away, come back, swarmed again. They had knocked on the door of every house, including Number 13, whose occupant was the Mrs. Murchison who was high on Johnny's list, just under Viktor Baumann. He had given the charge of that house to her. And how would it lead back to Baumann, anyway?

No. That was one thought too many, as someone once said. If he kept trying to see too far into the future, if he asked himself too many questions, he'd be paralyzed. He finished the report; it was basically what Phyllis had said at the scene, here in more detail, but with no surprises. Her eye had traced the bullet on its quick journey, had set forth various other attributes, such as the dehydration and malnourishment (neither life threatening, at least not at this point).

It was only the surface these villains cared about — the bisque-doll skin without traces of makeup, the shiny hair. The seductive power of the untouched. Why was innocence such an enticement?

He sat there for what felt like hours and was surprised that only half an hour had passed. It was nine-thirty. He would go to the Yard. Johnny Blakeley might be there; Johnny was known to keep long hours. No wife, kids, mortgage. The married ones envied him.

His desk was a blitz of papers. As if this was the dustbin man's last dump. Johnny sat, everything about him askew — tie, hair, desk. He was smoking some low-tar faux cigarette whose smoke spiral Jury's eye followed longingly.

Seeing this, Johnny pushed the pack toward Jury.

"No thanks, I quit."

"Ah. I tell myself several times a day I'll quit."

"Well, don't."

"That bad, is it?"

"Worse."

Johnny grinned and then reverted to what they'd been discussing. "You don't stand a chance in hell of getting a warrant, Rich, not even with the shooting death of a child. There's simply no way to prove she came from that house. I mean, more so than the other houses on that street. Hell, maybe not even *that* street."

"Get a warrant for all of them, then."

"I'd like to shake the hand of the judge who'd do that."

"So would I." Jury laughed. "If you haven't been able to, I certainly couldn't. No, I didn't even consider trying to get a search warrant."

Johnny leaned toward Jury as far as he could with the corner of the desk between them. "Rich, you can't walk in there without one."

"You did."

"Yeah and I got knocked up the side of the head for it, too. At least I had a little justification: it's my investigation, has been for some time."

"But so it is mine, now, with this child murdered."

Johnny sat back. "True."

They regarded each other.

Johnny said, "You're crazy."

"Maybe."

"Bloody hell."

Jury knew what was distressing him. He couldn't go along. The Murchison woman would recognize him and that would queer the whole thing.

"How much closer," asked Johnny, "will this get us to Viktor Baumann?"

It was the same question Jury had asked himself. "It won't is my guess. On the other hand, it might. But that's not the main issue, is it? The kids are."

"The thing is, you won't get to first base, I mean, if it's your plan to —"

"It is."

"If you think . . . Look, anyone who sees one of those kids does so only with the blessing of Viktor Baumann."

Jury smiled. "Well, I have been thus blessed."

# 39

"I want you to stay in the car until I give the word."

Jury had told Cody about the warrant that morning.

"If this DI — is it Blakeley? — if he couldn't squeeze a warrant out of a judge after all the time and effort he's spent on this Hester Street house, how did you manage?"

"I didn't."

Cody frowned. "You're going in without one?"

"I am. Not the best career move, but it seems to be the only way to get in that house."

It was an ordinary-looking terraced house of brown brick in a row of others, and the only differences between them were the window curtains — lace, muslin, cotton — and the color of the front door, in this case, blue. The car sat across the street and down four houses.

He had given Cody breakfast that morning or, rather, Carole-anne had. She loved doing fry-ups in Jury's kitchen. It surprised him that Carole-anne liked to cook, liked to feed people and liked to eat. Boy, could she eat! Where those calories went to, God only knew. She must have had the metabolism of the cat Cyril. She could certainly bend herself into equally exquisite positions.

The kitchen was too small; they were eating in the living room, Carole-anne handing them their plates full of sausage, eggs and grilled tomato before cooking her own. Stone had followed Cody in and now lay at his feet, or, rather, at a point midway between his and Jury's, uncertain of where his loyalty should lie.

That's when Jury had told Cody about the warrant. Or lack of one.

Carole-anne had overheard this and said, "Don't you have to have one of them?" She stood, spatula in one hand, plate in the other.

"What?" said Jury.

"Warrants."

"Forget you heard any of this." Jury cut off a bite of egg.

"But don't you?"

"Yes," said Cody. "You do." He broke off a piece of sausage and gave it to Stone.

"Well, then, why're you going in this place without one?" Hand with spatula now on hip. She was indignant. In a sudden shaft of sunlight that fell across the room like a lance, her hair blazed as if it, too, would conflagrate under this outrage.

Jury sighed. "This is none of your business, Carole-anne. Forget it."

"Oh, I see. Well, just wait till you're in the nick and wanting visitors. That'll be none of my business, either." She wheeled and flounced back into the kitchen.

Jury called after her: "I could use some more sausage."

"Go kill a pig, then." Amid the clattering of pans and dishes she added, "It ain't none of *my* business."

Cody snickered and fed Stone another bite of sausage.

Then Carole-anne was back with the pan of sausages, two of which she rolled onto Jury's plate. "To say nothing of when you lose your job!" Now there was the segue into the hardscrabble lives here in Gerrard Road. Jury, Cody and Stone chewed their sausage and looked at her.

"The thing is, if you go to prison, well, Mrs. Wasserman won't set foot outside her door; you know how she is when you're not here. Oh, I'd probably be all right except for who gets your flat. *That's* really something to think about." Willing, apparently, to think about it right now, she sat down beside Jury, spatula still at the ready, raised like a little flag. "It could be somebody really dangerous, like a stalker, or some other crazy, like someone in a white jacket who says he's an orderly at that hospital you were in, but he's really the serial killer who's been euthanizing patients —"

Cody was fascinated; Jury thought of Nurse Bell.

"— who would probably do us in as we slept."

"Don't change the lock, then," said Jury. "You have a key and that way you could come in and look around, go through the stalker's stalking equipment or inspect the scalpels and hypodermics belonging to the hospital crazy."

She went on as if he hadn't spoken. "Or it could be some old slag from Soho or King's Cross with men popping in every ten minutes, or we might get a drug dealer that'd turn this place into a crack house. Well, we can't depend on Stan as he's away most of the time." Now she turned to Cody, busy eating his egg on toast. "And it wouldn't surprise me" — here she shook the spatula at him — "if all this was your idea."

Cody stopped chewing, eyebrows raised.

"It isn't," Jury said. "It's totally my own." He smiled and then poked some fried egg in his mouth. "So forget what we were talking about. The less you know the better." That, he thought, was chilling enough.

"Oh, *nice*." She got up and turned her head and started venting at the ceiling. "Bloody nice, that is, now I'm to be questioned and Mrs. Wasserman, too, I expect. So you've drawn us into your little scheme and now we're to be accessories!"

Jury looked from her to his plate and back. "Any more sausages?"

Cody objected. "I'm coming in." He started to open the passengerside door.

Jury shook his head. "No. If two of us try it, we won't get past the front door. Think about it, for God's sakes."

Cody nodded. "You're right. But —" He turned almost beseeching eyes on Jury, as if this were something he had to do.

"Don't worry. You'll know."

The woman who opened the door he presumed to be Irene Murchison. He had formed in his mind an indistinct picture of this woman running along the lines of the thin, hard-looking, tight-lipped house-keeper of Manderley. But she wasn't. Mrs. Murchison was portly, her complexion rosy, her eyes an unclouded blue. A cheap gold chain round her neck secured her glasses when she wasn't wearing them. She had brown hair, going to gray, rolled back from her face and neck and secured by pins, one of which she reached up to affix in its place. She was such an ordinary-looking woman, Jury thought it was almost scary. "Yes?"

The tone, Jury thought, was one of gentle inquiry. Beneath it there was no hint of misgiving. "Mrs. Murchison?"

"Yes?"

Jury had to go deep inside himself for a response he had to force himself to make. He settled for a smile he had trouble getting any warmth into. "May I come in? Mr. Baumann sent me."

That did get him through the door, but it did not get him recognition. She looked perplexed as she opened the door wider. They stood in a dimly lit hallway where a long, ornate wooden table was pushed up against busy floral wallpaper of tiny flowers and vines. "I don't believe I know the gentleman. Baumann, is that what you said?"

"Yes, that's right."

"And you've come about — ?"

Still playing the innocent. Well, he hadn't expected her to acknowledge the company she and Baumann kept. "About your coin collection. I understand it's quite something."

She smiled. "Oh, *that* Mr. Baumann. The collector. Of course, of course. Won't you come into the lounge?"

He followed her into the room at the left which was as ordinary as its owner. Unattractive furniture upholstered in dark brown and scorched gold, as if it had been rubbed too much by the sun. There were cups and saucers on one of the shelves that announced their provenance as Bognor Regis and Blackpool, A PRESENT FROM . . . written in gold across their surfaces. On a round mahogany table were a number of framed pictures. What she had come in here for was a large velvet-lined box that held perhaps fifty or sixty coins on the top shelf, clearly more on deeper ones.

"Tell me," she said, "if you were looking for any coin in particular."

That was it, Jury thought, the coded question. He studied the coins, hearing Baumann's voice: "I've only seen two of those since I started collecting." Centered on the top shelf was a coin identical to the one in the paperweight on Baumann's desk. "I see you have a Greek Tetradrachms."

"Ah, yes, a handsome coin. Quite valuable."

But it wasn't, not according to Baumann. He was surprised she hadn't been better schooled. This whole numismatist gig was what kept her running smoothly. On the other hand, why should she be as knowledgeable as Baumann? Nobody was coming for the coins.

Jury commented on the framed pictures. "Lovely girls."

"Do you mean my nieces?"

That's what she was calling these girls, then. "Yes, that's right."

From his wallet, he pulled out the card that Baumann had given him to give his secretary, Grace. He wondered how Baumann had found the Murchison woman. And was it Baumann himself (who Jury was sure could be incredibly charming to women), or was it the money (which must be ample) or was it the power? Imagine having dominion over eight or ten children; imagine holding their fates in your hand.

All of this came and went in a flash in the act of handing over the card. She raised her glasses to her eyes and read it. Jury knew the brief directive by heart:

*Give Mr. Jury whatever he wants.*
*VB.*

And on the other side was the usual wording of a business card.

Mrs. Murchison looked up at him. "I see. Yes, I'd be happy to help you. Won't you sit down for a moment while we discuss your, ah, preferences?"

Now she was smiling. He supposed she got a cut, a percentage, rather than a straight salary, or in addition to it. Considering the risks the woman was taking, it would be a sizable amount. But did she expect Viktor Baumann to come to her aid if the place was raided? Not bloody likely.

As he sat down on a love seat upholstered in a rough brown fabric, Jury said, "You seem to have a lot of responsibility here."

She had taken a matching chair and now nodded, smiling.

Pleased as punch, thought Jury.

"Yes, I'm wholly responsible; I'm on my own, except for a cook and someone who comes in every day to deal with problems. After all, a child can be, well, obstreperous. Do you have children, Mr. Jury?'

Jury tried to govern his expression, to make his face blank or bland, to freeze the little muscles around his mouth. Why this woman didn't sense it, the all-but-engulfing desire to strike out at her, he didn't know. It could be a total lack of both imagination and empathy. "No, I don't." Thank God was his thought at this moment. "I'm wondering about your fee."

"That depends, really."

On what possible what? How did one measure? He said nothing, merely waited.

"It's fifty pounds for the half hour, seventy-five for the hour." She smoothed her skirt, happy to have the transaction in her court. "Except if you want two girls, then add on another thirty."

Like a cab ride. Extra fare, mate? That'll be another quid, ta very much.

"There's age, too. What do you prefer in that regard?"

She leaned forward in her chair, looking at him with glittering eyes, looking in a beckoning way.

This transaction *excited* her. And he thought, of course, to take this sort of risk, one that could bring Johnny Blakeley to your door, anytime, day or night, prison looming, it would have to be for more than money, more than wanting to please Baumann. She would have to be attracted by the job itself.

Johnny had held forth at length about pedophiles and how they claimed what they felt for these children was love, pure and simple.

"Perhaps we could have a look."

He loved that "we."

She reached to a little table beside the chair and picked up a small brass bell that actually tinkled. Jury heard the sound of something sliding and another of what sounded like furniture being moved around. In less than a minute a girl stood in the doorway of the lounge. She looked fifteen or sixteen, tallish, blond hair held back by a pink velvet band, and looking at Jury. Hard as nails. He wondered how long she had been here. Years, he bet.

"Samantha," said Irene Murchison, "let's have April and Rosie in here."

What benign names. He thought of gardens — Heligan, Angel Gate, even the rear garden of the Islington house, not a garden at all except for the little patch of iris that Mrs. Wasserman tended in the mellow months of spring and summer. He thought of that when he heard the name "Rosie."

The girl said, "Yes, Mrs. Murchison," in a dead tone. She might have been sleep-walking.

Again, Irene Murchison leaned toward him with that glittering look. "Rosie just came to us. She's our little one; she's new. You know what I mean?"

The tall girl was back, one child on each side. The little one, who was probably five, perhaps six, looked at him curiously and stuck her thumb in her mouth. It was as if she had no inkling that the look of this man could snag her and cut her to pieces. Her look was almost expectant, as if there could be a treat for her in this transaction, that the man might have boiled sweets in his pocket.

The girl on the other side of Samantha, eight or nine, looked scared. For her to move even closer to the tall girl, who was without sympathy, affectless, only showed Jury how frightened April was. Samantha pushed her away and told her to stand up straight, which only made the younger one more frightened still. April mashed her face into Samantha's side. Samantha shoved her off. She had probably started out like these girls.

Now she was a handler.

Jury thought the suffering of the other girls was a consolation to her. Either that or a way to reenter their world, but this time with control. With power. She would become another Irene Murchison eventually, unless something stopped her. The poor girl was beautiful; he doubted she knew it or, if she did, didn't care or even resented her beauty because look, after all, what it had done for her. Sod-all.

"What do you think?"

"They seem very nice, but —"

Mrs. Murchison nodded briefly at Samantha and the older girl led the others away. "You'd like to see the others, then?"

"I would, yes."

"Then let's just go round to the girls' room; yes, that's the easiest way."

Jury rose with her and they left the front room and reentered the dim hallway that led from the foyer to the back of the house. The long table was pulled out from the wall. The sliding sound he had first heard came from a pocket door in the wall. But it was measured and papered to look exactly like the rest of the wall and was, hence, all but invisible; that accounted for the pattern of the wallpaper. The room itself, when they'd stepped into it, was very narrow but very long. From the outside, he doubted anyone could tell this room was here, except one might wonder at the lack of a window. A person looking for a secret room might discover it. Otherwise, anyone on the other side of this patterned wall could languish here forever. It was like a hideous fairy tale. Well, then, he was going to be the prince, kids, like it or not.

Jury did not know what he had expected — strident voices, unruly behavior, the place a mess? He was not prepared for this silence, this orderly, neat room. Ten little girls, including the two Samantha had returned here (she herself being gone) were either sitting on their cots, each cot looking freshly made, or standing by them. Rosie stood at the end of this room with an older girl, older merely by virtue of being ten or eleven. The girl was holding Rosie's hand. April, the other girl brought into the lounge by Samantha, stood by the first bed. She and the other girls looked at Jury and then immediately dropped their eyes. He could tell from the tensing of their bodies they wanted to run. Fight or flight. Neither was possible here. They probably hoped that if they kept their eyes lowered, if they didn't look at him, he would not then look at them. They would be invisible, like the invisible line in the wallpaper on the other side.

Where did they come from? Had they been lost? Had they been lured? Had they been sold? Abandoned? Wandering the streets? Abducted from playgrounds, public parks or paths? How many children went missing and stayed missing in this country every year?

He looked down the row of beds and half expected to see Flora. Of course, Flora in the pictures he'd seen had been four. Now she would be seven, and that could have made a big change. He looked from face to face. With their shuttered eyes they reminded him of the stone effigies of children he'd seen in churches and cathedrals, the titled ones, dead at an early age, lying beside the stone duke or duchess. He remembered the two he had seen in a Hertfordshire church — little girls with their stone hands clasped. What had killed them? Disease? Fire? A stray shot? A fall from a roof or high window? What? He was reminded of this looking at the two at the back, Rosie and the older girl who had been holding her hand.

It was Rosie who broke away and did a skipping sort of run toward him while the older girl called "Rosie!" But Rosie stood there and gaily asked: "Can I go upstairs? Everybody gets to but me."

He looked down at her. "Yes, of course." Then he looked at the girl who was so protective and who looked now beside herself with misery. "And her," said Jury nodding toward the one at the back.

"Pansy!" Mrs. Murchison called her.

She came quickly, looking almost relieved that she could go with Rosie. It startled him that even in such dire circumstances as these and at danger to herself, she could still feel protective. But then hadn't he seen instances of this in adults, too? A man rushing into a burning building to save a stranger? It was what he had faith in, he suddenly realized, glad he had faith in something.

"Pansy's been with us for two years, haven't you, dear?"

Did the woman honestly think Pansy would look at her with affection? Pansy didn't look at all.

Every time this woman opened her mouth, Jury wanted to shut it by force. Every word she spoke poisoned the air around them. She called for Samantha again.

Samantha gestured for Jury to precede her; she told him to take the third room on the left. It would have made more sense for her to go ahead with the two girls, but it was clear why she didn't. Mrs. Murchison wouldn't want to make the client uncomfortable by having him witness to any struggle, any holding back of the girls. Jury could hear behind him that something like that was just what was going on between Pansy and Samantha. Finally, though, they all reached the third door and Pansy had been sorted. Now she took little Rosie's hand and they went into the bedroom. Jury followed.

The room was large, the furniture dark and heavy, just like the furniture downstairs. Never a child's room, but then it was not a child's life. He remembered houses he'd seen in one investigation or another, the little girls' rooms — pink walls, pink comforter, soft stuffed animals, white organdy — a room dressed like a ballerina. Never this. Before they sat down, Pansy walked stonily to a closet, opened the door and waited. For him, apparently. He walked round the foot of the bed and up to where she stood, thinking he was to hang his clothes in here. No, that wasn't it. What he was looking at was an assortment of little clothes. Costumes was more like it. It was a walk-in closet. He walked in, shoved the hangers back and forth, saw a gingham dress with an apron and a small rolling pin hanging on a cord, a sailor suit, a bright red tiny bikini, a black evening gown. Vast differences. Pansy watched apprehensively. He looked at her and shook his head. He walked out and shut the door. He had not yet removed his coat, which was lined with fleece and warm. But he wouldn't do it now, right this moment. Disrobing in any way, even removing a coat, would look like a threat.

Rosie was humming and stomping around, playing some private game, until Pansy grabbed her hand and whispered for her to stop. Rosie stuck her thumb in her mouth again.

At least there were a few trappings of what should have been a kid's world: books. Several were lined up on a freestanding bookshelf of the sort one sees sitting outside a book dealer's in good weather. Jury searched the shelf, hoping they were genuinely children's books that didn't hide among their pages some sort of pornography. He ran his fingers along the spines until he came to Maurice Sendak. He smiled. Maurice Sendak was surely the greatest thing to happen to children since the stamping out of smallpox. And Maurice Sendak's kids did a fair amount of stamping and stomping around. Rosie would love it.

They hadn't moved; they still held hands. Jury held up the book. "Let's read."

Gravely, Pansy looked down at her flowered frock, its puffed sleeves and smocking.

Jury shook his head. "No changing clothes, Pansy. We're going to stay in the clothes we stand up in." He smiled. "We're going to read a story, maybe two stories, and that's all we're going to do."

When she saw the cover of the book, Rosie jumped up and down and broke from Pansy's grasp. He could almost read Pansy's mind. A trick, a trick. It had to be a trick, a new awful game, everybody taking off his clothes. It would come clear in a few moments.

There was a bench beneath a window that faced the street and its dreary view of the terraced houses on the other side. Jury sat down and gestured to the girls to sit down. Pansy sat Rosie on the end of the bench and stationed herself between Jury and the little girl. It was the only heartening thing he'd seen in this place, Pansy protecting the new littlest girl. It could so easily have gone the other way; Pansy could so easily have turned, after two years, into another Samantha.

Jury opened the book and showed them

the first illustration. He read what text there was, surprised the story was about a vanished child. Maybe Sendak was better equipped to solve this case than police.

"Next page." He wanted the girls to turn the pages. Pansy was unaware of this, afraid it was part of this awful game, or what would soon become the awful game, a game of which she hadn't been told the rules.

Rosie stepped closer and turned the page, mashed it back as if it were the only way of controlling it. Jury continued to read and Rosie and at last Pansy turned the pages properly, and the story, like the child, was revealed.

Jury couldn't have said which of the three of them was the most enthralled. He had read most of Maurice Sendak's books, read them standing around Waterstone's or Dillards or Hatchards. This artist knew more about children than any social worker he'd ever talked to.

Rosie was extremely worried about the goblins. She did not like the goblins and was nervously looping her yellow hair round her finger. That reminded him of Lulu, only Lulu's hair was dark and uncurlable.

Most of the way through the book, perhaps reminded of the cold by the storm brewing in the pages, Jury felt the room was chilly. He hadn't noticed before because of his fleece-lined coat. Looking at what might be called an ornamental fireplace, he saw a small electric heater in the grate. It had two bars, neither of them red.

"Aren't you kids cold?"

Pansy answered. "I'm always cold in this house."

Jury took off his coat and held it first for Pansy to put an arm in the right-hand sleeve, then for Rosie to put her arm through the left. Now they were joined together. Rosie giggled. Even Pansy looked pleased. They held the coat tight around themselves.

They told Jury to finish reading the story, and he did, with Rosie standing and Pansy sitting, awkwardly maneuvering the coat between the two of them. They looked, for the first time, warm.

The goblins brought in a baby made of ice to replace Ida's baby sister. The ice, of course, started melting and Rosie didn't like that at all. Pansy told her not to worry; it'd all come right in the end. It did. Ida had to go out and rescue the real baby from the goblins, which she did, and vowed that she would always take proper care of the baby from here on in.

Pansy looked at the book after Jury finished speaking. Then she thought awhile as Rosie wavered from one foot to another as if she had to pee. Childless himself, Jury hadn't that much experience of children, but he thought it was rare for one to sit and ponder a problem.

Pansy said, "I know what happened."

For one starburst moment, he thought she was going to offer a solution to this case for him, tell him what had happened to Flora.

She said, "The older sister was supposed to take care of the baby, but she didn't. Probably she wanted the goblins to get the baby." Pansy paused. "It's like Samantha, only Samantha stopped with the goblins. And stayed."

"The baby ran off." Rosie piped up. "I will, too."

"No," said Pansy. "It didn't run off; it was stolen. And you can't run off, anyway, Rosie, so stop thinking about it."

"I can. I can sneak into the hall when she's not looking. Then I can open the door, like Alice did, and run. I can." Rosie was on the verge of tears.

Alice. Jury felt his heart lurch. "What happened to Alice, then?"

Rosie came closer, put her hand on Jury's knee, and whispered, "She ran into the street and got —"

"Rosie! We're not to talk about it!"

Pansy looked genuinely scared. No wonder.

"I don't care!" said Rosie.

Jury asked, "Was it Samantha who ran after her?" Another child.

Rosie nodded hard.

Pansy clamped her hands over her ears, wanting to hear none of this.

"Okay," said Jury. "We won't talk about it."

Rosie nearly wept. "But I can, I can." She was still back with running away.

He put his hand on her yellow head and ruffled the hair. "I know *you* can. I don't think you'll have to."

Pansy looked at him, puzzled.

Rosie had picked up *Where the Wild Things Are* and was stuffing it into Jury's hands.

"One of my favorites," he said. Actually, it was. "Okay. Sit down." This time there was one child on each side (only Rosie in the coat now, looking very much like a Sendak child) and both of them were leaning against him as he read the tale of Timmy and the grotesquely funny monsters, whom Timmy set out to sea for and joined. When they all started cavorting around, Pansy and Rosie got up and imitated them. The two girls copied the expressions of the wild things, made their hands into claws and stalked each other. And nearly fell down giggling.

"Now listen to me; here's what I want you to do."

They drew close.

"In a minute we're going downstairs, the three of us. It's important you both look very tired and sad."

"I'm not," said Rosie. "I'm not sad." She picked up the first book lying on the bench beside Jury. "You could read this again. Only leave out about the ice baby."

She did not want to go downstairs.

"Why don't you take it with you?"

"Okay, I will. But I'm still not sad."

"*Pretend*," said Pansy. "He means to *pretend*, Rosie."

"That's right. If you don't look upset, Mrs. Murchison will wonder and we don't want that. We need five minutes to get ready. What about the other girls, Pansy?"

"We always have to stay in that room. There's a telly but we mostly fight about what to watch. There's games and stuff, but we don't feel like playing. The only times we get to leave the room is when we eat and when we get to go out in back for fifteen minutes."

Rosie was making a face over one of the illustrations. "I didn't like breakfast. The eggs were all runny."

"We get to eat at a table in the kitchen, three of us at a time and Samantha sits with us, or Eddie. He's horrible. They're supposed to watch us so we don't cause trouble. But Samantha does let us talk as long as we don't get too loud. Only, there's not much to talk about except — you know — bad stuff, and nobody wants to talk about that. It's too scary."

It was the deepest blush Jury had ever seen. Pansy looked down at the floor, ashamed.

Jury said, "It's okay, Pansy. You've done nothing wrong. It's they who've done it. How many girls are here now?"

"There's nine. I counted them," said Rosie. She was frowning at another page, probably at the ice baby.

"There's ten," said Pansy. "You left yourself out."

"I don't like the food," she said again, in case they'd forgotten.

Jury asked, "Does Mrs. Murchison really start the girls this early?" He was looking at Rosie.

"Yes. But Rosie's the youngest. Me, I was seven." Again, Pansy's face went hot red, like the bars of the stingy electric heater.

"You've been here two years?" Jury tried to sound matter-of-fact; he didn't want her feeling any more ashamed than she already did.

Still, she looked anywhere but at Jury. Then she said, "Samantha's been here five. April's been here three. Longer than me."

"All right, listen. Rosie, listen to me." Rosie popped her face out of the book and pretended to. "After we go downstairs, I want you both to go back to your room and tell the others to put on their coats —"

Pansy was astonished. "But they only let us have them when we go outside; she keeps the coats somewhere in a closet. We go out back in the garden for fifteen minutes. There's no flowers, though. It's got a high fence."

"Does Samantha watch you?"

"Her and this man Eddie —" She looked as if she wanted to spit. "Both watch us. They tell us to play, but we just sit. There's nothing to play with and we're too tired anyway. So we sit on the steps or stand by the fence. It's all we do. It makes Eddie mad. I don't know why."

"It's all about control. Only now, we're the ones controlling things. Do you have blankets on your beds?"

She nodded.

"Then tell the girls to bring them to wrap themselves up when they get outside."

Her eyes widened, this time with recognition, and although she worked her mouth, she could hardly speak. They were going out; they were leaving this place. "How can you . . . how can we — ?"

Jury took out his warrant card. "I'm a policeman." Wide eyed, Pansy slapped her hands on her face, staring at him. Even Rosie raised her eyes from the book to look. He went on, "There's another policeman in a car outside. We're getting you girls out. All of you are going to leave, if you're careful to do what I tell you."

Rosie went back to looking at the book. Into this brief and frozen silence she said, "I think I'll be an ice baby. They only melt." She paused and looked at Jury almost beseechingly. "It's better than getting stolen." She was looking at Jury for confirmation of this hard decision.

"It's better not being either." Jury took out the cell phone and punched in the number. "Wait ten minutes and come in." He snapped the phone shut.

Going down the stairs, Pansy and Rosie were putting on a show, Pansy looking desperate and holding her arms across her stomach, Rosie doing a good job of pretend weeping. He wanted to applaud them both.

It made Mrs. Murchison, standing at the bottom of the stairs, smile. She gave Rosie a little slap on her bottom, saying, "Now go on with you, girl. You're all right."

The two, without so much as another look at Jury, pulled the table out, slid the door back and went into their prison room.

Mrs. Murchison said, "That's over the half hour, so I'll have to charge you for the whole hour." She beamed as he drew out his wallet, brought out two fifty-pound notes. Then she added, in a whisper, "But I expect it was worth it."

Years in the job had taught Jury incredible self-mastery. Otherwise, he would have killed her where she stood. He handed over the hundred. It was the transaction; he wanted money to change hands. If this ever had a flaming chance of coming to court. Then his years of self-mastery melted away like the ice baby. He flipped his ID open, shoved it close to her face.

"*What?* Police?" She backed away. "You can't walk into a person's house like this. Where's your warrant? You never showed me any warrant —"

He slammed her up against the wall. "This is my warrant!"

She flailed, arms going everywhere.

"Wait till my solicitor — I'll be screaming police brutality, you just wait!"

The little girls, each with her blanket, were filing out of the back room with looks that ranged from joy to utter disbelief. When they saw Jury with his forearm cutting across Murchison's throat, they stopped dead.

Jury let her go.

"Eddie!" she yelled.

The girls were dithering, beginning to laugh.

Jury looked around to see a thin man snaking round the other side of the staircase, apparently come from the kitchen. He was pointing a .45 at him. "Okay, mate. Back off."

Jury dropped his arm and stepped back. The girls on that side of the staircase backed off, too. Jury could understand why: Eddie was one of the meanest-looking men he had ever seen, with a long pocked face, testament to an old battle with acne, and a nose and mouth that looked thin and sharp as knives.

"You okay, Murch?"

Murch was better than okay. With renewed fervor and a few tugs at dress and corset, she strided in *in medias res:* "Coming in here without a warrant, just you wait, when Mr. Baum—" She stopped, realizing she had named him. "We'll have your badge and your job and don't be surprised when we drag you and the whole Metropolitan Police Force into court! Here you are, giving all them a bad name!"

Jury smiled. "Maybe, but it was worth it."

Eddie let fly with a little invective of his own, happy in the knowledge that he had the only gun.

Only he hadn't.

What Jury had taken for a shadow deep in the stairwell wasn't a shadow. Cody? Had he had the prescience to go around —

A gun fired and Eddie looked surprised and started to turn when another shot caught him in the turn and he slithered to the floor, a strand of blood snaking down his chin.

Mrs. Murchison yelled. The little girls moved forward in a wave.

Samantha stood there behind Eddie with

the gun at her side looking at Jury not with her earlier cold detachment, but helplessly involved.

Mrs. Murchison made the mistake of opening her mouth. "You! Wait till he gets ahold of you! You'll be sorry —"

The gun came up again but this time the shot was thwarted by ten little girls swarming between Mrs. Murchison and Samantha. They yelled, sang her name jumping up and down like the wild things in the book. *"Samantha, Samantha, Samantha!"*

She had saved them all; she had saved the day. Some were weeping with joy.

Jury moved through them to take the gun from Samantha's hand. Her face, skin the color of porcelain, looked crazed, as if it might come apart at any moment. He put his arm around her, her head on his shoulder. "It's all right, Samantha. Everything will be all right now. Look, you've saved all of us."

The ring of the bell had changed to a relentless pounding on the door. Pansy went to open it. She seemed near gleeful that a stranger stood there.

Cody walked in. "What the hell, guv? What the hell's been going on?"

He was immediately surrounded by little

469

girls, two of them swinging on his hands.

Jury didn't answer the question; he saw that Mrs. Murchison was edging into the lounge, which she could very quickly lock. The telephone was in there. "Cody!" He nodded toward her.

Cody made a lunge that had them both on the parlor floor. The kids whooped and hollered as if it was the most fun they'd had in years. It probably was. Cody got up, yanked her up without a care for ripping the silk and shoved her against the wall in the same lock that Jury had had on her a few minutes ago.

The kids started in again, this time with *"Cody, Cody, Cody, Cody."* Another savior. How many saviors were there and all at once? There seemed to be no limit to freedom. They were swinging their blankets in the air like small matadors.

"Hey, guv?"

"What?" said Jury, who was bundling Samantha into his coat. She was clearly in shock.

"Should I restrain her?"

"Of course."

"No cuffs, no rope, okay." He shrugged and delivered a right to the Murchison chin that sent her down the wall like Eddie, only still alive. Worse luck. Cody beamed.

The girls shouted. Better and better. What other delights were in store? Rosie was jumping up and down like a cork.

With Murchison "restrained," Cody said hello to the girls and held out his arms. They fairly flew at him, but he was strong and they couldn't get past.

Jury smiled. Cody Platt, snooker player, copper, catcher in the rye.

# 40

Chief Superintendent Racer was all over it: his nemesis, Richard Jury, like Richard the Second and Richard Nixon before him had been, so to speak, relieved of their command, that is, suspended, so was Jury to be just about any day now, pending further investigation.

Jury was in Racer's outer office with Fiona. He was studying the cat Cyril — definitely not a quick study — and said, "He likens it to a deposition or a dethronement, doesn't he?"

"Hasn't been in this good a humor since he made chief," said Fiona. " 'Flagrant abuse of police protocol,' indeed!" That was from some memo or other that had crossed her desk. She had said it so many times, she had memorized it. "Shocking, that is. Absolutely shocking! Makes me sick, it does." To indicate the scope of her shock and sickness, Fiona zipped up her sponge bag without even applying powder and blush. All she had done was to skim on a little lipstick, merely tipping her hat to beauty. The bag she shoved into a lower drawer. "And you can tell how upset Cyril is."

Actually, Jury couldn't. Cyril was at the moment engaged in his morning toilette, second only to Fiona's in time consumed. It was as if he were licking each ginger hair into cat-dander resplendence. Dander, he had once told Fiona, was in the saliva, not the fur. He had no idea how he knew this, never having owned a cat or a dog. He felt suddenly bereft, as if they had all up and died on him.

"I think I'll get a dog — I mean, if I'm going to be home a lot."

Cyril stopped in his labors and looked up sharply.

Fiona whispered, "Why'd you have to go and say that in front of Cyril? You know how he is."

No one knew how Cyril was. Cyril was too smart by half, smarter than Racer, but then that only took half. The decision to park Jury by the side of an unmapped road had been taken with amazing swiftness. Well, there wasn't much doubt he'd done what he'd done. In any event, he played his own role up in this grievous "flagrant abuse of police power" and played Cody Platt's role down. Jury had said he didn't see why there had to be an investigation at all, as he was willing to admit to his part in bringing the Murchison woman and her cohort Eddie Noon to their knees. Literally. But someone had to put his imprimatur upon the affair. Someone had to set the seal.

Jury worried about Cody, for he was of course part of it, though not as big a part. But as far as Jury was concerned it had been worth it. He knew Cody felt so too, perhaps even more than Jury did. The most worrisome thing was whether they could drag Baumann into court. Whether Murchison would give him up. Or indeed what would be admissible in Irene Murchison's case, considering the "premises" had been unlawfully "breached." That stuff had been going on for years; a little girl had been shot who had run from the house. There was probable cause for the police to enter the house, Jury thought, not, however, unwarranted.

As of now Jury sat unsuspended, here with Fiona, enjoying the click of computer keys, the snap of a compact (she having second thoughts about her shock and sickness) and Cyril washing. He was about to submerge himself into Yeats's "cold companionable streams" when Racer came through the door.

"For someone who's about to be suspended, you're spending a lot of time on your backside around here looking happy."

"I can't seem to tear myself away."

"Ha! Well, enjoy it while you can, Jury — 'this realm, this plot, this blah blah blah.' "

" 'This England.' You're certainly up on your Shakespeare."

Racer continued to treat Jury's possible suspension like a dethronement, as if Jury were handing over his crown to Bolingbroke. He gestured with his arm like a theater usher, hurrying Jury into his aisle seat. Jury hesitated for two seconds, giving the cat Cyril his chance to get in and get on with it. What really kept Cyril going was not Jury's smile or Fiona's sponge bag or tins of sardines, but Chief Superintendent Racer's ongoing attempts to trap him with elaborate, Rube Goldberg cartoon inventions. It would be for a human something like watching the Pyramids being built, stone by stone, just for you. Yes, Cyril's was a bracing life, a life lived on the edge — quite literally, as one of his favorite perches was the molding around the tiny recessed lights Racer had had installed when his office was remodeled as Harry's Bar and Grill. Jury saw the tip of a ginger tail twitching up there (no one knew how he managed to get up there in the first place) while Cyril plotted and looked down to see what Racer had planned for him.

"The Cornwall business. It's of no more interest to us, so stay out of it."

"Oh, but it is of interest. Viktor Baumann's involved there, too."

"If you're talking about these children, that's part of Organized Crime, that's SO1, the pedophilia unit. Isn't that your friend Blakeley's case? Over in West Central? Before you stuck your oar in?"

"My oar was little Alice Smith, the child shot in the back. That's my case, if you remember. This is all down to Viktor Baumann. God knows what else he's been getting up to. I'm just hoping he doesn't have more houses like that one. The Devon and Cornwall police think he might have abducted his daughter three years ago —"

Racer interrupted. "That's nothing to do with us. You closed the Alice Smith case. The child was shot by one of the other girls. The same girl who murdered the pimp" — he fussed a manila folder around until he came to it — "Eddie Noon. Got charges as long as your arm. This girl's pretty good at shooting people in the back, isn't she?"

Jury winced. Was the man laughing over this? Racer, for the moment, sobered up. "God, but what's it coming to, kids killing kids?"

"She probably saved my life." What was going to happen to Samantha? Anything'd be better than what it was before. Just to be rid of her, just to be rid of her . . . Samantha had repeated it like a litany. She had actually smiled.

Unable to fix on an appropriate response to Jury's saved life, Racer mumbled something and put the folder in his out box. "So we're shut of this, Jury."

"No, we aren't. Part of it's still open — as I've been saying —"

"That part is Devon and Cornwall police. As for you, my lad, pending further inquiry —"

He was a broken record. Jury stopped listening and watched Cyril, who had maneuvered himself around the room in the cat-size space (it might as well have been purpose built) between the wall and the outer edge of molding. He was now sitting in his favorite spot over Racer's desk. This

477

was the spot from which he'd made many three-point landings onto various parts of the desk. He sat now washing his paw and waiting his moment.

How many ways could Jury say it? The man had cloth ears. "As I've said — sir — the missing —" or dead, Jury didn't add "— child is Viktor Baumann's daughter. She was four years old. One of the reasons I went into that house was to see if he was keeping her there."

"What? The man's own *child?*" Racer washed at the air with his hands, palms out as if to keep Jury and Jury's sick ideas at bay.

"It goes on."

"In the States it goes on. Not here."

This earth, this realm, this England.

Sure.

Johnny Blakeley was still stationed at West End Central where part of the pedophilia unit was housed. It was there that Irene Murchison had been taken. She'd been in one of the interrogation rooms off and on over the last thirty-six hours. They could hold her on a score of charges; she was "garbage," Johnny said. What Johnny was after was an admission that the whole setup was Viktor Baumann's.

"Hell of a setup it is, too," Johnny was telling Jury an hour later over drinks in the Crown. "Viktor's friends — well, she didn't tell me precisely that, but it's obvious, isn't it? 'Very particular gentlemen.' Her words. The woman talks like she just stepped out of a Galsworthy novel, which is not, I hasten to add, her real milieu."

"These 'gentlemen' — meaning 'customers'? I'm thick today, as I just left Racer's office."

Johnny snickered. "It's Viktor's mates, isn't it? The ring. I want some names, man. How can this woman be willing to take the fall for this, Richard?"

"Women have been doing it for centuries."

"Hell, she's got to be twenty years older than him."

Jury shrugged. "She's a pivotal character in his life; she sees the whole thing runs smoothly; she keeps the girls in line." More like scared into submission. Jury could not forget the deathly quiet when he looked into that room. The unearthly silence. No child should be frightened into silence. "She's not doing this against her better judgment, remember. She likes it. She likes it a lot." Jury drank off his lager.

Johnny signed to the barman, held up two fingers. The barman nodded. "She's not giving him up, Rich," he said again.

"She admitted she knew him, though." Jury was watching a desultory game of snooker between one man covered in tattoos and another who had a musician's fingers. The musician lobbed the green ball into a pocket. Smatttering of applause. He thought of Wiggins and Cody Platt. He said, "I didn't screw everything up for you, Johnny, did I?"

The barman knifed foam off Johnny's Guinness. "My God, no," Johnny said. "What you and that Cornwall cowboy did was pretty much what I've been trying to work out how to do for months. Well, now we're sorted." Johnny smiled broadly, lifted his pint as if in a toast.

Cowboy. Jury smiled, as he lifted his.

When Jury walked into the lab, Phyllis Nancy was speaking into a mike suspended above the table in the middle of the room. A stream of blood ran from the body along a depression around the table and dripped into a chrome bucket. The cold blue light that emanated from a source he couldn't identify gave the place the look and feel of an outer space experience. She might have been an alien of higher intelligence performing an autopsy on an earthling.

Her hands were covered in blood, but her white coat was as clean as glare ice. He wondered how she managed that trick. But then he remembered that Phyllis knew the parameters of everything, the limits, the boundaries. There was an element of magic in this. Or perhaps it was something not at all magical. Jury (and a number of others) knew that the sight of blood made her sick. Forget med school — nearly everyone there went a little woozy on his or her first encounter with a diced-up body. Only, they got over it. Phyllis hadn't. When she started out, she said as soon as she made the first cut she would have to make for the toilet and throw up. After that she could manage the rest of the autopsy. Soon, she could get through half of the autopsy before she had to throw up, and then nearly all of it until the nausea hit her. Now (she had told Jury) it didn't happen until after she had finished. "It's incredible improvement, considering; one day I'll have tapered off until the nausea has stopped altogether."

Jury had laughed. "You make it sound like giving up smoking."

She considered this. "No, smoking is much harder to give up."

It was all a great joke; Phyllis thought so,

too. A coroner who couldn't stand the sight of blood.

"Why are you in this business, then? It's like Hannibal being afraid of walls or Nelson afraid of water. It's so hard on you, Phyllis."

"Not really. Just a few moments of discomfort. And a little embarrassment, granted."

"You take it all so calmly."

"But so do you when you find a body in the street, like little Alice Smith, facedown in her own blood. You have at least to give the appearance of calm."

Right now, she looked up from the table. He could still tell her eyes were green behind the plastic protective glasses both she and her assistants wore.

"Richard!"

"Hello, Phyllis." He nodded toward the table. "Is this one of your all-nighters?"

"Not now it isn't. I assume you have something in mind."

He smiled. "I do. Dinner. I know you don't eat before an autopsy."

She stripped off the gloves and discarded the mask in one fluid motion, then said to her assistant, "You can finish up."

It was that about Phyllis which made

482

him smile just thinking of it. She could always make you think she'd been waiting for you. And only you.

She started toward him and then stopped, her hand on her chest. For a moment she looked at the floor, then lifted her head and said, "Just wait here. I won't be a tick." And she hurried off.

To the toilet, of course.

They ordered salads to start and duck as an entrée.

While Jury was inspecting the wine list (about which he knew next to nothing) the sommelier arrived with a bottle of burgundy whose wax-sealed cork looked a thousand years old and probably went for a pound for every year.

"Thanks, but we didn't —"

The sommelier smiled and cut him off. "No, sir. This is with Mr. Rice's compliments."

"Oh," said Jury.

"My word," said Phyllis. "How very nice of him."

The sommelier continued: "Mr. Rice asked me to choose after you'd ordered. You're having the duck; I think you'll like this." He applied a straightforward opener to it, twisted and pulled up the cork. Then he poured a little into Jury's glass.

Jury sipped. "It's wonderful."

"Thank you, sir." He poured. He left.

"Mr. Rice," said Phyllis, "must really like you." She frowned a bit. "That name sounds familiar. Do I know him?"

Jury nodded. "You met him. Nell Ryder. Cambridge."

"Of course."

"Vernon Rice was her stepbrother." He looked into his wineglass. "He really loved her. He really did." Why did he keep repeating things lately? As if what he said was too much to say only once. He felt stupid about it. "I called him to get in here tonight. Aubergine usually has bookings weeks ahead."

The waiter had come with their salads, set them before Phyllis and Jury with what seemed invisible hands, come and gone while Jury was saying this. Jury looked at his salad, appetite suddenly gone.

"It's Nell and all of these girls, isn't it?"

"What?" He raised his eyes.

She smiled at him but didn't answer. But the question was strangely comforting. Perhaps he needed some sort of understanding about what he felt. His appetite returned as suddenly as it had left.

She said, "You saved those little girls."

"I might have freed them, but I didn't save them."

"I don't know. It might amount to the same thing, freedom and salvation. You certainly saved them from hell on earth."

"One, maybe. Rosie, her name is. I think she might have been the only one who hadn't yet been flung at some man like a piece of meat. Rosie." He smiled, remembering.

"No one can fling them at any man now, Richard. You took a terrible chance. Your job, your future on the line. Don't tell me you should have done more."

Forking up a piece of lettuce topped by a nut he didn't recognize, Jury said, "I should have done more."

Phyllis sat back in the banquette. "You should have killed this Murchinson woman? Is that what you mean?"

"I almost did. And I'm almost sorry I didn't."

"But she's necessary, isn't she?"

Jury drank his wine. "Yes, I guess so. She's the best link to Baumann, although there are others: the men who patronized the place. She'll give those names up if it means a deal."

"What are you going to do? Do you think you'll need a solicitor or what?"

"I'm not thinking that far ahead. I don't have time for this nonsense about my job. I'm going back to Cornwall in the morning."

She nodded. "Do you think this little girl is still alive, then?"

"A few days ago, I didn't; now I do." He didn't know why; no new evidence had presented itself.

Phyllis looked at her plate. "You're taking this case very personally, aren't you?"

"Maybe. If you got this involved with your work, what in hell would you do?"

She glanced around the room and back at him. "I guess I'd throw up."

# 41

"Very clever, Superintendent," said Viktor Baumann, lighter raised to his cigarette, clicked on and dropped into a vest pocket. He inhaled deeply. "But then I've heard you're a clever man."

Was Jury supposed to ask him how he knew that? Who Baumann's contacts were? Perhaps even someone in the CID informing him? "Not by half, Mr. Baumann. After all, you're still sitting at your desk, comfortably smoking."

Baumann smiled a Byzantine smile that suggested layers upon layers of meaning — charm, sweetness, melt-in-the-mouth flakiness of a French pastry. Nothing in the smile to hint at the cold calculation running it. No wonder he drew women to him — the pretty Mary Scott, Lena Banks, and even the dreadful Irene Murchison. Even, possibly, little girls, until it was too late.

"No reason I shouldn't be. Comfortable,

I mean. Whoever this woman is you have in custody —"

"The 'whoever' clearly knows you."

"Which is not the same as my knowing her, is it?"

"Why would she have done what the business card told her to do if she didn't know the name on it?" Jury had taken it out and dropped it on the desk.

Baumann spread his arms wide, taking in the whole doubting universe. "I've no idea. Did the direction on the card — was it introduced by a 'Dear' — what did you say her name was?"

Damn him. "Irene Murchison."

"Right. Well, did it say, 'Dear Irene,' et cetera?" He leaned forward. "Mr. Jury, if that card was ever brought into evidence, you and the prosecution would be laughed out of court. In case you've forgotten the card's original intention. My secretary Grace would certainly recall it. Shall we have her in?"

Jury gestured, and the hand moved away from the intercom. "What will you say, then, when Irene Murchison talks?"

"The Murchison woman can talk until she's blue in the face. It's nothing to do with me. Also, I hear your own role in this business is highly irregular. I understand there's to be an inquiry." The smile returned.

"What happened to your daughter?" Jury slammed that across the net to wipe the smile off the man's face (which it did) and at most to surprise Baumann into an unguarded response.

"I beg your pardon?" The mock friendliness gave way to true iciness.

"Your daughter, Flora. What happened to her?"

"You know what happened. We've been around on this before."

"True, but you didn't tell me then, either."

"That's ridiculous. She was abducted, as you know."

"By you?"

"Of course not!"

"What about Lena Banks, then?"

"What about her? We were good friends, I'm not denying knowing her. I didn't deny it when you brought her up."

"You used her; she was the one taking the chances, wasn't she?"

Baumann sighed. "Mr. Jury, you are both sentimental and dramatic; you're also overlooking at least one thing. Lena Banks was acting in her own interests, not mine. I'd no idea she'd gone to the Scott place."

"What possible interest could this woman have in Declan Scott or Angel Gate? He didn't know her; no one knew her."

Baumann said, smooth as silk, "You seem to be forgetting the very thing you told me — that Lena Banks was known to Declan Scott under another name. Fox, wasn't it? Georgina Fox? So she did have an interest in Mr. Scott, one I knew nothing about." He sat back, looking pleased with himself.

Jury said nothing. He was close to losing it. Then he thought of little Alice Smith and didn't. "You can be as smug as you like, Mr. Baumann. Irene Murchison won't hold out forever. They never do."

Baumann shook his head, his mouth so tightly drawn he looked as if it could spit bullets. "I'm calling this harassment, Superintendent. I know the commissioner."

"So do I."

For the first time, Baumann looked both uncertain and angry. "You bring up Flora in the context of this pedophile ring. Are you suggesting that I used Flora in this —" He paled.

There it was, the unguarded response. Not that Jury needed to be convinced of Baumann's running this ring, but had he been innocent of it, he wouldn't have made that leap to Flora. He couldn't have; it would be unthinkable that a man would serve his own daughter up on a platter.

He tried to regain his insouciant pose, but he knew he'd put a foot wrong. "What sort of a fool do you think I am?"

Jury leaned closer. "I don't know what sort. I only know you are one. Any man driven by a need, a compulsion is a fool by definition because his ability to act rationally is out the window. You're addicted, Viktor; you're addicted to little kids; you need them as much as a heroin addict needs to shoot up between his toes. You and the men you supply; your ring of pedophiles: I'll bet they're top of the line businessmen, not as powerful as you, but still well known, well off, well connected and dirty as they come." Jury leaned farther across the desk. "So you're way off the charts on this one, Viktor, when it comes to abuse. You're not using coke or heroin or whores; you're using little children to satisfy your addiction, you and the rest of the sick bastards who come to you. Dante doesn't even have a circle of hell for that. I know because I checked. Don't think for a moment you're going to get away with this, you son of a bitch." Jury turned and walked to the door.

"I'm ringing the commissioner, Mr. Jury."

Jury turned and smiled. "Give him my best."

# 42

The next morning he called Johnny Blakeley.

Johnny said, "She didn't name Viktor Baumann, but she rolled on seven of the others; we brought them in, prominent businessmen in the City. They're cheek by jowl with Baumann, only they haven't admitted it yet. The sons of bitches. It's amazing how these people can convince themselves they do no harm; indeed, they function to do good to children. Have them understand their 'sexuality.' A kid five years old, for chrissakes."

"You're pretty certain somebody's going to name Viktor Baumann?"

"You can take it to the bank. Because just imagine how much these men want the publicity; it would ruin them. So that's what I'm going with: first one that rolls on Baumann gets immunity and anonymity."

"Why in hell would they feel any loyalty to Baumann anyway?"

"They wouldn't." Johnny thought for a moment, then said, "Unless he managed to keep his hands clean; unless they really don't know who's behind it."

Jury said, "Ah. But being part of it, that would be half the fun, wouldn't it? The illicit sharing. Sitting around in your club with whiskeys and cigars with the others in the Baumann club, talking about it."

"We've got all of these eyewitnesses. Nobody wants to make these kids testify, but can you imagine how this would play in court? The testimony of these ten little girls? No. They'll all try to plead out; they wouldn't have a hope in hell in a trial. This older girl —"

Jury heard papers being shuffled and filled in the name: "Samantha Burns. I'm getting Samantha a solicitor."

"How about yourself, Richard?"

"You mean do I have one?"

"Yes."

"Not yet. I have an appointment with somebody in an hour."

CS Racer asked Jury the same thing, but with a noticeable lack of Johnny's sympathy.

"I have an appointment to talk to Pete

Apted," said Jury, he made a show of looking at his watch. "In fifteen minutes."

"Bringing in the big guns, are we?"

"We are. We'll need them."

Racer looked at Jury with suspicion. Was he or was he not being mocked? "Why're you smiling? You're not taking this whole mess seriously? Letting the Yard in for a hell of a lot of embarrassment? Egg on our faces, that sort of thing?"

"I'm just letting a smile be my umbrella."

The smile was for the cat Cyril, who was currently perched on top of the bookcase to Racer's right. It was another favorite seat. Cyril was looking down and his tail was twitching. Twitch. Twitch. A sign that this interview would soon be over.

"Well, you'll need something better than an umbrella this time, laddy. God! How could you have been so stupid?"

To Jury, the interesting thing was the underpinning of anxiety in the chief superintendent's tone. He told Jury again and again, just as he was doing now, saying the same things over and over as if this ritual barrage of words would somehow expunge the danger. Something like a religious chant. Racer did not want to rid himself of Jury as much as he liked to think. Jury served too many purposes, not the least of which was his clear-up rate. No one had a better record.

Now, Racer would get up out of his chair to pace with hands folded behind him, imitating a man in deep thought. It was this moment that Cyril had trained for. With Racer standing behind his chair, Cyril launched himself from the bookcase, made a graceful arc in air and landed on Racer's shoulder. Then he jumped down and fled from the room.

Fast on the cat's heels (but never able to catch him), Racer was yelling at Fiona: "Have animal control up here! Where is he? Where did he go? I'll kill him."

Jury sat peacefully, taking in the shouting and crying and swearing as all in a Cyril-day's work. If he chucked the job, he would miss it. Oh, well. He got up and went through to the outer office and joined the melee.

Racer insisted that Fiona was hiding the cat.

The funny thing was, Racer would miss Cyril, too.

# 43

"Does that detective know?" Lulu asked.

She was referring to Jury. "Does he know what?" said Melrose, tamping down earth.

"Where the Child Thief took her?"

"I've told you there's no such person."

"There was for Flora. Where is she, then, if you're so smart?"

Melrose considered beating his head with the trowel. "Okay, I'm not smart then. Certainly not as smart as your detective."

"She isn't dead."

At least the poor child didn't have to face death down. Yet. "Of course she isn't."

Lulu was bouncing a remnant of turf on her hand. "How do you know?"

Roy thought the turf was a ball and jumped for it.

"How do I — ? You just said yourself she wasn't dead."

"I know why I think she's not. But why do you think so?"

"A hunch. Intuition." He stood up. "Enough of this. I'm going in for tea."

Lulu made sure she'd get there ahead of him and ran.

Melrose walked out of the small garden and toward the old gardener, who was seldom seen here. He rarely came round except when the Macmillans weren't here. He had propped his ladder against the statue of the boys with buckets and appeared to be inspecting the turfed steps.

Melrose could not recall his name. Maybe he'd never known it. Heartily, he said, "So what do you think of the steps?"

The old man turned, scowling. "Piss poor, ah calls it. Looks like a dog's dinner, this lot. Thought Mr. Scott 'ad better sense. Fire in a bucket, ah calls it."

"He does, he does —" Melrose's eye was facing the boys with buckets against which the ladder was leaning. He thought for a moment. "Might I just use that ladder?" He didn't wait for an answer. As he put his foot on the first rung, he thought that one might need something to stand on to retrieve an object, but not to toss it in. He needed to climb up only four steps before he could actually look in the higher bucket.

There it was, the gun. He knew nothing about guns, but thought this one was probably what they were looking for. With his handkerchief over his hand, he reached in and pulled it out. He rushed pass the puzzled gardener into the house to telephone Jury.

"Newcastle, up in Tyne and Wear."

"When will he be back?"

"Should be back tonight, I think. I could get in touch with him —"

It probably had something to do with his cousin's death. "No. It can keep. Thank you."

Melrose walked up the steps to the white incidents van. A uniformed policeman sat at one of the desks reading a book about golf. When did he ever find the time to play? Another sat at the back. He was on his cell phone.

"Where's Commander Macalvie?"

The uniform turned and asked, "Ian, where's the boss?"

Ian shrugged. "I think he's in Launceston."

"You'll want to tell him about this." Melrose took the gun, wrapped in his handkerchief, from his pocket and put it on the desk.

"Bloody hell," said the uniform.

Ian lurched up. "Is that the gun that killed the Banks woman?"

"Well, it's *a* gun. But I'm not into ballistics. I *think* it is, but there again . . ."

Gingerly the uniformed policeman turned it around. "It's a .22," he said over his shoulder to the one named Ian. "Where the bloody hell'd you find it?"

Melrose tilted his head in the direction of the garden. "Back there. In a bucket."

# White Crosses

# 44

Leaving early in the morning would mean he could come back the same day, perhaps catch the same train as he'd taken a few days ago.

"It's Dickie," Brendan had said the night before. Dickie was the sixteen-year-old son who, as far as Jury knew, hadn't been in trouble before, certainly not been nicked by the police. Or had he and Jury simply wasn't aware? "Police got him down at Washington Wallsend station. His boss accused him of thievin'. This bloke that's foreman of this gâteau factory outside Washington. Okay, the boy did nick a couple of gâteaus, said it was for a friend's birthday party, but for God's sakes, is that a reason to call the Bill?"

Jury remembered passing that gâteau factory. Clean looking, very modern, gave the locals a lot of jobs. Brendan had once told him the employees were always afraid the off-site owner, a nasty, mercurial man with a habit, might close it down, but the factory apparently went chugging on. So he told Brendan he could be in Newcastle the next day; he'd get there at eleven. Could Brendan just meet him at Newcastle Central?

"Indeed I could. Thanks — it's really good of you, Richard; I know how busy you are."

"Not too busy to help out, Brendan."

Which, he supposed, was the attitude he should have taken all along.

The 8:30 got him into Newcastle at 11:36 and Brendan's car was waiting outside the station. Jury climbed in and Brendan started talking right away.

"Should we go to the police station straightaway?"

Jury thought for a moment, said, "No. Let's check out the gâteau factory. Maybe I can have a word with this Frank — what's his name, again?"

"It's Frank Vinson. I don't know if he's foreman or manager or what, but he runs the place. The bloke who owns it, though, he's a real shit. He's an alcoholic and does drugs. I met him once in a pub over there. It's as well he lives in London. Dickie says

504

it's common knowledge he's mixed up in drugs and such."

"You told me about him. Do you know his name?"

"Finnegan." Brendan was maneuvering the car round a turn to the bridge when he looked at Jury. "Do they all have to be fuckin' Irish?"

Jury laughed.

The place was in between the village of Washington and Old Washington. Jury remembered seeing it on that long-ago day when he'd met Helen Minton. He'd passed it going toward Newcastle. It was a long, low building, well kept up and had a reputation for turning out quality pastry for supermarkets such as Waitrose and for treating its workers well.

Only this instance, Jury suspected, was not an example of that. "You stay in the car, Brendan. You'd be more of a threat to Frank than I would at this point."

Brendan nodded.

Jury was directed to Frank Vinson's office by a cheery-seeming woman in a plastic cap, one of the workers on the floor who'd left for a smoke.

Frank Vinson was a biggish man, pleasant enough looking but with very sharp eyes that a poor lad like Dickie would not want cutting him a look. Frank had a decided lack of enthusiasm for coppers, which wasn't surprising given his connection with a villain like Finnegan. Jury would bet Vinson had been in and out of Borstal since a lad. He was from London and probably wasn't taking too well to this part of the country; for a lively Londoner, Tyne and Wear could be like Siberia, couldn't it?

Jury did not tell him he was here unofficially, just letting Vinson think that for some incredible reason, New Scotland Yard was interested in Dickie Malloy. Why on earth?

Jury didn't fill in the blanks for him, but instead asked, "Is somebody leaning on you, Mr. Vinson?"

Frank Vinson whipped those sharp eyes round at Jury quick enough to cut. "Dunno what you mean." He lit another cigarette from the butt of the one he was now stabbing out with a ferocity that would go more with the fire brigade's trying to extinguish the flaming plant.

"I think maybe somebody is," said Jury. "Finnegan maybe? Were there shortages? Something along those lines?"

Frank pulled open a desk drawer and

withdrew a pint of high-class courage. Remy. Then he rooted out a shot glass, poured and drank it back. "Look, any trouble with the books, it's not down to me." He leaned toward Jury, as if in confidence and repeated it, slowly. "It's not down to me."

Jury looked round the office, nodding slightly, shaking his head, nodding again, as if assessing the situation. Then he said, "Well, let me put it this way, Frank: I don't really think it's down to Dickie Malloy, either. Actually, I think there are all kinds of things going on, wouldn't you agree? My thinking is it's not down to either of you. It'd be much easier on everybody if you'd just drop the charges against this kid. There'd be no reason for any of this going any further, if you take my meaning, Frank." Jury smiled.

"Yeah. Well." Another cigarette, another shot of Remy, and Frank agreed.

Jury got in the car. "Not to worry, Brendan. He's seen the light."

"What? So what did he say?"

"He's dropping the charges. Let's go to the station. I know a DS there, or I used to."

Brendan was wreathed in smiles as he

started up the car. "What in hell'd you say to him, man?"

"Nothing."

Which was, to all intents and purposes, quite true.

At the Washington Wallsend station, Jury asked if DS Roy Cullen was still with them and was told yes, except it was Detective Inspector Cullen now, and Jury was pointed to the rear of the room where Cullen sat talking on the phone. He ended the conversation when Jury dropped into the chair beside the desk.

"Nice to see you again, Inspector. You deserve the promotion."

"C'm on, man, it's nearly a decade. If I'd not been promoted, I'd have nowt and been out on my arse."

Jury laughed. "True, but that isn't generally a reason for promotion."

Cullen was chewing gum just as slowly and methodically as he had when he'd been Detective Sergeant Cullen, resolutely resisting Scotland Yard's sticking its nose into Northumbria's police business. Now, however, the stolen gâteau business was hardly worth a nod, and him a detective inspector, for God's sakes. He nodded toward the phone. "I've just had Frankie

Vinson on the phone, telling me he was dropping all charges against Richard Malloy. Nice." In an unnice tone. "You had a little talk with him?"

"Nothing to speak of. Oh, come on, Roy. Somebody, probably Finnegan, is leaning on Frank, so he leans on this poor lad. So can we take the boy home now?"

Cullen shrugged. "Be my guest."

Dickie Malloy, a thin, gaunt boy with sad eyes, at first seemed to be shivering with fright until he realized it was Jury with the PC who unlocked the cell.

"Uncle Richard! Where'd you come from? What's going on?"

"Your dad's waiting, Dickie. Let's go."

In the car, Dickie sitting in back, Jury turned around and looked at him. Dickie seemed brimming over with relief. "Listen, Dickie, no more gâteau parties, okay?"

Dickie nodded with great enthusiasm.

Brendan laughed and bumped the car over a speed bump. "I never did know police to act quick on anything, but that sure was."

"Oh, we're quick as can be," said Jury. "Drop me back at Newcastle station."

★ ★ ★

At the club car's refreshment stand he bought a cup of tea, the counterpart of the earlier cup of coffee he'd discarded in the station. Back in his seat, he regarded the woman and boy across the aisle. The mother (at least that's who Jury assumed she was) was chewing gum avidly and reading what appeared to be, given its lusty cover, a romance novel. Concentrating on the book, her tongue pushed out a ribbon of gum and then curled to pull the gum back in.

The boy with her might as well have been on the moon for all the attention he got. He had a little metal car that he rolled about on the seat as he made a little blubbering noise that Jury imagined was meant to be the car's engine springing to life.

Jury leaned his head back. In another minute he felt eyes staring at him, the boy across the aisle trying to engage him. Jury was trying just as hard to disengage. He wanted nothing to do with any stranger at this point, nothing. But the eyes were wrestling Jury to the mat. He looked over.

The boy smiled. He looked to be seven or eight, with spiky hair the same brown color as his mother's, but blue eyes that belonged to nobody. They were the bluest

510

eyes Jury had ever seen, eyes that would make the boy memorable even if the rest of him faded into oblivion. He was holding the little car. Jury's look was interpreted as an invitation, and he crossed the aisle.

"I have a car," he said, holding it up for inspection.

"I see you do. What kind is it?"

"It's a Jaguar. I think." He frowned at the car as if it were not living up to his investment.

Jury took it and looked it over as if pondering the question of the car's make. "It could be a Porsche, too."

The boy had propped his elbows on the armrest of Jury's seat and was resting his chin in his hands. "What kind of car do you have?"

"I don't."

This appeared to knock the boy for a loop. A grown man who didn't own a car? "But you have to. How else can you go round the pubs?"

"You can walk, can't you?"

Here was an exquisitely monstrous notion. The boy made a face.

Jury asked, "What kind of car do you drive, then, when you go round the pubs?"

"Me?" He clapped his hands to his chest. "I don't have a car or go to pubs.

I'm not old enough." But he seemed pleased to be included in the driving and drinking population.

"Really? Then how old are you?"

The boy held up his hand, splaying the five fingers, which he turned into a fist and then held up three fingers.

"Five? That's nice," said Jury.

The boy was outraged by this error and the dimwit who couldn't count. "Eight! Look." Five fingers went up on one hand, three fingers on the hand holding the car.

"Ah! I was wrong. Sorry."

He was immediately forgiven, as the boy returned to his former stance, pressing his hands down on the armrest to keep his balance. "I'm going to London."

"London? Then you're on the wrong train, mate. This one's for Swansea."

Openmouthed, the boy stood ramrod still, locked into the position of the horrified and disbelieving. "Never! It's going to London. It's you that's on the wrong train!"

It was interesting that the boy didn't go to his mother for confirmation of the train's destination. Jury glanced over at her, still chewing gum, curling the lock of hair, reading her book. Like a character depicted on a frieze. Even her movements, so repetitive, seemed frozen in time. Had the boy given up turning to his mother for verification of what he was led to believe was true?

"That's mum. She don't mind."

Doesn't mind what? That they were hurtling through the night, aimed not at London but at Swansea?

"Bet," said Jury, digging around for change and taking a pound coin from his pocket. "Bet you it's going to Swansea."

"Okay, only —" The boy didn't have a pound to bet. Then he looked at his toy Jaguar or Porsche, and said, "I'll bet this." When Jury agreed to this, the boy said, "If you're on the wrong train, are you just going to keep going?"

Interesting question. "Don't have much choice, do I? This is the Swansea Express, anyway."

The boy was all over it. "Express" was something to sink his teeth into. His tone grew almost belligerent. "Why'd there be an express train to Swansea? It's not big enough."

"How do you know? You've never been there, I'll bet."

That stopped the boy momentarily. He had no rejoinder. But he would keep up his end nonetheless. He had London in his favor.

"Why are you so certain I'm wrong and you're right?" asked Jury. "Did you buy the ticket?"

"Me? A course not. Mum bought it. I heard her say London."

"Well, then it might be the right ticket, but still the wrong train." The boy frowned. Again, Jury found it interesting that he didn't ask his mum for backup here. It could be that he wouldn't get it, or would get it, but in a cross voice. But it also could be that for the boy, not being 100 percent sure of the train's destination threw him into a state of suspense that was not unpleasant. His small furrowed forehead and blue, blue eyes protested against such uncertainty, but not enough to make him turn away and ask someone else (the man reading a book? the elderly lady sitting knitting?) and put it behind him. He would enjoy the fabrication; he would enjoy being part of it. Kids liked to be safely scared, as at a fair, sitting in a little boat that winds through a tunnel of horrors — skeletons popping out at them, doomed creatures with lighted heads — yes, a child would gladly pay his fifty p or pound for the thrill of being scared.

From his expression, Jury knew that the boy was growing less and less certain of

London. He crossed the aisle to get the ticket stub stuck on top of the seat by the conductor. (The mother was all oblivious.) He looked at it and stuck it back with a frown. For he knew (as Jury had said) that the ticket proved nothing.

Down the aisle, just come into this car was the attendant rolling his tea trolley. Here was a chance! The pale-looking young fellow would most certainly know where this ambiguous train was taking them! The boy watched him, his skin going as pale as the attendant's.

Jury said, "You'll have to get out of the aisle to let him pass. You can sit over there." Jury indicated the seat facing him.

The invitation was accepted. The boy squirmed around to look at the progress of the tea trolley, which was making good time because there were so few passengers. "Want some tea or biscuits or anything?" asked Jury.

The boy shook his head, still biting on his lip. The tea trolley was nearly abreast of them and he got up quickly and went to the window, his back turned on Fate.

The attendant stopped. He listed the offerings, in a sweet manner, and Jury said, "I'll have a Kit Kat. No, make that two Kit Kats. Thanks." He paid for them and the

515

trolley moved on; the boy stayed for another moment at the window, where nothing could be seen but the dark. It was a full moon, the boy announced, and returned to his seat.

He thanked Jury for the candy and waited to see what Jury would do with his. Jury tore back a piece of the wrapper and then so did the boy. They both took a bite. Jury said nothing about the attendant, but the boy was leaning over the seat, craning his neck to watch the tea trolley out of sight.

"I should have asked him!" Too late now. "He'd'a known."

Jury smiled. For Swansea had set up shop in the boy's mind.

"What's there? I mean in Swansea?" said the boy.

"Well, there's a fair, usually. You know, with a carousel, Ferris wheel and all that."

"Has it got bumper cars? That's my favorite."

"Oh, yes. Two different lots of bumper cars."

His eyes widened. "Wow. Do you go there?" He added, in a disappointed tone, "I guess you're too old for that."

"You're never too old for bumper cars."

The boy nodded. "I won't be, not even

when I get to be twenty. Or thirty." His eyes widened at this seemingly impossible number of years. "It's not as big as London, either. If you got lost in London, well, I guess you'd stay lost."

"Oh, I could find you."

The boy looked dubious. "I think you'd stay lost. But I guess in Swansea you wouldn't."

"No. You definitely wouldn't." Jury looked down the aisle. Here came the most authoritative figure of all, the one who had incontrovertible proof of the destination of this train. Jury was afraid the conductor would bark out the news that London was coming up next. "Here's the conductor coming."

The boy whipped his head round to see and then slid off his seat and returned to the window to gaze out on darkness. He spoke about the moon. "You should see it! It's huge."

The thing was to keep up one's end. Winning was so far off the mark that the boy wasn't thinking about it. He had London in his corner, but Jury had worldliness. He knew more about such things; age granted him power, perhaps enough even to divert the course of the tracks. So in a way they were equal.

In this sense they were, indeed, magicians. It was the rabbit popping out of the hat that was important, not how the rabbit got there in the first place. Children could do this better than adults: keep the balls in the air, the body suspended, the tiger at bay. For truth must be held in abeyance. No matter how slight a one, Swansea must still be a possibility.

The train was slowing, the buildings now creeping past, the stolid brick and cement of city buildings and spreading railroad tracks, and there was no longer a means of denying that here was London. Passengers were rousing themselves from magazines and papers. The boy's mother was looking around with a baffled frown as if her child had disappeared largely to make her life more difficult.

The conductor was bellowing the destination as they chugged into King's Cross. The boy looked around the back of his seat, over the armrest at the conductor, then turned back and clutched his red car.

He was wondering, Jury was sure, what could be salvaged. Oh, there was a pound in it for him, but reward for being right had gone out the window long ago. This was London pure and simple, and his mother was registering his presence with a nagging "Joey! Come on, love." She was cross and trying to get their things together.

Joey said, "Okay," glumly, and gave Jury a look that could only be described as imploring. Game over. They could have kept it going had the train not put them down here; he could have gone on forever, as long as a game could go on.

He stood in the aisle as his mother got their belongings sorted, some stuffed into a carryall. To Jury he said, in a totally disheartened manner, "I guess I won." Talk about a Pyrrhic victory!

For winning was not the point, and Jury knew he'd best hold on to that pound somehow. He said, "You know, I'm not so sure you've won." He took out his warrant card and one of his business cards. He handed the card to the boy. "My name's Richard Jury. I'm a policeman, Joey."

As Joey's mouth fell open, his mother said, "Well, come on, then. We can't be stopping in the aisle all day." She started toward the front of the car, leaving Joey behind like a forgotten suitcase.

Jury rose, too. "Here's the thing. Sometimes police have to divert trains originally bound for somewhere else —"

Joey's eyes and mouth were perfect Os,

as round as the moon. He said in a wondering tone, "Like Swansea, you mean? This here train was meant for Swansea?"

Jury nodded. "Could be. So you hold on to your car and I'll hold on to my money and we'll see how this game plays out." He pulled out his small notebook, clicked his ballpoint into action. "What's your last name?"

Joey gulped it out: "Holden."

Jury smiled and thought of Cody Platt. He wrote the name down, said, "When I get wind of the train's actual destination, I'll let you know. We'll get this sorted, not to worry." They were moving up the aisle and Jury put his hand on Joey's shoulder. "Don't you worry; the game's still on."

What a willing suspension of disbelief was Joey's! His sad look was brightened by a big smile as the three of them descended to the platform. Then Joey's mum pulled him along, Joey pulling against her hand every dozen steps to turn and look back at Jury and wave.

In memory, Jury heard again the woman at the reception following the funeral, saying, "She was only your cousin; it could've been worse."

Worse? No, there is no worse, unless maybe it's on the moon. And before King's

Cross station canceled out the night sky, he looked up and thought about the pull of the moon, the receding of tides, the place where the worst can be measured.

Ahead, the boy was little more than a stick figure. But then the figure paused, its tiny hand waving. Jury waved back.

And then he knew.

# 45

"That's impossible," said Macalvie, after a few moments of silence.

"I don't think so." Jury had called Macalvie as soon as he'd got back to Islington.

"But Declan Scott surely would — ?"

"No, not necessarily. Think of Lena Banks. Scott hadn't a clue who she was."

"True. But he hadn't seen her for over a year." On his end, Macalvie turned from the phone to give directions to someone. He came back and said, "They couldn't keep it up. Nor for all that time."

"I think they could."

Again, Macalvie was silent. That was three times in one phone conversation. It had to be a record for Macalvie.

Jury said, "I'll be back in Cornwall in the morning. With Cody." Jury smiled. It was almost as if everybody was a kid these days, doing kid things.

"What's going to happen?"

"That's my lookout."

"What about Cody?"

"That's both of ours. It's mine for dragging him into it."

"When I talked to him he sure as hell didn't sound 'dragged' into it. He talked about it as if it were his finest hour."

"Maybe it was."

# 46

Pete Apted sat in his rich rosewood, mahogany, leather-lined office, finishing an apple. He was in his shirt sleeves, with his feet on the desk, and tieless, looking more like some rock group promoter than the barrister he was. Pete Apted had turned down a knighthood because (he claimed) it would make him appear unapproachable.

"Well, you *are* unapproachable," Jury had once told him, "except by a few of us brave souls and the solicitors who bring you cases." Jury had first met up with Pete Apted through the largesse of Jenny Kennington (but that book would remain closed, which pained him), who had retained Apted to defend Jury in an absurd murder charge. And Apted had in turn defended Lady Kennington on a charge that was not absurd.

Pete Apted shied the apple core at a wastebasket strategically positioned for just that purpose. The core went in; Apted pumped his arms in victory. "I keep moving it back." He took his feet off the desk, some sort of bow to decorum. "Superintendent, you do have a way of turning up. Who is it this time? You? Her? Neither?"

"Neither." Jury smiled. "Although it does involve me, but my part isn't criminal. The girl's name is Samantha Burns. She shot and killed a five-year-old girl."

Nothing shocked Pete Apted, but a lot of things brought on that woeful expression. "Kids killing kids. Is that becoming the national pastime?"

"She also shot a pimp named Eddie Noon. Saved my life, that did."

"Good for her. There's sympathy, right there."

"There's a house in Hester Street run by a woman named Murchison. Was run I should say, for she's now in custody." He told Apted the story.

Pete Apted looked at him in silence for a while, said, "These little girls, where are they?"

"Social services is looking after them at the moment." Jury hoped the girls would be kept together until something more permanent was arranged for each of them, but he supposed there wasn't much chance of that.

"Samantha had been in that house for how long?"

"Since she was nine or ten."

"There's even more sympathy. Now, what about you?"

"I went in without a warrant."

"Oh? That was smart."

Jury sat forward. He felt he had to explain himself to Apted; he always did. "This house has been under investigation for a long time. A DI named Blakeley who's with the pedophilia unit has been trying to work up enough evidence for a warrant. He was sure, when the little girl was shot, that whoever did it came from that house. Once Blakeley managed to get into the place, but not past the Murchison woman. It's very, very tightly run." Jury sat back. "I got in."

"Warrantless. None of what you discovered will fly in court, but you know that."

"Of course. The first order of business was getting those kids out."

"Exigent circumstances."

"But the 'circumstances' have been there for a long time."

"You didn't know that." Apted got another apple out of the bag, got up and pushed the wastebasket farther back.

# 47

Lulu, who was tossing a ball to Roy, met up with Jury between the fountain and Melrose's nicely turfed steps. Roy bounded ahead. "Hello." She pointed to what Jury was carrying. "What's that?"

"Mr. Plant's gardening tool. The Black Diamond secateurs."

Finding it to be a tool, she lost interest. Then she took Jury's hand. "I was just helping with the mead planting."

"No you weren't, you were playing ball, you and Roy."

She disdained this ball playing. "Oh, that was only in between. Come on." She pulled at his hand and they walked along the path to the little interior garden. "See this?" She pointed to a deep purple-blue pansy. "I put this first because it's got the most color. Then this, and this, and this." In turn she pointed out the paler shades, down to lavender.

Poor benighted pansies, Jury thought. Handled to within an inch of their lives. "That's a pretty arrangement, but don't you think Mr. Plant, as he's the expert, should be permitted to keep to his own design?"

"No." Lulu looked up at Jury as if she'd expected better from him. "His colors are all mixed up. Lie down, Roy."

The dog paid no attention, just went on looking at them with his tongue hanging out.

Jury sat down on the bench and crossed his arms. "Tell me something, Lulu. Did you like Flora?"

Lulu, head down, was scuffing at the soil around the pansies. She nodded. "You already asked me that."

"I know. But you might have changed your mind."

She frowned. "Well, I haven't. She was nice."

"You used to play with her at your aunt's house in Little Comfort?"

"Her mum brought her over." She stopped the scuffing and came to the bench and leaned on the arm. "We played cards sometimes."

Jury sat there for a moment, his arms folded across his chest. "It's been, I expect, all in all and despite what must have been the dreadful difficulty at the beginning, a lot of fun."

She stopped swinging on the bench arm and stood still, frowning. "What's been fun?" Her tone was blank, unpuzzled and also unconvincing.

Jury opened his arms. "All of this: you and Roy and your aunt. Angel Gate. The gardens, the sky." It was a sterling blue. The place was gorgeous with the light streaming through the trees and spreading to the flower beds.

"Oh, I don't care," she said.

Had she caught on just then and, like Joey, was prepared to play it out? Jury smiled. Had she or hadn't she? He felt as if he were being taken. It made him smile, really, that he was being handed a song and dance by a seven-year-old girl, that he was being hog-tied, blindsided and swindled. "Did you usually win at cards?"

"Always. I always won." Now she had grasped the arm of the bench and was leaning back.

"You know what you should be?"

"Uh-uh. What?"

"A Vegas blackjack dealer."

"That's funny. What is it?"

"Well, as soon as you find out what it is,

go be it because you'd be sensational. Everyone would be watching you. Las Vegas is a palace of games. You're seven now. By the time you're seventeen you'll have the city at your feet."

She looked down at her feet as if wondering whether she'd like a town at them. She pursed her lips. "What kind of games?"

"The kind that require quick thinking and a poker face. The kind where you don't give anything away." He leaned closer. "And the kind where, if you're clever, you hedge your bets."

Lulu was being acrobatic by turning her back to the bench and leaning over the arm, her face turned upside down. "I don't know what you mean. What's Lost Vegas?"

"Las Vegas is a town where everyone gambles. You know, makes bets and wins a lot of money. Or loses. You can win thousands of pounds on one bet. Or lose it."

"Can you bet fifty p?"

"Any amount. But what you could do is work the blackjack table. Probably, you'd want to change your name because Lulu doesn't sound much like a Vegas name. You like French names. You named your dog 'Roi.' Yours could be something like Genevieve or Fleur."

"No. I've always hated that —" Quickly, she stepped back, pressing her hands against her cheeks. Staring.

"You've always hated Fleur? How's that?"

"You tricked me!"

Jury looked at the sky. "Oh, I don't know. Entrapment, maybe."

"Come on, Roy! We're going!"

Jury rose before Roy did. "Oh? Where are you going?"

"To the kitchen. For our tea!"

"May I join you?"

"No!" She marched off.

Roy sat looking up at Jury in an uncertain way and then took off after her.

And Jury followed.

# 48

Had her aunt been there in the kitchen, the child would certainly have told her — warned her — but Rebecca Owen was nowhere about. But Declan Scott and Melrose Plant were about, both standing by the sink, both drinking mugs of tea.

Declan said, "Mr. Jury, I've had Commander Macalvie on the phone. He said he was coming over from Launceston. He should be here soon."

Melrose raised his mug in a gesture of greeting, but said nothing.

Lulu was busy shaking dog food from two boxes into Roy's little dishes. She added what looked like scraps of scrambled egg saved from breakfast.

Melrose said, "The way you feed that dog, he's going to get fat."

"He needs lots of food. He's had a terrible life." This came from the pantry, where she was putting back the boxes.

Declan looked at Jury and rolled his eyes. "I wasn't aware of that, Lulu." When she appeared again in the doorway, he said, "I assumed Roy was fortunate. At least for a dog. You got him from a litter of royal puppies, or so you said."

She hunkered down and shoved the dish with the egg on top (which the dog had been ignoring) directly under his nose. "I told you that Roy was taken away by Gypsies before he hardly had a chance to see the inside of the palace."

"Oh, sorry, I'd forgotten that detail."

"Yes, you did. You probably forgot" — and here her eyes looked daggers at Declan and Melrose, with an extra jab of them at Jury — "all of it. So Roy had to go around like a beggar's dog, hoping someone would remember." This was a hands-on-hips pronouncement.

"I'm sorry, Lulu. I am. I'll try to treat Roy with more, uh, respect in the future."

She looked at him through narrowed eyes. "There's three of you. You should've paid more attention to him. You should have remembered. Come on, Roy!"

Roy, remembrance of his fall from grace and favor not being as high on his list as it was on Lulu's, went on chomping his food.

"Come on, Roy! It's your last chance!"

Roy didn't care anymore about last chances as he did for first. He chewed.

Huffily, she said, "I'm leaving!" and turned and stomped from the kitchen.

Declan poured the remainder of his tea down the sink and said, "I think I should inquire as to the source of this trouble. We might avoid a beheading."

"You never can tell," said Jury. He looked at the pot and asked, "Any more tea?"

"What happened? You were out there for a good twenty minutes with Lulu," said Melrose.

When Jury told him, Melrose first looked astonished, but then he laughed. "Of course, of course. It explains a lot of things, such as why Rebecca Owen would get so anxious at some of Lulu's remarks. Afraid she was going to give the whole thing away."

"I'd have been anxious, too. That little girl likes to play at the edge too much."

Melrose said, "Mum and dad and auto accident, that was one expert contrivance, right down to the newspaper. I should have wondered about the next of kin." He shook his head.

"Incidentally, nice work with the gun. What put you on to the garden sculpture?"

"It was the gardener, the old one —"

"Mr. Abbot?"

"Yes, yes. He was nattering on about the turf and said among other things 'fire in a bucket.' I was standing there with that bronze sculpture in my line of vision. I guess the penny dropped."

Jury nodded. "They're running it through ballistics."

"About Lena Banks —"

"Ah, yes. 'The poor plain thing.' You said that several times."

"About Lulu."

"That's the point, isn't it? It could so easily have been said about Lena Banks. How dramatically different she looked from Georgina Fox. We had to get Dennis Dench to verify that they were one and the same. It was strange —" Jury stopped when Rebecca Owen entered the kitchen, carrying two brown sacks of groceries.

"Oh, hello," she said cheerily. "I've just got back from shopping."

Melrose went to her and took the brown bags, heavy with cans and produce. After he'd set them on the counter, he said, "I'm off to see my turf one last time, then it's to Northamptonshire this afternoon." He finished his tea.

"Good. I'll hitch a ride," said Jury.

Rebecca scraped a lock of hair back from her forehead and said, "I'm so sorry you'll be going, Mr. Plant."

"It's been my pleasure, Miss Owen." He turned and walked out into the gardens.

She picked up the cold teapot and asked Jury, "Did you have tea, then? Or shall I make some fresh? I'll do that. I'd like a cup myself."

"Can't I help you with those groceries?" Jury moved to the counter.

"Yes, if you could just reach these ones up to that high shelf. You're so tall. I have to get a stepladder to do it. The rest can go in that cupboard."

He deposited cans of beets and corn on the shelf, then took the sack to the narrow cupboard by the frig. As he was carefully placing them, and without looking at her, he said, "Miss Owen, you haven't been quite straight with me, have you?" He turned and smiled at her.

She was staring at him, the tin of tea in her hand. "Pardon?"

"How did Lena Banks or Viktor Baumann discover who Lulu really was?"

"Yes, how did they?" The new voice was Macalvie's. He stood in the kitchen doorway, Platt and Wiggins right behind him.

She looked first at Jury, next at Macalvie, then at Platt and Wiggins. Jury thought the poor woman looked not so much anxious as heartbroken, as if she knew this day was coming, but couldn't believe it was here.

Macalvie went on. "Because we know you shot Lena Banks." He pulled the gun from his overcoat pocket and set it on the long table. "Mary Scott's gun, isn't it? Shooting Lena Banks, that would be the clear reason, indeed, the only reason you would have been driven to do that, to take such a hell of a chance."

Jury put his hand under her elbow, steered her to a chair. "Sit down, why don't you." She seated herself heavily, and he sat beside her, looking as if he too were under fire.

Macalvie waited, and when no word came from Rebecca, said, "She threatened to take Flora, didn't she?"

Rebecca Owen nodded, cleared her throat, and said, "It was Mary's idea. That day in London when she met Lena Banks at Brown's. It was a kind of blackmail, really; the Banks woman said that for a considerable sum she might be able to keep Viktor Baumann from doing something about Flora."

" 'Something' meaning what?"

"She didn't say; it was an insinuation. 'Something' probably like what was supposed to have happened — abduction. Ironically, it was what police thought he had done. Mary was terrified also because she had this heart condition and if she were to die, there'd be nothing to stop Viktor Baumann from gaining custody of Flora. After all, he was her father. Mary would have paid up if she'd had the money. The woman wanted half a million pounds, she said. So that day in Heligan Gardens Mary told Flora that I was to pick her up and take her to Little Comfort and she, Mary, would see her that evening and explain it all. Just to go with me and be a good girl. I went to the Crystal Grotto and kept out of sight — there were very few people there — until I saw the two of them. I changed her blue coat for a brown one and put a scarf round her head and we left by way of one of the service roads. It's the way I got in. If any of the people working there saw us, we wouldn't be able to go through with the kidnapping story, of course. We'd have to wait awhile and try something else.

"Flora wasn't bothered by this. She has an amazing presence of mind for a child. She's really very strong."

Jury said, "You'd have no trouble convincing me of that."

"Well, she took it all as a game, didn't she? Flora was to stay with me until Mary could decide what to do. Then she could go back to Angel Gate. But then Mary died suddenly. I really didn't know what to do. Flora herself was afraid of her father; if playing this game would keep him away, well, she was glad to play it. She loves her stepfather."

"Wait a minute," said Macalvie. "You said Mary Scott would have paid this money to Lena Banks if she'd had it. She might not have, but her husband certainly did."

Rebecca shook her head. "He wouldn't have done it. He would have got the police involved."

"And he'd have been right," said Jury. "So Declan Scott was never told?"

She shook her head.

"God," whispered Macalvie. "You let him go on for all this time — ? Considering how much the man has lost?"

Rebecca bent her head. "I felt I had to; it's what Mary wanted. As long as there was any danger of Flora's being found out, I was to keep her with me. So that's what I did. But don't think I didn't feel for him. That's why I decided to let her come here with me."

"But how could this little girl go along with this?" Macalvie was baffled.

Jury said, "It was the game; it was keeping all those plates in the air."

Macalvie frowned. "What in hell does that mean?"

Jury smiled. "It was seeing how far she could go. It was delightful — tempting fate. Once in a while Lulu would drop a little clue — right, Miss Owen?" Rebecca nodded and half smiled. "Such as telling us there's a place named after her. Which there is: Flora's Green. Would we be smart enough to pick up on something like that?"

"She made me very nervous; I was so anxious she'd give herself away."

"Yet here we were, policemen, detectives, who couldn't sort it. Lulu would hold out until the last card was played. Literally. She'd make a great card sharp."

Cody smiled. "I see what you mean. And I didn't even see —"

"Leave that." Macalvie glared at both of them.

Wiggins said, "But this Lena Banks, Miss Owen. What happened there? How had she, or they, found out that Lulu wasn't Lulu?"

Rebecca turned away. "The white crosses."

Jury frowned. "You mean the ones Flora painted on the trees out in front?"

She nodded. "They had a private detective following me for some time. Viktor knew me, you see. He knew how devoted I was to Mary. When Lulu and I were at Angel Gate, the Little Comfort cottage was empty. He couldn't get inside but he could look around, which he did. Along a path in a little wooded area he found trees with white crosses on them. I didn't even know it."

"Your private detective," said Jury, "was probably the itinerant tree man who came to the door one day and asked Declan Scott if he wanted those trees cleared, the ones marked with white crosses. And Declan laughed and told him, no, the white crosses were done by his daughter."

"I'll be damned," said Macalvie. There was a pause. He asked, "Why would you shoot her here? This means you put Declan Scott in the frame for that murder."

Rebecca shook her head, "I didn't know that. I had no idea she was also this Fox woman. What I hoped was that you'd make the connection with Viktor Baumann."

"How did you know there was a connection?" said Cody. "You didn't know the woman; nobody here did."

"Lena Banks told me. There was no reason not to. The point is: I had to acquiesce; there had to be the appearance of acquiescence. I could have told you that Viktor is not a man who takes things by force. He wouldn't kidnap Flora; he would never drive up and force her into a car. Of course he wouldn't. The man's a sociopath, isn't that obvious? He needs to sustain the illusion that people know he's right and go willingly." She paused and took a deep breath. "The gun was Mary's; I doubt Declan even knew she had one. You can imagine how she'd feel that she needed one, can't you?"

Macalvie nodded. He looked, Jury thought, as if he hated the job, but still had to follow through. "You'll have to come with us, Miss Owen."

Cody dragged the handcuffs from his belt, unwillingly. But Macalvie shook his head and Cody put them away. The three of them walked through the dining room, Jury making a fourth, but following behind.

They sat at a table in front of the fireplace playing cards — Declan, Patricia Quint and Lulu. Jury couldn't seem to think of her in any other way. She was Lulu. Pat Quint was laughing and giving Lulu a little swat with her cards. The three of them were so much at ease that Jury knew Lulu hadn't told them. Yes, she would keep it up as long as she could, wouldn't relent, wouldn't show her hand, wouldn't call. Jury had to admire her. Just like Joey.

Declan heard the approach of the others and looked around over his shoulder. He frowned. "Rebecca?" He rose, as did Pat Quint and Lulu. She was pale; she rushed over to Rebecca and grabbed her hand. She was jumping as if in some attempt to find a supporting ground. Then she stopped and that determined look came over her face. It was sad to see a look hardening the face of a seven-year-old girl. She said: "Didn't you tell them we just made it all up? You — we — never did anything?"

Jury marveled at Lulu's quick inclusion of herself in the action.

"We made it up. It's only a story. I'm really Lulu and nobody's after me. It's a game!" She flared at Macalvie but it was Cody she started hammering with her fists.

Declan put an arm around her chest, pinning her to him. "It's okay, Lulu. I'm sure nothing will happen to Rebecca."

Lulu had broken free. She was jumping again. "But it was only a story! Tell them!" She hung on to Rebecca's hand.

"I'll be all right, Flora —"

"No! I don't want to be Flora! I want to be Lulu!"

Patricia Quint was openmouthed.

Declan froze. "*Flora?* What on earth are you talking about?" He looked from Lulu to Rebecca Owen.

She said, "I'm sorry, I'm truly sorry, Declan. I couldn't —"

But what she couldn't was lost in silence until Macalvie said, "Let's go" and led Rebecca Owen to the door.

Declan knelt down and studied Flora's face that looked, for the first time since Jury had known her, as if it were crumpling into tears. "It'll be all right, Flora. I'll make sure nothing happens to Rebecca. You stay here with Pat."

He was getting into his coat when he said to Jury, "What will happen to her?"

"I can't say for certain, but I would imagine the circumstances would make her very sympathetic in a trial." Jury was walking with Declan to the door. "Mr.

544

Scott, there's just one thing I don't understand."

At the door, Declan turned. "What's that?"

"I know people see what they expect to see, and Flora was made to look completely different as Lulu, probably as different as Lena Banks was from Georgina Fox. But I don't see how you wouldn't have known."

Declan Scott smiled slightly. "What makes you think I didn't, Superintendent?"

# Man Walked
# into a Pub

# 49

"I can't imagine, Superintendent," said Agatha, "why you would want to spend any more time in Cornwall than was absolutely necessary. You recall the last time we were there, surely."

Jury speared a sausage, and Melrose drank his tea. Melrose raised an eyebrow. "Recall what, exactly?"

"The whole dreadful business."

Melrose stopped drinking his tea long enough to observe, "I should cut out my tongue for saying it, but I feel a strong presence of Henry James."

Jury snickered and chewed his sausage.

"And even though it's been three months since your accident, Superintendent —"

Melrose cut her off. " 'Accident,' Agatha? You make it sound as if he'd fallen off his bike."

Agatha sighed and layered up another

scone half with blackberry jam and clotted cream. "Don't be ridiculous, Melrose. I'm not minimizing his being shot at."

Jury smiled. "I'm fine, Lady Ardry. Right as rain. Or will be if Martha has any scrambled eggs left."

Agatha smirked. "Martha's getting too old to cook."

"Agatha, refresh my memory, will you? Precisely why are you here at nine in the morning?"

"Why?"

"Yes, that's more or less what I said."

"I always look in to see how you are around this time." She huffed up, chagrined.

Melrose loved that "look in." "No, you don't. You come here for your elevenses, not your nineses."

"Well, I have something particular to report, but as you're not interested —"

What interested Melrose at the moment was his horse going by and looking in the dining-room window.

Jury followed his line of bafflement, looking over his shoulder. "What's Aggrieved doing out there?"

"That's the first question. The second is, who's the other horse?" For a white horse had followed Aggrieved past the window.

"That," said Agatha, "is the information I wished to impart."

Melrose was for once all ears. So was Jury, who stopped in the middle of his last sausage. "Impart, for God's sakes."

Agatha held out for five seconds by delicately patting her mouth with her napkin. "The horse belongs to Mr. Strether."

"And who in hell is he to be up here getting Aggrieved out of bed?"

"Horses sleep standing up," said Jury as he contemplated his empty plate.

"Don't you start in," said Melrose. He turned back to Agatha. "Well?"

"If you'd stop shouting, I'd tell you."

Pleased as punch she was with herself. "I wasn't shouting. This is shouting!" His vocal cords took off.

Ruthven came rushing in, looking alarmed. "M' lord? Is something wrong?"

"It's all right, Ruthven. I was just demonstrating a shout." Ah! Ruthven would know! "Who the devil's that other horse out there?"

"That would be Mr. Strether's m' lord. Mr. Momaday's up on Aggrieved."

Knowing all of this was her fault, Ruthven gave her a frigid look.

"But what's this Strether person doing here? Is he some friend of Momaday?"

"No. I believe it was Lady Ardry who invited him."

Melrose turned to her again. "I don't get it. Why? The man's a complete stranger."

"Not to me," said Agatha. "And I thought your poor horse would enjoy it."

Jury sniggered. Then he asked Ruthven, "Do you think Martha has any more eggs and sausages left?"

"Absolutely," said Ruthven, taking Jury's empty plate.

"Enjoy — ? What? That he now has a playmate?"

She produced a martyred sigh and ate her scone, wordless for a blessed change.

Melrose threw down his napkin and got up. "Come on," he said to Jury.

"Come on where? I haven't finished breakfast."

Agatha chortled. "At least here's one person you can't order around!"

Jury rose and slugged back his coffee. "Sure he can."

Melrose was talking to the man on the horse, who sat quite high in the saddle. He reached down his hand to shake Melrose's hand. Wouldn't common horse courtesy ask that he at least slide down from it?

He said, "Lambert Strether, sir, from Slough."

Melrose turned to look at Jury, who merely shrugged.

"Lambert Strether, you say?"

Now Strether did hook his leg over the horse's rump and come down. Beaming. His teeth glittered. He shook hands with Jury and said, "I see you're well read."

"He is," said Jury, inclining his head toward Melrose. "I'm not."

Strether turned to Melrose. "The name means something to you?"

"It means something to a lot of people."

"My mother adored Henry James."

Melrose looked at Jury. "Is Henry James adorable? I wouldn't think so."

"Lambert Strether is the protagonist of *The Ambassadors*." Strether aimed this nugget of information at Jury as if Jury were sitting in the front row, mostly asleep. "It's rather embarrassing, the name, when I meet educated people."

"Then why didn't you change it to Fred or Digby or something?"

"Trevor?" said Jury. "Trevor's always good."

This suggestion seemed to confound Strether, who opened his mouth but couldn't think of a response.

"Leaving the name aside, what are you doing here, Mr. Strether?"

"Why, I met up with Lady Ardry, who claimed this was her family seat."

"It is, but she's not sitting in it. But why's my horse out here with a saddle on? That suggests someone's been riding him."

"Your groundsperson, your caretaker was up on him, but he suddenly recalled something he had to do."

"Yes, like getting off my horse. That would be Mr. Momaday."

Jury fed Aggrieved a sugar cube and, feeling a bit sorry for the white horse for having to cart such a pompous arse around, fed him one, too.

"But tell me, Mr. Strether, what are you doing in Long Piddleton?"

"I'm looking around."

"I can see that. But what is your larger, wider mission?"

Strether looked blank and then, catching on, said, "Oh, you mean why I'm in the village? I'm looking for property."

Jury looked at Melrose and tilted his head upward in the direction of the hill.

"Really?" said Melrose. "Not much to invest in around here, though there is a pub up there that did a smashing business until it closed."

Strether looked off in that general direction. "Why did it close if it was doing so well?"

"Owner relocated," said Jury, with a snicker.

"Perhaps I should see it, then."

"Perhaps you should," said Melrose. "It's called the Man with a Load of Mischief."

"Interesting."

"The renovation, that'd be a bit pricey as it hasn't been lived in for so long."

"Oh, that doesn't signify. No, price is not a problem. I own so much property."

"What's he all about?" said Melrose that afternoon as he and Jury passed Miss Broadstairs's cat, Desperado, asleep on top of her garden wall. Melrose poked him and the cat shot up, tail twitching.

Jury said, "Whatever it is, it's not what he says. The jacket didn't fit, the cuffs were frayed, and did you see the shoes?"

"I didn't, Sherlock, no."

"Heels run down like mad. I wouldn't be surprised if he had newspaper in them to hide the holes."

"What was he doing?"

"At Ardry End? Casing the joint, I expect."

Melrose stopped by the pond where ducks were scooting this way and that. "You mean I'm about to be robbed?"

"Don't get so excited over it. He's probably only looking round to see who has a few quid to make it worth his while."

Melrose didn't follow this. "For what?"

"My guess is he's a con artist. A confidence man."

They crossed over the street. "Wait. I'd forgotten the contest! Strether, yes, he's the one who inspired the Henry James contest."

Jury stopped and looked up the cobbled street to the old pub sign and the mechanical Jack. His trousers were in need of a coat of turquoise paint. "I see. The Henry James contest. You know, that's about what I'd expect of your pals." As they walked on, he asked, "Do they ever do anything constructive?"

"Of course not. We none of us do." Melrose waved to Miss Crisp across the street who was setting another chair outside her secondhand furniture store. It was directly across from Trueblood's Antiques and made a nice contrast. "And stop talking about them as if they weren't your pals, too."

Jury smiled. "Oh, they're quite definitely mine."

They turned into the Jack and Hammer where Jury was warmly greeted, first by Dick Scroggs and then by the group at the table in the window. Diane Demorney even set down her martini long enough to give Jury a ginny kiss. Vivian Rivington tried to do this but failed, missing his cheek by a few inches since she had to lean over the table. She gazed at Jury as if he'd just tossed an armload of roses at her feet. It was hard to tell about Vivian.

"You're in time to judge the competition. Melrose told you about our little contest. Or do you want to enter yourself?"

Trueblood asked this so earnestly that Jury laughed. "I'm afraid I haven't read enough Henry James to imitate him."

"Not *read* enough?" said a startled Diane, who appeared to be tasting the word carefully, as one might a portion of something dangerous, like puffer fish. "Dear God, you don't think *we* have, do you? I read the beginning of *The Portrait of a Lady* where they're gathered for tea on the lawn, in spite of its being late enough for drinks. I question whether Henry James had his priorities straight."

Jury tossed his coat on a neighboring chair and sat down by Vivian in the window seat and looked around at all of them. "If you haven't read him, how can you parody him?"

Joanna Lewes, their resident writer of romance novels, said, "We all read, you know, something or other a long time ago, and Marshall copied out a page of *The Ambassadors*. You see, this man walked into the Jack and Hammer —"

"You mean Mr. Lambert Strether?"

"Right. So he seems such an idiot — I can't imagine the real Lambert Strether barging in on a tableful of people who were having a good time without him, can you? So we've got this contest going where each of us has to write one sentence — it'll have to be fairly long, if it's in the style of James."

"Don't forget the important bit," said Vivian.

Jury said, "I'm glad to hear there *is* an important bit."

"Do you want to enter?" asked Trueblood. "Entry fee is one pound fifty."

"I sincerely doubt it. But I have first of all to hear the important bit."

"I'm in," said Melrose, slapping two pound coins on the center of the table and taking back one fifty p piece.

Trueblood supplied Jury's answer: "The sentence has to begin 'Man walked into a pub.' Those words must appear in your sentence. The only variant allowed would be 'the' put in place of 'a,' as in 'Man walked into *the* pub,' instead of 'Man walked into *a* pub.' Want to put up a quid? Winner takes the pot."

Diane shook her head. "Winner takes most of it; runner-up gets the fifty p pieces."

Jury was about to improve on his earlier sarcasm, when Mrs. Withersby ("girl of the moment," Melrose said), waving a bit of paper, yelled, "I got it; mine's done."

Mrs. Withersby (Dick's char) cleared her throat, which was no mean feat, considering her two-pack-a-day habit. She raised her voice and recited: "Man walked into a pub and pissed hisself before he got to the bar." She chortled, thinking that wonderfully funny.

Jury did, too. He looked at the people around the table as they looked at Mrs. Withersby, as if they were considering her entry.

Trueblood said, "Just leave it on the table for the vote."

"No you don't, me flamin' friend. I holds on to it. Someone could nick it right out of the pot."

"I assure you, Withersby, old trout —"

People did not "assure" the Withersbys of the world of anything involving money or drink. She wanted it where she could see it.

"It stays with me!"

Diane asked a question that was spot-on. "How could anyone steal something you've already read aloud?"

Withersby just gave her a dismissive backhand wave and walked off.

"Who else?" asked Trueblood.

Vivian raised her hand like a timid school girl. "I have one."

"Fire away!"

"A man walked into the pub, who, upon first glance appeared, with his open countenance, forthright, but whose interlocutor found him to be holding a prodigious quality in abeyance."

"Wow! Brilliant," said Melrose. What does it mean, though?"

"It means the man first appeared to be aboveboard and honest, but he wasn't. He was holding something back."

"Then why," asked Diane, "didn't you just say that?"

Trueblood heaved a sigh. "Diane, that's probably what they kept saying to Henry James. His own brother even said that to him. I'm sure it was Henry James's contention that he *did* say it."

"Oh." Diane took another sip.

Trueblood informed the latecomers, Melrose and Jury, that this was another part of the competition: you had to be able to explain what you wrote.

"I don't see why. Henry James never did. I mean if you're so dumb or daft you don't understand what he's saying, well, he's not going to translate."

Jury came in at this point. "You see your initial problem? Henry James would never say 'A man walked into a pub,' or 'the' pub. Did Henry James actually ever use the verb 'walked'? To say nothing of the noun 'pub'?"

Joanna got a little testy. "You're not even competing. I don't think you should be giving an opinion. I've got mine done." She rattled the single sheet of paper as if shaking it alive.

"Ah!" said Trueblood. "Let's hear it!"

" 'A man walked into the pub,' said Woodmount, and before we could even begin to contemplate his purpose, showed it in a beguiling light."

They looked at her. "Interesting," said Trueblood.

Vivian said, "So you're using 'man walked into the pub' as something being said by your character?"

"Yes. Thought that was rather clever." She smiled.

"I'm ready," said Diane. She read: "A man walked into the pub and ordered, in the tone of one who was used to having his wishes translated into charming action, a vodka martini."

Trueblood tossed down his pencil, and there was general argument over this. "There weren't martinis, then, were there? I don't think there were martinis around until the 1920s or even 30s. Much less were there *vodka* martinis."

Diane gave a little laugh. "Don't be absurd."

Theo Wrenn Browne said, prissily, "Life doesn't proceed on your wishful thinking."

"You're right," said Diane, raising her martini. "It proceeds on this."

Melrose said, "Martinis have been around since at least the 1880s. I'm sure Henry James must have drunk his share."

"I doubt it," said Diane, "or he wouldn't have put his characters — to say nothing of his readers — through that boring tea on the lawn scene."

In the midst of this fracas, the inspiration for their game walked in — or, rather, carried himself in. Lambert Strether. He approached the bar and ordered a drink.

"How pleasant," said Strether, cruising with his drink to their table and waiting for an invitation to sit down, which wasn't forthcoming. "I took your advice, Lord Ardry —"

As if, thought Melrose, they were chums.

"— and am seriously considering making an investment in your pub."

"The Man with a Load of Mischief?" asked Vivian, alarmed that her past might come back and snap at her heels.

"That's the one! I've been in touch with the estate agent already."

Joanna, who'd been penciling something into her sentence said, without even looking up, "Then you'll be disappointed." For a writer of genre fiction, Joanna's mind moved with remarkable swiftness. "Because my offer's already on the table."

Strether was quite visibly angered by this, but he checked himself. "They didn't tell me that. Why didn't they?"

"Who did you talk to?"

Strether searched his mind. "Abigail someone."

"Oh, that one. No, it's another agent who's handling the sale."

Around the table, all eyes stared at Joanna for this trick. Admiring the rabbit she'd just pulled out of the hat. Whatever Strether was up to, Joanna was taking point, game, match.

Strether said, "Well, that rather leaves me out, doesn't it?"

She had not actually looked at him, but now she did. "It would seem so."

"I daresay there must be other property to invest in. A pub struck me though as especially, well, convivial."

Trueblood snapped his fingers and said, "You know, I think I've got just the place for you. It's about two miles out, just off the Sidbury Road. Little pub called the Blue Parrot. Now, the thing is, it's not formally on the market; the agent got an exclusive listing. As for the proprietor, he's a bit of an odd old thing, bit of a wide lad, if you ask me. Might have another little business on the side." Trueblood winked and lay his finger against his nose.

Melrose Plant rolled his eyes. Did people outside of P. G. Wodehouse actually make that sort of gesture?

"His name's Trevor Sly — good name, I'd say. He's being peculiar about the sale. He doesn't want people to know he's selling up. Ridiculous, what? Wants to sell the place but wants it kept secret. If it's a pub you want, nothing's better than the

Blue Parrot. Why, we could drive you over if you like and you could have a look round." He gave Strether an amiable smile.

"That's decent of you," said Strether, but he looked a tad uncertain.

Jury assumed the uncertainty came from having his real estate dealings taken out of his control. "You know, you'd best be careful, Mr. Strether."

"You're Mr. Jury? Is that right?"

"It is."

"Do you live in this charming village yourself?"

"Unfortunately, I live in not-so-charming London. I'm with New Scotland Yard."

Talk about a sudden step backward! Strether's foot was almost out the door.

So Jury put it on a little thicker. "A superintendent —"

Another step back.

"— with the fraud squad."

There were smiles and nods all round the table. Strether was making a show of looking at his watch, and got out, "Is it that late? I've got to —"

But Jury wasn't about to let him off so easily. "I'm here because of a report of real estate swindles in the area."

"It's bad," said Trueblood. "This Mrs.

Oliphant, poor woman, put down fifty thousand pounds on a cottage in Sidbury and wound up with a deed to nothing. The so-called seller of the property didn't own it in the first place."

"Shocking," said Joanna. "And there was — what *is* her name? The woman who thought she was buying half a bed-and-breakfast that didn't exist?"

Diane, who'd been looking across the street, said, "Oh, you mean Ada Crisp." She worked a cigarette into an onyx holder. "We all can be so gullible, can't we?"

Lambert Strether mumbled his good-byes and was off like a shot.

They all looked at one another, pleased as punch.

Jury said, "Who needs Henry James?"

# 50

Jury felt a need to walk, as if any walls would be too confining. He was in the City again, on Ludgate Hill. He passed few people, odd, since this would be rush hour, when all of these buildings dumped their employees into the street, a fate which it actually amused him to think he might be sharing, perhaps on a permanent basis.

The whole incursion into the ignominious Hester Street house wouldn't have amounted to much had Cody not clipped the old girl on the jaw. But then Jury had hardly been a model of behavior. He was perfectly aware of the wisdom — or lack of it — of getting Cody into a situation like that.

So he was up for a reprimand, which was probably all he was up for, despite Racer's lavishing so much attention on Jury's being hung out to dry.

Jury wondered sometimes what kept him

going. Sarah would have said that, wouldn't she? He felt his dead cousin like a shadow along the pavement, stretched to a point beyond recognition. Yes, that was what Sarah would say and had said on more than one occasion: I really don't see what keeps me going. He could hear her as clearly as if she had been walking beside him.

He walked down Ludgate Hill into Cheapside — he always seemed to gravitate toward the City in these past months and postmortem moods. The hospital, the Grave Maurice, Mickey Haggerty — he told himself not to go there — Vernon Rice. He wouldn't mind having a drink with Vernon, dinner even. He thought this was a constructive idea, something to keep him from glooming away. The people he passed had their cell phones stuck to their heads like a third ear. He took his out and realized he didn't have Vernon's number and information was no good as he was ex-directory. Still he was encouraged by this small shift in his outlook, this more positive behavior. He put the cell phone away and turned into Martin Lane and then into the first pub he came to.

It was a pleasant pub, with a lot of dark paneling and the light from the overhead chandelier playing off the black beams. The few customers gave Jury the impression of being regulars, probably because they looked so comfortable, sitting together or even alone.

He took one of the stools at the bar and ordered whatever was on tap. When he got his drink a man sitting a couple of seats away raised his glass and said, "Cheers." Jury nodded and raised his own glass. He was just as glad that the man hadn't intended his salute as a prelude to conversation. While he would have welcomed conversation with a friend, he wasn't eager to engage in small talk with a stranger. The half dozen customers at the bar drank in silence, except for the one talking to the bartender. There would be, he supposed, a more boisterous crowd as the night wore on.

It took him half an hour to drink two pints and to order a third, after which he felt his mood lightening. All it would take to make the transition from maudlin to relatively tranquil would be a cigarette. Everyone else was smoking away.

His mind went back to Declan Scott, who had explained to Jury, over the telephone, his going along with this dissembling.

"Did Flora know you knew?"

"You mean Lulu?" He laughed. "No, of course not. You see, she needed it. Flora had come to need the masquerade. She needed to believe she was fooling everybody, she needed to feel safe. And she felt safer as somebody else. That was crystal clear to me."

Remembering this, Jury just shook his head. Talk about a man of Jamesian sensibility!

Down the bar, the barman laughed. The sound was almost raucous in the comparative stillness. It seemed a disruption. The few customers looked up or over at the barman. Jury yawned. Two pints had surely been enough for him; he hadn't needed this third, had he? It was going to put him to sleep. He felt drugged. This made him smile, the idea of it. Here he was, totally anonymous, and with no police business to take care of. Everything had wound down, except for his future, which didn't really bother him.

As he sat staring at his third pint, another customer walked in, and, looking as if he was used to the place, took the stool beside Jury, giving him a brief nod before holding up two fingers as a request to the barman, who nodded.

This man was very well dressed in a black cashmere coat and scarf and a suit definitely not off the rack. There were also gold cufflinks. The stranger's whiskey arrived, but he did not look too happy about it. Jury decided it wasn't the fault of the whiskey (given the man knocked it back with no trouble), but the fault of something more deeply ingrained.

The barman came along with the bottle — expensive stuff — and refilled the man's glass as he asked, "How're you keeping, Mr. Johnson?" He asked this with a touch of deference, or perhaps simply care.

"Fine, thanks Trev."

The barman, Trev, refilled the glass, smiled and went back down the bar.

Jury would have preferred no names, as they intruded upon this little island of anonymity he had been enjoying.

Mr. Johnson brought out a silver cigarette case, extracted a cigarette, tapped it on the case and lit it with a silver lighter. Jury watched this maneuver with envy.

Johnson apparently saw this and interpreted it correctly. "Care for one? You look all out."

"Oh, I'm all out all right. Have been for over two years."

The man smiled. "You quit, did you?"

Jury nodded.

"If this bothers you too much, I can put it out."

Jury was surprised by such consideration. "Nice of you, but I enjoy vicarious smoking."

Johnson laughed. "I've tried to quit but can't seem to manage it."

"Understandable. The thing is you never get used to it. At least I don't." Jury drank his beer.

"It helps, along with this" — Johnson raised his glass — "to get you through the day."

"Sometimes I wonder if the whole purpose of life is simply getting through it."

Johnson laughed again, let the laugh lapse into silence. After a minute of this he said, "Whatever the purpose, I don't think we have much control over it."

Jury frowned. "I don't know if I agree with that or not. Let me think."

Johnson smiled a little and let him think.

Jury said, "But do you mean we're controlled by external forces?"

"Some. But I think it's more internal forces. The unconscious. I don't think we know why we're doing what we're doing most of the time."

"Hmm." Jury was only partially aware he'd been studying his empty glass, wondering when he had drunk it all, until Johnson said, "Let's have another." He signaled to the barman, Trev.

Jury sat up. "I think I've had enough, actually."

Johnson laughed again. "No you haven't." When he caught Trev's eye, he made circles in the air over the empty glasses.

When the fresh drinks arrived, Jury said, "I still don't know. Cheers."

"Cheers. Fair enough." Then he extended his hand. "Incidentally, I'm Harry Johnson."

"Richard Jury." Jury shook his hand. "At times, I think we're waiting for a story."

"A story?"

"You know, the way we used to when we were kids. Not just at bedtime, but anytime, wanting a narrative to take us out of things. Even if we make it all up as we go along. That's what some sleep experts say we do with dreams."

"What do we do?"

"Well, some say dreams are meaningless, that they're just mental detritus, or debris left over from that particular day's wreck. But the question this raises is this: if the dream's actually meaningless, just the day's leavings, then what about the narrative? Why are dreams stories? No matter that the images are strange or exotic or unreal — why is there a story, why do events follow one upon the other?"

"Good question."

"So the dream experts answer it by saying, oh, well, the dreamer supplies the narrative. The dreamer makes up the story himself."

Harry Johnson thought about this for a moment, then said, "But doesn't it come to the same thing? The dream still means something because it's the dreamer himself who's linking the images together, if you see what I mean."

"Absolutely."

They sat in silence for a moment. Then Harry Johnson said, "If you want a story, I'll tell you a story — though I can't explain it, or tell you the end; there isn't any end."

"Sounds intriguing."

"Oh, it's intriguing, all right."

"Go on."

"It happened to a friend of mine. This person, who was the luckiest person I've ever known — you could almost say was hounded by good luck — lost everything overnight."

"Bloody hell. You mean in a market crash, something like that?"

"No, no. Not money. I mean he lost everything. He woke up one morning and found himself sans wife, son, even his dog. He did not know what had happened, and of course no one would believe him and he had no idea what to do. He considered going to the police, but what in hell would he say? They wouldn't believe him, I mean wouldn't believe the wife, the son, the dog had simply disappeared; well, you know how bloody-minded police can be —"

"I do indeed." Jury smiled in a crazy kind of way.

"Right. Families don't all of a sudden disappear — I mean, unless some psychopath walks in and murders them all. He told me he felt he was living in a parallel universe, that his wife and son were in one and he was in another."

"Then what did he do?"

"He hired the best private detectives. They found nothing, not a trace. There was simply no trail." Harry stopped, took out another cigarette, offered the case to Jury again, and Jury again refused. "That was a year ago."

"And — ?" It struck Jury suddenly, the answer to the question he had glumly posed to himself earlier: what kept him going? Here was the answer: curiosity. He waited for Harry Johnson to fill in the blank after "And — ."

Harry lit his cigarette, blew out a stream of smoke and said, "The dog came back."

Jury stared. "This is a joke, right?"

Unsmiling, Harry Johnson said, "No, it isn't. The dog just came back." They were both silent for a moment while Harry Johnson seemed to be collecting himself. "So do you want to hear the rest of it?"

Dumbly, Jury nodded.

*Man walked into a pub . . .*